Land Beyond the Horizon

OTHER BOOKS AUTHORED BY JULIA DROSTEN:

The Lioness of Morocco
The Girl with the Golden Scissors
The Elephant Keeper's Daughter
Land Beyond the Horizon

Das Revuemädchen
Die Seidenrose
Die Löwin von Mogador
Die Honigprinzessin
Die schwarze Taube von Siwa
Die Elefantenhüterin
Das Mädchen mit der goldenen Schere
Der Duft von Zimtblüten

ABOUT THE AUTHORS:

Horst and Julia Drosten write together using the pseudonym Julia Drosten. They live in the picturesque Münsterland region of Germany and have always wanted to write books. They find the research to be almost as much fun. For *Das Revuemädchen* they have flown in a historic biplane and for *Die Seidenrose* they have been pampered by an aesthetician. Before writing *Die Honigprinzessin*, they became beekeepers; for *The Girl with the Golden Scissors*, they traced the streets of 19th century Vienna, and for *The Elephant Keeper's Daughter*, they visited Sri Lanka to spend time with wild elephants.

All three books were bestsellers on Amazon.

LAND BEYOND THE HORIZON

JULIA DROSTEN
TRANSLATED BY CHRISTIANE GALVANI

©Julia and Horst Drosten
All rights reserved. No part of this book may be reproduced or used in any manner whatsoever without our express written permission.

This is a work of fiction. Names, characters, organizations, places, events, and incidents are either products of the authors' imagination or are used fictitiously.

©Cover Design: Horst Drosten
Photo Material: Shutterstock: Elina Pas, old ship sailing in the Baltic Sea;
Horst Drosten: Branches with flowers, colonial building in Galle, coast of South Africa
Academie Royale des Sciences, Mappe-Monde, 1700

Translated by Christiane Galvani

Edited by Dr. Elizabeth DeNoma, and Maura McGurk

"Winds they blow, ships they go
Far to foreign lands.
Just the sweetheart stays behind
Crying on the sands.

Please don't cry, wipe your tears,
Think of me and of the time
When you'll be mine again.

Silver and gold, whole trunks full,
I'll bring back with me.
Silk and lovely velvet things
When I return to thee."

(Loosely based on a Scandinavian folksong)

CHAPTER ONE

TÜBINGEN, DUCHY OF WÜRTTEMBERG, 1786

"So, this is the thanks I get? You rotten bastard!"

With that and a hefty kick, Hannes Hiller found himself transported through the open gate of Tübingen Town Hall and into the marketplace. He landed with his right hip on the edge of the mallet that he kept in the sack attached to his belt. The pain nearly took his breath away.

Still dazed from the impact, he was scrambling to his feet when he was grabbed by the vest and yanked upwards. He tried to free himself, but his attacker was not only big and heavy, he was also strong as an ox.

"You confounded blackguard!" Hannes heard him shout.

He felt himself shoved onto the well-stocked table of a butcher offering up his wares on market day. The next thing he knew, he was grabbed by the scruff of the neck and had barely enough time to close his eyes before his face was pounded into a bowl of fresh chicken livers.

"Damnation!" the butcher bellowed. "Be gone, all of you! Now!"

To show his serious intent, he swung the meat cleaver he had only just used to cut up a piece of pork. Several housewives moved away fearfully.

Hannes picked himself up, turned around, and felt the clenched fist of his attacker land squarely in the middle of his face. His eyes watered and he tasted blood. He ran his tongue along his teeth to see if they were all still there.

In the distance he could hear his fellow journeymen and the apprentices. They leaned out of the second-story windows of the town hall and watched him fight with Master Sigwart.

"You really had that coming, you dope!" Anton, the senior journeyman, roared. Some bystanders clapped loudly.

A stranger stood in front of the guard house by the marketplace. He observed the commotion as he chewed a savory roll, he had bought from a baker's stall. He raised his eyebrows with a mocking smile.

"What is it that young fellow's done?" he asked the guard, whose curiosity had prompted him to trade the warmth of the guard house for the November cold.

"Well, it seems that Hannes has once again chased a skirt, only this time the skirt belonged to the wife of his master, Sigwart," the guard explained. "He's a real ne'er-do-well, Hannes is. He just can't leave the women alone."

"I could think of quite a few men who'd be glad not to be bothered by their yokemates after a few years of marriage," the stranger remarked. "But judging by his reaction, I take it Master Sigwart's wife is quite a desirable woman?"

The guard nodded.

"A pretty young thing." His face took on a pained look. "A man doesn't have one like that to himself for long."

A small group of students, visibly tipsy, stumbled out of, the Golden Lamb tavern.

"Hey friends! Look over there. Looks like it might be a nice little spectacle!"

"It's just gone noon," grumbled the guard. "At this hour they belong in the lecture hall."

"What'd you do, give those plump breasts of Sigwart's wife a good kneading?" one of them shouted. The others broke into roars of laughter.

The master swiveled around, his face a dark red.

This was the moment Hannes needed. Like a ram, he thrust his head full-force into his opponent's stomach. Sigwart reeled.

His fall was broken only by the stone parapet of the decorative fountain in the square. Neptune spouted water behind him.

By now a large crowd of onlookers had assembled. Every blow, every hit, by the two brawlers received a loud round of applause.

"That's enough!" The guard's right hand clutched the handle of his rapier.

The stranger stopped him. "Wait!"

"It is my duty to preserve the public peace here, sir!"

"Do you not want to know who's going to win the fight?" The stranger winked at him.

The guard lowered his rapier, grinning.

"Whenever Hannes and the old hothead go for each other, all bets are off. One is strong, the other is swift and wily."

While Hannes was not as brawny as Sigwart, he was a good thirty years younger and considerably more agile so that, slowly but surely, he gained the upper hand. He landed a well-aimed punch in his adversary's abdomen and was about to strike again when, jumping forward, he slipped on the wet cobblestones and began to lose his balance. The master immediately lunged at him, and wrapped his arm around the younger man's neck, putting him in a headlock. Next, he took Hannes by the belt and flung him over the parapet and into the fountain.

Those standing closest were splashed and they shrieked as they moved away. They were quickly drenched again because Sigwart nimbly leapt over the parapet to attack Hannes again as he lay in the water.

"You are expelled from the guild! You will never again find employment, you ... you dishonorable weasel! In the pillory is where you belong!"

He grabbed Hannes by the throat with both hands and pushed him down, under the surface of the water.

Hannes was submerged in the ice-cold water. He kicked and fought with all his might. But the master had him in an iron grip until he almost drowned. He desperately thrashed around until he succeeded in twisting onto his stomach. He bent his knees and pushed up, trying to free himself, while the older man straddled him. Then he arched his back and, like a bucking bronco, cast off his tormentor.

The master landed on his well-padded behind when he hit the water. With lightning speed, Hannes swung around and, as soon as Sigwart surfaced, he knocked him out with a well-placed uppercut. Then he took the unconscious man and heaved him over the parapet. The master landed on the pavement like a wet, motionless sack.

Hannes bowed to the spectators with a mocking smile and turned to the apprentices and his fellow journeymen, who gawked at him sheepishly.

Triumphantly he shouted the motto of the carpenters' guild and added, "A carpenter is known by his chips!"

The guard adjusted his black bicorne and stepped forward.

"Master Sigwart! Hannes Hiller! By the authority vested in me, I arrest you for disturbing the peace and for public brawling!"

The stranger intervened.

"Feel free to take the master away as soon as he regains consciousness. I shall lay claim to the other offender in the name of His Serene Highness, Duke Carl Eugen."

The guard hesitated. He had, of course, noticed the stranger's dark blue coat, the white breeches, and the high black boots of a Württemberg officer. Yet in their subservience to the sovereign, they were equals. He was still formulating his reply when the strange officer turned from him and shouldered his way through the crowd.

The officer approached Hannes as he washed his bloodied face in the fountain.

"That's the problem with beautiful women, is it not? They turn your head. But you, Hannes Hiller, are an impressive fighter."

He gave the young man's muscular appearance an approving look.

Hannes straightened up and wiped his wet brown hair from his face.

"Since you already know my name, may I inquire, what is yours?" There was a defiant look in his dark eyes.

The stranger lowered his head slightly.

"Von Langsdorff, Grenadier Captain of His Serene Highness, Carl Eugen."

"And what, may I ask, is your interest here, Grenadier Captain?" asked Hannes, as he wrung out his vest.

"Don't you want to join me for a nice mug of something before you catch your death of cold out here?" Von Langsdorff gestured toward the Golden Lamb. "On me."

"But you'll be wanting something in return!"

"An amusing story, that's all," the captain countered magnanimously. "Such as how a lusty young fellow like you ended up in such a backwoods place as this?"

Hannes knit his brows. His village near Stuttgart might deserve such a term, but surely not the venerable town of Tübingen, with its renowned university and the stunning castle high above the Neckar River. Nevertheless, the strange officer's words had piqued his interest. And besides, a bit of warmth and a nice brandy sounded good.

He glanced over at the master, who was still dazed and being propped up by the senior journeyman. The little fling with the master's wife and the brawl had cost Hannes his employment and his earnings. And he had forfeited his place to sleep in the master's garret. The feeling of triumph over having won the fight faded. He thought of his mother, and wondered what she would think of all this, as the last of his exhilaration dissipated. His mother was a widow and his father, who'd also been a carpenter, had left them penniless. To see to her basic needs, Hannes had been sending her a good part of his earnings. Without those few kreutzers, she would end up in the poorhouse.

He swallowed hard and looked at von Langsdorff, who had been studying him. He was willing to bet all of his tools that there was something behind this stranger's invitation. But if it meant he got one or two goblets of brandy out of the deal...

Hannes took a deep breath. "Agreed, Grenadier Captain."

"One jug of brandy for this valiant young man and me!" the captain shouted to the innkeeper, who was sorting mugs and bottles on a shelf behind the counter.

Von Langsdorff quickly surveyed the room before heading to a small table with two chairs by the fireplace. Using the tip of his rapier, he shooed away a fat black cat that had been dozing in front of the crackling fire. Then he pointed to one of the chairs before taking a seat on the other. By now the innkeeper had placed two pewter vessels on the counter and was filling a jug from the tap of a small keg.

Hannes sat down gingerly. His body ached as though the master had used a log as well as his fists to pummel him.

This was his first time in the Golden Lamb and he looked around curiously. Tradesmen, farmers, and merchants from the market went to the Kronenschenke on the other side of the market square to celebrate, to play dice and occasionally to brawl. The Golden Lamb was the locality for burghers.

The inn was well patronized. Some people were playing *ombre* at an oak table. Three professors wearing black gowns and powdered wigs debated at another. A lone guest sat hunched over a weighty tome in the back of the room and, seated in an alcove, the apothecary from the neighboring pharmacy and the pastor from the Church of St. George were eating sweet and sour tripe stew, and washing it down with a quarter liter of wine.

The only woman in the place was the barmaid, a pretty, buxom little thing who was wiping the counter with a wet rag. Upon locking eyes with Hannes, she smiled pertly at him and straightened her bodice. He winked at her and she quickly laid down her rag, took the full jug of brandy and the two vessels and sashayed over to Hannes and von Langsdorff.

"Don't you want to remove your wet clothing? Here, I'll help you."

She placed the jug and pewter drinking vessels on the table, while looking lasciviously at his broad chest.

"Oh, I surrender to your advice," he laughed. She leaned over and tugged at his kerchief. "Whoa, not so fast!" He took hold of her wrist.

"Back to work!" the innkeeper barked.

"Well, is he supposed to come down with a fever, drenched like that?" she countered.

"Perhaps the young lady would not mind bringing him a blanket instead of undressing him in the middle of the taproom," von Langsdorff suggested.

"Go ahead. I'm not going anywhere," said Hannes. He playfully slapped her on the hip and she bustled away with a giggle.

The innkeeper continued to grumble until von Langsdorff threw his bulging leather wallet on the table and the coins inside jingled.

"It seems that you appeal to the fairer sex." The grenadier captain took the jug and filled Hannes' goblet to the rim.

Hannes was flattered, and grinned. "Well, at least I know where I'm going to sleep tonight."

"She is fair and beauteous, that barmaid." The captain raised his glass. "To women and their virtues!"

The smell of the fruit brandy was enticing. Hannes emptied his goblet in one gulp and immediately felt the warming effects flow through him.

Von Langsdorff refilled his mug at once.

"With all due respect, young man, getting caught flirting borders on folly."

"You're right, Grenadier Captain. But still, I enjoyed it." Hannes began his second brandy while the captain still nursed his first.

Hannes' thoughts began drifting to his frequent trysts in the laundry room with the master's wife, while the master lay

13

snoring in the marital bed. This had long gone undetected until earlier that day, when they had become reckless. At midday, when the stew was being served, the mistress had whispered to Hannes, telling him to meet her in the broom closet later. That little exchange had not gone unnoticed by her jealous husband. Just as Hannes loosened the mistress' bodice to kiss her resplendent white breasts, Sigwart had stormed in.

"What are your plans now, with no work and no pay?" Von Langsdorff refilled Hannes' brandy.

"Move on," Hannes shrugged.

"There aren't too many work sites in the winter," the officer pointed out.

"There are many repairs that need doing in the cold season. The beams of the Tübingen Town Hall aren't the only ones affected by wood worm."

Hannes sounded more confident than he felt. His traveling book, which contained all the certificates of his previous jobs, was locked in the guild chest, the guardian of which was Master Sigwart. Without these certificates he was unlikely to find work.

"Here, wrap this around you." The barmaid returned and handed him a blanket of coarse wool. Then she placed a pewter bowl filled with water on the table, dipped a corner of the blanket in it and dabbed his bruised face.

"How's that now, sir?" She leaned forward and allowed Hannes a good look into the *décolletage* of her bodice.

"A wondrous view!" The brandy blurred his vision, but he could see quite clearly that the girl's breasts were round and firm like two luscious apples.

He took hold of her hips and said, "I know of something else you could do for me."

"First, the young lady is going to get us another jug of her excellent brandy."

Von Langsdorff placed a coin on the table. "For your service."

The girl's eyes grew wide. The silvery thaler was quite a bit of money, at least four kreutzers. She quickly slipped it into her apron pocket, took the jug and left.

"So, have you completed your journeyman years?" von Langsdorff inquired.

"Yes, Grenadier Captain. Three years and one day." Hannes took his brandy and drank from it.

"And how old are you?"

"I'll be twenty-two in February. If I may ask, sir, why are you interrogating me?"

The barmaid returned and placed another full jug on the table. She gave Hannes a suggestive look and walked away, swinging her hips.

Von Langsdorff was about to replenish his drink but Hannes raised his hand.

"I've had enough. If I have any more, I won't have a chance with the girl."

"Surely a vigorous young man will be up to it!" Von Langsdorff filled Hannes' goblet to the brim.

Hannes nodded, took the goblet, and emptied it.

Von Langsdorff leaned across the table. "That young wench over there is quite fair, but there are women on this earth who are ravishing enough to make you think you've landed in paradise."

"Oh yes? And where do I find such women?" Hannes slurred.

Von Langsdorff gestured. "Such exquisite females don't come cheap. What does a carpenter make in one month? Six gulden? And you don't have even that much anymore."

Hannes was silent. This aristocratic officer did not need to know that his entire fortune at that time amounted to no more than twelve kreutzers, sewn into his vest. Tomorrow was payday—though not for him.

"I know what you're thinking," said von Langsdorff. "All that hard work, year in, year out, and in the end it's barely enough to keep body and soul together."

Hannes stared into his drink with glassy eyes.

"I can help you," he heard von Langsdorff saying conspiratorially. "All you have to do is say yes and I will help you on your way to paradise. You will have wealth and prosperity and the world's most beautiful women at your feet."

"Arise! Arise!"

Hannes shot up, groaning, and grabbing his aching head. The loud voice pierced his skull. Frigid morning air flowed over his skin. He shivered. Closing his eyes, he reached for the cover but instead of the woolen material his fingers found soft, warm flesh.

"Eeehhh!" A piercing shriek rattled him. He squinted reluctantly. A young woman sat next to him on the narrow cot. She was naked, with her arms crossed protectively over her breasts, and her eyes wide open in shock. Water ran down her naked body. At first, he had no idea who she was but then he recognized the barmaid from the Golden Lamb. How had he landed in this bed with her?

"Get dressed, you good-for-nothing! Hurry up!"

Cold water splashed his face. Hannes snorted and spat.

"Curse it! What was that for?"

He felt as though he had been thrashed by the master all over again but at least he was now awake. He shook himself like a wet dog and opened his eyes once and for all. The gray light of morning shone through a hatchway under the gable of a cramped garret. Next to the cot stood a man who looked vaguely familiar.

The man wore an immaculate officer's uniform, highly polished boots and a black bicorne on his powdered hair. In his right hand he dangled a woolen blanket from the tip of his rapier; in his left, he held the now-empty water jug. He casually tossed the blanket over the girl and placed the jug on a small three-legged stool.

"We have a contract, you and I," he said.

Hannes had no idea what he meant, nor did he care.

"Leave us, and let me sleep!" He reached for a corner of the blanket.

"Oh no, you don't!" The officer hit his hand with the flat edge of his rapier.

"Damnation! Have you gone mad?" Hannes began to cough and promptly gagged. He tasted bile and felt as if he had eaten a pound of rotten meat. His parched throat burned like fire.

"Enough of these antics. Get on your feet!" The officer used his rapier to pick up Hannes' clothing, which lay strewn in an untidy heap at the foot of the cot, and threw it at his head. Then he withdrew a few coins from his coat pocket and threw them into the barmaid's lap.

"You did a commendable job looking after him!"

As Hannes turned around, he saw how she gathered the coins with lightning speed. He seized her fist and pulled her fingers apart until he saw three silver coins in her palm.

"You have betrayed me!" he cried out in disbelief. Her lips quivered but she returned his gaze defiantly.

"Stop your complaining! You should be thanking me! For I have managed to get you a job as a carpenter," the officer interrupted. "And in case you don't remember to whom you owe this debt of gratitude: Von Langsdorff is my name. Grenadier Captain von Langsdorff; it is I you have to thank."

Hannes let go of the girl and held his aching head in his hands. Slowly, he began to remember fragments. He had fought with the master and a strange officer had invited him to go drinking. And was it true that later they had signed a contract? Hannes bristled. *Could I actually have fallen for the military's oldest trick?*

"So that's why you were so generous with the brandy!" he gasped. "But you'll be sorry, you wait! Damnation!" Anger swelled in him. He clenched his fists.

"Easy does it, young man!" Von Langsdorff pointed the tip of his rapier at Hannes' throat.

Hannes reluctantly lowered his arms. "I can't have been drunk enough to strike a deal like that!" he groaned.

Von Langsdorff drew a deep sigh. Then he withdrew a sheet of paper from his coat, unfolded it and held it up.

"This is your military service contract: Johannes Hiller, born on February 25, 1765 in Weilersbronn, has committed himself to serving for five years as battalion carpenter in the newly established Infantry Regiment of Württemberg."

Hannes stared at the paper. The letters danced in front of his eyes. He found reading difficult, particularly in his extremely hungover condition, but he recognized his clumsy signature next to the red seal at the bottom of the document.

"Sweet Mother of God! Five years! And you conspired with him!" he snapped at the barmaid.

She sat silently, clutching the coins to her bosom.

Cursed drinking! What have I let myself in for? He got up, slipped into his knee breeches and shirt, and stepped into his boots, which were still wet. He tied his shoulder-length hair at his neck and tried to remember what had happened. Alas, he could not. The greater part of the previous day was erased from his memory.

"You didn't do so badly. As a tradesman in the field, you'll be earning ten gulden a month. Honor and glory for the taking. And remember: women love men in uniform." Von Langsdorff waved the contract in the air.

Hannes considered his possibilities, not an easy task with his throbbing headache. Truth be told, he did not relish the thought of risking his neck for the power plays of some duke. On the other hand, the pay was enough to ensure that his mother had a life free from cares in the little house that his father had built. And then there was that matter with the women. He had often noticed how infatuated women were with men in uniform.

"And you swear that those ten gulden are actually in the contract?" he asked.

The grenadier captain nodded emphatically. "In addition, the regiment will supply you with a complete uniform, weapons and rations. If you get sick, the regiment's barber surgeon will take of you."

"There's one thing I don't understand," Hannes said as he pulled on his vest. "Duke Carl Eugen is not waging a war at the moment. Why does he require a brand-new regiment?"

Von Langsdorff tugged on his gloves. "I explained all that to you before you signed the contract. But if you insist, I will explain it to you again once we're on the way."

"Why not now?"

"There's no time. We must leave."

"Leave? Where're we going?"

"Ludwigsburg. That's where the regiment is forming."

Hannes nodded slowly. "Agreed. But first, you must fulfill three requests."

"Be careful, young man," von Langsdorff grumbled.

Hannes, who was about half a head taller, approached the grenadier captain. He placed his hands on his hips and looked at the officer. "First of all, I am ravenous and I understand that the breakfast at the Golden Lamb is tasty and satisfying."

Von Langsdorff hesitated. "All right," he eventually agreed.

"Secondly, I need my warm jacket. I left it at the worksite in front of the town hall and I obviously cannot go back there. Have it brought to me while I am having breakfast."

Von Langsdorff thought for a moment. "I'll keep you company while you breakfast, and have someone fetch your jacket. What else?"

"I want to say goodbye to my mother."

Von Langsdorff was losing his patience. "We don't have time for pleasure trips. The regiment must be formed and ready to march as quickly as possible."

"These are my conditions. Should you refuse, I shall disappear before you've drawn your rapier." Hannes said firmly. Following his father's death, his mother had had to rely on him for her livelihood. She would be distraught if he disappeared.

Von Langsdorff groaned, "Where does your mother live?"

"In Weilersbronn near Stuttgart, right along the route to Ludwigsburg."

The captain's face relaxed. "Well, in that case, there is nothing to prevent you from saying farewell to your mother."

"I'll take your word for it." Hannes tromped toward the door. The girl called out to him, "Come back any time! I enjoyed it."

Hannes ignored her and closed the door behind him.

CHAPTER TWO

DUCHY OF WÜRTTEMBERG, 1786 – 1787

While Hannes and von Langsdorff breakfasted on barley porridge and a mug of watered-down wine, the innkeeper's son fetched Hannes' jacket from the town hall. Before they finished, a sergeant with eight men in tow appeared at their table. He snapped his salute.

"Respectfully report, Grenadier Captain, the new recruits are ready!"

As Hannes took stock of these hungover young men, he realized that he had not been the only one to have fallen into the recruiter's trap.

After the regiment, accompanied by von Langsdorff, departed on foot, he learned that almost all the recruits were craftsmen and sons of farmers. Only one was a student who had composed a defamatory song about the territorial sovereign, Duke Carl Eugen. He had opted to go into the military to avoid prison. Two of the young men had traded their sentence in debtors' prison for this stint in the military. Five of the recruits had had the same experience as Hannes: a strange officer had invited them for a drink and when they woke up the next morning with a throbbing headache, they found out they had become soldiers.

Eventually, von Langsdorff shared with them the reason for the infantry regiment of Württemberg. While the regiment was technically the duke's, he had rented it out to the Dutch East India Company, *Vereenigde Oostindische Compagnie*, or VOC. The Company needed protection on the way to the Kaap de Goede

Hoop, the Cape of Good Hope, in South Africa, where their ships berthed on their way to and from East India. In Kaapstad, Cape Town, the ships replenished provisions, discharged crew who had fallen ill, and carried out any necessary repairs.

"Your work at the Cape is going to be pure relaxation," von Langsdorff insisted. "There are no pirates and you will have no problems with the natives."

"That begs the question whether the VOC has too much money or whether you're not telling us the entire truth, sir," Hannes remarked. Some of the other recruits voiced their agreement.

"Far be it from me to tell you lies. Do you not know that this honorable Company, as the merchants call it, is the richest and mightiest trading company in the world? They own three thousand ships that transport spices, silk, tea, and porcelain from East India and sell them throughout Europe. Maintaining a regiment is child's play for them."

"Still, I don't believe that this honorable Company has enlisted us for its amusement," Hannes persisted.

"Have I told you that the Company has built brand new barracks for the regiment? Do you remember what I told you in Tübingen about the women?" Von Langsdorff winked at him conspiratorially.

Hannes grumbled but the other recruits pricked up their ears and besieged von Langsdorff with questions. He did not hesitate with his answers and before long there was a lively discussion.

The march was exhausting, as the unremitting rain turned the street into a muddy mess. Before long, some of the recruits complained because von Langsdorff, the only one on horseback, kept a brisk pace. Their uniforms were drenched and their boots were the worse for wear. The men's discontent was growing but a sergeant marched behind the group and saw to it that none of them tried to steal away.

Whenever they passed through a village, more recruiting officers joined them with other young men. By the time they reached the Filder Plain shortly before Weilersbronn, their group had grown to thirty soldiers and five recruiters and officers. At last, the sun emerged from the low-hanging clouds and bathed the vineyards, potato fields and harvested fields in a soft golden light.

Hannes' mother lived in a tiny mudwalled house at the end of the village road. A chicken coop leaned against the back wall. The last turnips and heads of cabbage were visible in the beds of the little garden. The hazelnut trees had been harvested and the leaves of the raspberry bushes and apple trees had been raked into a tidy heap.

Hannes stepped up to the fence and rested his hands on the warped slats. The little house was more rundown than he remembered. The paint on the shutters was peeling, the mud walls needed a coat of paint as well, and the wood shingles on the roof were in a sorry state.

The narrow door to the chicken coop opened and Hannes' mother stepped out. She held an empty seed bowl. Her brown dress and apron were old and worn but Hannes was relieved to note that she looked healthy and her wrinkled face seemed alert and alive. When she noticed the group in front of her house, she stopped in surprise.

"Greetings, Mother!" said Hannes.

Her eyes grew wide. "Good God, boy! Why are you not in Tübingen?" She looked at the curious villagers, the recruits, and officers.

"God Almighty, now I understand! So, you've been snagged. They were here, too, and picked up young men on the Filder Plain for the duke's new regiment. They picked through the hay stacks and slit open the beds and if one of them wouldn't go willingly, they pulled out their rapiers."

Looking directly at von Langsdorff, she spat on the ground. "Your job is a disgrace!"

With that, she turned on her heel and hurried toward the house. Hannes saw her wipe her eyes with the tip of her shawl. He quickly opened the gate, rushed after her and embraced her.

"They even dragged August Eberle from the sickhouse," she lamented. "And yet the poor soul doesn't even know how to tie his boots."

"But August is only sixteen," Hannes cried out in astonishment. "He's much too young."

"Well, that doesn't bother those high and mighty gentlemen! They'll take anyone they can get." She raised her head and froze.

"Look at you! Did the recruiters do that to you? Is that how they got you to join?"

"Don't worry, Mother," he tried to soothe her. "Would I let anyone force me to do anything? I want to join the regiment!"

"Silly boy, you don't know what you say." He felt her rough hands glide over the scabs and bruises on his face.

"If they didn't do it, you must have been in a fight again! Did you join them to avoid going to prison?"

"Methinks she knows her son well!" von Langsdorff cackled on the other side of the fence.

"Mother, please believe me! I look forward to my service. I'm going to see the world and have adventures."

"Adventures are for fairy tales. But you were always one to act first and think later." She took his hands. "How long will you be away?"

"Five years."

She looked at him aghast. "Before those are over, an old woman like me is going to be dead and buried. That's if you return at all!"

"Of course, I'll return," he retorted. "We'll see each other again, Mother! Strong and sound as you are!" He laid his arm around her and led her to the bench by the front door.

"You know, it takes quite a bit to harm me."

They sat down. His mother pulled a cloth from her apron and noisily blew her nose. "Could you not have sold yourself for just one year?"

"No, I could not," he explained patiently. "The regiment will be stationed in South Africa. One year will almost have passed before we even arrive."

She let out a piercing cry. "They're sending you to the end of the world, are they?" She shook a clenched fist in von Langsdorff's direction.

"You are an evil man! Snaring my only child with your talk! Oh, but there'll come a time when you'll have to account to God for your actions!"

Murmurs of approval could be heard coming from the villagers and recruits.

"Really now, my good woman!" Von Langsdorff replied peevishly.

"Please calm down, Mother. South Africa is a beautiful spot with a pleasant climate. A nice place to live."

Hannes thought about everything he had learned on the long trek about this mysterious place at the other end of the earth. None of the officers had ever been there and many of the new recruits had never set foot outside of Württemberg. Still, they all had had something to say about South Africa. His mother, too, had clear ideas about the place.

"Don't talk nonsense, boy! A place full of savages and dangerous animals is what it is. You weren't here that summer when the troupe with the menagerie stopped off. They had beasts of prey with yellow fur, big as three grown wolves and fangs as long as my hand! And those Negroes! Godless black-skinned monsters is what they are." She pulled her shawl close.

Hannes took her hand. "The yellow predators are called lions. And as soon as one of them gets close to me, I'll teach it a lesson with my shotgun. And the Negroes are not monsters but human beings. South Africa is big, Mother, much bigger than our Württemberg. There is room for many people and animals. Imagine, there are antelopes, which can jump better than our goats, and elephants as tall as your house, and striped horses that you cannot ride, called zebras."

Along the way, he had also learned that South Africa was home to palm-sized spiders, venomous snakes as thick as one's arm, as well as enormous lizards with protective scales that devoured every other animal that ventured too close. That was information he chose not to share.

"Striped horses!" his mother exclaimed. "Don't you toy with me!" Again, she wiped her eyes with the corner of her cloth.

"See to it that nothing happens to my boy," she warned von Langsdorff. "Otherwise, I'll go to the duke in Ludwigsburg myself and bring charges against you."

"You won't have to, Mother," Hannes interjected. "I won't be living in the wilderness but in a town on the Cape of Good Hope. Only white people live there. The captain says that the only Negroes are the slaves that the white people keep."

Von Langsdorff had also claimed that the female slaves were exotic beauties whose sensuality verged on licentiousness. But, of course, that was another detail he withheld from his mother.

She nodded hesitantly, trying to come to terms with the inevitable. At last, she rose and walked over to the fence.

"Help me understand one more thing, sir." She looked sternly at von Langsdorff. "Why does our duke need a regiment in South Africa?"

The grenadier captain took a deep breath and picked at a few invisible threads on his uniform jacket.

"His Serene Highness has concluded an agreement with the reputable Dutch East India Company in Amsterdam and—"

"Speak to me in a way I can understand!" She flashed angrily at him. "Or are you some know-it-all and don't want me to understand?"

Hannes intervened, "The regiment is the duke's but we serve the Dutch East India Company. Our job will be to protect the trading post that the gentlemen merchants use for their ships."

"So, as I understand it, the duke is selling his country's children to the Dutch! He has no desire to dirty his own hands when he needs money for his palaces and mistresses, does he?" Hannes' mother was disgusted.

Von Langsdorff lifted his hand.

"Madam, I urge you to contain yourself, lest you end up in the fortress of Hohenasperg."

Hannes yanked his mother away from the fence.

"Mother, I've concluded a favorable contract with decent pay, more than what Master Sigwart paid me. Ten gulden every month! I'll send it to you because the regiment provides for me and I won't need it. You'll have a good life, Mother. Much better than now!"

"That's just on paper! Or have you seen a single kreutzer of your pay so far, huh?"

"Not yet, Mother. But we're about to get paid in Ludwigsburg. That means new shingles for your roof before the winter wind starts blowing across the Filder Plains."

"The fence needs repairing too." She looked over at the warped slats.

Hannes removed his knife from his belt and slit open the seam of his jacket, causing some coins to fall out. He collected them and placed them in his mother's hand.

"Here are twelve kreutzers. You'll get more soon, I promise."

"And what about you?" she asked as she slowly closed her hand around the money.

"I don't need anything." He swallowed hard. "I told you. The regiment will provide for me."

Von Langsdorff turned his horse around.

"It's time."

Hannes nodded sorrowfully. By now the sun had set. Soon it would be dark and they still had to set up their tents for the night. He enfolded his mother in his arms. She stifled a sob.

"These heartless people won't even allow a son to spend his last evening at home with his mother."

He kissed her gray hairline.

"Don't cry, Mother. I am making my fortune. You'll see."

She stepped back from his embrace, reached under her bodice, and pulled out her only piece of jewelry. It was a chain with a small silver cross that her father had given her on the occasion of her confirmation. Hannes had never known her to remove this necklace. Yet at this moment she pulled it over her head and hung it around her son's neck. Then she took his face in her hands.

"May God be by your side always and may you never lose hope while you are far from home."

Snow lay on the streets and in the squares of Ludwigsburg, the duke's residence, that last Saturday in February. Still, the sun shone and the birds sitting in the leafless trees sang as though they knew that spring was near.

After morning roll call, all nine hundred sixty-two soldiers, seventy-eight non-commissioned officers and thirty-eight commissioned officers of the 1st Battalion of the Württemberg Infantry Regiment marched to the garrison church to attend the farewell service conducted by the army chaplain, Master Spönlin. Afterwards, they marched to the palace, where the duke and his retinue were to witness the solemn consecration of the flag.

Despite the wintry cold, the streets, and the square in front of the palace were teeming with people. They sang a song composed especially for the soldiers by the poet Christian Friedrich Daniel Schubart on the occasion of their farewell:

> *"Onward brethren and be strong,*
> *departure day is here!*
> *A heavy weight upon our souls*
> *as on the lands and seas we go,*
> *to scorching Africa."*

Their voices could be heard all the way in the main courtyard, where regimental commander Colonel Baron von Hügel paced back and forth in front of the regiment and gave a speech about soldierly virtues and discipline. In front of the *corps de logis*, which housed the state apartments, sat the duke and duchess, surrounded by their household and guests, who sat in armchairs specially set up for the occasion.

A little warmth would be nice, Hannes thought as he wriggled his freezing toes in his buckled shoes, which were made of exceedingly thin leather. His uniform, consisting of a dark blue jacket, white knee breeches, a white shirt and vest, while impressive-looking, hardly provided enough warmth. His leather helmet with the black horse's tail was too tight and painful. As an army carpenter, Hannes also wore a work apron and a long-handled axe.

The uniforms and weapons for the battalion had arrived just one week before. In general, the garrison's preparation for the recruits had been abysmal. There had been neither furniture nor cooking implements when they arrived in late November. Before long, rumors began making the rounds that the duke and the merchants of the honorable Company were disputing the division of costs down to the last kreutzer.

"Cold," a voice next to Hannes said plaintively. August Eberle was rubbing his arms. He, too, had been assigned to the second of the ten companies of the 1st Battalion. Of course, the recruits were under orders to stand still and look straight ahead, but three months of drills had failed to teach August to obey orders. Hannes assumed that he simply did not understand what was asked of him, and blows and kicks from the non-commissioned officers had not taught him anything either.

"Quiet!" Hannes hissed. "You'll end up with a real beating if you're not careful. And put your arms down."

August nodded eagerly and obediently placed his hands by his side. A little while later, he began shifting from one foot to the other. Hannes looked over at the duke. It was the first, and most likely the last, time that he would meet him face to face.

Duke Carl Eugen sat enthroned on a gilt ceremonial armchair. His plump cheeks jiggled with his every move, and his fur-trimmed velvet coat with the broad sash of medals was tight over his round belly. In his younger days, this man was rumored to have been quite a *bon vivant*, who had almost ruined the duchy with his many love affairs and ostentatious court. Hannes thought that he bore a great resemblance to the pug that his second wife, Duchess Franziska von Hohenheim, held on her lap. Sitting next to the duke, she conversed quietly with the woman on her other side, the wife of the regiment commander, the Baroness Anna Maria von Hügel. She was an elegant lady with a feathered hat and long, white powdered curls.

The colonel finished his address and returned to his seat. Then the duke rose and extended his right hand. An adjutant immediately rushed over and handed him a rolled parchment. Carl Eugen opened it, remained motionless for a moment, and then declared in a loud voice:

"We, Carl Eugen of Württemberg, hereby permit every officer, non-commissioned officer and common soldier, be he a fusilier, grenadier or cannoneer, craftsman or musician, if he is not willing to set out on the journey to South Africa, to leave the regiment here and now, without fear of punishment or persecution!"

There was utter silence as the duke handed the paper back to his adjutant and returned to his seat. Everyone seemed stunned by this unexpected announcement. Hannes wondered what the twist might be to such a generous offer. A soldier behind him had no such misgivings.

"That's what I call a gift!"

He stepped out of line, followed by two others. They gave their weapons to a sergeant and left the courtyard, unimpeded.

The thought of being a free man gave Hannes a painful feeling of longing. No standing at attention for hours, no drills. No shouted orders he was obliged to follow, no matter how senseless they might seem. He took a deep breath, thought of his mother and how happy she would be if he left the regiment. But how would he provide for her? Without a job and his certificates?

Quack, quack, quack. Three ducks flew across the courtyard, loudly flapping their wings, a female followed by two drakes.

"Nice birdies!" August enthusiastically waved his arms.

The duke noticed, and, not accustomed to such lack of respect, he stiffened. The duchess tried to soothe him by gently placing her hand on his arm. Hannes noticed how some of the guests tried to hide their amusement by averting their faces. Baroness von Hügel covered her mouth but her shoulders shook as she suppressed her laughter. Her husband's expression, however, was almost more horrified than the duke's.

The colonel's adjutant hastened before the regiment and shouted, "Attention!"

Instantly, all the soldiers, non-commissioned and commissioned officers stood at attention. Only August craned his neck and followed the ducks with his eyes as they flew in a big circle over the battalion.

"Nice," he repeated, spellbound. "Nice birdies."

"Quiet!" Hannes elbowed him hard but August paid no heed. He was mesmerized, watching the loudly quacking ducks head directly toward the duke, flying so close that they almost brushed the plume of feathers on his hat.

"Ha!" he laughed and slapped his thighs. "Haha!"

The duke and his retinue froze.

"Attention! Eyes front!" the adjutant screamed. The startled company sergeant rushed over to August and rammed his fist into his face. The boy's laughter turned into a scream of pain. He stumbled and fell. The sergeant was about to kick him but was prevented by Hannes' swift action. He pushed the man aside and kneeled down next to August, who, holding his face with both hands, whimpered, and rolled from one side to the other. Hannes removed his kerchief and dabbed the boy's bleeding nose. Then he took him by the arm and yanked him to his feet.

"By God, if you want to stop getting walloped, you've got to silence yourself!"

"These miscreants are to be punished most severely for their insubordination!" Colonel von Hügel bellowed. "Take them away!"

The sergeant drew his rapier. Hannes tightened the grip on his axe. No one was going to punish him for helping a poor devil who did not even understand what was going on around him!

"My lord!" The voice of the Baroness von Hügel could be heard clearly in the tense silence of the courtyard. "I entreat you to show mercy."

"Hold your peace!" commanded her husband as he turned away from her. "You do not understand military discipline."

"My sentiments exactly," the duke barged in as soon as he had recovered from the shock. "Discipline and order are of the utmost importance in a regiment."

"We can all attest to the fact that the discipline of these soldiers is beyond reproach," the duchess now spoke up. "To be sure, one of them made a mistake. But it came from a feeling of joy and," she paused, "inexperience."

"And the other recruit carried out a laudable act of compassion," added Baroness von Hügel.

The duke shook his head so vigorously that his double chin shook.

"I beseech you with all my heart," the duchess asked softly yet emphatically.

"Very well. Just for you, Franzele." Carl Eugen gave a brief nod to Colonel von Hügel. "Begin the consecration of the flag."

It seemed as though von Hügel gritted his teeth but then he raised his arm to give the order.

Footmen arrived and arranged a long table in the space between the battalion and the guests and brought along hammers and nails. Again, orders were shouted. At the sound of a drum roll, officers brought forward two wooden poles and the two battalion flags and placed them on the table.

A corporal selected four soldiers to hold the flagpoles. The chaplain blessed the flags, took the hammer and, in the name of the Holy Trinity, struck the first nails into each of the flagpoles. Next came the regimental commander and the highest-ranking officers. Finally, the duchess and Baroness von Hügel stepped forward. As patronesses of the flag, it was their task to strike the last two nails.

While the sovereign's wife approached her duty with solemnity, the spouse of the regimental commander watched the soldiers. Her eyes rested on Hannes and August, who stood at attention not too far from her. August anxiously stared straight ahead, dried blood smeared between his nose and mouth. Hannes sensed that he was being watched. He turned his head slightly and met the gaze of the officer's wife. *A fine-looking woman*, he thought.

She smiled, as though she had read his mind. The rise in the little beauty mark on the left side of her mouth betrayed her.

The spectators applauded. The duchess had successfully driven in her nail. Next, it was the baroness' turn. With a solemn bow, an officer handed her the hammer and a nail. She gave him a grateful nod, stepped over to the table and placed the tip of the nail on the flag. She lifted the hammer and lowered it on to the iron head, but it slipped. The nail lay on its side, spent and useless. Hannes grinned. He had seen the mishap coming because she had swung the hammer like a handkerchief.

The baroness was not abashed in the slightest.

"How clumsy of me!" she cried out with a smile. "Perhaps one of these gentlemen has some expertise and might be willing to assist me?"

At once, two officers stepped forward, and yet she pointed to Hannes.

"He looks like the right one."

Colonel von Hügel grew red in the face and leaned forward as though he were about to lunge at Hannes. It was only the duke's presence that prevented it. However, everyone could see what he thought of his wife's choice of the very soldier who had come within a hair of being thrown in prison.

Hannes thought he must be dreaming. Never before had a lady of high society, an aristocrat who was part of the duke's court, shown any interest in him.

Ignoring the baron's furious glances, he stepped up and said, swollen with pride, "I would be honored to assist you."

He took a new nail, smoothed the flag on the pole and placed the nail on the flag. The baroness smiled and gave him her slender left hand. Hannes gently placed it on the nail.

"Hold it tight, my lady."

"Shall I fear for my fingers?" she asked.

"Not if you trust me, my lady." He stepped behind her and leaned over her shoulder. Then he placed the hammer in her other hand.

"Use care!" He strengthened his grip and skillfully aimed three blows into the wood.

"What a pleasure it would be to be guided more often by such strong hands as these," she said over the roaring applause. "At the back of the *corps de logis*, there is a side entrance. Be there on the strike of eight," she added softly.

Shortly after dark, his fellow soldiers had fallen asleep, Hannes climbed out of the narrow window of the dormitory of his barracks. Fortunately, the window faced the street so that he did not risk encountering the sentry guarding the entrance. He ran through the quiet nocturnal streets to the ducal residence. At a safe distance from the guard house, he scaled the wall surrounding the palace and its gardens.

Despite the darkness, he was able to make out the projections, wings, towers, and alcoves of the vast palace without difficulty thanks to the light burning in most of the many windows. The *corps de logis* was not far and he had no trouble finding the small door in the back.

On the stroke of eight from the palace chapel, a tiny crack appeared in the door and an arm waved him in. Inside, a darkly clad female figure was waiting. He could not make out the face since it was almost entirely obscured by the cape of her gown. He assumed her to be the baroness' chambermaid. She placed a finger on her lips and motioned him to follow her. They quickly ascended the stairs. Candlesticks mounted in iron sconces threw their flickering light on the bare gray stone. Hannes was a little disappointed to see nothing of the pomp of which the duke was so fond. Clearly, this was the servants' entrance.

On the second floor they turned down a long, narrow corridor before stopping in front of a plain wooden door. The woman knocked three times before motioning Hannes to enter and silently closing the door after him.

He found himself standing in a lavish, square room. The only light, coming from a crackling fire in the fireplace, radiated a welcome warmth after the drafty hallways. A giant crystal chandelier was suspended from the middle of the ceiling. On the walls hung mirrors, and portraits of people he could not recognize in the scant light. On the dressing table by the window sat diverse jars, little boxes, and brushes, flanked by two porcelain amphoras. The most prominent piece in the room was the large bed to his left. Its posts were carved, its canopy was high, its heavy red brocade drapes half-closed. A pair of delicate slippers lay carelessly discarded on the rug.

Hannes cleared his throat.

"Baroness?"

A muffled laugh could be heard coming from the bed and his heart began to beat wildly. He was not inexperienced. He had discovered the charms of the fairer sex after his parents apprenticed him to a master in Vaihingen. But never had an aristocratic lady tried to seduce him.

"Remove your garments and come to me," a voice purred. He noticed a movement and saw the naked legs of a woman. The rest of the body remained hidden behind the brocade curtain.

His arousal grew as he beheld the well-shaped legs and small feet. He swiftly slipped out of his clothes and sat down on the bed. Anna Maria von Hügel pushed the brocade curtain aside. She lay before him on a mountain of pillows, her curly hair coiled around her marble white breasts. Her skin glistened in the twilight and her body seemed to consist only of enticing curves.

She surveyed his broad shoulders, small waist and muscular legs and her smile broadened.

"I knew that the sight of you would not disappoint," she observed.

She stretched out one arm and pulled him close, using her other hand to free his hair from the ribbon and ruffle it. He smelled the intoxicating scent of her perfume and, aroused, leaned forward to kiss her.

"Just a moment, my young hero. We are going to savor this tête-à-tête."

She gently pushed him away. It was only then that he noticed the little table on the other side of the bed. Its top had a recessed basin from which the necks of two bottles protruded. She rolled on to her stomach, took out one of the bottles and pressed it against his naked chest. He gave a start at its cold temperature, and she laughed.

"There is ice in the basin. Have you ever tasted champagne?"

He shook his head. She leaned over the edge of the bed and reappeared with two glasses and a small knife.

"It tastes like nectar and ambrosia when it's well chilled. And naturally this heavenly drink comes from France, where they understand the art of living better than anywhere else on earth." She shook the bottle a few times and handed him the knife.

"Cut the string."

He obediently cut the thin twine wound around the cork. There was a deafening bang and the cork flew high into the air.

"Sweet Mother of God!" Hannes recoiled. The champagne spumed and ran all over his fingers.

"Champagne is effervescent," she explained, quite amused. "It stirs the blood and makes desire sparkle."

She held out the glasses. He filled them carefully and was about to have a taste before she stopped him.

"I'll show you how to relish this divine nectar. À ta santé!"

She toasted him, placed her head back and emptied the tulip-shaped glass in one gulp. Then she wrapped her arms around his neck, pulled him close and kissed him greedily. He opened his lips and felt the champagne, cool and sweet, flow from her mouth into his. She released him.

"Now it's your turn."

He took the glass, threw his head back and drank as he had watched her do. He kept the last mouthful and kissed her deeply and urgently. Beads of champagne rolled from her lips and down her neck. He followed their trail with his tongue all the way to her erect nipples. She took hold of his hair with both hands and pulled him up.

"Love me," she whispered. "Love me long and passionately."

Much later, as the flames in the fireplace were dying, they lay in bed in a close embrace. Anna Maria's fingertips traced the muscles of Hannes' upper arms.

"Your body reminds me of a Greek hero," she noted. "What is the trade that made you so strong?"

"I learned the trade of carpentry." He freed himself from her embrace and sat up.

She placed her right hand on his back.

"You want to leave already?"

"The last time I got in the way of a husband, my lady, I received a real thrashing."

She laughed. "Do not distress yourself about my husband. We are bound by mutual respect, not sensual pleasure. All my husband asks of me is discretion."

Hannes raised his eyebrows. After his experience with Master Sigwart, he harbored some serious doubts about the magnanimity of cuckolded husbands. But then again, what did he know about the customs of the high-born?

Anna Maria lifted the second bottle of champagne out of the ice, opened it skillfully and filled both glasses.

"The bond I have with the baron concerns the welfare of our three sons. They will become officers, like their father. Our youngest is currently a student at the Hohe Carlsschule in

Stuttgart. He's only nine and already away at school. I miss him terribly."

Her expression became gentle and Hannes began to think that he would cherish Anna Maria for her maternal affection alone.

He emptied his glass and waited for her to refill it before he said, "And to think this evening almost didn't happen, my lady."

"I do believe you find me irresistible."

"I do indeed, as you know by now. And yet I was on the point of taking His Serene Highness up on his offer to leave the regiment."

"That would have been regrettable. Was I the reason you decided against leaving?"

He smiled. "In a way, my lady, though it was mainly August and the ducks."

She nodded slowly. "I understand. Truly, you have a good heart, Hannes. But tell me, why were you so ready to turn your back on the regiment?"

He considered his reply, wondering about the wisdom of sharing his motivation with, of all people, the spouse of the regiment's commander. But then he recalled that it was she who had intervened on behalf of August and himself, and he decided to trust her.

"Well, my lady, a recruiter, a von Langsdorff, promised the world to me if I signed up to serve. Now, I am not a fool and I know that not all that glitters is gold. Yet after three months of sleeping on a straw mattress under a flimsy blanket in the bitter cold, while getting paid not a single kreutzer ... my lady, it has given me to think. The men say that von Langsdorff pocketed thirty-five and the duke as much as one hundred sixty gulden for each one of us recruits. It's only us soldiers who are not getting what's coming to us!"

He shook his head emphatically and continued, "I went to the sergeant and demanded an explanation. What I got was a piece of his mind! He told me to silence my complaints and threatened me with his stick. All of this came back to me when I heard His Serene Highness' offer, and I told myself that I was a fool if I continued to bear such treatment."

He emptied his glass and wiped his mouth with the back of his hand.

Anna Maria gazed into the dying embers.

"Surely the recruiter did not force you to sign? You could have stayed a carpenter, I am sure?"

He laughed sheepishly.

"Von Langsdorff was overly generous with the brandy, my lady, and I can hardly remember how I was recruited. I stayed with the regiment because of the pay. Ten gulden a month is good pay, which I have already promised to my mother. She needs it desperately." He looked at the glass in his hand.

"Well, at least I'll see something of the world."

She placed her hand on his arm. "Your motives for staying were honorable. Remember that when you're tormented by doubts."

"My lady, I'm still owed thirty gulden, my pay for the last three months. I feel as though I've been sold at market, like a piece of meat."

Her mouth twitched but she quickly lowered her gaze.

"I'll lend you the money."

Hannes stared at her in disbelief. While he was certainly aware that she was of her wealth, he was stunned that, just like that, she could offer a sum that represented, for him, a small fortune. He swallowed hard.

"I am grateful to your ladyship, and your goodness hath nearly forced me to silence. But I cannot possibly accept this money."

"Because I am a woman?"

He avoided her gaze and remained silent.

She stroked his cheek.

"I think highly of you, Hannes. It pains me to know that your mother has to suffer without your help. You are a proud man and I respect that. If you do not want to accept my money, I will ask my husband to write a letter asking the Company to release the recruits' pay. Be patient. Merchants are a tough and stingy breed."

He placed his right hand on his chest and lowered his head.

"You are an honorable woman, my lady, in this matter, and one whose company I will surely miss."

"But why? I will be accompanying my husband to South Africa."

Another surprise.

"My lady, you are not only honorable but also bold!"

"Well, as bold as a man, I hope. Besides, I know my strong protector is nearby."

She leaned toward him and kissed him. As she released him, the clock in the palace chapel struck midnight.

"It's the twenty-fifth of February now," he said. "My birthday."

"Happy birthday!" she exclaimed and embraced him. "How old are you now?"

"Twenty-two."

"Such a tender age," she said as she looked him over softly. "It would please me to grant you a wish for your birthday. A gold pocket watch, perhaps?"

He thought for a while. Of course, a woman like this could fulfill all sorts of wishes but he did not want a delicate gem that he had to guard all the time.

"I'm not too adept with the quill," he finally said, a little embarrassed. "Would you help me write to my mother to let her know that I am well?"

"You have no wish for yourself?" She was taken aback. "Not even for more trysts like this?"

"But will we not have more in South Africa anyhow?"

"You appear to rate your amorous talents quite highly, don't you, Hannes?"

Smiling, she slipped out of bed and into elegant, revealing bedclothes made from the sheerest and most expensive silk. Then she disappeared to an adjacent room. A short while later she reappeared with an ink pot, a quill, and a sheet of paper.

"Get up, lazybones! You must tell me what to write to your mother before you go marching off to Holland."

CHAPTER THREE

AMSTERDAM, THE REPUBLIC OF THE SEVEN UNITED NETHERLANDS, 1787

Jan Pieter de Groot ran down the three steps of the Amsterdam Town Hall and threw a glance at his pocket watch. At the same time the bells in the ridge turret of the neighboring Nieuwe Kerk, the New Church, began to ring.

Two o'clock! He snapped the watch shut angrily and returned it to his coat pocket. It was extremely rude to keep a director of the Dutch East India Company waiting. Unfortunately, his appointment with the commissioners of the Wisselbank and the city magistrate had lasted longer than anticipated. They had discussed the amount of silver guilders that were to be sent as trade coins with the fleet to Asia. He was responsible, as Finance Inspector, for imprinting and sending the coins and thus had to take part in these discussions. And now he hoped that the *bewindhebbers*, the administrators, at the *Oost-Indisch Huis*, the East India House, were also running behind schedule. The Lords Seventeen, the Board of Directors of the Dutch East India Company, had been conferring every day ever since the ships of the spring fleet had returned from Asia in March.

While the cargo was unloaded at the berths in the Zuidersee, the governing body deliberated over its next purchase order, the construction of new ships and the amounts of dividends for the shareholders. In addition, the auctions of spices, cotton, silk, porcelain, silver, tea, and coffee at Europe's major trading centers were being prepared. At today's session, the Lords had been discussing how to fill the vacant positions on the board.

A dreary gray sky hung over the roofs of the city. The month of April had been marked by a constant thick drizzle and today was no exception. De Groot hunched his shoulders and pulled his bicorne deep over his face.

"Read all about the betrayal of the Orangists!"

Someone suddenly pushed a paper under his nose. He turned around and saw a boy of about twelve years of age, shielding his flyers from the rain inside his jacket. "All the information you need for just one stuiver, *mijnheer*." He grinned in anticipation.

De Groot glanced at the sheet. It depicted two pigs with the faces of Stadtholder Wilhelm V and the mayor of Amsterdam, Willem Gerrit Dedel, eating together from a feeding trough. The text underneath referred to the secret negotiations that Dedel had held with the stadtholder. For years, Amsterdam and the Republic of the Seven United Netherlands had been involved in a bitter conflict. The United Republics supported the Democratic Patriots while the monarchist supporters of the stadtholder called themselves Orangists. The warring factions were in deep opposition to each other in Amsterdam and the city was periodically torn apart by unrest.

De Groot retrieved a copper coin from his pocket. But when the boy wanted to hand him the pamphlet in return, he refused.

"Get yourself a decent job and make something of yourself."

The usually busy Dam square, surrounded by the town hall, the Nieuwe Kerk and the Damrak Canal, was almost deserted. The merchants, wrapped in their cloaks, attended to the few maidservants and housewives who braved the weather to make their purchases. A few beggars sought refuge under the walls of the Nieuwe Kerk and a fellow relieved himself under the steps of the old Weigh House.

When he reached the canal, where the barges were being moored as they were every day, he could hear behind him the rhythmic steps of heavy boots walking to the beat of drums and a man's voice shouting commands. As he looked over his shoulder, he saw a company of soldiers march across the square under the command of a lieutenant. The white and red plumes on their hats told him that they belonged to the Free Corps of the Patriots. The boy selling propaganda in front of the town hall ran toward them, waving his cap.

De Groot walked on, shaking his head. He left Damrak Street with its tall, narrow merchants' buildings on the left and turned west on to Kalverstraat. Publishers, printing presses, engravers, book, and art merchants had their shops along this street. Scattered among these were coffee houses, where business and politics were enthusiastically discussed.

De Groot was headed to an establishment with a name almost impossible to pronounce, Quincampoix. It was the meeting place for enlightened and democratically-minded Amsterdamers. De Groot was not a habitual patron but he didn't want to be seen at this upcoming meeting, so he'd agreed to meet at Quincampoix, rather than one of his usual haunts. He had been asked for this meeting without an explanation, but de Groot believed he knew the reason.

He pushed open the door and was met with the loud hubbub of voices and the usual mixture of the smell of tobacco, sweat, stale air and, of course, coffee. He anxiously scanned the exclusively male crowd of patrons gathered around tables and on benches. A visit to a coffee house was not prohibited to the fairer sex, per se, yet to be seen there would be was damaging in the extreme to the reputation of any respectable woman. Aside from serving staff, women were rarely seen in these establishments.

De Groot let his eyes wander across the room at the artists and art dealers conducting their business. Two of the guests were engrossed in their game of chess and a few others read the newspapers provided. Directly in front of him a group of young writers vociferously debated whether the stadtholder would be successful in persuading his brother-in-law, Frederick William II of Prussia, to invade the Republic of the Seven United

Netherlands. But de Groot was unable to spot the person he had come to meet, perhaps because of the poor lighting. The small leaded glass windows did not allow much light into the room. He closed the door and headed to the bar, walking across the floor dusted with sand.

"*Goedendag, mijnheer.* I am Roos. Would you like something to drink?" the young woman behind the counter greeted him. She poured hot coffee from a large pot into several ceramic cups. The seductive aroma of freshly ground coffee beans caressed his nose.

"Good day to you, Roos. My name is de Groot. I have reserved a table for myself and *Mijnheer* Alewijn. Has he arrived yet?"

"No. But I did arrange a quiet place for you, as you requested." The young woman pointed to a table in the back corner. A mid-height wooden partition provided the most privacy possible, as well as a good view of the door.

"Well done." De Groot nodded approvingly. He pointed to the cups in front of him. "I'll take one now."

Roos pushed a steaming cup across the counter with a smile. Her round cheeks were crimson. Behind her was an open fire that spread a stifling heat. A kettle with softly bubbling coffee hung from a hook over the flames.

"Is that you in this portrait, Roos?" De Groot looked up at the small square oil painting that depicted a young woman with a serious expression, starched white bonnet and a neat lace collar. It was flanked by other paintings, mostly of sea battles and landscapes. De Groot had been told that many of the artists paid for their coffee in paintings. He supposed it to be a lucrative deal for the innkeeper, who was sure to sell these works to other patrons at quite a profit.

"Yes, *mijnheer*," Roos replied hesitantly.

"Well, wench, if you permit me the observation, you are far fairer and more virtuous in the flesh."

De Groot winked at her, took the cup, and went over to his table, followed by the curious gazes of several people. At first glance, his lanky frame looked quite modest and frugal in the simple black suit with the white neckcloth. But upon second glance, the acute observer would recognize that the knee breeches, vest, and coat were made of Turkish camel hair and the neckcloth of the finest Chinese mulberry silk.

De Groot sat down on the bench against the back wall, placed the cup in front of him on the table and retrieved his snuffbox from his coat pocket. Almost all the other patrons smoked their tobacco in wood or clay pipes. De Groot preferred snuff. While opening the box and relishing the aroma of the fragrant ground leaves, he focused on the impending meeting.

Frederick Alewijn belonged to the Amsterdam Chamber of the Dutch East India Company and was its most powerful director. De Groot had known him for a long time. After repeatedly lavishing praise on Alewijn for his accomplishments and recommending numerous lucrative financial transactions, de Groot had managed to coax from him a nomination for the vacant position of Director of the Amsterdam Chamber. He hoped Alewijn had requested the meeting to inform him that he—de Groot—had become the successor.

Being named Director of the Amsterdam Chamber would represent the crowning achievement of his almost thirty-year career at the Company. In this position he would be subordinate only to the Lords Seventeen of the Governing Body. There would be almost no limit to his power and authority in decision-making. And he could easily come up with the six thousand guilders in VOC shares that he would be required to pay at the time of his appointment. He would recoup that amount in no time, thanks to the generous dividends which the Company traditionally paid.

The door of the Quincampoix opened and a middle-aged gentleman entered. He wore a jacket conspicuously embroidered with gold braids, velvet knee breeches and shoes with gold buckles. The wig with the curls over his ears was immaculately powdered. He folded his umbrella and placed it in the corner next to the door. Then he pulled out a pamphlet from inside his jacket.

De Groot quickly tucked away his snuff box, got up and waved. The gentleman nodded briefly and headed in his direction; chin raised. Unlike the other patrons, he did not order his coffee at the counter but gave Roos a little hand signal instead.

"Greetings, *Mijnheer* Alewijn." De Groot bowed, though not too deeply. After all, he expected to be almost an equal of Alewijn's soon.

"*Mijnheer* de Groot." Frederick Alewijn nodded slightly and looked out the window. "Good heavens, what awful weather!"

He sat down opposite De Groot and placed the pamphlet next to him on the bench. "I saw the Stad Cavalerie galloping to the Dam. You had business at the town hall this morning, didn't you? Do you know if there is anything new afoot?"

De Groot told him about seeing the Free Corps of the Patriots and the flyer with caricature. "I suppose that the militia are going to demand Dedel's dismissal as mayor."

Alewijn snorted with displeasure. "These democratic ideas are spreading like wildfire and are disrupting our business. Heaven knows I am no friend of the Orangists but as an honorable trader wanting to go about my business, I have no choice but to support the stadtholder."

De Groot was prevented from answering by Roos, who showed up holding a tray with a cup of steaming coffee, a sugar bowl, and a pair of silver tongs.

"Hooy the apothecary delivered the sugar himself this morning, per your request."

"I do hope that you are in good health?" de Groot inquired as soon as Roos had left.

"Well, at least ever since my doctor prescribed Caribbean sugar, my gallbladder has troubled me much less frequently." Alewijn placed three lumps into his coffee. "And you? How are you?"

"Very well, thank you for asking. Merely my stomach," de Groot's hand involuntarily traveled to the area in question, "troubles me after a heavy meal."

"And may I inquire after your delightful daughter?"

"Bethari is studying art at the Amsterdamse Stadstekenacademie."

"She is a student at the Amsterdam Arts Academy? I had no idea that women were admitted to study there."

"Why not, if they are talented?" de Groot retorted. In fact, the administration of the school had admitted Bethari only after a more than generous donation from him, of which his daughter suspected nothing.

De Groot continued, "I have submitted several of her works to influential art dealers without revealing that they were painted by a woman."

"And what was their verdict?"

"They praised her work for its power of expression." In reality, the dealers had described Bethari's paintings as too outré and eccentric for the general market.

"Once she's a wife and mother, she'll have to divert her ambition to her husband and children."

De Groot took a sip of coffee. "Bethari is only seventeen. I'm not rushing her to get married." He decided to direct the conversation to the actual reason for the appointment. "I trust today's meeting at the Company was to everyone's satisfaction?"

Alewijn bit on a lump of sugar. "We received word of the first auctions. Unfortunately, the proceeds were not as the Lords had hoped."

"That is extremely regrettable," de Groot mumbled. Of course, in his position as Finance Inspector, he had long been aware that the monetary situation of one of the world's most powerful trading companies did not exactly look rosy.

"The calamitous war with England has shrunk our financial reserves. And had we not lost our trading monopoly for cloves and nutmeg to those damned French, there would be less cause for concern. But the price drop since then has been a tragedy."

"We must maintain our East Indian markets at all costs," de Groot noted. "Perhaps we can manage to get the States General to send an armed fleet to protect the colonies."

Alewijn shook his head. "The supreme command over the armed fleet rests with the stadtholder and he is currently in Prussia to persuade the king to invade the Netherlands. In addition, I doubt that parliament will appropriate additional funds for the necessary ships. What is needed now, if we are to secure the future of our trading Company, is men who are experts. The Lords Seventeen are of the same opinion."

"Well said, *mijnheer*." De Groot was about to burst with anticipation. He struggled to put on an appropriately humble demeanor.

Alewijn went on, "You are such a man, my dear de Groot. Consequently, I have mentioned your name to the Lords with respect to a special matter. It is a very delicate and precarious affair. It is critical that it be implemented effectively if the trading Company is to return to the path to success."

"Always at your service, *mijnheer*," de Groot replied smoothly. Truth be told, though, he was bewildered to hear Alewijn speak of the position of director in these terms.

Alewijn smiled, thin-lipped.

"I'm glad to hear that. Then there is nothing that stands in the way of your being sent to East India."

"You desire me to travel back to Java?" de Groot asked, utterly dumbfounded. He wondered if he might have misunderstood in the babel of voices surrounding them. When he was younger, he had been stationed as the Company's auditor in the colonial capital, Batavia. But it was highly unusual for a man of his stature to be expected to leave the comforts of life in Amsterdam and head to the tropical hell of Asia.

"You are leaving for Ceylon, not Java," Alewijn explained.

De Groot studied him intently and when he saw the steely glint in Alewijn's eyes, he realized that the man could almost read his mind. That blackguard, was actually enjoying his dismay! Still, de Groot was not quite ready to give up on the idea of a misunderstanding.

"I am convinced that the Lords Seventeen will understand that I am perfect for another function," he declared in a firm voice. "My knowledge and years of experience are a perfect match for the job requirements of a Chamber Director."

Alewijn gave him a pitying look.

"My dear sir, it was I who recommended you for the position in Ceylon. The board members trust my judgment implicitly and are entirely in agreement. They expressly request your being posted there."

De Groot struggled to keep his composure. It was entirely clear to him that he was being cast away, relegated to an as yet ill-defined role in a colonial outpost, far from the seat of power, let alone the comforts of home. As he took a sip of his cold coffee to buy time, he feverishly tried to think of a way out. Refusing an assignment from the Lords Seventeen would mean the end of his career. Still, he tried.

"I am an old man. What could I possibly accomplish for the Company in Ceylon?"

Alewijn guffawed as though de Groot had just told the most amusing joke. "You are fifty-two years old! A man in his prime." He signaled Roos to bring them both more coffee.

"This assignment does not require youthful strength and valor but experience, wisdom and determination. The trading company finds itself in crisis. Not only has our business been harmed by the war with England, but the conditions of the peace settlement have been a disaster. We lost the Coromandel Coast to the English and, with that, the production facilities for the lacquer furniture that we had been selling so profitably. Now it is of the utmost importance that we protect our remaining markets from the competition. If not, we're finished. The issue is this, my dear sir: there are signs that our cinnamon monopoly is in jeopardy."

"How say you?" De Groot opened his eyes wide. "From what evidence do these thoughts arise?"

"Twenty bales of Ceylon cinnamon were put up by the British East India Company at the latest London spice auction."

De Groot froze. Twenty bales corresponded roughly to a weight of one hundred forty pounds. He knew that it was worth the significant sum of seven thousand gulden.

"Something like that is possible only with the help of traitors," he determined.

Alewijn nodded.

"You have put your finger on it most precisely, my good sir. And I know that you possess exactly those qualities that will be needed in order to salvage the extremely important cinnamon monopoly: in addition to acumen, most important are unscrupulousness, greed and proclivity for corruption."

Despite the heat in the coffee house, de Groot felt a shiver run down his spine.

"My dear Alewijn, I don't understand."

"Don't try to play me for a fool," Alewijn snapped. "The Company is well aware that for years now you have been taking out loans from our Orphan Chamber without repaying them. You have been taking the money to buy large amounts of wares in East India on your own account, take up cargo space on the Company's ships and then sell your ill-gotten goods back to us. Thus, your fraud is threefold."

De Groot hung his head in silence. He had been intoxicated by it all—the business successes, the recognition for his achievements, the money, the career advancement. He had craved more and more. And now the time had come for him to pay for his rapacity. He knew that he was not the only swindler in the ranks of the Company. There was widespread smuggling and private trading. Bribes were exchanged for favors and appointments. Finance inspectors and auditors forged accounts and helped themselves to the seemingly endless wealth of the Company.

"The Lords have been aware of your side deals for some time. If you make an effort with this assignment, they are willing to overlook your transgressions."

De Groot thought feverishly. The posting to Ceylon frightened him. When he was younger, the prospect of a good career, success and money had enticed him to Java. Now, at his age, he feared the long, arduous sea voyage and the tropical climate of East India.

"I am not available for this assignment," he said firmly. "I plan to submit my resignation to the Company, and to retire."

Alewijn took a sip of coffee, pulled out a small embroidered handkerchief and dabbed his mouth. "You will do no such thing, my dear de Groot—unless you want to ruin your daughter's future."

"My daughter?" de Groot look at him in shock. "I exhort you, sir, to leave Bethari out of this."

"I'm afraid that will not be possible, de Groot, if you decide to be obstinate." Alewijn folded his handkerchief and returned it to his pocket.

"Perform admirably, and the Lords will abstain from punishing you. However, if you fail, your property will be confiscated—as compensation for your offenses. Your shame will be the talk of the town and the best houses will close their doors when they hear your name. Not to mention that you can abandon any hope of snagging a husband from a prominent family for your daughter. And that's what you're after, is it not?"

De Groot lowered his head.

Alewijn leaned against the back of the bench and studied him thoughtfully.

"Take your daughter with you to Ceylon. I am sure she will be happy to return to the tropics. Her mother was a native, wasn't she?"

De Groot curled his lip and clipped his words. "Bethari was born in Batavia, not in Ceylon, and her mother was Indonesian."

The barest of pauses indicated his surrender.

"When is the departure scheduled?"

"In May," Alewijn replied. "The Company has acquired a new regiment—two thousand men—from the Duke of Württemberg. Reinforcement of an additional one thousand men is planned. It will support our resupply camp on the Cape, just in case the English or the French decide to try to get their greedy hands on it. The 1st battalion is currently on its way to Vlissingen. You and your daughter will be accommodated on one of the ships. I will send you a procuration document giving you complete authority to act on behalf of the Company. If necessary, you will receive military support from our new regiment."

Before de Groot could answer, the door of the coffee house flew open and three young men burst in.

"The Patriots are assembling in front of the town hall! They are about to hand in a petition demanding the removal of Dedel and all Orangist councilmen! It has the signatures of sixteen thousand Amsterdamers. Shipyard workers are on their way and if they clash with the Patriots, there will be blood."

De Groot rose hastily. "Please excuse me. I must go to my daughter!"

The Amsterdam Arts Academy, where Bethari was at that moment taking art classes, was, like the offices of the councilmen and magistrates, located in the town hall building on the Dam.

Alewijn, too, rose.

"*Vaarwel, Mijnheer* de Groot." He watched the young men continue to disperse the latest news from the center of town.

"Do not allow yourself, *mijnheer*, to forget that I am making it possible for you and your daughter to leave this country before there is an uprising, and the Prussians strike. You will do well to be grateful for this courtesy."

CHAPTER FOUR

AMSTERDAM, THE REPUBLIC OF THE SEVEN UNITED NETHERLANDS, 1787

De Groot turned, and shoved through the crowd that began to invade the Quincampoix, chattering with the latest news.

"Hail, you!" He beckoned a boy lounging around the entrance.

"Run to the Kaizersgracht Street to the house with the two reclining lions at the door. My servant will open for you. Tell him *Mijnheer* de Groot sends you. Instruct him to come with a carriage to the back of the town hall. And hurry!" He pressed a stuiver into the youth's hand. Then he hastened to the Dam.

There was still a heavy mist in the air that had wet the cobblestone streets. De Groot almost slipped on one of dozens of flyers that lay about. People jostled him as they poured out of the side streets and alleys. Many of them sported red and white ribbons on their clothing or red and white plumes on their hats, in order to be recognized as adherents of the Patriots. Some of them held clubs or stones.

The noise increased as de Groot approached the Dam, the square in the center of town. The beating of drums could be heard. A chorus of voices demanded that Dedel be handed over to the mob, calling him a traitor, a fat pig, and a greedy drunk. It was clear that the mayor was as despised as the stadtholder.

The Dam, practically deserted only a few hours ago, was filled with men, women, and children. The Free Corps marched through the area where the market stalls usually stood. The horse-mounted members of the town watch posted themselves along the edges of the Dam to observe the events.

De Groot pushed and shoved his way to the town hall. He recognized some of the leaders of the Patriots on the steps of the main entrance. One of them held a stack of papers, which de Groot assumed to be a petition the man meant to submit to the council members.

A sturdy guard armed with a spear blocked de Groot's further progress.

"This is as far as you go, *mijnheer*," a sturdy guard man informed him.

De Groot recognized some of the leaders of the Patriots on the steps of the main entrance. One of them held a stack of papers. De Groot assumed it to be a petition the man meant to submit to the council members.

De Groot decided to try to enter from the back entrance. There, where a medieval rampart once stood, he found a narrow street between a canal and the town hall. Here, too, he was met by people trying to get to the Dam. People rammed into him and insulted him. He eventually reached a narrow door in the middle of the rear wing. It was locked. He angrily pounded on it. The hatch opened and the guard's face appeared.

"Oh, it's you, *Mijnheer* de Groot!"

"Permit me entrance! I must reunite with my daughter."

"But of course, *mijnheer*." The hatch closed and the door opened.

De Groot rushed inside. "How goes it here? Is everything secure?"

"Yes, *mijnheer*, your daughter is safe, I guarantee it," said the man as he quickly bolted the door.

To the right and left of him, each corridor subdivided into many others. Prison cells and the court room lay behind some of the massive doors with iron locks. De Groot hurried to the second floor.

Here lay the political heart of the city. In the center was the Citizens' Hall, with its marble-covered walls. Rows of doors led to the different offices: the mayor and judges, the vault, the offices of the Wisselbank and the administrative offices of welfare for orphans and the poor. Chancery clerks, secretaries, councilmen and magistrates rushed back and forth; de Groot could hear muffled voices behind closed doors. Absent were the citizens who would usually come to the various chambers with their concerns. The faces of the civil servants were unusually serious.

De Groot's anxiety grew. Taking two steps at a time, he bounded to the upper floor, where the art academy's two lecture halls were located. The walls along the corridor were covered with the students' works, one of Bethari's among them, which portrayed de Groot's servant Rufus in a white turban. His ebony-colored countenance shone before a green background as though it were bathed in sunlight. The servant's thoughtful gaze appeared to follow the viewer. When de Groot had first seen the painting, he had been shocked. In his opinion, depicting a Black man, and a slave at that, as so self-assured, contravened divine order. Yet Bethari's instructor had declared the portrait a job well done.

Rufus brought Bethari to her class by coach every morning. Normally he collected her every afternoon as well. But de Groot did not wish to wait; he needed his daughter safely at home before any bloody clashes occurred in the streets. He opened the door to one of the lecture halls, expecting to find his daughter, but the hall was empty, save for a plaster statue of a boy with an apron draped around his hips to conceal his sexual organ. De Groot felt a fit of pique wash over him. Bethari was supposed to be there for a life class, using the plaster model for studies of the human body. One of the conditions de Groot had placed upon her studies was that she was strictly prohibited from studying live models, as the male students did. De Groot harrumphed and left the room.

He pushed open the door to the drawing classroom. Seventeen heads turned at once, among them that of Professor Frans and that of a young man under the ceiling chandelier, posing nude, as a hero of the ancient world. And there was his daughter, sitting among the other students, holding a piece of sanguine chalk in her right hand, and balancing a drawing board on her knees!

"Bethari!"

De Groot was so enraged by his daughter's disobedience that he almost forgot what was brewing outside on the streets.

"Father! Why are you here? Where is Rufus?"

Bethari beamed at him without the slightest hint of a guilty conscience. She had a bright blue silk scarf wrapped around her shiny black hair and wore one of those new shirt-like chemise dresses made popular by the French queen and, which was, in her father's opinion, outrageously revealing. But Bethari had prevailed against him as she so often did, just as she had ignored the fact that he had forbidden her to draw live models.

"*Mijnheer* de Groot!" Professor Frans, Bethari's favorite teacher, rushed over to him. "Let me explain."

De Groot spun around.

"Woe! Sir, why do you allow my daughter to jeopardize her good name like this?"

The professor, who was convinced of Bethari's talent and never missed an opportunity to praise her, lowered his head. However, de Groot suspected that he was only feigning shame so as not to further anger him, as de Groot was an important patron of the academy.

De Groot looked disapprovingly at the young model, who hastily slipped into his breeches, and then at Professor Frans.

"You have brought shame on my daughter! There will be consequences to this outrage. And Bethari, you will accompany me as we take our leave!"

"Why do you punish me, Father? Because I claim the same right as any male students?" She angrily stuffed her drawings in her portfolio.

He shook his head.

"We must get home. There is an uprising brewing in front of the town hall."

He had no sooner finished his sentence than they heard the sound of breaking glass somewhere in the building. The students jumped to their feet and looked at the door with alarm. De Groot took Bethari's hand.

"The Patriots are demanding the mayor's resignation. The town guards and the Free Corps are even now on the point of assembling and it seems the dock workers also make their way to the Dam. As soon as they come upon the Patriots, it will be bedlam. Send your students away, Professor! Lo! Class is finished!"

The barouche waited for them behind the town hall. Rufus opened the door and assisted Bethari in climbing in. Then he took his seat next to the coachman. Their journey, which ordinarily took only a few minutes, required considerably more time today as the narrow streets along the canals, were hopelessly congested. It appeared that every able-bodied Amsterdamer was making his or her way to the Dam. One man charged the carriage and pounded on the window, right in front of Bethari's face.

At first, she recoiled, but then she screamed at him, "Wellaway, you oaf!"

The man looked at her, dumbfounded, and kept running.

"Bethari, these people are dangerous," de Groot admonished her. "You mustn't antagonize them further." He knocked on the partition.

"Driver, carry on!"

The two horses broke into a trot and a little while later they reached their house on the Kaizersgracht Street.

"Rufus, light the fireplace in the sun parlor," de Groot ordered. "And bring a glass of port for me and a hot chocolate for the mistress."

De Groot removed his wig, exchanged his coat for a loose dressing gown and his buckled shoes for felt slippers, and repaired to the sun parlor. Bethari stood by the window there, looking into the small rose garden that separated the residence from the carriage house and stable. She, too, had swapped her high-heeled shoes for comfortable slippers and had draped a shawl around her shoulders.

The sun parlor was a small, intimate room of which both father and daughter were fond. On the walls hung Bethari's art work, from her inexpert childhood paintings to the drawings and paintings from her time at the academy. Persian rugs de Groot had acquired from a dealer in Batavia covered the floor. A lacquered cabinet displayed his collection of Chinese porcelain. In the corner stood a desk which he used for correspondence. During the cooler seasons Bethari often sat by the fire with a book. In the summer months, she enjoyed being in the rose garden just outside, one of her most favorite spots. There, she set up her easel and painted in the shadow of a copper beech, whose dense leafy branches reached over from the neighboring property.

She turned as her father entered the parlor. Her dark, almond-shaped eyes flashed angrily. "Father, you take exception to my drawing a live model and make me look a fool in front of my fellow students? When I've long known what a man looks like undressed and as God created him!"

De Groot stared at his daughter in disbelief.

"Child, that cannot possibly be!"

"In fact, I came by my knowledge right here!" She pointed to the carriage house. His eyes followed her outstretched arm and he froze.

In the alcove next to the entrance to the building stood a life-size, classical statue of a satyr. Its physique was as impressive as the live model at the academy, including the male body parts. De Groot began to understand that his daughter, whose modesty he had tried to guard so carefully, had obviously studied the satyr thoroughly.

"Dear Father!" She placed her hand on his arm. "Do not look as if you had just seen this statue for the first time!"

"My dear, in a way I have." He was shaken. "I commissioned the statue based on the art of classical antiquity. It is of great value, though I never considered its ... objectionable aspects with regards to impressionable young ladies."

Bethari laughed. "Well, thanks to this satyr, I know quite well what distinguishes a man from a woman."

"Such talk is sinful, child! Never let anyone outside of this house hear you speak like this!"

She jutted her chin forward.

"Anyone outside of this house! Father! I know well that those self-appointed moralizers of this town already disdain me because I'm not buxom, blonde and pale like a Dutch woman."

The Amsterdam society rumor mill had been churning for some time because of the exotic looks Bethari had inherited from her mother. Some swore that de Groot's deceased wife had been a slave, while others insisted that he had made her acquaintance in a bordello in Batavia. Many of them viewed the fact that Bethari was the only female student at the city art academy as evidence of the loose morals she must have inherited from her mother. If the city gossipmongers were to discover that Bethari painted from a live male model, it would be even more grist for their mill. None of these people had ever met her mother, as she had died in Java, never to set foot in the Netherlands, but that mattered not.

"You cannot give people more reason to gossip," de Groot said. "Your behavior must be beyond reproach at all times. If not, you will damage yourself and your future."

"Oh really, Father." She made a dismissive move with her hand. "You speak of my prospects on the marriage market. That may be important to you but I care not a whit. I want to become a good painter. And that includes studies of live models. It does not turn me from the righteous path."

De Groot snorted and retrieved his snuff box from his pocket.

"Since, thanks to our statue, you are already familiar with the male anatomy, why not utilize the modestly covered plaster figure of the young boy?"

"Because I wish to depict reality, Father," she retorted. "Human beings are different and not all are built as flawlessly as the model at the academy today."

A log in the fireplace snapped. De Groot frowned.

"Why does Rufus tarry with our refreshments?"

"You are overly harsh with him, Father." Bethari sat on one of two armchairs strategically placed before the crackling fire, with a small round table nearby. De Groot took the other seat. As he settled, then took a pinch of tobacco between his thumb and forefinger and moved to use it.

Bethari watched him with great interest.

"May I try some, Father?"

He looked at her indignantly, but was spared the trouble of a reply because at that moment, Rufus entered. He wore the same white turban as in the portrait Bethari had painted of him. With it he had paired a strawberry-colored jacket with brass buttons, blue velvet breeches, white stockings, and black buckled shoes. He balanced a silver tray with a steaming porcelain cup, a glass of dark red port wine and a plate of pastries.

"Sir."

He placed the tray on the small round table and handed the cup to Bethari.

"It smells delicious!"

"I asked cook to add some rose water and vanilla to the chocolate."

She beamed at him.

"Thank you, Rufus. If you like, have cook give you some as well."

He bowed slightly but left the room without replying.

"Bethari, you may not offer a servant something meant for the master and mistress," de Groot admonished her. "He's going to start considering himself as one of us."

"Oh, is he not?" she asked defiantly.

"Where did you come by such foolishness?" de Groot grumbled.

"That is the opinion of all the students at the academy. And it is mine as well. We believe that you should emancipate Rufus and pay him for his work, Father."

His expression soured.

"Child, you know not of which you speak."

"Father, it is what seems right. Can you not see that all humans are born equal?"

"Rufus will leave the moment I emancipate him. And then who will look after you?"

"I do not need a chaperone, Father. I am grown up. I believe that Rufus should be free to come and go as he pleases, just like you and I. He would not run away, since he could have done that long ago, had it pleased him."

De Groot regarded his daughter sternly.

"I sincerely hope that you have not discussed this fiddle-faddle—this supposed equality of all humanity—with Rufus."

"Perhaps I should," she retorted.

Rufus had been part of her life ever since she could remember. He came from Madagascar. As a boy he had been sent to Batavia on a merchant ship and bought at auction by her father. At the time de Groot had been looking for a companion for his wife and a playmate for his two-year-old daughter.

Rufus had continued to care for the little girl after her mother's death. When they returned to the Netherlands twelve years ago, de Groot had brought the servant with them. There were several other households in Amsterdam in which slaves from the East and West Indies had been brought along by their owners. Some had emancipated their slaves. De Groot, however, deemed that unnecessary; he thought a slave was too valuable to be freed just like that.

"What has caused such a bad temper in you today, Father? Are you worried about business?" Bethari hesitated, thought with a furrowed brow for a moment and then inquired, "Were they not seeking to fill the director's position today at the meeting at the East India House, the very same that you had hoped to get? Oh, my goodness! I have a feeling—" She broke off.

De Groot cleared his throat.

"Alas, I was not given the vacant position on the Amsterdam Chamber. *Mijnheer* Alewijn informed me today."

"I am so sorry!" She looked at him compassionately. "And you were so sure you would get it. How disappointed you must be."

"I thank you for your sympathy and kindness, daughter." He smiled sadly. "I shall seize this moment to impart even more news."

"What is it?" She looked at him anxiously.

De Groot had not taken another wife after Bethari's mother's death. As Bethari grew older, he had become accustomed to discussing his hopes and worries with her. However, his disciplinary transfer to Ceylon and the reasons for it were something he was not willing to share with her under any condition. Still, he could not conceal the entire truth from her.

He took a gulp of port.

"We are to leave Amsterdam."

"I beg your pardon, Father?" She stared at him in disbelief.

"The Company is posting me to Ceylon. We will depart in May."

"To Ceylon? In May?" Bethari slammed her cup on the tray. "Just when Professor Frans is planning to exhibit my painting *A Day in the Life of a Weaver's Family* in this year's competition at the academy. He says it's an excellent opportunity to make future buyers aware of me as an artist. Turn down this assignment, Father. Please!"

"That is impossible."

"Why? You are a man of importance, not a simple clerk whom these Lords can move around as they please!"

De Groot suppressed a groan. He hated to disappoint his daughter. He sought subterfuges. "By any practical measure, it will be serendipitous for us to be out of the country soon. You saw yourself what happened in the city today. If the Prussians truly do invade, there will be a revolt, the outcome of which is uncertain."

"You are destroying my future as an artist with all your pessimism!" She wiped her eyes with the back of her hand.

His feeling of guilt intensified.

"You need not quit painting simply because we quit the Netherlands. Imagine all the artistic inspiration that will come to you in Asia. You have always wanted to paint *plein air;* there will surely be opportunities for you there."

As a little girl, Bethari had drawn in the sand of the courtyard with a twig. In the kitchen, it was pictures in the flour on the kitchen table, made with her finger. She scribbled all over the walls with the kohl stick her mother used to make up her eyes. When she was five, she took an interest in her father's quill and ink pots. The day she enhanced one of her father's carefully written letters with a drawing of something she called "monkeys playing" was the day that de Groot had extracted a promise that, henceforth, she would use only paper and pastels for drawing. Later on, in Amsterdam, he added canvases, brushes, oil, and mineral pigments to blend colors. And at the tender age of fourteen, she had managed to persuade him to allow her to attend the Amsterdam Art Academy.

"We will sail from Vlissingen," he went on. "First to the Cape of Good Hope and from there, on to Ceylon. Rufus will accompany us. I am sure you will be pleased about that."

She shrugged her shoulders.

"Pray, what business have you in Ceylon?"

He had not given any thought to what he would say to Bethari about that. At last he said, "I have been charged with supervising the Company's cinnamon trade in Ceylon. You know that the field operations are always supervised by someone from the motherland."

Much to his relief, she seemed to accept this explanation. He quickly added, "I had hoped it might please you to return to East India."

She stirred her chocolate.

"I've not yet been to Ceylon but perhaps I shall enjoy exploring a new world there." She took a sip but made a grimace because the chocolate had grown cold.

"What will happen to our house, Father? Will you sell it?"

He shook his head.

"This house is your heirloom, my dear, the place to which you can always return. I would never sell it. Nevertheless, we shall not stay in East India forever. As soon as my assignment is completed, we will return home."

"Many years will have passed before then," she replied, despondent.

He fell silent and studied the picture Bethari had painted last winter. It depicted the courtyard of their house in Batavia, overgrown with orchids, jasmine, carnations, and eucalyptus. She had painted the colors and overabundant life that exist only in the tropics with light, fluid strokes. The plants stretched toward the light and glistened as though recently washed by the rain, whereas the blossoms and leaves on the ground wilted and abandoned themselves to decay.

Every time he looked at the painting, he found himself transported back to Batavia. He could almost feel the heat and oppressive humidity on his skin, and could vividly recall the opulent life and ever-present death there. He marveled at how his daughter had managed to capture these impressions so aptly on the canvas. She had been only five years old when they left Batavia.

He cleared his throat.

"I expect us to return home in two, three years at the most. If at that time, you still wish to become a painter, I will permit you to finish your education at the academy."

CHAPTER FIVE

VLISSINGEN, THE REPUBLIC OF THE SEVEN UNITED NETHERLANDS, 1787

"Stop!"

Hannes jumped up and dropped the rag with which he had been cleaning the stock of his gun.

But August had already dipped his right hand into the kettle hanging over a fire in the barrack yard. His shrill cry made not only the other soldiers spin around, but also the sergeant in charge of the nearly nine hundred men of the 1st battalion. Colonel von Hügel had ordered the men to clean their guns, in preparation for a solemn ceremony the next day, when the men were to take their oath to the Dutch East India Company. Their weapons and uniforms needed to be impeccable for the occasion.

"Lo! It's our muttonhead August!" a grenadier shouted. "Who else would stick his hands in boiling water?"

The soldiers nearby laughed loudly.

Shaking his head, the sergeant remarked, "A one such as you truly deserves to be slapped for this stupidity. Yet if I punished you every time you earned it, by my oath, I should never have time for anything else. Return to work, men! You know what the colonel expects from us."

Hannes grabbed the whimpering August by the shoulders and shook him lightly.

"Stop mewling like an infant! Or do you want everyone to laugh at you? And now try once more to take hold of the barrel, only this time with the tongs. They're not lying next to the kettle as decoration, you know."

He shoved the boy in the ribs.

"Yes sir, Hannes!" August hastily reached for the wooden tongs.

"You use this to take the gun barrel out of the water," Hannes explained. "That's right. Now put the barrel on the table over there. But don't touch it again until it is cooled."

"Are you a female, Hiller, a tib? Or why is it you have such motherly feelings for our little simpleton?" an artilleryman cleaning the barrel of his small field gun teased. Again, roaring laughter rang out.

"Take care, you, or you'll get a taste of my motherly feelings!" Hannes snarled at him. He was heartily sick of his role of August's protector but ever since he had helped him in the courtyard of the Ludwigsburg Palace, they had been joined at the hip. The other recruits and officers bullied August. When it became too much, Hannes intervened, and thereby also ended up being the butt of their jokes. But more than one comrade had become acquainted with his fists and Hannes had earned the men's respect.

"Calm yourself, Hiller!" the artilleryman raised his hands defensively.

Hannes took one of the rags lying on the work table and tossed it to August.

"Be sure to clean it properly. While the inside of the barrel dries, clean the butt. And then you take the oil," he pushed a can across the table, "and lubricate all the metal parts. Do you understand?"

August nodded eagerly and grasped the cloth.

"Yow!" He winced in pain. The skin on his right hand was reddened and had formed blisters.

Hannes examined the hand and frowned.

"This must be treated." He summoned the barber surgeon. "Do you have some ointment for him?"

"You heard the sergeant," the barber surgeon replied after throwing a cursory glance at the injury. "He must deal with it." With that, he walked away.

Hannes shook his head silently. Then he told August, "Listen to me. You disappear to the latrine and piss on your hand. It will clean the wound. After that, you report to the infirmary."

The boy nodded and slunk away slowly across the courtyard into the barracks, where the latrines were located.

He's thin as a rail, thought Hannes, *and still bone-weary.*

The thirty-three-day footslog from Ludwigsburg through the Margraviate of Baden and then France had taken August to the edge. The officers had spurred the recruits on without mercy. Marches of eight to ten hours a day on muddy streets, in thunderstorms, rain, and bitter winter cold were the rule. Rarely were they given days of rest or sufficiently dry and warm places to sleep at night. Hannes and August had spent many a night out in the open. Their field rations consisted of stale beer and barley broth. And those were sparse, at that. They passed a few days in the northern French coastal town of Dunkirk before the battalion crossed over to Vlissingen in the Netherlands. These days of relative rest still had not been enough time for August to recover his full health.

Some had had it even worse. Twenty-one men had died on the way and more than one hundred lay in the sickhouse in Vlissingen. Hannes was fortunate to have a robust constitution and had gotten away with a mere head cold.

He began to focus on the details of his gun, which he had taken apart in order to clean. Now he began to reassemble the different parts. As he pushed the barrel into the shoulder stock, he reflected on how weary he was already of his service in the regiment.

The rations had improved in Vlissingen and the soldiers were able to rest. But their days were still made up of the same monotonous drills, marching exercises, and sentry duties, all of which bored Hannes. He did not enjoy the officers' and corporals' strict control. He longed to be his own man again, to be free.

He approached the sergeant with his reassembled muzzleloader.

"Respectfully report that I am returning my weapon to the arsenal." The sergeant nodded indifferently.

Hannes stored the gun in the designated area of the arsenal. When he straightened his back, he caught sight of a door, behind which was the entrance hall of the barracks. From there, a wide gate led to the street. He looked around the courtyard furtively. His fellow soldiers were busy with their work, paying him no attention. The sergeant had taken out his pipe and tobacco and tugged at the tie fastening of the pouch.

Hannes took a deep breath and slipped through the door into the deserted hall. In the center, a staircase led to the second floor. On the left side of the door was a window. On the right side two soldiers in a guard house chatted quietly. They did not notice Hannes as he darted silently under the stairs. When they laughed loudly, he seized the opportunity to run to the window and dive headlong through it, landing on a narrow strip of grass. He listened and heard the guards laughing. No one seemed to have noticed him. He knew from the marching exercises that by heading east, the street led to town; heading west, it ended at the ocean. Hannes stood and ran in the direction of the sea.

It had been a long time since he had felt this happy and free. Like a bird that had escaped its cage. He inhaled the briny air and tilted his head back. Fluffy white clouds slowly moved in the blue sky. Seagulls screeched as they flew overhead.

When the battalion had gone ashore at the Port of Vlissingen on April 17 after a two-day ship's journey, the weather had been rainy and stormy. But it had soon improved and today, the first of May, it was almost hot. Luckily, the fresh breeze blowing from the North Sea provided cooling relief.

Hannes reached a tall, grass-covered dam, which he had initially mistaken for a rampart. But he had since learned that it was a dike, which protected the land from the ocean's savage, often deadly, force.

He strolled among the sheep which, guarded only by a dog, grazed on top of the dike. Several windmills stood near each other, their sails turning steadily with the air, the wooden beams creaking. Growing up, Hannes had known only water mills. Fascinated, he watched the round caps of the Dutch mills turn with the sails, in the direction the wind blew.

The harbor lay ahead of him on the left. Hannes had never seen so many ships as in Vlissingen. Powerful and massive with three tall masts, they anchored in the large harbor. Cannon barrels peeked out of the portholes. He observed the small launches ferry supplies and people back and forth. The Dutch East India Company owned several rows of warehouses along the pier. Behind those were the dockyards, where the great ships known as East Indiamen, and the maneuverable smaller luggers, were built and repaired.

Standing on the ridge of the dike, Hannes could see the infinite, silvery gray water. He had first laid eyes on the ocean in Dunkirk. From there, they traveled to Vlissingen in the smaller ships known as coasters. While at sea, they had been caught in a storm which tossed their ship around like a toy. Hannes had been both intrigued and frightened by the raw, wild strength of the waves. The sea never slept. Even on a calm day like today, the waves broke continually on the sandy shoreline.

Spontaneously he took off his uniform jacket, shoes and stockings and tied everything into a bundle. He ran down the dike over the sand into the ice-cold North Sea. Like a playful little boy, he splashed with his feet in the water and fished for seaweed and seashells in the shallow waves.

Eventually he emerged from the water and sat in the warm sand. He took hold of his right foot and ran his thumb over the many callouses. As a test, he filled his shoes with sand, raised them one after the other, and watched the grains spill out as though through a sieve.

He had noticed the first holes in his shoes after just ten days on the march. Eventually, he and his fellow soldiers all limped along on their bloodied feet. The rest of their uniform was in no better shape. The leather helmet offered little protection from the rain—certainly less than the tricorne hats that many of them had worn as civilians. The cheap material used for their uniforms had worn threadbare before they had even arrived in Dunkirk.

"This is rubbish! Just about good enough as a cleaning rag," one of his fellow soldiers had declared after examining the fabric carefully. The man was a former tailor and knew whereof he spoke.

On the beach, Hannes put his shoes aside and propped himself up with his elbow in the sand. When he squinted, he could make out the tiny contours of several three-masters on the horizon. He wondered if they were heading to the East Indian or American colonies, or coming from there.

The following day, the battalion was to take the oath of loyalty to the Dutch East India Company and as soon as the winds were favorable, the regiment would set sail for South Africa.

In spite of all the adversities, Hannes still felt a great desire for adventure, though not all the soldiers shared that feeling. More than two hundred recruits had absconded during the march, forcing the officers to double the number of guards. Most of the desertions had occurred in the Margraviate of Baden, which offered protections for military men. There, if a soldier desired to leave military service, he had only to enter a neutral building. Once inside, he was a free man and could not be forced back into the battalion. The residents of the Margraviate took this protection seriously; they lined the streets and tried to offer protection for any recruits who felt ready to bolt, even under the vigilant eyes of the officers. Many residents even opened their front and barn doors.

They all still awaited their pay, which, according to Hannes' calculations amounted to a tidy sixty gulden by now. He wondered if the Baroness von Hügel had kept her word and asked her husband for the advance, and whether the colonel had rejected her request. He could not ask her because he had not seen her since their tryst at the palace in Ludwigsburg. He had heard that she had traveled to the Netherlands by ship on the Rhine and was staying in Vlissingen with her husband. But he had no idea how to find her and speak with her privately.

He put on his stockings and tattered shoes. Even though it was difficult to leave this momentary freedom behind, he had to return to the barracks before the sergeant or the other soldiers noticed his absence. He grabbed his jacket and stood up.

"*Beweeg je niet*! Do not move!"

He turned around, surprised. He had not noticed anyone approach. The voice belonged to a young woman sitting on a folding stool. On her knees she balanced a board with several sheets of paper. In her right hand she held a pencil. Next to her stood a tall, dark-skinned man in a white turban, holding a parasol over her head. Hannes did not know what she had said, for she had spoken in Dutch.

The woman again said something, which he understood no more than her first words. She gesticulated in an agitated way.

At that moment the wind picked up and the top sheet on her board flew up. She tried to grasp it but it quickly flapped out of reach and in Hannes' direction. He leapt forward, and managed to just grasp it, though his momentum propelled him onto the sand, on top of it. When he stood, he realized the paper had been completely crinkled.

The young woman uttered a cry of disappointment and said something that sounded like a scolding, to his ears.

"No good deed shall go unpunished," Hannes grumbled. He looked at the paper in his hands and froze.

"Egad, it is my very likeness!"

The young woman had sketched him as he lay stretched out on the sand, contemplating the ocean. She had succeeded in capturing, with sparing, light strokes, not only his outward appearance but also his meditative mood. It was so accurate that he almost felt uneasy. Incensed, he waved the paper.

"Why did you not ask for permission to draw me?"

The lady's eyes grew small. She began to answer but the dark-skinned man stepped in front of her and pointed the parasol at Hannes.

Hannes raised his hand in a calming gesture.

"Be still, my friend." He hardly wanted to risk having this beanpole of a man ram the iron tip of the parasol into his ribs.

"Rufus, *niet*. No."

The young woman laid a hand on her protector's arm and he lowered the parasol. She was a delicate slip of a girl, but the look she gave Hannes was resolute. Her dark eyes sparkled and her skin shone in the golden sunlight. The gusting wind gathered up the thin white fabric of her skirts to reveal glimpses of narrow hips and well-shaped legs. She did not wear a hat in the style of the day; rather, she wrapped a shawl tight around her head that still allowed her long black hair to flow from underneath.

"You are German?" She asked him in his own language, in the guttural singsong peculiar to the Dutch.

He began to feel himself charmed, though in an unfamiliar way that he had never before encountered with other women. He bowed.

"Hannes Hiller, at your service, miss. I am a Swabian, first and foremost, as that is my home region, but I suppose you can call me a German as well. Where did you learn to speak my language so well?"

"I learned German because we frequently have German guests at our home."

Lo, she was married! Her husband had to be a merchant, or a governmental official, if they hosted foreigners from German-speaking areas. Hannes was bewildered to notice the disappointment this realization aroused in him. The fact that an interesting woman was married had never bothered him before.

"You look like a vagabond." She surveyed his untidy ponytail and shirt hanging loosely out of his waistband.

"Yet you are in uniform." She nodded to the jacket in Hannes' hand. "Are you one of the German soldiers who arrived in Vlissingen two weeks ago?"

It annoyed him to be compared to a vagabond.

Gruffly, he retorted, "I signed on with the Infantry Regiment Württemberg, something I consider most honorable. You, miss, on the other hand, are someone who creeps up on innocent people and secretly makes drawings of them. Shall we speak further of honor?"

Her dark eyes flashed. "There's no need to take that tone with me!"

"No indeed, milady! I simply do not wish to be the subject of a drawing without my permission!"

Again, he looked at the sketch and was struck by how precisely she had captured him. It was almost like looking in a mirror! He rolled up the paper.

"What are you doing?" She stretched out her hand. "Give me my drawing and be on your way."

He shook his head emphatically. "Your drawing, milady, belongs to me!"

"That is absurd. I am the one who made it!"

"And I am the one pictured in it!"

She looked at him indignantly. "I have heard that you soldiers are an uncouth lot. But let me tell you something, sir, I draw whom and what I please! Come, Rufus, let's away."

She turned and trudged away through the sand. The darkskinned man threw an angry look at Hannes. Then he folded the chair and hurried after his mistress.

Hannes entered the barracks the same way he had left it.

Most of his fellow soldiers had finished cleaning their weapons. A few artillerymen were still at work, heaving the barrel of a small four-pounder on the mount. The sergeant stood next to them with a red face and screamed at August:

"Stand at attention when I speak to you! Where is Hiller?"

The boy pulled up his shoulders and covered his ears. He had wound his uniform kerchief around his burned hand. Hannes ran across the courtyard and saluted the enraged officer.

"Here, sergeant!"

"Hiller! Why did you leave the battalion?"

"With your permission, sergeant, I needed desperately to relieve myself. It was a matter that could not be postponed." This excuse had just come to Hannes.

The sergeant snorted angrily, "You mean to say you have been sitting on the latrine for an hour? Do you take me for a totty-headed fool?"

"Never, sergeant! But with the grub we get here, an hour on the latrine is nothing." The artillerymen, who had been following the spectacle, smirked.

The sergeant looked Hannes over with narrowed eyes.

"I shall overlook it this once."

"Yes, sir!" Hannes saluted again. The sergeant turned to August.

"Why do you stand around, gawking? Assemble your weapon!"

The boy hid behind Hannes in fear. Hannes suppressed his irritation with him and followed his inclination to help.

"With your permission, sir, I'll show Private Eberle how to assemble his weapon."

"Certainly not!" the sergeant thundered. "That is something this dolt is going to do himself even if it takes all night!"

"I feel quite sure he knows how to do it," Hannes countered, against his better judgment. "But he cannot hold anything with his scalded hand."

"So what! The life of a soldier is not that of a topping fellow!"

Hannes took a deep breath. He would have loved to kick first the sergeant and then August in the behind. Instead, he took the boy's injured hand and peeled away the kerchief. Although Hannes was gentle, August whimpered like a dog being

75

whipped. Hannes himself was shocked; the hand was bright red and covered in blisters.

"Look at this, sergeant. He must be examined by the barber surgeon."

The sergeant took hold of August's arm and pulled him to the front. "If he doesn't learn to tolerate an injury like a man, he is not suited for the life of a soldier."

Exactly, thought Hannes. *Someone like August has no business being in the military.*

But he did not wish to receive further punishment for standing up for the battalion bumpkin. The sergeant jabbed August in the back.

"If your gun doesn't look spick and span at the ceremony tomorrow, ninny, you'll find yourself in prison until we embark!"

Those words gave Hannes an idea.

"Sir, the Lords from the Company shan't be too pleased to see injured men serving in the regiment. Surely, you do not want such exposure in front of Colonel von Hügel or perhaps even the duke?"

"What say you?" The sergeant gave him a wary look.

"The other day you yourself told us that members of the board and important officials of the Company will attend the ceremony."

"Soldier, there will be almost nine hundred men present. A couple of scalded fingers are but child's play and shan't be noticed."

"Yet what if they do notice, sir?" Hannes asked slyly. "If the wound gets infected, it may require amputation of the whole hand. Then August will not be useful as a soldier and the gentlemen directors will think that the Duke of Württemberg has fobbed off unfit recruits on them. Do you want to risk besmirching the honor of our sovereign?"

The sergeant clenched his teeth, angry to be cornered in this way. And yet he did not wish to attract the colonel's anger, much less the duke's.

"Private Hiller!" he bellowed furiously. "You will assemble Private Eberle's weapon without delay, and return it to the arsenal! I will hold you responsible if you might make even the slightest error! And Private Eberle, you will accompany me to the infirmary at once!"

The battalion's oath-taking ceremony took place in the barracks courtyard in the bright sunshine. The recruits had erected a dais and guest seating under a canopy. To the left and right, the flags of the regiment and the Dutch East India Company flapped in the wind. August, his scalded hand treated with ointment and bandaged by the barber surgeon, joined the battalion in marching into the courtyard.

Hannes watched with interest as the guests assembled under the canopy. Five elegant gentlemen sporting old-fashioned, long wigs appeared first. Colonel von Hügel and his wife took their seats behind them. Anna Maria toyed with her fan while examining the rows of recruits; from time to time, she leaned into her husband and whispered something. There was nothing to indicate that she had noticed Hannes, nor did he expect her to, given that there were almost nine hundred military men in the courtyard.

He felt resentment rising in him. He had trusted her to appeal to her husband, and still, day after day passed and none had received their contractually promised pay. He wondered if she had made the offer on a whim. He did not find it honorable in the least.

The two last guests stepped on the dais, a dainty young woman with a colorful scarf wrapped around her dark hair and a gentleman, past the prime of his life, dressed in black. The young lady greeted the other guests with a graceful movement of her head and took her seat next to Anna Maria von Hügel.

Hannes was surprised to recognize his beach acquaintance from the previous day. He wondered about her appearance at this event. Then he scrutinized her companion. *What makes a young, beauteous lady marry such a dotard,* he wondered. Colonel von Hügel and the other guests greeted him deferentially. When he sat down, she gave him a bright smile and he placed his hand on her cheek, full of the pride of ownership.

Money doesn't smell, Hannes thought.

A drum roll rang out. Colonel von Hügel rose, bowed briskly to the Dutch dignitaries and began his speech. Hannes wondered if it were French, which he knew to be the language of the upper classes, though a common carpenter's journeyman like him could not understand it.

But then the Colonel switched to German and solemnly declared that today, the 1st Battalion of the Infantry Regiment of Württemberg would be formally handed over to the service of the Dutch East India Company. Next, he introduced the guests: the five elegant gentlemen were directors of the trading company, while the old fellow, called de Groot, was its finance inspector.

The Colonel also read a letter from the Duke of Württemberg in which the sovereign used many gracious words to express his good will to the Lords, the directors, of the trading company. One of them, along with the colonel, recited an oath in Dutch and German, which the soldiers repeated, word for word.

"The 1st Battalion of the Infantry Regiment of Württemberg is hereby handed over to the service of the Dutch East India Company," the colonel proclaimed. "I release the soldiers from duty for the rest of the day. Embarkation begins tomorrow, and as soon as the wind is favorable, we shall set sail."

Hannes was dumbfounded. *And where is our money?* he thought. *Our sixty gulden?*

But the Colonel made no mention of the outstanding payments. The Dutch, too, sat in their seats with dispassionate smiles. Baroness von Hügel idly fanned herself.

Anger got the better of him. He would not stand this treatment, this fiddler's pay, for another moment. With determination, he took two steps forward and shouted so loudly that men in the last rows heard him:

"I have a question!"

Eight hundred ninety soldiers and officers, as well as the guests under the canopy, stared at him. Colonel von Hügel's mien hardened. His face turned deep red.

"How dare you? This disrespect is outrageous!" he screamed.

But Hannes had no fear of authority, especially when he was angry.

"When shall these honorable, hard-working men be paid?" he called out, loudly and distinctly. "We've not seen a balsam since we were recruited."

The Colonel gasped and was about to answer when a second soldier interrupted.

"He's right. I also want to know when we'll receive our due!"

"Yea! And I!" a third intoned.

"If you continue to take us for fools, you'll be sorry!" a fourth screamed.

The shouts of approval filled the courtyard and none of the officers intervened. That did not surprise Hannes. There were rumors making the rounds among the recruits that the officers had not seen a single gulden of their pay either. Afraid, de Groot tried to exit the dais and take his wife with him, but she freed herself with an indignant expression. When her husband again tried to collect her and flee, she snarled at him angrily.

The directors of the trading company huddled with the finance director de Groot in intense conversation. Anna Maria von Hügel, partially concealing her face with her fan, animatedly discussed the turn of affairs with her husband, but the man of action soon had enough. He pushed aside his wife, yanked his pistol from his belt, and ran to the front line of the battalion.

"Silence! That's an order!" He raised his arm and fired into the air.

The shot echoed against the walls of the barracks, instantly silencing every voice. The soldiers stared at their commanding officer with a demeanor borne of belligerence rather than anxiety.

Colonel von Hügel returned the weapon to his belt. His hate-filled gaze bored into Hannes, who realized at that moment that he had just made a bitter enemy.

He had insulted the commanding officer, of all people, in front of the entire regiment and distinguished guests. He had technically incited a revolt among the recruits and he was most certainly in danger of harsh punishment. Hannes had heard tales of imprisonment, floggings, even the dreaded running of the gauntlet.

And yet he remained convinced that it was the men's right to demand their due. If they fulfilled their part of the contract, should not the Dutch East India Company fulfill theirs?

"Why have the men not received any pay?" asked a bright female voice with a lilting accent.

Hannes could hardly believe his ears. The young artist, who had no connection to the regiment, was the last person from whom he expected support. But there she stood in front of her chair, upright and resolute.

The Dutch continued to huddle animatedly together. At last, de Groot stepped forward and announced, "The Honorable Lords of the Dutch East India Company will withdraw to consult with commanding officer Colonel von Hügel."

"Don't take too long!" a soldier shouted from one of the back rows. "Not one of us shall step foot on a Dutch ship before we've received our pay!"

"You cannot continue to tup us this way!" bellowed another.

"Colonel von Hügel will be given our answer tomorrow morning," de Groot declared. "And as a sign of their good will, the honorable directors will provide an extra serving of brandy."

There were shouts of triumph until Colonel von Hügel raised his right hand.

"The brandy will be dispensed once the battalion has been dismissed according to regulations."

He summoned an adjutant and gave him an order. The officer saluted briefly and ordered several sergeants forward. Following brief instructions, the sergeants fanned out, located the regiment's rebel spokesmen, and led them away. None of the other soldiers protested—either they were afraid of suffering similar consequences or mollified by the prospect of additional brandy.

The adjutant addressed Hannes, "Step forward, private!"

Reluctantly, he complied.

The adjutant pulled his rapier and hit Hannes on his upper arm with the flat edge of the blade.

"Come!"

"You mustn't hurt Hannes!" August stood next to the man he had chosen as his friend and protector.

"Be gone with you, before there's an accident!" The officer pointed the rapier at him.

"Hannes always helps me," August insisted. "You mustn't hurt him."

Hannes quickly placed his hand on the boy's back. "Nothing shall happen to me," he said, though he was none too sure.

The adjutant shoved Hannes before the commanding officer. Colonel von Hügel scrutinized him coldly. Still, his lips remained pressed together and his face red. Hannes returned his gaze without batting an eye. He hoped and prayed that the colonel had not gotten wind of his intimate encounter with his wife in the palace at Ludwigsburg.

"Name?" the Colonel bellowed. Hannes lifted his chin.

"Private Hiller!"

The commanding officer narrowed his eyes before turning to his adjutant.

"Private Hiller will appear before the Council of War. Until a verdict has been reached, I sentence him to confinement in a darkened cell. Take him away!"

CHAPTER SIX

VLISSINGEN, THE REPUBLIC OF THE SEVEN UNITED NETHERLANDS, 1787

Two sergeants dragged Hannes to the barracks and pushed him down a staircase into the basement. One of the sergeants took a lantern from a hook on the wall and lit it.

They led Hannes down a long passage with an iron barred door at the end. Behind it lay his cell, as cramped and tiny as the bear cage he had once seen in a traveling menagerie. There was no straw on the bare mud floor for a bed, nor so much as a bucket to relieve himself either.

A hefty kick transported him into the cell. Then the door was shut and bolted behind him. The two sergeants disappeared, taking the light of the lantern with them.

Dazed, Hannes picked himself up.

The blackness was impenetrable. He carefully groped his way along the stone wall, one hand next to the other. Eventually, he crouched in the corner, wrapped his arms around his knees and asked himself why in the world he had not availed himself of the opportunities to escape from the regiment. The journey to paradise the recruiter had promised was turning more and more into a nightmare of deception and drudgery. And he could not even give von Langsdorff a piece of his mind; the recruitment officers had long since left.

Hannes rested his head on his knees and closed his eyes. He was hardly a coward but the thought of his mother having to make do without his pay, maybe having lost all faith in him, brought tears to his eyes. Maybe they were tears of anger against

Baroness von Hügel, who had failed him so abysmally. Here he was, sitting all alone in the dark, save for the mice scampering all around him. Strangely, the sound of their little feet broke through his sorrow.

At one point the wooden door at the other end of the passage opened to reveal the yellow light of the lantern. A sergeant approached and pushed a piece of bread and a jug through the bars.

"How long will I have to waste away here?" Hannes asked. "Has there been a verdict yet?"

But the sergeant disappeared without so much as looking at him.

Hannes crawled to the bars, groped for the bread, and sniffed it. It was clearly moldy and the inside of the jug smelled foul.

Bread in your pocket is better than a feather in your cap, is what his mother had always said.

Better eat it before the rodents do, he thought, and bravely bit into it. The bone-dry bread almost got stuck in his throat. He forced himself to drink a few mouthfuls of water. A little while later, his stomach revolted and he vomited in the corner of the cell.

His gut hurt. He curled up into a ball on the floor, and groaned in recognition when he heard a crinkle under his shirt; he had folded the young Dutchwoman's drawing and tucked it under his shirt instead of throwing it away. Now he slid his hand to his chest and lightly fingered the paper. He reminisced nostalgically about the ocean, the sun, the soft warm sand, and the young woman.

She had shown great courage in her blunt criticism of the powerful dignitaries of the VOC. He turned over in his mind how a stranger, a young lady of society, no less, cared enough about a tag-rag and bobtail group such as this assemblage of poor, mercenary recruits to speak up on their behalf. Meanwhile, his commanding officer, had purposely fed him rot-gut rations and foul water, and deprived him of the dignity to even relieve himself like a man. Eventually Hannes dozed off, waking with a start when he heard the key turn in the squeaky lock of the wooden door at the end of the passage.

The door opened and the light of the lantern blinded him.

Surprisingly, a female voice said, "Please wait outside for me."

The hairs on the back of Hannes' neck stood up. He knew that voice. Then he heard the guard.

"Are you sure that you do not wish me to accompany you?"

"It is as I told you," the woman responded impatiently. The door closed and the light neared his cell. Hannes forgot about the pain in his abdomen, scrambled to his feet and grabbed the iron bars. He recognized the cloaked figure who placed the lantern on the floor and threw back her hood.

"Hannes!"

"Baroness. I didn't expect to see you here. Should I be honored?" His voice vibrated with the anger he felt about her broken promises.

She waved her hand. "What is this smell?"

He smiled derisively.

"I crave your forgiveness if my accommodations offend your nose, but my stomach is not accustomed to such delicacies as are served here."

She gently placed her hands around his fingers, which still grasped the iron bars.

"How fare you?"

"My lady, I fare just as you may imagine a man would fare while being punished for demanding his rights. How long have I been left to rot here?"

He withdrew his hand from hers and wiped his brow. He had lost all track of time in the darkness.

"You have remained here one day. It is evening; the sun has just set."

"You should not be here, my lady, for I had a look into your husband's eyes. If he hears that you have paid me a visit, my situation will only worsen." He stopped short. "Is the underlying reason for my incarceration that the Colonel has learned of our rendezvous?"

"Of course not!" She looked at him, bewildered. "I have told you, that matters not; my husband and I have no ardent fires between us."

Hannes thought of that afternoon in Ludwigsburg. He had enjoyed wooing the Baroness von Hügel, under the pretext of hammering the nail in the flagpole; it had made him feel flattered, strong, and irresistible. And yet, the lady's husband had no choice but to watch helplessly, else provoke a scandal. In retrospect, he could imagine how the cuckolded von Hügel may have felt.

I wonder if the Colonel wants to teach me a lesson? I would, if the shoe were on the other foot.

Hannes looked into the Baroness' eyes. "Do you know anything about the others, my lady? Are they still imprisoned?"

She nodded.

"The Council of War has decided. Over three days, they will each be given fifty blows on the backs of their legs."

Harsh punishment, he thought, *but tolerable.*

"And I?" he asked. "Has my punishment been determined?"

She placed her hand over her mouth as though trying to keep the words from coming out, and for one moment he felt fear.

Then she said, "The Company and my husband have come to an agreement regarding the outstanding pay."

"Why only now?" He crossed his arms. "Or was your vow in Ludwigsburg not followed by action?"

She raised her chin. "I keep my promises and I asked my husband for an advance for you soldiers. He assured me that he would take care of it. When I heard yesterday that nothing had been paid yet, I was shocked."

"And, will we receive our due?"

She nodded tentatively. "For now, each soldier will receive four gulden."

Hannes threw his head back and laughed out loud.

"Four gulden! Now that's what I call a successful negotiation! 'Tis a fraction of what the Company owes each of us!"

"The Company clothed and fed the battalion on the march, as well as here in Vlissingen. Those costs have been deducted from the pay."

"Sweet Mother of God! We were pressed into serving these conniving dogs. They had to provide for us!"

"Apparently, the terms of the contract the duke has entered into with the Company are different. That is what my husband told me. I can assure you; he was deeply troubled by the injustice."

Hannes only grunted.

She continued, "Do not get in the mulligrubs; four gulden are better than nothing. You shall receive the rest of your pay in South Africa. That is what my husband negotiated with the Company."

"My lady, are you trying to pull my low-born leg?" He angrily pounded the wall of his cell with his fist. "That recruiter von Langsdorff told me that we would be paid in Ludwigsburg. Promises made by you and your ilk are worth less than a measly copper kreutzer!"

"The other men were happy about the announcement," she countered, bewildered. "I heard that they no longer refuse to embark."

"Even the animals receive better treatment than we. If I had met with these bloodsuckers, I would have seen it through," he replied bitterly. And his mother in her small cottage with its leaky roof was still waiting for her money!

"You are most unfair," she said reproachfully. "Initially, the directors of the Company had planned to pay you only two gulden. My husband, with his persistence, managed to double the amount."

"Damned duplicity." The words slipped out of Hannes' mouth. "My lady," he added.

There were several seconds of oppressive silence between them. Suddenly she reached through the iron bars and placed her hand on his bristly cheek. "You were very brave today on the barrack yard. Never forget that."

Astonished, he looked at her and noticed that tears shimmered in her eyes.

"Why do you say that?"

She avoided eye contact with him. "I have to go now. But I will pray for you."

When he was alone again, he remembered that she had not answered his question about whether the Council of War had determined a punishment for him.

"Private Hiller!" Regimental recruiter Grenadier Captain von Langsdorff stood before Hannes, smiling broadly, and handing him a sheet of paper.

"Sign it and you shall not be sorry!"

"Don't do it, boy! Can you not see that he's in league with the devil?" Hannes spun around and saw his mother; whose eyes were swimming in tears.

"On your feet, you good-for-nothing." The recruiter swung his leg and gave him a forceful kick in the ribs.

Hannes awoke with a cry of pain, started up and hit his forehead on the lantern swinging directly in front of his face. Blinded by the light, he flinched and tried to orient himself.

"Hurry up, private."

The lantern swung to the side and Hannes could see the sneering, laughing expression of the company sergeant. All at once, he remembered everything: his arrest, the dark cell, the visit from Baroness von Hügel and her cryptic parting words, "I will pray for you."

He got up with difficulty. His body ached. He had to prop himself up against the wall because he was so stiff. In that moment, he noticed a second sergeant, standing in the open cell door and holding a rope. He stepped behind Hannes, tied his hands, and shoved him into the passage.

"Where are you taking me?" asked Hannes.

The two men grinned. "You'll find out sooner than you like," said one.

They led Hannes up the stairs and into the barracks hall. One of them opened the door to the courtyard and the other pushed him into the open. He shuddered as the cool, moist air washed over his body. After one day and one night in complete darkness, the gray early morning light hurt his eyes. It took him a few seconds to make out shapes and contours. Then he froze. The entire battalion had assembled in the courtyard, in formation in two groups. The soldiers who had been arrested with him stood separately. In the middle of the yard, one aisle remained clear all the way to the front; at the end of it stood five men, waiting. Hannes recognized the regiment commander accompanied by his two adjutants. The army chaplain, Master Spönlin, and the doctor in charge of the 1st Battalion, Major Liesching, had taken their positions. The drums rolled, then pounded out a marching rhythm as the sergeants led Hannes along the aisle. The soldiers in formation presented their weapons and stared through him without emotion. Only his fellow soldiers in custody sought eye contact with him. Furtively he took stock of their bloodstained breeches, evidence of their punishment. Their expressions worried Hannes. Were they empathetic, regretful, or perhaps even dispirited? He could not tell.

The sergeants stopped him in front of the commanding officer.

"On your knees!" the company sergeant ordered while brutally pressing him to the ground.

The drums fell silent. Von Hügel looked intently at Hannes. His lips pressed into a thin line; his chin jutted out. One of the adjutants stepped up to the colonel, saluted and handed him a piece of paper. Von Hügel unrolled it and held up the densely inscribed sheet. Hannes made out several signatures and a seal.

"Private Hiller!" von Hügel thundered. "As commanding officer of the Infantry Regiment of Württemberg and president of the Council of War," he pointed to the men to the right and left of him, "I find you guilty of the charges of insubordination, refusal to obey orders and incitement to revolt. I hereby condemn you to death by firing squad!"

Hannes felt a shock run through his body. "No!"

He tried to jump up but his tied hands changed his center of gravity and caused him to lose his balance. Two sergeants threw themselves on him anyway, and he fell headlong on the ground. One of the men grabbed his hair and used it to yank his upper body into a vertical position, while the other pressed his shoulders down. Hannes resisted with all his might. He managed to free himself with one painful lurch. His head upright, he looked straight into the commanding officer's eyes.

"Who hath given you the right to pass such a sentence on a man who had simply demanded his—"

"Silence!" von Hügel flared up. He turned to the assembled soldiers, spittle flying from his mouth.

"I forbid anyone to ask for clemency for this delinquent. Anyone disobeying my order will be sentenced to death! Take him away!" He made an abrupt movement with his hand in the direction of the sergeants.

The two men dragged Hannes to his feet. His heart raced and his knees shook. He could not comprehend the sentence the Council of War had passed. Like a refrain, four words resonated in his head: *It is not true. It is not true. It is not true.*

One of the adjutants opened the bullet pouch on his belt, took out a bullet and approached Hannes.

"Your hand, private!"

Half dazed, Hannes stretched out his right hand and the officer laid the bullet in it. Then he and the second adjutant stood before the prisoner. Master Spönlin and Major Liesching lined up behind them. Von Hügel took his place at the head of the little troop.

The trumpeters played the signal and the eight people strode through the aisle, led by the colonel. When they reached the second company, Hannes heard a hoarse shout that ended in a stifled gurgle. He turned his head and saw that one of the men held August's mouth shut. The boy watched him, wide-eyed.

Hannes clutched the bullet. He could hardly believe that each step was taking him closer to death. He had not even lived yet, and now everything was supposed to be over? He briefly contemplated making a break for it. But he stood no chance in the presence of almost nine hundred soldiers who were ready to fire.

The group stopped in front of the barracks, exactly at the spot where Hannes had stepped into the daylight not even half an hour ago. The clergyman and the doctor stood next to him. The adjutant who had given him the bullet now took it back and passed it to von Hügel. He watched as von Hügel took out his pistol and loaded it. Then the other adjutant approached and bound his eyes with a black cloth.

Again, the drums rolled.

Mother, please forgive me, he thought, full of despair.

He felt fear and hopelessness like never before in his life. Almost involuntarily, his lips began to move.

"The Lord is my shepherd," he whispered. "*I shall not want. He maketh me to lie down in green pastures: he leadeth me beside the still waters...*"

The drums fell silent. He heard the cocking of the pistol. His eyes filled with tears and the words came tumbling out of his mouth more and more loudly,

"*Yea, though I walk through the valley of the shadow of death, I will fear no evil: for thou —*"

The air was pierced by a deafening bang. Hannes jumped with fright. Something warm ran down the inside of his thigh. His knees gave way and he fell to the ground.

For a few seconds, everything around him was still and dark. Then he became aware that someone was fumbling with his blindfold.

I'm alive? he thought in disbelief. But that was impossible! The death sentence was carried out, he had heard the shot.

Surely, he had to be wounded. But why did he feel no pain? Had fear robbed him of his senses?

The blindfold fell from his face.

From his place on the ground, he saw only a single pair of legs in leather boots stood before him. His eyes wandered upward and eventually met Colonel von Hügel's inscrutable gaze.

"Private Hiller, you are pardoned!"

Von Hügel turned on his booted heel and stomped off.

Hannes turned on his back and saw the cloudless sky, which he had thought he would never see again. A shiver went through his limbs and he felt a coldness spreading in his abdomen. He knew he should be relieved, grateful, and happy but instead he felt paralyzed. Even the thoughts in his head were frozen. He lay on the hard ground in front of the barracks like a dead man.

CHAPTER SEVEN

ON THE ATLANTIC, 1787

Bethari pushed aside the thin sheet and sat up in her bunk. The air in the narrow cabin was stifling and much too hot to sleep. She turned her head and looked outside through the rectangular window where the ocean and the night sky merged. The full moon was reflected on the dark water surface, large and unusually red.

She could hear the water splashing against the side of the wooden ship. The bell on the deck gave two short rings. The sound repeated four times, each time with a brief interval between the rings. The bell indicated the start of the midnight watch or perhaps that of the first daytime watch, which began at four in the morning. Either the night would last another eternity or soon a new, oppressively long day under the torrid equatorial sun would begin.

For two weeks the *Drie Gebroeders* had been as though nailed to the lead-gray ocean somewhere between Africa and South America in an area that Captain Schwarz called the "horse latitudes". These were windless regions surrounding the globe, north and south of the equator. They owed their name to the Spanish conquistadors' habit of throwing their horses overboard, once potable water for humans and animals became scarce.

One week earlier at dinner, Captain Schwarz had assured her that, even without wind, they were moving forward on the ocean currents, albeit very slowly.

"How many ships have been in this situation and have had their passengers and crew die miserably of thirst?" she had asked him.

"Only a novice dies in the horse latitudes," he had answered. "I have been traveling the seas for thirty years and I know the oceans like the back of my hand. The horse latitudes are narrower in some areas than others. The nautical charts show me exactly where those areas lie. Trust me, milady, we will soon reach the trade winds. Then the sails of the *Drie Gebroeders* will be transformed into wings and will carry us to Brazil in no time. From there the winds will take us to the Cape of Good Hope."

Despite these encouraging words, a few days ago the captain had given the order to ration water. Today Bethari had caught him inspecting the slack sails of his ship with an anxiously furrowed brow.

The *Drie Gebroeders* was the flagship of a fleet of five great three-masters that were to take the 1st battalion to South Africa. Three months earlier, the ship had sailed from Vlissingen in bright, early summer sunshine. Their journey had taken them from the North Sea into the Atlantic, along the coast of France, Portugal, and northwestern Africa. It had been a joyful ride. Seagulls and other sea birds followed the ship; Bethari observed dolphins playfully jumping out of the water in front of the ship's bow. Once she had seen the water spouts of whales in the distance. Yet after the Cape Verde Islands, the winds had become weaker and weaker until they had stopped altogether. At the same time, the heat had picked up. It had become so unbearable that even the pitch between the planks was melting.

The first time Bethari had felt fear was ten days ago, when a sailor had died of fever and exhaustion. Since then, the Grim Reaper had taken three more crew members and five soldiers. Her father was sure that the men had consumed bad water and ordered Rufus to boil theirs.

All at once her narrow cabin seemed intolerable to Bethari. She decided to get up and go to the bow. Maybe being there would give her the feeling that the ship was moving forward after all. She put on her slippers and a dressing gown. She carefully opened the door and peered out. The lantern hanging from the ceiling shed a yellowish light on the deserted passage. Her father's cabin was directly across from hers, and next to it, that of Colonel von Hügel and his wife. The captain's cabin and his chartroom were located behind that, with the officers' quarters underneath.

Bethari was relieved to see that Rufus was not there, as he would surely have prevented her little escapade. At the beginning of their journey, he had slept on a mat outside her door but since they had been bobbing up and down in the horse latitudes, he had been sleeping in the open, somewhere on deck.

Bethari padded along the passage. She crossed the captain's mess with its long table, where the captain ate with the chief officer and chief mate, her, her father, the von Hügels, the regiment's physician and the pastor, Master Spönlin. She groped her way in the dark and hit her head on one of the chicken cages, setting off a startled clucking. She hastened to the afterdeck. But even outside, the air was completely still. It was almost as hot as in her cabin.

She looked at the helmsman. His hands lay idle on the mighty wheel. Next to him stood one of the two steerers. Another sailor sat in the crow's nest of the main mast. All of the *Drie Gebroeders'* sails were hoisted in order to pick up even the slightest wisp of wind. Bethari could hear how the slack rigging hit the masts. The wooden hull creaked softly.

I wonder if we'll ever reach shore? she thought uneasily.

"Tis forever since we've encountered another vessel," the helmsman said at that moment. "Four hundred souls alone in this watery desert."

The steerer answered, "How are we supposed to encounter another vessel when there's no wind and none of us is moving?"

The helmsman hesitated, "It's just … this cursed ship…"

The steerer grunted and pulled out his snuffbox.

The helmsman went on, "Have you never heard that there's a frigate with black sails cruising in these latitudes? It needs neither wind nor current. It is Death and his bride, Nightmare, sailing in it, seeking ships like ours, which are caught up in the doldrums. If they find one, they roll the dice to decide what to do with the living. If Death wins, the people on board must die, if Nightmare wins, they will be forever scarred by the curse of this encounter."

Bethari felt a tingling on her scalp and could not help but look out at the ocean. It was a dark and motionless expanse.

"Everyone knows that ships can't move across the ocean without the power of the wind!" she said out loud.

Startled, the steerer and the helmsman turned around then quickly averted their gaze.

Perhaps her attire embarrassed them.

After a long silence, the steerer replied, "You ought not be here in the middle of the night, milady."

She raised her hands by way of apology. "It is so very hot. I thought I would suffocate in my cabin. I am hoping that it will be more tolerable at the front of the ship." She started for the steps leading to the middle part of the upper deck.

"Begging your pardon, I cannot permit that!" The steerer took a step as though to block her.

"Of course, you can. You just can't say anything to my father about it." She nimbly slipped past him and ran down the stairs. Luckily, the men did not pursue her as she scurried under the sail of the main mast and across the cleanly scrubbed planks.

To her left, two longboats were fastened along the railing. Before her, steps led to the foredeck. She could hear the soft bleating of the goats in the enclosures under the steps. The animals were there to provide milk but if the wind did not pick up soon, they would be slaughtered to save their water rations.

She placed her right hand on the railing and stopped short. Hannes Hiller stood at the portside railing. He wore a soldier's travel uniform—wide, calf-length pants and a linen shirt. His gaze was fixed on the ocean. His hands grasped the railing as though he were ready to leap overboard. And yet he did not budge.

She had watched from afar how he had helped the shipwright to replace cargo covers. She liked the way he made himself useful while the other soldiers sat around or played cards.

She had noticed that he was different from his fellows at the oath-taking ceremony in Vlissingen. She had felt an affinity when he had spoken up before the regiment commander and demanded the outstanding pay they were owed. She, too, had the determination to fight for what she wanted and was willing to flout the rules to achieve her goals.

Hannes Hiller had received a harsh punishment for his audacity, of that she was sure. Yet when she asked her father about it, he curtly answered that the punishment had been commensurate with the offense.

At least he had eked out a small advance for the men. That, too, she knew from her father.

She jumped when she heard the clacking of ladies' shoes behind her and hurriedly ducked into the small space between the two longboats. Baroness von Hügel rushed by her hiding place. She carefully stuck out her head and saw the regimental commander's wife run up the stairs and across the foredeck to Hannes.

Anna Maria von Hügel and she were the only women on board. They got along well. Anna Maria was intelligent and well-read and a good conversationalist. She had examined Bethari's drawings and had impressed the young artist with her informed comments. They often sat together on the afterdeck with their pads and drawing tools, sketching and chatting.

Bethari knew how much the Baroness missed her three sons. She wrote to them every day and could hardly wait to put the letters on a homeward ship at the Cape of Good Hope.

But what was the connection between the wife of the regiment commander and a common soldier? But why would the wife of the regiment commander meet with a common soldier in the middle of the night? The only connection Bethari could yet see was that the soldier had been ordered before the Council of War, and convicted, by the woman's own husband.

Bethari watched in astonishment as the Baroness spoke insistently with Hannes. He moved away and stared at the ocean, but Anna Maria would not be rebuffed. She laid a hand on his arm and whispered something to him until he suddenly spun around and brushed her hand aside. Anna Maria uttered a muffled cry and stumbled backward.

Bethari instinctively turned toward the afterdeck. The mainsail blocked her view of the two men at the helm. She waited anxiously but nothing happened. Neither the helmsman nor the steerer seemed to have noticed what was happening on the stern deck. Bethari quickly turned around again.

She could only vaguely make out Hannes' face. He spoke and gesticulated animatedly. The Baroness seemed ill at ease. She tried to interrupt him but with a severe move of his hand, he bid her be silent. Bethari was very keen to know what the two were arguing about, but she was unable to make sense of the few scraps of conversation that she did pick up.

At that moment Anna Maria turned around and ran down the stairs of the foredeck. Bethari was able to duck under the two longboats just in time, before the heels clattered by her.

"Madam! What is the matter?" she heard the helmsman's voice. He did not receive an answer, at least not one that Bethari could hear. The sound of the heels died away.

Slowly she straightened up and peeked over the top of the longboat at Hannes. He stood with his hands on the railing as though the Baroness had never shown up, as though their altercation had never taken place.

"Miss!" a voice behind her whispered. Startled, she turned around. "Rufus!"

The upper body of her servant loomed over the side wall of the rear longboat. Obviously, he had spent the night in there. The clatter of the Baroness' shoes must have awakened him. He rose to his full height, adjusted his turban, and carefully climbed onto the deck.

"Please allow me to accompany you to your cabin." He offered Bethari his right arm.

She looked back at Hannes. "I would give anything to know what Baroness von Hügel wanted from him."

"Begging your pardon, miss, but that is something you ought not to be asking yourself."

"He appears distressed," she said softly. "What could it be?"

Rufus placed his hand on her arm. "Let us go. I think he would not like to know he was being watched."

Hannes had lost himself. He was alive, certainly. But the carefree, daredevil part of his being had died in that fateful moment when he thought he had been executed.

The new Hannes failed at the simplest tasks. He seemed to be unable to stop his thoughts from returning to his near-death experience. He was powerless to control his all-consuming rage against Colonel von Hügel. He had never felt as helpless as at that moment. He no longer laughed or joked with the men but instead withdrew from them. By now they avoided him and looked at him warily, as though he were a ghost among the living. The only exception was August, who admired him as much as ever.

"I like you, Hannes!" he declared again and again, but it offered Hannes no consolation.

During the day he distracted himself with all sorts of work. He had practically forced his help on the ship's carpenter. Luckily, there was always something on board in need of maintenance or repair. But in the stillness of the night, he feared the weight on his being would suffocate him. He lay awake in his hammock, listening to the breathing and snoring of the other men. He tried not to think about the dungeon where he had been locked up in the hours before his mock execution. Whenever he did doze off, he would wake with a start and the feeling of a heavy stone on his chest preventing him from breathing. Most of the time he would escape to the upper deck to relieve his anxiety.

Hannes looked out at the boundless ocean and tried to repress the memories of the prison cell, evoked by the dark confines of the ship's interior. The sailor on night duty had grown used to the sight of him and left him alone.

Yet, this night he was prepared to end his misspent life.

Jump overboard, he told himself as his hands clutched the railing. *Then you will finally be at peace.*

And yet he did not jump. Muddled thoughts of his mother and a tiny glimmer of hope stopped him from taking that final, liberating step.

"I've been waiting for this opportunity."

He whirled around. Anna Maria von Hügel stood behind him. Of all people, it was the wife of the man who had used his position as commanding officer to sentence him to death. He inhaled deeply and tried with all his might to conceal the tremor in his voice.

"Leave me be."

"I must know how you fare." She stepped next to him. "I am so very sorry about what happened to you. But remember: you are alive!"

An uncontrollable rage surged up in him. He had to restrain himself from screaming at her.

"With all due respect, you are using words with which you are utterly unfamiliar."

She winced and for one moment he hoped that his incivility had driven her away. But she said, "My husband had no choice. He is responsible for the discipline of the entire regiment. You have to understand, soldiers who rebel endanger the order of regiment."

"It is rebellion now, my lady?" he said in a strained voice. "When you visited me in my cell, you called it courageous."

She laid her hand on his arm. "The Colonel had to be strict with you. But then he showed you clemency by sparing your life."

He slowly turned to face her.

"You knew of my mock execution when you came to my cell?"

She lowered her gaze and fell silent. Renewed rage flared up in him. Had she been a man, he would have used his fists on her.

"Why did you not warn me? Is your heart made of stone?"

"My husband is the commanding officer. I am not allowed to undermine his authority."

He violently brushed her hand away from his arm.

She shrunk back. "I could hardly preempt my husband!"

"Maybe he didn't impose that punishment merely because I demanded the rightful pay for us soldiers but because he knew of our little rendezvous," he snapped at her. "I suppose that thought never entered your noble little mind, did it? You wouldn't be here otherwise. Or is it all the same to you if your husband gives me another taste of his 'clemency'?"

"You're being unfair." Her lips quivered.

"Leave me," he snarled. "And never return!"

She looked at him silently for a moment. Tears streamed down her face. She shook her head, turned, and ran away.

Alone with his thoughts once again, he tried in vain to calm his churning emotions. He swore to himself that he would never again go near a married woman.

Still, for many years he would be forced to be under the command of Colonel von Hügel—at his mercy, away from home, from people to whom he could open up. This realization brought on a feeling of suffocating anxiety.

The only way out of this trap was suicide.

Again, he clutched the railing and tensed his muscles for the jump. And again, he was incapable of taking this final step.

He gazed at the moonlight reflected in the sea and tried to remember the last time he had felt happy and carefree. That afternoon in Vlissingen came to mind. He had not thrown away the drawing by the young Dutchwoman. Hannes felt under his shirt and withdrew the sheet. He unfolded it and studied the drawing. How hopeful, strong, and self-confident, unstoppable he looked then. But now he knew better.

His throat felt dry and tight. He crumpled the paper in his hand and was about to throw it overboard, when he lowered his arm again. Was he really ready to throw his life away? To give up on himself? Slowly he unfolded the creased sheet and stared at the former Hannes.

I want to be myself again, he thought. *I want to be the person I was!*

He felt a waft of air blow across his neck and hair.

The wind was coming up.

Three weeks later the *Drie Gebroeders* passed the island of Fernando de Noronha. Shortly afterwards, Bethari saw the coast of Brazil for the first time. But another week would pass before they arrived at the harbor of Porto Seguro, which was protected by rocky reefs.

Fishermen's huts lined the beach. Behind these grew a dense, dark-green forest. The town of Porto Seguro sat on a hill north of the harbor and consisted of little more than two churches, long storage sheds and a cluster of small wooden houses.

The *Drie Gebroeders* had taken longer than anticipated for its journey to Brazil. Captain Schwarz immediately had the supplies of fresh water, bread and meat replenished. In addition, he put abundant fresh fruit on the menu. The ship's doctor and Major Liesching treated numerous patients suffering from bleeding gums, dizziness, fever and exhaustion, all symptoms of the dreaded mariners' disease, scurvy.

Bethari was amused as she watched the soldiers eye and sniff the bananas and oranges set before them. In contrast to the men, she was well acquainted with exotic delicacies. The Dutch East India Company transported fruit from South American plantations to Amsterdam and sold it through specialized merchants for a lot of money.

In addition to the large trading vessels, there were numerous ships from Guinea, the Pepper and Ivory Coasts. They carried Africans to be sold as slaves for the sugar cane plantations, as well as the gold and diamond mines in the interior of the country.

Bethari stood on the upper deck with her father and Rufus as one of the slave ships was unloaded. The men wore iron rings around their necks, and their hands and feet were shackled with chains. Women and children were allowed to walk freely. All of them seemed listless and bone-weary. They wore nothing except a loincloth. Onshore the traders were waiting to examine their teeth, eyes, touching their entire bodies without the slightest sign of discomfiture.

Bethari looked at Rufus. His dark face showed no emotion. Then she looked over at her father. Jan Pieter de Groot had taken out his snuffbox.

"Father, did you buy Rufus on a market like this?"

"Where else?" he replied blandly. "Slaves are sold on the slave market."

"And did you also look into his mouth and examine him from head to toe?"

"How else was I going to find out if he was healthy?"

De Groot took out some snuff, inhaled, and grimaced with pleasure. Rufus stood by the railing, completely still and giving no indication as to whether he had heard the exchange. She frowned.

"Rufus?"

"Yes, miss?" He turned toward her.

"Can you still remember how you came to us?"

"It was as the master said. He bought me on the slave market in Batavia."

"And do you still remember Madagascar?"

"I am sorry, miss. That was long ago and I was still very young."

"Rufus!" De Groot's voice sounded severe. "My jacket for dinner is still in need of being brushed out."

"Yes, sir." The servant bowed slightly and hastened away.

De Groot turned to address his daughter indignantly, "I beseech you not to give Rufus silly ideas, Bethari. He has a good life with us. Much better than those poor devils will ever have." He pointed to the newly arrived slaves.

She raised her chin. "And yet you bought him like a piece of cattle."

While the *Drie Gebroeders* was anchored in Porto Seguro, she was cleaned thoroughly and all necessary repairs were made. The mood among the sailors, soldiers and passengers was cheerful, almost exuberant. That was due not only to the sun and warmth of Brazil. Everyone felt relieved to escape the tight quarters onboard and the uncertainty of being at sea. One could see that the soldiers, especially, were happy not to be cooped up in the belly of the ship any longer. During the four-month journey thus far, they had been allowed on deck for only thirty minutes twice daily.

Bethari had not seen where they were put up on the ship but she had asked Rufus about it. He had told her how the soldiers lived on the two decks. The lower of the two sat below the water and was deprived of all daylight. On the deck above that, the men had to hang their hammocks from the forty cannons that the *Die Gebroeders* carried in case of a pirate attack. It was oppressively tight everywhere. No one was able to stand up straight and it reeked of unwashed bodies.

Once, when they were still at sea, she had heard Captain Schwarz ask Colonel von Hügel to enforce discipline. Some soldiers had quarreled while playing cards. Gambling was prohibited, and brawling even more so. Once the sergeants had separated the culprits, von Hügel had sentenced them to twenty lashes each. Bethari had heard their cries from below deck and again wondered what Hannes' punishment had been in Vlissingen.

She had felt a strange connection to him, ever since she had first seen him and felt compelled to capture his likeness on paper. She watched him almost daily in Porto Seguro when the recruits rowed to shore to drill on the beach, or when he assisted the ship's carpenter.

"Do you see that soldier over there? The one who is sawing a beam with the *Drie Gebroeders'* carpenter?" she once asked the baroness, as they sat and drew on the afterdeck. "Everyone else on the ship is enjoying the warmth and the freedom to move around here in Brazil. But he always looks sad and depressed."

The commanding officer's wife looked up briefly from her easel.

"Are we not all a little depressed now and again, far from home as we are?"

CHAPTER EIGHT

OFF THE COAST OF SOUTH AFRICA, 1787

Four weeks later the *Drie Gebroeders* put out to sea with a steady westerly wind and forty days later the watch in the crow's nest reported that the African continent lay ahead.

"If all goes according to plan, we shall reach our destination tomorrow morning," Captain Schwarz announced. He stood with Bethari, her father and the von Hügels on the afterdeck and looked to the northeast with his spyglass. The sun slowly sank into the ocean. White foaming crests sparkled in the last of the daylight. The colonel asked for the spyglass and squinted through it.

"Are we not sailing too far from the coast to be able to navigate with precision?"

"Certainly not!" Schwarz took back the spyglass. "Close to shore lie many reefs just below the surface of the water, that would slash open the ship. And then there is the danger of being hit by a rogue wave and capsizing."

"What is a rogue wave?" asked Bethari.

"A monster wave with immense power. It bounces off the rocky coast and hits all the ships that are sailing too close to the coast. Just look at the sea foam on the bluffs over there. The *Drie Gebroeders* could easily be smashed against the rocks."

"It does not appear so dangerous from here," von Hügel remarked.

The captain shook his head as if to say that only an inexperienced landlubber would make such a statement. He was about to answer but de Groot forestalled him.

"The ocean has taken untold numbers of ships and thousands of lives off the Cape. Do you notice how even a big, heavy three-master like this, dances on the waves?"

"Indeed, and we are easily two hundred nautical miles from the mainland.," Schwarz agreed.

"I can feel it," the baroness said. "Since the lookout reported sight of the coast of Africa, the swells have been getting choppier."

As if to confirm her statement, a wave rolled underneath the ship and made the bow rise up. It seemed as though the *Drie Gebroeders* had been lifted by an invisible hand, briefly making her stay on the crest before sinking her deep into a valley of gray water. All of them lost their balance and clung to each other.

"God almighty!" Anna Maria gasped. "Please excuse me; I must take my leave and retire." She stumbled away with her hand covering her mouth.

Captain Schwarz had a compassionate look on his face as he watched her leave.

"The Cape of Storms turns the stomachs of even veteran sailors' upside down. I shall have a bucket brought to your cabin for your wife."

At dinner, both the baroness and her husband were absent. The captain excused himself, as he had to supervise the taking in of the sails because the wind had grown into a massive storm. The cook did not serve the customary soup, and the meat course had no gravy. De Groot and his daughter ate out of bowls, rather than plates, and they were forced to hold their drinking glasses firmly in their hands. Bethari had great difficulty in not spilling the wine on herself. Now she understood why all the big and heavy pieces of furniture had been screwed down onboard. The ship bucked the waves like a wild horse.

After dinner she lay down on her bed. She did not don her nightgown because she was sure she would not be able to sleep a wink.

She listened uneasily to the storm that raged around the ship, making its wooden hull creak. Unsecured objects flew about, clattering and rattling. The boatswain's whistle shrilled.

Again and again, they climbed the crest of a wave and, immediately after, pitched into the depths of the trough on its backside. Waves broke over the ship and for one brief moment, the *Drie Gebroeders* lay perilously on her side. The pitching motion threw Bethari against the raised side of her bunk, and she cried out. Immediately thereafter, the ceiling lantern, already swinging wildly, extinguished itself.

She leapt out of bed, striking her right leg on the edge. As the *Drie Gebroeders* again rolled, she fell flat on her face. The pain brought tears to her eyes, and her knee burned like fire. The cabin door flew open and crashed against the wall.

"How fare you, miss?" Rufus burst in and squatted down next to her, holding a lamp. Dazed, she raised herself up.

"I bumped against something, that is all. How fare you?"

"Very well, miss. Please allow me to assist you." He put his hand under her arm and pulled her to her feet. The ship rose and fell again.

"Yow!" Bethari doubled over in pain. "I can hardly bear any weight on my right knee."

"Please permit me to carry you to your bed." He put his arm around her waist but she resisted.

"No, Rufus. I want to go to Father. Is he in his cabin?"

"The master is on deck with the captain."

"Then take me there."

"I must advise against that, miss. It is so stormy outside that you would be blown overboard. Please stay inside."

"No!" Bethari shook her head defiantly. She would not remain alone in her cabin for anything in the world.

"In that case, I will take you to the captain's mess and bring the master there." Rufus' tone let her know that he would not tolerate any objections.

"Very well." She nodded acquiescently, linked arms with him and took one step.

"*Vervloekt!*" Her face distorted in pain, she collapsed. "I cannot and will not stay here. Let us proceed."

They inched their way forward, through the seesawing corridor. Bethari supported herself against the wall on one side, and leaned against Rufus on the other. The servant had a firm grip on her waist and lit the way with the lantern in the other hand.

"Do you remember, miss, how we were caught in a storm off Cape Agulhas on our way back from Batavia? You were still small and fearless. You did not even get seasick."

She shook her head.

"I am sorry to say that I remember not much of our time in Batavia, nor of the passage to Amsterdam."

They eventually reached the captain's mess, and Rufus turned to her.

"I beg you, miss, please rest you here while I seek out the master."

Bethari was none too pleased to be alone again. Through a window, she watched the sea foam wash over the deck and shadowy figures brace themselves against the force of the water. Eventually, the door was thrust open from the outside at the same time a bolt of lightning struck. Voices yelling orders were drowned out by the ear-splitting thunderclap. De Groot stumbled into the room.

"Bethari, what on earth are you doing here?" He stared at his daughter as though he had seen a ghost.

"I was looking for you, Father." She limped over to him and threw her arms around him, even though he was soaked.

"What is the matter with you, child?" he asked, with concern in his voice.

"It is nothing to cause worry," she said, trying to calm him. "I just bumped into something. Rufus said you were with the captain."

De Groot smoothed her hair.

"We will no longer go into port at Table Bay; the storm would shatter us on the shore. Schwarz wants to head into Vaals

Bay. It's located next to Table Bay and is fairly well protected on both sides by promontories. The VOC uses it as its winter harbor."

Bethari looked up into his troubled face.

"What do you mean by 'fairly well protected'"?

De Groot made an effort to project confidence. "Schwarz is experienced. He has sailed around the Cape in both directions more than a dozen times. And he shall do it again."

"Hi-yo! You, come up here!" a sailor urged in broken German. Hannes turned around.

"I am needed here."

Bedlam had broken out below deck as well, though the sailors, Hannes, and the ship's carpenter put their backs into their work. One group of sailors used marker poles next to three of the pumps, and measured the water line on board. Another group, pumped out water from the vessel's hold as fast as they could. Hannes and the ship's carpenter had been trying for hours to repair a broken crankshaft on the fourth pump. The carpenter raised himself from his crouching position and exchanged information with the approaching sailor.

"The mizzen mast is damaged," he reported to Hannes. "Go with him and help repair it. I cannot leave this task."

Hannes followed the sailor into the open, and the storm almost knocked them off their feet. Within seconds, Hannes was drenched. A few lights still flickered on deck. Officers shouted orders, barely penetrating the howling of the wind. Sailors made their way forward along tethering ropes, climbing the masts to take down the sails in order to assess the damage. It took two helmsmen to keep the *Drie Gebroeders* on course. Hannes took hold of one the tethers. It took all his strength to reach Schwarz. The captain clung to the mizzen on the afterdeck. The longboat lay at his feet.

"I'm here, Captain," Hannes shouted against the wind. "What can I do?"

Schwarz swung around, his wet hair plastered to his head, water running down his face. The storm made his voice almost inaudible.

"The longboat ... not secured ... flew like a cannonball against the mast. Men all well."

The planks under Hannes swayed as he surveyed the damage. The massive oak mast had not been broken in the impact but had been splintered at eye level. Sooner or later, the storm or the waves would fell it.

"Must be strapped ... need stable posts and supports, rope, pitch and a few strong helpers ... light."

The captain nodded and shouted orders. Then he handed Hannes a rope which was tied to the mast on the other end.

"Tie this to yourself ... until now ... no man overboard ... you ... shall not be the first!"

Upon Schwarz's command, four sailors rushed over. They gathered wood, a roll of hemp rope, a bucket of pitch and various tools from the carpenter's shop below deck and dragged them to the damaged mast. Two sailors fetched special safety lanterns with unbreakable horn windows and attached them to a post to create the necessary light. Hannes cut the beam with an axe; the men smeared it with pitch and wrapped it with the sail. The wind threatened to throw them off their feet. The strong waves made Hannes feel nauseated, but not afraid. He had felt numb for so long that it almost felt good to him to take on the sea and the storm.

"I did all I could," he shouted at Schwarz, who had been watching. "With ... luck ... arrive ... Bay."

"Well done!" A tremendous wave hit the ship. Still, the captain succeeded in slapping his shoulder. Schwarz put his hands around his mouth, shouting, "All of you have earned an extra portion of rum!"

The loud screams of the chief officer broke through the raging storm.

"The watchman reports lights, portside ahead!"

The captain whipped out his spyglass and looked.

"Not the Northern Lights, I hope?" a sailor cried out. "A ship that sees the Northern Lights is doomed," another panted.

Hannes peered over his shoulder and saw a flickering light in the distance. The flickering disappeared after a few moments but a faint light remained.

Schwarz's bellowed demands pierced the night, "Rudder hard a-starboard! All men aloft! Set sail!" Away with the spyglass. As fast as the swaying ship allowed, he rushed to the helm. The two helmsmen anxiously stepped aside when he took hold of the helm with both hands.

"The storm is going to shred you to bits!" the chief officer cried out.

"Follow orders!" Captain Schwarz snapped at him.

"Yes, Captain!" The officer rushed away.

Hannes loosened the rope around his body. With several other sailors, he braced himself against the storm to direct the halyards to the wind.

For just a moment, the storm seemed to ease. All men stood still and look to the dark horizon.

"What is that?" Hannes called out. At that very moment the tempest seemed to start up again, only stronger and louder than before. Gusts from every angle blew into the swelled sails above him and shredded them. A mighty tremor shook the ship and threw Hannes off his feet. A wave crashed over him. Cold, salty water streamed into his mouth and nose. The next wave took him with it.

Hannes cursed himself for loosening his tether as he struggled against the power of the water. He crashed into a cabin wall on the afterdeck. Wave after wave flowed over him, first from one direction, then from another. He was powerless to stop his body from sliding along the deck, and back again. He heard a mighty crash. The ship lurched and Hannes eventually realized that the motion had ceased. The storm raged on but the constant swaying stopped. The ground underneath had turned into a steep incline.

Was the ship still moving at all? Completely disoriented, Hannes rubbed the salt water out of his eyes and tried to straighten up. Each one of his bones hurt but since there seemed to be no fractures, he was able to lean against the wall behind him and slowly get to his feet. He strained to peer into the darkness. At that moment the clouds broke and a pale moon appeared, illuminating the destruction.

The *Drie Gebroeders* no longer lay flat in the water. Bizarrely, the stern was now the tallest part of the ship; the *Drie Gebroeders* looked as though she were headed down the crest of a wave, yet was frozen in the midst of this effort.

Almost directly in front of Hannes' feet a large hole appeared in the afterdeck, and he could see the upper part of the mizzen mast protruding through the splintered planks. The wave had broken it, picked it up and bored it into the deck. Hannes' trained carpenter's eye noted that his repair to the mast still held. However, the sailors who had helped him with the repair were nowhere to be found. He continued his surreal inspection, discovering that the *Drie Gebroeders*' bow lay considerably lower than the stern. The mainmast and foremast, which had proudly towered above the ship, were now reduced to splintered stumps; the yards and sails had vanished. Hannes was horrified to realize that people lay everywhere among the debris. A few of them numbly tried to scramble to their feet, slipping and sliding on the steep and wet deck. Most did not move at all. One of the helmsmen lay slumped over the wheel.

"My ship," the captain moaned, his face distorted by pain. "A damned rogue wave's dealt her the death blow."

"What say you, Captain?" Hannes asked anxiously.

Schwarz turned around slowly. "A monster wave has washed us onto a reef that has penetrated the hold of my ship like a bayonet."

"The *Drie Gebroeders* has been slit open?" All at once, Hannes comprehended the severity of the situation. "My fellows are below deck! And the carpenter and the sailors are at the pumps!"

He stumbled over to the hole in the afterdeck and kneeled down. Everything below was pitch black, though he heard groaning. A few voices called out, "Help! Get us out of here!"

Hannes leaned into the hole. "Stay calm, men. Help is on the way."

He looked around anxiously. Where was von Hügel? Even though ordinarily he avoided the commanding officer as best he could, at this moment he wished that the colonel would show up and give orders to rescue the soldiers from this hell.

"Out of the way." The captain pushed him aside and crouched down in front of the hole. "Boatswain! Are you down there?"

For several seconds they heard nothing but the groans of the injured, but then a voice called out from the hold of the ship, "Yes, Captain!"

"How bad is the situation?"

"Sir, the impact tore the cannons out of their mounts. They rolled over many of the men and crushed them. And the water is rising because the pump deck under us is flooded. It has reached one foot high now."

"Damn!" Schwarz panted. "Did any of the men from the decks below you make it up?"

There was a long pause.

"No, Captain."

"Tell the survivors that we shall get them out and on land again!" Schwarz got up. "By God, I do not yet know how we will do it. But we must try." He turned to Hannes. "We need light. Get me some lanterns and dry tinder, my box has gotten wet. And pray to God, man, that we do not lie too far from shore. We must quit the ship before it splits apart!"

Hannes stumbled forward and pushed open the door to the cabin area. A light flickered dimly. He could make out human beings among the toppled chairs and broken china. They huddled against the back wall of the captain's mess, near the open door leading to their cabins. He recognized de Groot's servant, de Groot himself, as well as Bethari. The servant kneeled on the planks, holding the lamp. De Groot crouched next to him. Bethari lay stretched out on the ground. Her head rested in de Groot's lap. She did not move.

"At last! I had thought we lay here, forgotten!" De Groot gestured desperately toward his daughter. "She hit her head on the wall and now she won't wake up."

Although he had spoken to Hannes in Dutch, Hannes had learned a few scraps of the language during his work with the ship's carpenter. He wanted to help Bethari, but he was on a mission for the greater good of the group.

"Sir, three hundred of my fellow soldiers are trapped below deck and await our help. Give me your tinderbox and the lantern. We need light," he explained in broken Dutch.

"And what about Bethari? She is injured."

"You and your servant are with her."

"I want the ship's doctor or the regiment's barber surgeon to examine her."

"Sir, the two doctors, should they still be alive, are needed for the injured soldiers and sailors!" Colonel von Hügel had appeared in the doorway leading to the cabins.

"But my Bethari," de Groot stammered.

"She will wake on her own." Colonel von Hügel pushed past de Groot. Anna Maria appeared behind him. Her hair was tousled and she looked the worse for wear but seemed unharmed. Von Hügel told her to sit with de Groot, Bethari and the servant, then moved to Hannes, his brow furrowed with anger.

"Why do you not help the men?" he demanded to know.

Hannes raised his chin. "The captain has ordered me to get him some tinder and lanterns so that we may have some light during the rescue."

"I have a tinderbox." Von Hügel patted his jacket. "Now don't stand around, soldier. Come with me!"

Once set in motion, the rescue efforts proceeded rapidly. Captain Schwarz, Colonel von Hügel and the chief officer worked as hard as Hannes and the sailors. First, they pulled the tip of the broken mast out of the hole. Then Hannes fashioned a ladder out of some broken chair legs and a rope, and lowered it to the deck below. One by one the survivors climbed up and sank in exhaustion onto the planks of the afterdeck. One of the first to emerge from the hole was August. "Gramercy, you're alive!" Hannes cried out when the boy's disheveled head appeared in the opening.

"Hannes!" August embraced him boisterously. "You're here!"

"Did you hurt yourself?" Hannes held him at arm's length and looked him over. "Any wounds or pain?"

"I am in one piece!" August assured him, but his face grew serious. "There is so much water down there. And many people are hurt."

"Only prayer is going to help most of them now." Master Spönlin crawled into the open and got up with a groan.

"Major Liesching is doing his best but he cannot perform miracles."

CHAPTER NINE

OFF THE COAST OF SOUTH AFRICA, 1787

Hannes helped until dawn to rescue the injured from the lower deck. He held the light while the doctor tended to the wounded, tore blankets into strips for bandages, and made stretchers out of hammocks and poles. Captain Schwarz ordered that the bodies not be thrown into the ocean for fear of attracting sharks, so they left the dead soldiers and sailors in the lower deck.

Many men had lost their lives when the cannons rolled over them. Among the survivors, Hannes saw crushed limbs, open wounds and splintered bones protruding from arms and legs. The injured whimpered and groaned; some screamed with pain. Exhausted soldiers and sailors gathered on the middeck and afterdeck, many of them with bandages, improvised splints on their legs and arms, or unevenly fashioned crutches. Of the one hundred sailors and three hundred recruits of the Infantry Regiment of Württemberg, two thirds had lost their lives and many were so badly wounded that they were unlikely to survive the next few hours.

Hannes encountered August by the portside railing, peering at the coast.

"Hello, my friend."

He leaned over the railing and saw, in the deep, the reef that had doomed the *Drie Gebroeders*. A few seals lay on the limestone which had been polished by the ocean. Waves, several meters high, driven by the wind, towered on the rocks before crashing in a bow of white foam. Several crates and barrels bobbed up and down on the water. Hannes guessed that many more had been washed overboard and swallowed up by the seas. August had tears in his eyes.

"Do you see the people, Hannes? Drowned and dead. And the lovely goats too."

Hannes followed his gaze. Half a dozen dead bodies, sailors who had been washed overboard during the storm, and three dead goats lay among the debris on a narrow strip of sand on the shore. Behind this sad and gruesome scene, the hillside rose gently to become a ridge. Craggy cliffs framed the small beach, continuing along the endless stretch of shore. Waves still surged as far as they could see.

Just a few more meters and we would have been trapped, thought Hannes.

The lifesaving shore was barely a ship's length away from them but climbing the rocky shoreline was impossible. Besides, any swimmer would be shattered on the rocks before arriving there. They did have a chance, however, thanks to the small stretch of sand.

Captain Schwarz, too, clung with one hand to the portside railing, looking at the coast through his spyglass. Next to him his chief officer, the von Hügels, the de Groots, and Rufus struggled to keep their balance. Bethari leaned heavily against her servant. She looked pale and exhausted in the bright morning light. On her head she wore a stained bandage, which she held with her hand. The wind tugged at her dress and her long black hair.

Schwarz lowered his spyglass and turned to the others.

"We have drifted past Vaals Bay," Hannes heard him say. "Roughly six to eight nautical miles."

"How do you know that?" von Hügel asked.

"I have compared the coastline with my nautical charts."

"Will no one from the harbor know that we are stranded here?" Bethari asked. Schwarz nodded.

"The lady displays unfailing intuition. We are left to our own devices."

There was a pause. Then von Hügel asked, "Can we use the longboats?"

"They either went overboard last night or were destroyed by debris," the chief officer explained.

"And the remaining ones, can they be repaired?" the colonel inquired.

"Are you joking?" the captain snapped at him. "Those are no more than driftwood! And yet—" he took a deep breath, "we must leave the ship before it breaks to pieces."

"It will break to pieces?" the baroness called out in dismay. Hannes instinctively moved closer to the group.

"Can you hear the *Drie Gebroeders* creaking? She will not last much longer in the surf." Schwarz's voice sounded constrained.

Hannes listened intently. Aside from the crashing of the waves and the rush of the wind, he heard the creaking sounds of the beams, bending under the water's pressure. It sounded as though mighty bones were rubbing against each other. He shuddered. As a carpenter, he knew what wood sounded like shortly before it burst asunder under pressure. He looked out at the ocean and in the direction of the bow. The entire front deck was flooded; some of the waves even washed over a part of the upper deck. The figurehead at the tip of the bow had become invisible.

"How much time do we have to evacuate the ship?" the baroness wanted to know.

The captain did not answer.

"I will see to the recovery of the money chests," de Groot said. "Have a few of the sailors and this regimental carpenter here build a raft so that we can take the trunks to shore."

This brought Schwarz to life.

"A raft?" he screamed. "Do me the courtesy, my good man—observe the ocean! How, by the grace of God, will you guide a raft through this surf? And one that is laden with chests full of coins? Have you no idea how much something like that will weigh? If it doesn't sink right away, this raft of yours will shatter on the rocks! First and foremost, we will save people from this ship. You can locate your damned silver at the bottom of the bay after this is all over."

De Groot placed his hands on his hips.

"The Lords Seventeen will be most displeased to hear that you were willing to surrender to the ocean thirty-seven trunks filled with silver gulden belonging to the VOC, *Mijnheer* Schwarz!"

Schwarz inflated his chest.

"So, you plan to make a report to the Lords? Please send them my most gracious regards, *Mijnheer* de Groot, and do not neglect to mention that more than three hundred sailors and soldiers lost their lives."

De Groot drew a deep breath but Bethari was quicker.

"The captain is right, Father. Let us focus on the people and not the money."

"I, too, give top priority to the rescue of the remaining soldiers," von Hügel stated.

"But how will we reach the shore without a raft or a longboat?" his wife interjected.

"We will build a slide," said Captain Schwarz. "But first I require three strong swimmers."

"I most humbly volunteer for the task," Rufus said as he stepped forward. One of the sailors volunteered as well.

The colonel surveyed his surviving soldiers and paused when he saw Hannes.

"You, soldier, will go as well!"

He is not satisfied with what he has done to me already, Hannes thought bitterly. *He will never tire of tormenting me. If I disobey the order, he'll punish me again. If I follow it, I'll end up as shark bait.* Again, he was overcome by a fierce rage. Had it been up to Hannes, they would have settled their feud like men, with their fists, once and for all. Instead, von Hügel relished wielding his power as commander to not only belittle Hannes, but put him in danger.

You will not succeed, he thought and clenched his fists so hard that his hands hurt.

Schwarz beckoned the three men and pointed to a jagged limestone cliff on the coast.

"Listen with great care, men; I shall explain to you what you have to do. We will stretch a rope from the ship to that rock. And for that, the three of you will have to swim to shore. One of you will take a tether to which the rope is attached." He looked at Hannes. "Will you do it?"

Hannes nodded.

"On shore, you three must pull on the rope and wrap it around the rock. Because it weighs a hell of a lot, it will require all three of you. You," indicating the sailor, "will fasten the tether. Make a round turn with two half hitches. That will fasten the knot."

"Understood, Captain," the man answered earnestly.

"And where will the other end of the rope attach?" Hannes wanted to know.

"We shall attach it to the stump of the mizzen mast. We will also require a towing rope which must be brought ashore for the slide."

"I shall do that," Rufus volunteered.

"Very well, we shall begin."

"One moment, Captain," the baroness interrupted. "Do you mean to say that you expect us to make our way over the ocean, hand over hand, along a rope?"

Schwarz shook his head. "Not quite. You will have hold of the slide as well."

"With all due respect," de Groot spoke up, "this seems a great risk to me. The storm still perseveres. We shall be blown into the ocean with such a device!"

The captain gave him a hostile look.

"If you have a better suggestion, *Mijnheer* de Groot, that involves neither raft nor money chests, by all means, let us hear it. Otherwise, you are free to go down with the *Drie Gebroeders*."

He breathed deeply and continued more calmly to the rest of the group, "I have seen this done before, and the structure is this: the big rope will form the main part of the slide, leading from ship to shore. Two smaller ropes will form loops. A stable post that is not too thick will lie in these loops and form a handle of sorts, which shall hang from the big rope. Two cords are required, one for a brake, one for pulling the slide. We shall hang onto the post and glide to shore, one by one."

"That will not be easy." Von Hügel frowned and chewed on his lower lip. "But it seems like the only feasible way."

"Take two greased iron rings and pull them over the heavy rope. And hang the loops with the slide on that. That way the structure will glide more easily along the rope," Hannes suggested. "I expect the rings on which the chains of the ceiling lamps hang should work."

"Excellent idea, soldier!" Schwarz praised him.

Von Hügel glowered at Hannes but nodded briefly.

"Will this structure support a hammock?" he asked the captain.

"Probably. Why do you ask?"

"We'll use that to transport the two ladies and the injured. We'll also use it to take provisions, guns, and ammunition to shore. After all, we still must make passage all the way to Cape Town."

"Yea," Schwarz remarked. "We'll take our ship's medicine chest as well then."

"Are there any savages in the area?" von Hügel inquired.

The captain nodded.

"The Khoi and the San. The Khoi roam with their herds of cattle. The San are hunters and gatherers of wild fruit, exclusively. Both are accustomed to dealing with Europeans and are mostly peaceable. Shall we start now?"

De Groot demurred once more.

"Surely the Company's silver can be taken ashore in the hammock."

"Are you starting that nonsense again? First of all, we have not time to convey silver coins over the ocean and secondly, my sailors will most certainly not haul the chests to Cape Town for you," Schwarz said, incensed.

"Nor shall my soldiers!" von Hügel declared. De Groot pressed his lips together and dispensed with any further discussion.

Schwarz clapped his hands.

"In the water, men. Time begins to run out. Take great care not to hurt yourselves on the underwater reefs. Blood attracts sharks."

Hannes, Rufus, and the sailor took off their jackets, shirts, shoes, and stockings. Hannes carefully wrapped the young Dutchwoman's drawing in his folded clothing.

"Take good care with this," he bade the sailor to whom he gave the bundle.

Then he tied the rope around his middle and stepped to the railing. Below him the water rushed over the reef. The surface appeared smooth, but there were clearly dangerous jags lurking below.

The distance to shore was not great, but the waves towered up to two meters. They were of no great consequence to a ship, though they could easily swallow a human. And then there were the sharks. Although Hannes could see no telltale fins, he knew that the ruthless predators lurked at greater depths.

"These brave men have vowed to risk their lives for us. How shall we protect them from sharks?"

Recognizing the voice, Hannes turned to see Bethari, who had planted herself in front of Colonel von Hügel and fixed her gaze on him. Once more, she had given voice to Hannes' thoughts, as if she had heard them.

She is so different from her husband, he thought. He simply could not imagine what bonded the elderly finance inspector and his vivacious, young wife, yet it was clear to all that the de Groots were close.

Colonel von Hügel cleared his throat. "I fear it is impossible."

His gaze briefly wandered to Hannes at the railing. "We have no spears or harpoons."

"The two pistols on your belt are not wet," his wife interrupted him. "Can you not shoot sharks with those?"

Von Hügel looked at his wife coolly. "I can shoot at their heads or dorsal fins," he conceded, "if they surface, that is." He was obviously of two minds. After a pause, he added, "I shall call additional officers to protect the swimmers with their pistols. But I warn you, if they miss their target, the water will be teeming with sharks and our odds will be worse than before."

Shortly afterwards, von Hügel and three of his officers lay prone on the deck, their pistols ready to fire. As the three swimmers, Hannes, Rufus, and the sailor, lowered themselves from the port side, the seals hastily slipped into the water.

The granite rock under Hannes' feet felt cold. He took a tentative step as the surf sprayed over him. He almost slipped on the surface, made slimy by algae and water. He clutched the silver cross from his mother, which he always wore around his neck.

Just a stone's throw to shore. Give me strength, Lord, and watch over me, he prayed silently. A gust of wind took hold of him and pushed him forward, causing him to stumble and slip. Next, a wave washed over him and pulled him into the ocean.

The water was frigid. He felt his muscles tighten and fought his way to the surface with a few powerful kicks. Another wave washed over him, yet this time he was ready, and fought against it. The power of the sea was frightening and yet it pushed him forward, always in the direction of the shore. His eyes searched for their goal: the limestone spire to which they planned to attach the rope. After a while, he began to hit his stride.

Out of the corner of his eye, he saw the sailor, who swam a little behind him and seemed to have difficulty keeping his head above water. The de Groot's servant, on the other hand, swam with powerful strokes, at the head of the group.

The exertion began to take its toll; Hannes had the feeling his lungs were about to burst and his heartbeat pounded in his ears. Suddenly he heard screams from the ship:

"A shark! Swim faster! For God's sake!"

Panicked, he looked over his shoulder. One body length behind him, the sailor flailed wildly with his arms, a light gray triangular dorsal fin directly behind him.

"Open fire!" Colonel von Hügel roared. Almost immediately, the sound of gunshots rang out.

Hannes doubled his efforts. His arms and legs felt leaden but fear propelled him forward. Stroke by stroke he fought to get to shore, ever in fear of being attacked by the shark and pulled under water. He eventually saw that the de Groots' servant had made it, and not long after, his own feet also grazed the sandy ground. After a few more strokes, he was able to stumble onto the shore. Breathing heavily, he sank to his knees and looked back on the ocean. There was no sign of the sailor. The triangular dorsal fin had disappeared as well.

"How fare you, *mijnheer*?" a voice asked in Dutch.

He looked up to see Rufus' dark face floating above him. His concerned dark eyes peered at Hannes.

"One of us did not make it," Hannes panted. He noticed the long, bloody scratch on the servant's lower left leg. "You are bleeding."

Rufus nodded sadly. "I swam too close to one of the reefs and I am afraid that attracted the shark."

He extended his hand and helped Hannes to his feet.

Hannes said, "We have no time to brood over that. Let us get the rope over here. It will be damned hard since there are only two of us now."

He untied the rope from his middle and turned toward the *Drie Gebroeders*. From the shore, the once splendid sailer was a sorry sight. She was stuck on a rock. A deep gash could be seen on her starboard side. Water gushed into her interior. It would not be long before she irretrievably broke apart.

Some sailors had maneuvered a roll of cable onto the deck and tied it to Hannes' rope. They signaled that they were ready.

"Now!" Hannes nodded to Rufus.

Together they began pulling the length of rope. Hannes broke into a sweat, and his exhausted arm muscles burned hellishly at the effort. He thought he would lose his strength but with Rufus' help, the heavy cable slowly slid along their line, from the *Drie Gebroeders* toward the shore. At last, they retrieved it and wound the cable around the rock.

"Do you know how to make a sailor's knot?" Hannes asked the servant.

"I am sorry, *mijnheer*." Rufus shook his head. Hannes had watched the sailors making knots a few times but he could not remember how to make the complicated loops. He knotted and wound the end of the rope to the cable as best he could, then regarded his handiwork with a frown.

"You stay here and make sure that nothing gets slack, otherwise people will fall in the water," he instructed Rufus. "I will work the hoisting cable."

The servant nodded solemnly. "Yes, *mijnheer*."

Meanwhile on the ship, the sailors had greased two iron rings and pulled the cable through them. Next, they made loops in the smaller rope and pushed a pole through them. Then they wound the end of the cable around the mizzen mast.

Captain Schwarz stepped to the railing and cupped his mouth with his hands, "Are you ready?"

"Ready!" Hannes screamed back and waved his arms.

In order to test their contraption, they placed two chests of hardtack and Hannes' and Rufus' bundles of clothing into a hammock and pulled it across the ocean. The wind tugged at the hammock, swaying it back and forth. But Hannes, his feet in silt and seaweed, managed to maneuver the load safely to shore. He opened his bundle and was relieved to find the drawing Bethari had made of him; it was only slightly more crinkled. He quickly slipped his shirt over his head and slid the paper underneath.

Next, the women were to be brought to safety. Bethari was the first to climb into the hammock. The wind whipped her hair and pulled at her dress. She held the bandage on her head with one hand and used the other to cling to the slide. Hannes pulled the cable. Despite the greased iron rings, it was difficult to convey the load along the cable. He braced his legs firmly in the wet sand.

Suddenly a gust of wind blew under the hammock. It tipped precariously to one side and Bethari came within an inch of capsizing. She let out a scream and clung to the slide with both hands. Her bandage blew away but she managed to hang on until Hannes was able to re-stabilize the hammock. He leaned backward and pulled the cable with all his might. Shortly afterward Bethari arrived on land.

She swung her legs over the side of the hammock and was about to jump into the shallow water when Hannes lifted her and carried her to dry sand. She wrapped her arms around his neck and pressed her face against his shoulder. He felt her delicate small body through her dress, drenched by the surf, and her chest, rising and falling with her breath. He caught himself wishing he could have carried her much farther. If only she did not belong to de Groot!

"Mistress! How fare you?" Rufus ran over to them.

"I am safe and well. Mark you, I am not made of fine china!" She lifted her head from Hannes' shoulder and smiled at the servant. There was dried blood on her forehead.

Hannes gently put her down. She took one step toward Rufus and groaned, "My knee! I cannot put any weight on it!"

"Do you see that rock there?" Rufus pointed to a flat granite behind the rock spire to which the cable was attached. "You shall be more sheltered from the wind over there, miss. Come with me." He put his arm around Bethari and slowly led her there.

Hannes returned to the shore and took hold of the hoisting cable. The sailors had retrieved the hammock and re-greased the rings. Anna Maria climbed inside. The colonel wrapped a rope around her waist and fastened it to the slide. Then he gave Hannes a signal to start pulling. As though by a miracle, the wind did not blow so strongly during this maneuver and the baroness reached the shore without difficulty.

As Hannes helped her out of the hammock, she smiled and said, "All my life I haven't had as much excitement as I had these last few days. I think that's enough for a while."

But when the injured began arriving and Rufus laid them down at the other end of the beach, she saw to it that the men were as comfortable as possible and spoke to them encouragingly.

Hannes looked at the cable with great concern. It did not yet sag but that could change with the additional and continued weight on it.

The conveyance of guns, ammunition and the ship's medicine chest took place without incident. They were heavy enough not to be blown out of the hammock.

The sailors and soldiers with minor injuries and those without any injuries made it to shore unscathed, although some were tossed around by gusts of wind. August was one of them. Once he made it to shore, he helped Hannes with the hoisting cable. Colonel von Hügel was the last of the regiment to leave the ship.

"You owe me a debt of gratitude," Hannes said as the commanding officer jumped in the sand in front of him.

Von Hügel gave him a look filled with hate as Hannes blocked his path.

"I could have toyed with your life as you did with mine. But I did not."

For a while they stared each other down.

"Never forget your place," the Colonel hissed. Hannes remained immobile until von Hügel finally pushed him aside and trudged away.

A short while later the captain slid to shore.

"We did it. All the men are off the ship. Well done, soldier." Schwarz jumped into the shallow water next to Hannes, turned and looked at the wreckage of the *Drie Gebroeders*. The wooden hull creaked and squeaked. Two boards splintered above the hole.

"That is all," he murmured. "Soon the sea will take her. At least we were able to rescue all the survivors."

"Alack! Send it back for me!" De Groot appeared on deck and gestured wildly.

"Zounds!" the captain roared, "How in the world did he get there?"

"Did you not know he remained on board?" Hannes asked.

"No, damnation! I thought he had long ago come ashore; else I would never have abandoned the ship."

Hannes squinted, "His jacket looks most unusual, does it not?"

The captain eyed de Groot through his spyglass. "Yea, by God!"

"My mistress wants to know if everything proceeds smoothly."

Schwarz lowered his spyglass, and Hannes turned to face Rufus and Bethari, who looked at Schwarz accusingly.

"How could you let this happen, Captain?"

"Miss, had he not ignored my instructions and disappeared below deck to stuff his pockets with bags of coins, this would not have happened!" Schwarz snorted angrily.

"How can you make such a claim!" Bethari's eyes sparkled with indignation.

"Pray you, miss, take a look at his coattails. What do you think makes them stand up almost horizontally?" He handed the spyglass to the young woman.

She looked through it for a few seconds. Then she handed the instrument back to the captain.

"You are right," she said softly. "I must ask your pardon."

"It will be difficult to bring him ashore safely with the weight of the coins," Hannes remarked.

"We shall tighten the cable once more so that he does not land in the ocean," Schwarz determined.

"I fear it is too late for that," Rufus interjected.

Bethari, Hannes and the captain looked at the ship. De Groot had somehow recovered the slide, which he now held with both hands. His legs swung freely.

"Pull me to you, else I shall fall!" he screamed to Hannes in German.

Rufus and Hannes grabbed the cord and pulled with all their might. Two sailors helped, yet the farther the slide proceeded, the more the cord sagged. Halfway across, the Netherlander's feet hovered no more than a few hand's widths above the water.

"Can you not move the cord any faster?" Bethari asked impatiently. She stood in the shallow water and stared intently at her father.

Schwarz whistled and summoned one of the sailors. "The hawser must be tightened. Re-knot the cord to the rock!"

"Nay, that is riskier. Instead, several of us men shall hold it taut. That is how we shall bring him over."

The Captain clapped his hands to summon a few of the sailors. Together they took hold of the rope.

"Shark!"

The piercing cry rang over to them. A soldier pointed to the water where a large, triangular fin made its way like an arrow to where de Groot was suspended. Rufus and his helpers tugged on the cord in a race against the shark. The predator had almost reached de Groot when the cord became taut. The slide jerked back and forth and for a moment it looked as though the Netherlander would lose his grip. The shark's head shot out of the water, its gaping maw, with its razor-sharp teeth, opened wide. De Groot pulled up his legs just in time, and the predator missed him. Seconds later a shot rang out and the shark disappeared.

"He shan't prey on anyone again," Colonel von Hügel announced as he replaced his pistol in his belt.

When de Groot at last slumped into the wet sand, Bethari shouted with glee. She fell to the ground next to him and covered his face with kisses.

"We made it," de Groot panted and embraced his daughter. He stood and then helped her to her feet.

"Might I have a word with you, *mijnheer!*"

"Yea?" De Groot turned around and looked straight into Schwarz' face, which was distorted with rage.

"With all due respect, de Groot, you are a bastard!" With that, the captain reached back and gave the Netherlander a sock in the jaw that sent him backwards into the shallow water.

CHAPTER TEN

VICINITY OF VAALS BAY, SOUTH AFRICA, 1787

When de Groot reached the shore, the sun was low in the sky, as the rescue had taken the entire day.

Hannes was bone-weary. His arm muscles ached and his face was badly sunburned. His skin felt as though it were covered with a thousand ant bites because the wind relentlessly blew sand on it. His lips were rough and dry. When he ran his tongue over his mouth, he tasted salt. His stomach growled. He had eaten nothing all day and he was ravenous.

Even though he and other men had toiled hour after hour to bring what they could ashore, most of the supplies had been lost. That included not only the greater part of the silver coins belonging to the VOC but also most of the chests of weapons and ammunition, the de Groots' and von Hügels' baggage, as well as the regimental uniforms which had been stowed on the lowest deck. The water had rendered most of the food inedible. Hannes hoped that they would be able to subsist on wild animals and plants until they reached the Cape Colony.

Captain Schwarz had told them that they had drifted past Vaals Bay, which was adjacent to Table Bay and Cape Town. Hannes had no clue how far they were from their actual destination. He hoped that, given the many injured who urgently needed help, it would not take too long to reach civilization.

He sighed and studied their surroundings. While the beach was about one hundred paces long and thirty paces wide, it offered no protection at all. He felt a cold wind blowing, as the surf drenched his clothes and the sand assaulted his face. The cliffs to the west and east of the small cove were too steep to climb. To the north, the hillside rose gently, dotted with limestone rock of all sizes, and covered by wind-blown low shrubbery and bushes with yellow and white blossoms. Trees did not seem to grow here, save for a few knee-high specimens with trunks resembling columns, and sparse, dry branches.

A mountain range formed the horizon, which at the moment was cast in a blue hue, thanks to the waning daylight. Hannes thought their best chance lay to the west, where there seemed to exist a flat trough-like pass with craggy granite sides. He thought this was a possible passage, did there seem to be a possibility of getting to the hinterland. Suddenly Hannes became aware of something else: clouds of smoke rising from the foot of the steep cliffs. He hurried over to Schwarz. The captain and his chief officer sifted through the debris that had washed ashore.

Hannes heard him say, "Damnation, everything is wet. No good as firewood."

"I saw two axes among the guns we brought to shore," he interrupted. "We'll use those to chop off the wet outside layer of wood. Then we'll use the dry wood inside to kindle a fire and once we've got that going, we can add the wet wood."

"I must say, soldier, without your help today, we'd face a much worse situation right now," he said approvingly.

Hannes lowered his head. The praise made him happy but at that the same time, it embarrassed him. Being helpful came naturally to him. His work as a carpenter, often aloft on scaffolding, had shown him the necessity of depending on others and working as a team. He pointed to the smoke columns on the horizon.

"Speaking of fire, sir, there are several on the mountainside."

"Bushfire. They're common in this dry region. They don't usually last long and are limited to small areas."

"They present no danger to us?" Hannes asked.

"Yea." Schwarz gave him a good-natured pat on the back. "No cause for alarm, soldier."

By now the officers had counted the survivors. Only eighty-four of the four hundred people on board the *Drie Gebroeders* remained. August and a group of men used laths to dig shallow makeshift graves for the dead. Then they gathered rocks to create small grave mounds as protection from predatory animals and fashioned crooked crosses out of some ropes and pieces of wood, but truth be told, there were few graves because most of the casualties had found their final resting place at the bottom of the ocean. Master Spönlin said the "Our Father" for all these poor, dead souls.

The ship's doctor and Major Liesching treated the injured. Almost everyone had suffered one injury or another when the ship hit the reef, from bruises and bumps, to sprained and broken limbs, all the way to severe internal injuries that made survival unlikely in this rough environment, far from an infirmary.

Some sailors and soldiers built stretchers from pieces of the sails and planks that had washed ashore, while the two doctors bandaged the open wounds and splinted fractures. Major Liesching sutured the injury on Bethari's forehead. De Groot held her hand but she made no sound throughout painful procedure.

"You will be left with a small scar," said Liesching as he put away his instruments. "If you permit me the observation, you are an exceptionally brave young lady."

"A scar doesn't bother me at all," she replied with a dismissive gesture and stood up. "I have breath in my body. Many others were not so lucky. Rather, tell me how I may assist you in treating the severely injured."

"I would like to help too, major." Anna Maria appeared next to Liesching and looked at him expectantly.

"But Bethari! You yourself are injured!" De Groot tried to restrain his daughter.

"Let me go. Think you, honestly, that I will idly sit by and gaze upon the misery of others?"

She freed herself and limped away with the doctor and Anna Maria.

Hannes used one of the axes to chop away the wet wood from the beams that had washed up, and piled the dry wood under the cover of the rock spire. In the meantime, the ship's cook skinned three goats that had drowned while his helper built a frame. Hannes kindled a fire underneath, and soon the animals roasted over the crackling flames. Some of the men who had gone looking for water managed to find a small creek. Now they transported fresh water back to the camp using hats and caps.

When the goat meat was done, the castaways gathered around the fire. Hardly anyone had eaten a thing for a night and a day so that now they gladly helped themselves. In addition, there was hardtack, dry and hard as a rock. As there were no eating utensils apart from a few survival knives, they ate with their hands.

Hannes threw a furtive glance at Bethari. She sat on a round rock between de Groot and Rufus and gnawed the meat off a rib. Every now and then she wiped the fat and juices off her mouth with the back of her hand. With her disheveled hair and dirty dress, she looked more like a vagabond than the wife of a rich merchant. For his part, de Groot's jaw was red on the left side where the Captain's fist had landed. Chewing was obviously painful for him because he declined the hardtack, biting off only small pieces of meat. He moved his mouth slowly and gingerly. Hannes observed that he still wore the rope with the coin bags around his waist.

At that moment Colonel von Hügel asked, "Captain! Are you sure we are in the vicinity of Vaals Bay?"

All conversation and noise stopped instantly. Every eye found the captain.

"One hundred percent sure. As I told you already onboard the ship, I compared the coastline with my nautical charts. I recognized a characteristic cliff through my spyglass. It looks as though it's hanging from the western edge of Vaals Bay."

"Well, you were mistaken when you thought you saw Northern Lights and there were none," von Hügel remarked pointedly.

Schwarz glared at him angrily. "I never thought that the light phenomena were Northern Lights. I thought they were bushfires. When I saw the flames, I knew that the storm had driven us too close to shore and I tried to steer against it. It was our misfortune that the storm was too much for the *Drie Gebroeders*."

"But if those were really bushfires, why did we see them only briefly? A fire does not go out so quickly," Anna Maria argued.

"If the fire is burning in a depression, the flames can easily disappear from view," Schwarz explained.

"But who started the fires and why?" von Hügel persisted.

"Many times, all it takes is a lightning bolt. Sometimes flying sparks created by falling rock can start a fire."

"Or have people set the fires for slashing and burning?" de Groot interjected. "I am familiar with that from long ago in Java. That is how the farmers there gain new land for agriculture."

"That is another possibility." The Captain stroked his scruffy beard with his thumb and forefinger. "Perhaps they were set by the Khoi to make new pastures for their cattle."

"You mean to say that we are stranded in the wilderness, surrounded by savages?" Von Hügel's right hand instinctively moved to his pistol.

Schwarz smiled wryly. "You can let go of your pistol. If they had wanted to attack us, they would have done so already."

"They are here?" Von Hügel peered anxiously into the darkness.

Schwarz shrugged his shoulders. "I have not seen any but if they are close by, they have been watching us ever since we ran aground."

"Why did they not help us?" Anna Maria wanted to know.

"They have become wary. Not all of their encounters with foreigners have been altogether good," the Captain responded.

"As settlers claim their ancestral lands, they retreat farther and farther inland to find game to hunt, and pastures for their herds."

"Do you think that they will overcome their shyness and reveal themselves?" Bethari wanted to know. "I would love to make drawings of them. It is a shame that all my drawing tools went down with the ship."

Von Hügel stood up abruptly.

"Enough! Under no circumstances will I permit us to be surrounded or attacked by Khoi or San or anyone else! Where are the chests with the guns?"

"What do you have in mind, my good man?" Schwarz had risen as well. "I hope it's nothing foolish."

"I will send a reconnaissance troop to drive away these characters from this cove."

"You will do nothing of the sort. Darkness has already fallen. You and your people are not familiar with the terrain, and you are exhausted and injured. If you were to antagonize the natives in your current situation, you would find yourself disadvantaged."

"But it is the mission of the Infantry Regiment of Württemberg to protect the Cape Region," von Hügel insisted.

"The regiment's mission is to protect the Cape Colony," Schwarz corrected him. "And until we reach that, you are under my command."

"Gentlemen, please! Do not get agitated!" Anna Maria took her husband's hand and pulled on it until he reluctantly sat down.

"My dear husband, I am also of the opinion that nothing dangerous should be undertaken at night. Instead, let us discuss what is to be done tomorrow. Do you have a plan, Captain?"

"Indeed, I do." Schwarz, too, sat back down in the sand. "With all our wounded, it would take at least forty days, if not more, to walk from here to Cape Town. Fortunately, we are close to Vaals Bay. I know of a beach like this one, just one day's hike away. That is feasible. In addition, there will be sailing ships seeking refuge from the storm. When it gets dark, we will light a big fire so that they can see us. They will take us aboard and transport us to Table Bay."

"Well, that sounds simple enough," said the baroness.

"Too simple," her husband grunted.

"Are there no villages or settlements around here?" de Groot asked.

Schwarz shook his head. "There is only Simonstad on the other side of Vaals Bay. If there are any villages around here, it's going to be the *kraals* of the natives. And I know neither where they are nor if we would be welcomed there."

"Well, in that case, your suggestion sounds first-rate. Does it not?" Anna Maria nudged her husband.

Von Hügel nodded grudgingly. "But I insist on posting guards around our camp and on keeping the fire on all night!"

While the castaways sought places to sleep as close to the fire as possible, Colonel von Hügel assigned the first sentries. Hannes watched de Groot take off his jacket and solicitously cover Bethari with it. Apart from this gesture, his hands rested on the coin bags, which he had still not taken off.

Hannes shook his head and turned away. He had dug himself a shallow trough in the sand to guard against the encroaching cold temperatures. But he could still feel the wind blow across his body. In addition, he had the feeling that the air was getting more and more humid as the night progressed.

The colonel had not assigned him to stand sentry but, as so often was the case, he could not fall asleep. After several months at sea, he missed the constant creaking and swaying of the ship. With one arm under his head, he lay on his back and looked at the starlit sky.

It had been almost one year since he had fallen into the recruiter's trap in Tübingen, lured by the prospect of adventure and money. He would never have dreamed even in his worst nightmares that these adventures would include a mock execution and a shipwreck. Besides, he had not been paid a single kreutzer of his pay. As a convicted mutineer, he had not received the advance of four gulden that his fellow soldiers had been paid in Vlissingen. The accruing pay was recorded in the VOC's register of debts and set off against the costs of board and lodgings, weapons, and gear.

It pained him to think that he had been unable to send his mother the money he had promised her to repair her roof. Back home in Swabia it was almost winter and that was usually long, dark, and cold. Hannes was concerned that his mother might fall ill in her drafty little cottage. He resolved to write her a letter as soon as he arrived in Cape Town. He hoped that by that time he would finally receive his pay to be able to send it home. Should he speak to Anna Maria again, he wondered? But then he scrapped that idea. She had made it clear in Vlissingen that she could not be relied upon. And anyhow, after the mock execution he preferred to keep her at arm's length.

He was startled by a series of deafening crashes, louder than a thunder bolt.

"Good heavens!" he cried out and jumped to his feet.

He could see by the light of the fire that the sound had frightened everyone in the camp. Some hurried to the water while others ran along the beach, panic-stricken.

"Help! An earthquake!" one shouted.

"We're being attacked by savages!" someone called from another direction.

"Silence!" The captain's thundering voice drowned out the noise. "It's the ship. The *Drie Gebroeders* is breaking apart once and for all!"

Hannes strained to see the coast. The flames of the fire blinded him and the moonless night absorbed most of the contours, making it difficult for him to recognize the ship. But he heard her final groaning sigh and the little hairs on his forearms stood up.

There was no question of sleep anymore during this night. Hannes crouched by the fire, his arms wrapped around his knees, and stared at the ocean. The fog arrived with the morning. The billows were cool and moist as they came in from the water, creeping inland. There were moments when the sky was clear and, in those moments, Hannes saw the wreck of the *Drie Gebroeders*. Her bow had vanished. The stern was still poised on the cliff. Numerous planks had come away from the wooden hull of the ship. The rest looked like a skeleton.

When she broke apart, additional equipment and bodies flushed out of her hold. The bodies were waxen and bloated. Fish and other marine animals had already fed on them. A sickly, cloying stench filled the air.

Master Spönlin began to dig more graves; Hannes grabbed a piece of driftwood and helped. The preacher nodded gratefully.

"'Tis bad enough that these poor souls had to die far away from home. The least we can do is give them a dignified final resting place," he said. "The same is true for those three severely wounded whom the Lord called to Himself during the night."

As they pushed the crosses into the flat hill of sand, they heard angry shouts.

"Damnation! Those savages stole a crate of our hardtack during the night! Their footprints prove it!"

The cook stood, hands on hips, not far from the fire with von Hügel and the captain. All three stared at the sand.

"My adjutant reports to me that the sentries found traces of naked feet all over camp. They were small, however, like children's footprints."

Alarmed, Schwarz looked at him.

"Why did you not tell me before?"

"I did not want to cause a commotion," the Colonel answered. "Do you have any idea who we are dealing with?"

"Indeed, I do." The captain nodded. Before he was able to continue, one of the officers yelled, "Look out!"

At the same time, a second voice called out, "Savages! They're coming into the camp!"

Von Hügel swiveled around, his hand on his revolver. Schwarz grabbed his arm. "Don't!"

A group of approximately two dozen people appeared out of the bushes, where they had been hiding. They were shorter than the Europeans, wiry, and lissome. Their skin shimmered like the sand. Their short black hair was twisted in tight spirals close to the scalp. Their eyes were narrow and strikingly dark.

An elderly man, with a leopard skin thrown over his shoulder, led the group, escorted by warriors with wooden spears. A few women and children came next; all were naked except for leather loincloths and long necklaces made of wooden and bone beads.

"These are San bushmen," Schwarz explained so that all of the castaways could hear him. "Stay calm and have no fear. They are harmless."

"From your lips to God's ear." De Groot felt for the coin bags around his middle.

"I do not put much trust in the Lord in situations like this," von Hügel said. "All soldiers! Fall in!"

"Stay back! Or it will end badly," Schwarz flared up.

"Not for us," von Hügel retorted. "We have firearms. All they have is pointed spears."

"You are wrong. The points of those spears are dipped in deadly poison and the warriors who are armed with them rarely miss their targets. But these people are peaceful so long as we are peaceful. Last night they stole a crate of hardtack from us but they could just as easily have taken the clothes off our backs. We would only have noticed it when we were naked because bushmen have the ability to blend in with their surroundings."

"I am also quite sure that they have no hostile intentions," Bethari could be heard saying. "They have women and children with them."

Von Hügel looked at Schwarz. "I will wait and see. But the responsibility is yours."

The situation was tense as the group of San approached under the suspicious eyes of the castaways.

The leader stepped up to Schwarz and von Hügel and said something in a language consisting of clicking and clucking sounds. None of the castaways understood a word.

"Are they stuttering?" the Colonel asked the Captain, puzzled. Schwarz shook his head. "That's how all the savages speak around here."

"So, you understand them?"

"I'm afraid not. My contacts with the natives are confined to the Khoi, who come to the Cape Colony to sell their cattle and sheep and they speak a little Dutch."

Rufus caught Colonel von Hügel's eye. "Can you translate for us?"

"I regret I cannot," the Black man answered politely. "I can speak only Dutch and Malagasy. And a little bit of German, French, and Malay. I have never heard the language of these people before."

"Look!" Bethari called out.

The warriors stepped aside to make room for a young woman with a baby in her arms. The child wailed most pitifully and was not to be consoled even though the mother gently rocked it from side to side. The young woman stopped in front of the ship's doctor and Major Liesching. She laid her hand first on the baby's forehead and then on its stomach and shook her head with a worried expression.

"She seems to know that we're physicians," Liesching said, surprised.

"The Captain did say that they've been watching us since our ship ran aground," de Groot interposed.

"Obviously the mother is seeking medical advice for her child," the ship's doctor remarked and tentatively stretched out his arms. The young woman looked at him beseechingly and handed the little one to him.

"He has a fever." The ship's doctor felt the forehead and carefully palpated the abdomen. Again, the baby uttered the most heart-rending cry. "The abdomen is hard. Most likely it is in pain. We should bleed him to reduce the pressure in his body."

"And then we purge him," Major Liesching added.

"Bloodletting and an enema? You're going to kill the poor little thing!" Baroness von Hügel stepped forward and quickly took the baby. "Is there nothing better in the ship's medicine chest for a fever and a stomachache? You've got to treat a little baby like this gently and carefully." She leaned over the infant and tickled him under his chin with her finger.

"I bought some cinchona bark in Fernando de Noronha," said the ship's doctor. "It's helpful in treating a fever. I can spare a little."

"And ground kaolin should help with the diarrhea. I noticed that you have some in your medicine chest," Major Liesching interjected.

The two physicians prepared a paste by mixing the two medications with some boiled water and then administered it to the reluctant baby. A few minutes passed and the child grew quiet. His eyes eventually closed and he fell asleep. The baroness returned the baby to his mother's arms. "He will get well," she reassured her, smiling cheerfully.

Shortly afterwards, the bush people disappeared as quickly and soundlessly as they had appeared. The castaways packed up the equipment they had salvaged and placed the severely injured on the stretchers made of sail cloth and wooden sticks.

Bethari's knee was red and swollen and every step she took was extremely painful. It would be impossible for her to do a day's march through rough terrain.

"I can build you a sedan chair, miss," Hannes suggested.

He looked for a piece of cloth, a rope, and a few poles and, using the tip of a knife, began to poke holes in the cloth for the pieces of rope. She sat in the sand and watched him.

"You are very skilled with your hands."

He answered without looking up. "Before I became a soldier, I was a carpenter, my lady."

"It felt good yesterday to be carried ashore by you. Your arms are strong."

He did not reply, wrapped the cloth around the poles and fed the rope through the holes.

After a short pause she asked, "Will you and Rufus carry me on that seat?"

"If that is what you wish, miss."

"Are you always so sparing with words or is it just me that you don't enjoy talking to?"

The corners of his mouth twitched when he turned around.

She returned his smile. "You are really not such a *zuurprium*."

"A what?"

"A *zuurprium*. That's what we call a grouch, someone captious and disputatious."

"And that describes me, miss?"

"If you could see yourself right now, you would understand."

"Well, if you expect me to carry you all over the place, you should guard your tongue, my fair lady," he countered, but he was grinning and she noticed it.

"I never keep my opinions to myself."

"Miss, I had not noticed." He turned and walked away.

After a meager breakfast of cold meat and hardtack, Colonel von Hügel ordered his soldiers into march formation and addressed them.

"The worst of this journey is behind us, men. Soon we will arrive in the Cape Colony," he announced in a firm voice. "On our way, we will adjust our tempo to the slowest among us. By that I mean our fellows who carry the stretchers with the wounded. The bearers will be relieved every two hours. Additionally, I expect the healthy to care for the sick and the men to care for the women. No one will be left behind."

"There are all sorts of venomous snakes around these parts," the captain warned before he joined von Hügel at the head of the caravan. "They will most probably be frightened away by the noise we make. Still, we should all be cautious and watch where we step."

The two men had decided not to follow the steep shoreline but to head inland in a northwest direction. Schwarz' compass would help them stay on that course because patches of fog coming in from the ocean continued to obscure the position of the sun.

Slowly the column of castaways climbed the hill behind the rock spire and took the path to the pass, the only passage to the interior. Six soldiers with guns loaded and bayonets fixed, escorted the captain and von Hügel, who were followed by the stretcher bearers and wounded.

Hannes and Rufus carried Bethari. The servant went in front, Hannes in back. They did not need to be relieved as the fine-boned young Dutchwoman was light weight for the two men. De Groot walked next to her. Hannes observed how they laughed with each other and talked quietly. It was evident they were very close. He asked himself how it was that the woman had only just now flirted with him, Hannes, right under her husband's nose.

After they crossed the pass, the wind finally subsided. The more they moved away from the ocean, the warmer it became. The fog seemed to have gotten stuck in the mountains as well. When Hannes threw a quick glance back over his shoulder, he saw how the peaks shredded the white plumes.

Schwarz and von Hügel led the group through an extended valley with a creek. In the west it was bounded by a steep mountain range. In the east it rose gently. Wide, charred areas were evidence of recent fires. Time and again Hannes saw columns of smoke rising. The wind carried the smell of smoke to them but Schwarz assured them that the fires were too remote to represent any danger to them.

Between the scorched sections grew low bushes and shrubs. The yellow ones reminded Hannes of his mother's needle cushions. The purple ones looked like the heather that he knew from the marshlands and sandy plateaus of his homeland of Württemberg. There were no trees in the interior of the country either, aside from a few low-growing specimens, whose silvery foliage gave forth an intense scent of almonds.

"Last year, these fields were burned," Schwarz explained, before adding, "I have observed this phenomenon untold numbers of times when I visited the Cape. And every time I am fascinated anew." Hannes, too, was intrigued by how thoroughly and quickly nature renewed itself, seemingly unimpressed by wind and fire. His own experience had been similar. His mortal fear in the moments following his mock execution had almost destroyed him but, little by little, life was returning to his soul.

When the sun reached its zenith, the castaways rested by the creek. Hannes and Rufus put Bethari down by a flat rock on which she could comfortably sit.

"I thank you both." She smiled at Hannes and her servant.

"You must be thirsty. I will get water for you." Rufus bowed and walked away. Bethari stretched her legs, stiff from sitting, and grimaced with pain. "I would much prefer to walk but my silly knee will not permit me."

"I think I can manage to carry a little feather like you, miss" Hannes muttered.

She giggled. "A feather?"

"Yes, half a portion. A lightweight. Like you, I mean, miss." He rolled up his sleeves up to his elbows. "I'm thirsty. And I'm hot. If you'll excuse me, miss."

She watched him trudge toward the creek, kneel down and splash water on his face and neck. Her lips curled into a dreamy little smile.

There was nothing to eat except hardtack. They washed it down with ice cold water, which had an iron taste. Dragon flies with iridescent blue wings flew above their heads and small black lizards sunned themselves on rocks. In the distance they could see two grayish-brown antelopes the size of horses, with long, tightly spiraled horns and dewlaps on their lower necks.

"Those are elands," explained the Captain. "Their meat is tender and savory. A real delicacy. But the roast seal to which we will treat ourselves in Vaals Bay this evening isn't bad either. Seals spend the nights on the beach and are easy to shoot outside the water."

De Groot, breathing heavily, lowered himself onto the stone next to Bethari. He handed her the dripping wet neckcloth he had rinsed in the creek.

"Here, little one. You can cool your knee with this."

"Thank you." She took it, slid it under her dress and wrapped it around her painful knee.

"Along the coast I felt the wind in my bones and here I'm dying of heat." De Groot wiped his brow with his sleeve.

The captain looked at him mockingly. "Your silver coins are a heavy burden, aren't they, *mijnheer*? And utterly useless here in the wilderness. You can neither eat nor drink them. And yet their weight makes you sweat even more!"

De Groot paid no attention to him and instead beckoned the commanding officer. "I'd like a word with you, *Mijnheer* von Hügel!"

The colonel stepped over to him. "How can I help you?"

"I need a few of your men to carry my coin bags."

Von Hügel raised his right hand to ward off the request. "I already told you that my men would not be available for such a service."

"I'll offer you this one if you help me." De Groot touched one of the bags on his belt and raised it slightly. "There are fifty gulden inside."

Von Hügel contemplated the little sack for a moment. "For five bags, I'll entertain your request."

The Netherlander snorted with indignation. "Really! That's half a year's pay for you!"

Von Hügel raised his eyebrows. "What do you know about my pay?"

"I am Finance Inspector for the honorable Company, your employer! But because of my position, I am willing to show forbearance and to give you a second bag when we reach the Cape Colony."

"Two immediately, one in Cape Town," the Colonel replied, unblinking.

De Groot knitted his eyebrows. "I'll have to think about reporting this extortion attempt in my next letter to the Lords Seventeen."

"And in that letter, be sure to mention how your high-handedness impeded the evacuation of the ship," von Hügel shot back.

"Three bags and that's final!"

"Agreed." Von Hügel took a brief bow and left.

"You're giving the Colonel one hundred and fifty gulden and the men who lug the money for you get nothing?" Bethari asked angrily.

Her father pulled his snuffbox out of his jacket. "For a soldier, this von Hügel has surprisingly good business acumen."

"Please answer me! Why not give the men a few gulden for their services?" Bethari was not willing to let the matter rest.

He sighed. "Charity is fine if one can afford it. But we're talking about the Company's money here. I have the obligation to use it advisedly."

"And still you distribute it most unequally."

"Please, Bethari, cease pressuring me. You do not understand anything of business."

"Then explain it to me!" she persisted but he shook his head.

"The colonel just received one hundred and fifty gulden from me. Let him use that to pay his men."

After the meager meal and a short rest, the castaways continued their hike. When the sun was low over the western horizon, they reached another deep pass. After crossing, they saw before them a flat, sandy shoreline, similar to the one where the *Drie Gebroeders* had run aground. Behind it lay Vaals Bay. Hannes squinted. He believed he could make out the tiny outlines of sailing ships on the reflective surface of the water. Provided the bright light was not playing tricks on his eyes, help was close at hand. Just as the Captain had promised, several seal families lay on the beach. As soon as the humans came over the pass, they clumsily made their way to the ocean and dived underwater.

"There goes our dinner." De Groot placed his arm around his daughter's waist, lifted her out of her seat and carefully helped her to her feet. "Are you comfortable like that?"

Bethari stretched. "Yea, I am well. Much better, certainly, than the two men who have been carrying me over hill and dale."

De Groot turned to Hannes. "Thank you for that."

"That is all the appreciation you plan to show?" Bethari rebuked him. He grunted. But then he untied one of the bags, took out one gulden and gave it to Hannes.

"For you, soldier."

"Why, this is sheer madness!" Hannes joked, taking the coin.

De Groot pursed his lips. But then he took out another gulden. "That's enough now!"

"And you will not thank Rufus?" Bethari interrupted. "He carried me as well."

"Rufus has never had money," de Groot answered gruffly.

"I'll share with you." Hannes was about to hand one of his coins to the servant. Rufus' eyes grew large at the sight of the coin, then he slowly raised his hand.

De Groot barked, "Desist, soldier!"

Rufus shrunk back. "I'll attend to the night-quarters for the master and mistress." He turned and hurried away.

Hannes swung around. "What I do with my money is none of your damned business!"

"How I deal with my servant, on the other hand, is my business. And anyway, watch how you speak in front of a lady!" De Groot raised his hand. "I don't wish to hear any more about it."

Bethari looked at her father in disgust. "I am disappointed in you!"

Before he could answer, the captain appeared.

"Through my spyglass I have seen no fewer than two dozen ships with the VOC flag in the bay. A convoy returning to Europe from Batavia or Ceylon that has sought shelter here from the storm, no doubt. As soon as it is dark, we shall light our signal fire and they will notice us."

"Captain!" a sailor shouted and ran across the beach to him. "We have company!"

Six San warriors crossed the low pass, divided into pairs of two, each shouldering a long branch with a dead Cape grysbok hanging upside down. The warriors headed straight to Schwarz, placed their kill in the sand and left.

"How did they know we were here?" Hannes asked, annoyed. Throughout their hike, he had been on the lookout for visitors but had seen no trace of them.

"As I told you, they watch us." The Captain touched one of the animals with the tip of his boot. "The treatment of the child appears to have been successful. They brought us these bucks as a sign of their appreciation. The meat is very flavorful, much tastier than seal. Cook!" He gestured to the ship's cook. "Prepare our dinner!"

While the cook and a few helpers skinned and gutted the grysboks, which were not quite the size of deer, a few other men collected dry branches and brushwood and kindled a large fire. It was not long before the appetizing aroma of roasted meat filled the air.

Hannes took his portion of meat and sat next to August.

"Well then, did you get lots of blisters?"

The boy nodded sadly. "My feet hurt. But this food helps. It's very tasty."

Hannes was starving and ate heartily. He was surprised to discover that the meat was, indeed, very tender and fine-textured.

"A few more days and we shall sleep in real beds again," he told August, with a full mouth. "In the barracks of the Cape Colony. That is, if one of those ships in the bay sees our fire."

"I feel quite sure of it." Bethari gingerly lowered herself onto the sand next to Hannes and August. "Once it's dark, the flames will be visible throughout the bay. Hannes, you have been helping me so unreservedly ever since our shipwreck. Your goodness has nearly left me silent."

He turned his head and looked at her. Her dark eyes glowed in the eventide light like two pieces of coal and her gaze pulled him in. And the same feeling he had had when he carried her to shore the previous day came over him. He was attracted to her. Much more than he should have been to a woman who belonged to another man.

"Over there is your husband." He pointed to a few flat rocks on the other side of the fire on which de Groot sat with the captain, von Hügel and Anna Maria.

"Perhaps it is he who should be enlightened with regard to your feelings, miss, not I."

"My husband?" She looked at him, confused. "Who might that be?"

"Well, for heaven's sake!" he burst out. "Do you take me for a totty-headed fool? Why, de Groot, of course. You have his name!"

For a moment, she sat, immobile. Then she rose with difficulty and concealed her clenched fists in the folds of her dress to hide her rage.

At last she took a deep breath and said as calmly as she could, "I took you for clever, Hannes. But that was a mistake. Because you are, in fact, a simpleton, a great big *dwaas*! A fool! Has it never occurred to you that *Mijnheer* de Groot might be my father?"

CHAPTER ELEVEN

CAPE TOWN, SOUTH AFRICA, 1787

"Ow! Damnation!"

The ball shot through the air. Hannes tried to catch it but the hard leather orb slipped through his hands and crashed onto his chest.

"Aha!" August jubilantly jumped up. "Out!"

"I shall come for you next time!" To the mischievous amusement of the others, Hannes trotted to the edge of the field on which two teams of recruits competed. He was annoyed with himself for not catching the ball and he ignored his fellows' crowing.

As they did every evening, several soldiers played a round. After months of being confined on the ship, the men yearned for exercise. Spectators stretched out on the sandy ground around the field, smoking their pipes and chatting.

The men played in the back courtyard of the Kasteel de Goede Hoop, the Castle of Good Hope, where the accommodations for the fort's garrison were located, along with the bakery, and various workshops, for the blacksmiths, carpenters, and regimental tailors. For nearly five years, the fort garrison had been home to Swiss mercenary soldiers from the *Régiment de Meuron*. The men of the Württemberg Infantry Regiment had provided reinforcement, but the Swiss regiment was about to transfer to the VOC's East Indian colonies.

After the departure of the Swiss, the Württembergers would finally move into the large barracks immediately next to the Kasteel, though until that time, they made do with tent accommodations next to the piers in Table Bay. The officers stayed in furnished apartments all over town. Colonel von Hügel had rented a lavish house on the Heerengracht Street for himself and his wife. Jan Pieter de Groot had done the same.

Around the front courtyard of the garrison were the writing rooms of the senior VOC clerks. A passageway connected two courtyards; on one side was the governor's house and on the other, the apartments of his adjutants. The facility was protected by a wide moat with drawbridges as well as ramparts, walls and five bastions armed with cannons.

The castaways had been in Cape Town for almost two months now and still Hannes had vivid memories of the morning of their rescue. By the first light of day, he, and all those who were able-bodied, had run to the shore of Vaals Bay. Captain Schwarz had already scoured the horizon with his spyglass. All of them strained to hear the soft sloshing of oars. But Hannes heard nothing save the rushing of the waves, the squawking of the seagulls, and his own breath.

When the sun slowly rose over the hills and the gray water of Vaals Bay began to sparkle, he recognized a clunky ship's hull with the red, white, and blue flag of the Netherlands on the main mast, not too far away. People ran around on the upper deck. He heard the sound of the boatswain's pipe and saw the longboats being lowered into the water. The castaways broke out in jubilant cries of joy.

In the afternoon they went ashore in Table Bay. Here, too, Hannes could see traces of the storm: several stranded ships, smashed to pieces or split open on the reefs, with broken masts. Later he learned that during that night, twelve sailing ships had been destroyed or had sunk.

A few days after their rescue, Captain Schwarz and the surviving sailors left for the Netherlands on an East Indiaman. Some time later, more VOC ships arrived from Europe, bringing the rest of the regiment's recruits. Though some of the soldiers had died from fever and exhaustion on the journey, it was naught to compare to what the *Drie Gebroeders* had endured.

The recruits were most pleasantly surprised by how easy life in South Africa was for them. There was plenty of nutritious food and the weather was almost always warm and dry, except for the occasional strong wind blowing from the Atlantic. Most importantly, there was no combat action. Since the war with Great Britain had been lost three years earlier, the Netherlands was at peace with her European neighbors. The Khoi and the San did not represent any danger and their only offense was the rare theft of some cattle.

Therefore, there was little for the recruits to do aside from their daily exercises. Once, one of the companies had been ordered to guard a ship loaded with porcelain, silk and spices that had been stranded off the Cape. And in early December, on Governor Abraham Sluysken's birthday, the regiment held a military parade through the town.

Hannes dropped to the floor next to one of the soldiers, stretched his legs and propped himself up on his elbows. The soldier nudged him in the ribs and sniggered.

"Say, did you let that nicky ninny hit you on purpose?"

"Certainly not," Hannes grumbled. "He's got quite a punch. And his name is August, by the way."

"I meant no harm. Want a smoke?" The man held out his tobacco pouch by way of conciliation.

"Your farmer's herbs are too dry for my liking, and black as pitch too. My guess is that they are mixed with ferrous sulfate. I might as well smoke ground nails. But I am grateful, my friend." Hannes patted him on the shoulder. The recruit pulled his clay pipe out of his tobacco pouch. Hannes watched a few seagulls fly over the bastion walls, squawking.

He could see Tafelberg, Table Mountain, in the distance. He was fascinated by the long, flat-topped mountain that towered over Leeuwenkop, Lion's Head, in front and Duiwels Kop,

Devil's Peak, behind. From the Kasteel's courtyard the mighty crest looked quite close but Hannes knew that it was an almost two-hour march to the foot of the mountain. Today the plateau periodically disappeared under low-hanging clouds drifting in from the Atlantic. "Table Mountain's tablecloth" is what Capetonians called this phenomenon.

On the side of the mountain facing the town, Hannes had often noticed small fires after darkness. These were not bushfires, as he had initially supposed. One of the Swiss soldiers had explained to him that these were campfires set by escaped slaves. More than one thousand slaves lived in the town of five thousand inhabitants. Most of them belonged to the Dutch East India Company. They worked on the docks or took care of the trading company's vegetable garden, situated inland, behind the Kasteel.

Since Hannes had arrived in Cape Town, several ships carrying slaves from Madagascar or the French colony of Île-de-France had docked in the bay. The VOC needed the strongest of the men; the rest were sold in a square behind the Company's slave house. Hannes had heard that some of the officers acquired young mistresses this way.

Simple recruits like he could not afford such an extravagant lifestyle—although all, including Hannes, had finally received their first pay shortly after their arrival. It was just about sufficient for some of the most inferior tobacco, and beer diluted with sugar water. Prices for imported luxury goods were high and whenever many ships were harbored there, with their sailors yearning to squander their pay after many months at sea, the prices became astronomical. His ten gulden a month had far less buying power than Hannes had expected.

The sound of loud drunken singing returned him to reality. Half a dozen soldiers staggered through the gate between the front and back courtyards, as Hannes' companion lowered his pipe.

"Monkey's asses, just what I needed," he grumbled.

"Monkey's ass" was a curse word the recruits had learned on the Cape because of the many baboons native to the region. Initially the animals' bright red buttocks caused much hilarity and provided material for indecent jokes. However, after some of the apes had stolen the tobacco pouches of inattentive men, pulled the buttons off their jackets and bitten them mercilessly if they resisted, the baboons had become very unpopular. They were chased away with rocks whenever they appeared.

The Swiss soldiers were every bit as unpopular because they received considerably more pay than the Württembergers and treated them with corresponding haughtiness.

"Hello there, *Gschpändli,* fellows!" one of the Swiss men shouted. "Lo, did you have to stay home again? 'Tis a shame that only some of us can afford a pannychis the likes of which we had last night!" The remark referred to the bordellos and taverns of Schotsche Kloof, where the men preferred to disport themselves.

His companions laughed uproariously. One of them performed some swaying movements with his hips. The conversations on the courtyard fell silent; the ball players interrupted their game.

"Be gone, understrappers!" one of them snarled.

One of the Swiss soldiers waved two large terra cotta bottles. "I have here some excellent, very quaffable wine. It will tickle your palates. Much better stuff than watered-down beer. I might let you try some." He looked at the bottle and shook his head. "Now that I think about it, this tasty stuff would be wasted on sugar-beer guzzlers."

He pulled the cork from one of the bottles, put it to his mouth and emptied it. Then he belched heartily. His comrades crowed.

"That's it!" One of the Württembergers rolled up his sleeves. A few others followed suit. Within seconds, the hard, leather ball zoomed past Hannes and directly into the heckler's face.

"Bastard!" The man dropped the bottle and touched his bloody nose, grimacing with pain.

The Württembergers triumphantly advanced. "You've been asking for a thrashing, you pant shitters! And you'll get it!"

The Swiss men stood shoulder to shoulder, their fists raised.

"Mullocks!" screamed one.

"Monkey's ass!" retorted a Württemberger.

"Weasel!"

"Son of a whore!"

The squabblers stood nose to nose, pushing and shoving.

"Enough! Do you want us all to land in the lockup?" Hannes grabbed one of the soldiers by the scruff of the neck and pulled him away. Two other recruits also tried to separate the brawlers.

"When did you turn into such a fussock?" The man yanked himself free. "You used to handle two at once."

Hannes watched as the Swiss men took to their heels and sought their sleeping quarters as though they were relieved to have escaped serious injury. "Yea, well, I used to be stupid."

"A blunderbuss!" August shook with laughter.

Hannes gave him a hard poke in the ribs. "Make yourself scarce!"

The boy, half stunned, half offended, went on his way.

"What, we're not playing anymore?" One of the soldiers threw the ball in the air.

No one answered. The scene with the Swiss men had ruined the atmosphere.

"I'll be very glad when these pompous asses finally get on their way," one man grunted.

"Then they shan't rub our noses in how wonderful they are anymore," added another.

"I'd like to know why they get paid more than we do," the first continued grousing.

"They signed better contracts with the Company, that's obvious," a second man said.

"They didn't get screwed over like our duke."

"And don't forget that they can even leave their pay in the regimental coffers," the first one reported. "When they get home, they'll be receiving a tidy little sum of hard, Dutch gulden. Our pay is worthless Indies gulden."

"Yes, paper money that's just about good enough to wipe your behind in the latrine! Must we continue to suffer this pathetic deal?" a third man interrupted.

"Let's put up a fight!" one in the large group screamed. "We'll refuse to serve the Dutch fat cats!"

There was approving muttering from all sides. Their rage, long suppressed, was being vented.

"Stop this nonsense!" Hannes stepped between the men. "Your plan is doomed to fail. Have you forgotten what happened to me?"

"You were alone. There are many of us. They can't touch us!"

"I'm telling you, they have the upper hand. If you land before the Council of War, you will be found guilty of mutiny and sentenced. I'm not so sure that von Hügel will be content with a mock execution again."

"But how do you propose that we come into our own?" shouted another.

Hannes thought for a moment. "To fight the terms of a contract negotiated by the duke is difficult, if not impossible. But I know where we can earn some money." His eyes scanned the group of men. "Become *pasgangers*. Each one of you worked an honorable trade before he became a soldier. In the shipyards, in the stockyards, in the sailmakers' shops, the blacksmith's shops, carpenters' workshops or bakeries, everywhere around here capable men are being sought. I submitted my application to the High Command and it was approved. Starting next week, I'll work as a carpenter on the docks and get paid for it."

"You go right ahead and suck up to the nobility," one of the men grumbled. "But I wouldn't dream of breaking my back. I'll just end up being screwed over again."

"Everyone negotiates his pay with his master. For example, I'm getting paid in Dutch gulden," Hannes replied. "We have time, my friends. Why would we not use it?" He turned around and walked away.

Bethari entered her father's study. She balanced a tray with two half-filled wine glasses.

Jan Pieter de Groot looked up from his desk. "Since when are you part of the staff? Where is Rufus?" He frowned as he watched his daughter limp toward him. It was half a year since the *Die Gebroeders* had been shipwrecked but Bethari's right knee was still painful whenever she put weight on her leg.

"I told Rufus that I would bring the refreshments. Or do I interfere with your work?" She looked across the tabletop with interest at the scattered papers. Some were covered densely with writing, others with numbers. On the top lay a hachure map, representing the relief of the terrain.

De Groot placed his quill pen into a wooden box and closed the inkwell. Then he took a leather portfolio from the edge of the table and slipped the sheets of paper inside. "Of course, you're not disturbing me. Still, I must say I'm surprised at Rufus. He knows that your knee is not healed yet. And apart from that, I don't think it's right for you to do the work of a servant."

He rose, took the tray from his daughter, and brought it to his desk. Then he pulled a comfortable armchair next to his chair.

"Sit down, my dear. I'll ring for Rufus and ask him to bring a small footrest for you."

"Don't do that, Father, please. All you really want is to reprimand him. But it's not his fault if I don't listen to doctor's orders."

Major Liesching as well as one of the physicians on the Cape had examined Bethari shortly after their arrival. Both of them suspected a torn meniscus.

"I cannot understand why you don't rest. This way, your knee will never improve." De Groot watched his daughter support herself on the arms of the chair as she lowered herself.

"Oh Father, please don't scold me, at least not on my birthday." She carefully extended her aching leg.

158

He smiled contritely. "I feel guilty to spend so little time with you on your special day. But there is so much to prepare before our onward journey to Ceylon. And now tell me—how did you spend your afternoon?"

"I tried out my new painting supplies and blended a few colors. The pigments are of the finest quality." Smiling mischievously, she spread out her fingers and showed him the blue, red, green, and yellow stains. "I am so happy to be able to paint again at last!"

"I'm pleased that my present gives you joy." He leaned forward and stroked her thick, dark hair.

The shops in the Cape Colony did not carry art supplies. For weeks, he had sent Rufus to the harbor on daily missions to find out if a docking ship brought canvases, pencils, oils, brushes, and pigments on board. At last, a sailer had arrived, fully laden with luxury good from Europe. De Groot walked to the harbor himself to buy all the supplies his daughter needed. That morning at breakfast he presented her with his surprise.

"Well, then let us drink a toast to me on my birthday." She was about to reach for the glasses when he raised his hand. "You know my thoughts on young ladies' consumption of alcohol."

She gave him a reproachful look. "Do not treat me like a little girl. After all, I turned eighteen today."

He smiled at her. "I should begin looking for a husband for my grown-up daughter."

"Oh, there remains lots of time for that." She took one of the glasses and raised it, "*Voor goed,* cheers!" They clinked glasses filled with the golden wine of the Constantia Estate on the back of Table Mountain.

De Groot had rented the house from the widow of an affluent merchant, who had moved in with her son. It looked like a typical Cape Town house, with its whitewashed façade and green shutters. It had two stories with many rooms, chambers, and salons. On the walls hung mirrors and oil portraits of the previous residents. The family showed off its wealth in the china cabinets filled with Chinese porcelain. A delicate spinet stood in one of the salons and Bethari often played it in the evenings.

As a precaution against fires and unlike the older houses in the Cape Colony, this building had no thatched roof and only one hearth, in the kitchen. The temperatures were pleasantly summery at the moment but Bethari was certain that the residents would be miserably cold in the winter. The widow's seven slaves came with the house. Unlike in the Netherlands, it was not customary here to employ paid servants.

Bethari gazed out through the wide-open windows. The white curtains blew in the breeze and she could hear the rustling of the dark-green leaves of the mighty oak tree in the courtyard. She loved that tree. Its height and expanding crown reminded her of the copper beech in their garden in Amsterdam.

"Doesn't it feel strange to experience the most beautiful summer in the middle of February? I'm sure that at home there is snow on the ground," she said, lost in thought.

Her father studied his daughter, "Are you homesick?" She shrugged lightly. "I miss our convivial evenings, my friends, and my fellow students at the art academy. But this country is much too beautiful for me to feel homesick. These constant visits bore me, though. Mondays at Baroness von Hügel's, Tuesdays at the governor's wife's, Wednesdays at the apothecary's wife's and so on and so forth. Do you realize that the ladies here are actually somewhat leery of me? Around here, the people with dark hair and skin like mine are usually slaves." She glanced over at the desk.

"You have yet to tell me what the mission in Ceylon is all about."

"Cinnamon," he revealed. "The Company imports the world's best cinnamon from Ceylon."

"Fair enough," Bethari replied. "But what is your mission?"

Her father smiled wanly at her. "The Lords Seventeen wish me to inspect everything concerning the trade *in situ*: the yield, the costs of the transportation insurance, the protection of the warehouses, the transportation to the port and the loading onto our ships."

"Does the Company not employ on-site inspectors for these things?"

"That is correct. But even they need to be inspected now and again, and that is just about impossible to do from Amsterdam. You know how long it's been since we left home. And we haven't even reached Ceylon yet."

"What keeps us from continuing our journey?"

"Well, you know what happened to the silver which the Lords Seventeen entrusted to me."

"It's lying at the bottom of the ocean."

"Exactly. Five of the thirty-seven crates were intended to cover the costs of my mission. I gave Captain Schwarz a letter to take to the Lords. In it, I describe the events and request the delivery of replacement silver. Provided Schwarz reaches Amsterdam without delay and the Lords promptly make the necessary arrangements, the ship with the new money should arrive within the next one to two months. It is then that we will begin our onward journey."

Bethari turned the wine glass in her hands. He was beginning to hope that he had sated her curiosity when she asked, "Five crates of silver, that's a lot. Do you need the money to make people compliant? Or to extract information from them?"

He bit his lip and pulled his snuff box out of his jacket. How could he possibly have thought that he could distract his perceptive daughter with trivialities? Her questions had hit the nail on the head. Of course, he could not divulge that.

"We need capital for our living expenses. The rest is a reserve for anything unforeseen. After all, I'm still at the beginning of my calculations and I have no idea what awaits me in Ceylon," he said instead. He was well aware that he did not sound convincing at all. The money sacks that he salvaged from the *Drie Gebroeders* contained more than enough to cover their necessary expenses, in addition to all the comforts of daily life. He laid one hand on the leather portfolio.

She placed her empty wine glass on the tray and stood up. "In that case, I don't want to keep you from your work."

He, too, rose from his chair and took her in his arms. She leaned against his chest. "Promise me that you will not put yourself in danger, Father?"

He kissed her on the forehead. "But of course, I'll be careful. You know that."

She raised her head and looked at him. "I'll be glad to help you."

"You? No!" He laughed and pushed her away. "My business will only bore you. Tomorrow afternoon the Lodge holds its weekly meeting. I'll see Colonel von Hügel there. I shall ask him to loan me one of his officers as an assistant."

The following afternoon, when Jan Pieter de Groot stepped onto the Heerengracht, the bright sun reflected off the white house façades. The light hurt his eyes and his black broadcloth suit and vest, his shirt and neckcloth made him break into a sweat. He pulled his bicorne down over his forehead and hurried into the shade of the big oak tree that lined the street. He felt a little envious as he watched a palanquin being carried by two slaves. More than likely, behind those drawn curtains sat the wife of a well-to-do merchant. She was not subjected to the dust that flew up with every step he took on the unpaved street and ruined his freshly polished shoes.

There had not been a drop of rain for weeks. Potable water had to be laboriously obtained from a fountain on the main square, since the canals along the street were dry and stank abominably. De Groot pulled out his handkerchief and held it against his nose as he avoided a huge heap of cow dung. He was immediately surrounded by a swarm of fat blow flies. He waved his hands in exasperation. The most elegant residences and important public buildings were along the Heerengracht. It was a mystery to him why the governor allowed farmers and natives to use the town's stateliest street to drive their cattle to the slaughterhouse.

The nearer he came to the graceful white masonic lodge, the more members of the Brotherhood de Goede Hoop he encountered. De Groot belonged to a Dutch lodge but he was permitted to attend the meetings of the Freemasons of Cape Town. He utilized this opportunity regularly, for here he met all the powerful men in the city and learned firsthand who had been given a prominent position or what major decisions were pending. The governor belonged to the Brotherhood as did prosperous merchants, the apothecary, the doctor, and the judge. Important temporary visitors to the city like Colonel von Hügel or ships' captains in transit were invited to the regular dinner.

De Groot passed the Groote Kerk, the church, and the sickhouse. Almost directly across were the slave house and the garden belonging to the Dutch East India Company, surrounded by blackberry hedges. The VOC used the fruits and vegetables grown here to supply the crews of its ships.

He stopped and watched as Black men loaded baskets filled with cabbages, potatoes, turnips, and beans onto the wagons of some ox carts.

At that moment, Colonel von Hügel came around the corner of the slave house. De Groot raised one hand and gave a friendly wave.

"A good afternoon to you, Colonel."

Von Hügel bowed his head politely. "Greetings to you, *mijnheer*." He was about to walk on but de Groot cut him off. "How are you and your esteemed wife, Colonel?"

Von Hügel bowed his head briefly. "Excellent, thank you for asking."

"Splendid! Please be so kind as to convey my most respectful compliments to her."

Von Hügel had no choice but to continue on his way in de Groot's company. Initially, they made small talk. The Netherlander spoke of his trouble with an insolent slave. Von

Hügel inquired about his daughter. They agreed that the sunny, warm weather at the Cape was preferable to the rainy, cold conditions at home.

As they passed through the white portal, flanked by two tall columns, and into the lodge's courtyard, de Groot said, "I've been told that life for the regiment is quite pleasant here. Instead of wars, there is rest and nutritious food. Your soldiers surely are in the best of health."

"That is correct," von Hügel answered haltingly.

De Groot continued, "Not everyone can deal with so much idleness. It might even be harmful for some."

The Colonel looked at him warily. "My soldiers stand ready for any emergency at all times."

"That is commendable," de Groot replied affably. "I'm merely wondering if you might be able to spare one of your capable men for a specific mission."

Von Hügel put his hands on his hips. "What are you up to, *mijnheer*?"

De Groot took him by the arm and led him behind the thick trunk of an old oak tree. "It's nothing of great consequence. I simply need someone to lend me a hand."

Von Hügel wrinkled his brow. "What is hidden behind this specific mission?"

De Groot raised his shoulders. "Not unlike a military mission, my assignment must be kept in strict confidence. I can disclose only this much: it concerns our colony in Ceylon. I am expecting a shipment from Amsterdam and then I will continue my journey. And by the way, I was thinking of a young lieutenant. He should be intelligent, valiant and not without ambition."

"You can forget it! I cannot possibly spare any of my officers. Least of all, for a mission about which I know nothing."

Von Hügel was about to go but de Groot held him by the shoulder. "I fear, esteemed Colonel, you have no choice." He reached into the inside pocket of his jacket and took out a letter.

"The Lords of the honorable Company have authorized me to take any measures necessary to execute my assignment."

He unfolded the letter and held it under von Hügel's nose. The Colonel's gray eyes scanned the writing and stopped at the blood red seal at the bottom.

"You are a cunning—" He swallowed the rest. "I shall appeal to the Lords."

"You can certainly do that but you will not be heard." De Groot slowly took a deep breath. "I will simplify your decision, esteemed Colonel. You have had new uniforms tailored for the soldiers of the *Drie Gebroeders* and the payment from the Company is still outstanding, is that right?"

Von Hügel nodded reluctantly.

"What if I were to take care of the matter? I guarantee you that I will accept your price."

"Certainly, something I would take under advisement." Von Hügel's face lit up.

"As you know, I have lost most of the money I had brought with me," said de Groot.

"But the replacement has been ordered. As soon as it arrives, you will get paid. In return, starting tomorrow, one of your lieutenants will be at my disposal." He extended his right hand but von Hügel did not accept it.

"For how long will you need this assistance?"

"Until the end of my mission."

"Will you take the man to Ceylon with you?"

De Groot nodded. "I depart as soon as my money is delivered from Amsterdam."

Von Hügel stroked his chin with his thumb and forefinger. "I believe I may have just the appropriate candidate for you: Private Hiller. You will get information in the Kasteel on how to find him. As far as I know, he's currently working as a *pasganger* at the docks."

For a few seconds, de Groot stared at the Colonel, then he bellowed, "I have demanded an officer. And you have the nerve to palm off an ordinary soldier on me? And one who is a convicted mutineer to boot? After my generous concessions?"

Von Hügel smiled. "I knocked those mutinous ideas out of Hiller in Vlissingen. And you know that after the sinking of the *Drie Gebroeders* he proved himself to be a true soldier. He saved you from the sharks when you risked your life because of your rapacity."

"I won't stand for—" de Grout harrumphed. He shook his head and took a deep breath. "I have no use for a private who can barely read and write his name."

Von Hügel's face betrayed no reaction. He seemed determined not to miss the opportunity to rid himself of Hiller.

"He possesses far more than the skills you require. Did he not prove himself obliging when it came to transporting your injured daughter? It's up to you, *mijnheer*. Either you take Hiller or you'll have to do without an assistant from among my ranks. And now, if you'll excuse me."

He turned and left.

It was late in the evening when the colonel stood in front of his house and observed the façade, whose white color was faintly illuminated by the starlight. His gaze wandered up to a bay window in the middle, immediately under the steep roof. Yellow light escaped through the narrow gaps in the closed shutters. He chewed pensively on his lower lip. Then he opened the heavy front door.

The slaves had left a burning lantern on an iron hook in the hallway. He took it and climbed the stairs. The yellowwood floor boards creaked under his feet. When he reached the first floor landing, he saw his valet, who squatted by the door to his master's bedroom, head on his knees and arms wrapped around his legs. Soft snoring sounds revealed that he was sleeping. But when the heels of von Hügel's boots clacked on the floor, he woke up with a start.

"Colonel! I beg your pardon!" The man shot up and tore open the door to the bedroom. He followed his master into the room.

Von Hügel placed the lantern on the nightstand and waited for the man to slip the jacket off his shoulders before he sank on the edge of the bed heaving a deep sigh.

"I trust you had a pleasant evening, sir?" The valet hung the jacket on a hook and picked up the slippers from the floor beneath.

"I've had better." Von Hügel took off his hat and the powdered wig *en queue* and placed them next to himself. Then he extended one leg toward the valet. The man knelt down.

"Do you have any other wishes, sir?" he asked as he yanked the tight boot off the calf.

Von Hügel shook his head. "When you're ready, you may retire. Wake me early tomorrow at sunrise."

"Very well, sir." The valet took off the other boot and helped the colonel into his slippers. Then placed the hat and the wig on two stands.

"I wish you a good night." He bowed and disappeared.

For a few minutes von Hügel sat motionless on the edge of the bed. Then he rose, took the lantern, went to the door, and listened. The house was silent. Only the roof beams creaked. He opened the door and peered outside. A narrow strip of light shone under the entrance to his wife's bedroom. He quietly tiptoed across the landing and knocked on the door.

"Yea?" he heard Anna Maria's voice.

He entered and saw her sitting at her dressing table. She had pushed all her jars of cream, small bottles, and brushes to one corner. Before her she had a sheet of paper, an inkpot, a shallow bowl and sealing wax. Two envelopes were propped up against the frame of the oval mirror. A multi-branch candelabra stood in the middle.

"You're home late." She looked at him over her shoulder.

"The brotherhood had their dinner this evening and it dragged on."

The soft golden light refracted her wavy, loosely-bound hair. She wore a light nightgown of white muslin, the collar of which had slipped and revealed her well-formed right shoulder. Even after fifteen years of marriage, he still desired her.

"I had hoped to find you still up."

She rested her hand on a sheet of paper. "I'm writing to our children. I want to give the letters to Captain van der Holst tomorrow."

"You miss our boys."

Her face grew sad. "What mother would not?"

"I miss them too." He stepped closer. "May I stay a while?"

"Please." She pointed to a chair against the wall next to the dressing table.

"*Mijnheer* de Groot was there as well this evening. You know, the Netherlander working for the VOC." He placed his lantern on the floor.

"Yes." She turned her attention back to her letters.

"I've been asking myself why he is undertaking this long journey. Today he disclosed to me that the Company has sent him on a special mission to Ceylon."

Anna Maria dipped the quill into the inkpot. "What kind of mission?"

"He didn't want to say. But he demanded to have one of my officers as an assistant."

She paused. "Can he make a demand, just like that?"

"I'm not pleased about it but he has the full authorization of the Company. Still, I was able to lessen the impact of his request somewhat by agreeing to give him one of my common soldiers. Private Hiller." He studied her face intently.

She placed her quill in the bowl and turned halfway toward him. "Hiller has been a thorn in your side, hasn't he? That's why you're getting rid of him." After a short pause, she added, "But at least in Ceylon, he'll be safe from you."

The impact of her words on him was twofold. They diminished his authority as commanding officer and they proved that Hiller was important to her still.

"Every soldier needs a firm hand so that he follows orders at all times," he argued. "Especially Hiller. He's a mutineer at heart."

"What you did to him in Vlissingen was vicious. He was justified in demanding his pay."

"He made me look like a fool in front of the entire battalion and undermined my authority in front of the of men. After he had already cuckolded me in Ludwigsburg for all the world to see!" He slammed the palm of his hand on the table and made the flames flicker.

She cringed. "How could you ...?"

"Don't you dare lie about it," he interrupted her testily. "I remember the day of the consecration of the flag as though it were yesterday. This Hiller stepped forward in front of the duke and all of my officers, and you encouraged his impudence! That was an affront not only to you, a gentlewoman, but most of all, to me."

By now Anna Maria had turned to face him. "That was uncalled for."

Von Hügel waved off her objection. "And as if that had not been enough of a humiliation, you invited him to your bed chamber as well. Don't look at me like that. I've long known about it. Your maid and my valet share their gossip."

She lowered her gaze. "I've always feared that the reason you made him suffer in Vlissingen was jealousy."

He ran his fingers through his thinning hair. "My motives were base. That should not have happened. And yet Hiller needed to be punished."

Anna Maria leaned forward and looked directly into his eyes. "I have never known you to bear such grudges, my husband. You are an honorable man. Why are you still so cruel to Hiller?"

He swallowed. "You two have inflicted an irreparable insult on me. I will not tolerate him either in your presence or mine. This fellow acted as though he were the equal of princes. He is indifferent to family, rank, or ancestry. He knows no respect."

Mockingly, she pursed her lips. "Are not freedom, equality and fraternity among the precepts of the Freemason community to which you belong?"

"This Hiller is not to lay a hand on my wife! And my wife is not to encourage him!" He pushed the chair back, stormed through the room and slammed the door behind him.

CHAPTER TWELVE

CAPE TOWN, SOUTH AFRICA, 1788

Jan Pieter de Groot dodged an ox cart loaded with wood and nodded to the customs inspectors in front of the guard house which separated the town from the harbor.

Once again today, the traffic was backed up on the street, which was blocked by sailors and soldiers, captains, and officers, merchants, and pedestrians, horses, and carts. The two officers carefully inspected, counted, assessed the taxes and duties of everything the work slaves hauled off the big sailers and took into town. The hubbub would not let up until the fall, when the ships would move for the winter to the more protected port in Vaals Bay.

Today the entry was blocked additionally by a capsized cart. It had been loaded with wine barrels that now rolled across the street. Some had burst and the smell of alcohol filled the air. Slaves cleared the pieces out of the way and tried to move the damaged vehicle to the side while the driver pulled the reins of the oxen.

De Groot was relieved when he finally reached the harbor. He paused at a sailmaker's shop and stopped a slave who labored to push a cart of melons and lemons.

"Where can I find Master Willemsen's carpenter's shop?"

"Right over there, sir." The man pointed with his chin to a row of sheds. De Groot nodded and went on.

Along the wooden docks, the shops of carpenters and linen weavers, tinkers, and smiths alternated with long warehouses. At the very end, just before a small, rocky island where the prison was located, lay the slaughterhouse. The bellowing of the cattle that were driven here every day from the interior of the country mingled with the noise of the workshops. The wind carried the stench of excrement and blood. De Groot pressed his sleeve to his mouth and nose and hurried on with his head lowered.

Great East Indiamen were docked at the pier and anchored in the bay. In between, fishing boats floated on the waves and Chinese and Malay merchants rowed their boats, filled to capacity with fruit, vegetables, tobacco, and water barrels from one vessel to another.

A ship could lie in port for two to four weeks, longer for repairs, and the place teemed with sailors. They slept in tents near the pier. They were not permitted to set foot in the town but they preferred the taverns and bordellos in the harbor anyhow.

De Groot looked disapprovingly at a sailer belonging to the British East India Company which lay across from Master Willemsen's workshop. The superstructures were extravagantly carved, the tall, slender masts bobbed up and down in the breeze and massive cannons projected from the portholes. In the last few years, the English merchants had turned into the Dutch Company's most aggressive competitors. Their ships were fast, their captains daring and their soldiers had snatched the most significant trading posts along the coast of India and China away from the VOC. And now the cinnamon trade, firmly in Dutch hands for almost two hundred years, was at risk.

Slaves lugged one crate after another of Chinese tea and porcelain and bales of Indian silk from the ships. They stacked them on the pier while several sailors shielded the goods from passersby.

Well, that's strange, de Groot mused. Normally the English sailers were not unloaded in Cape Town; they stayed just long enough to take on provisions and fresh water. He also noticed that there was an unusual number of sailors on the pier in front of the ship. They did not talk and joke the way sailors usually did on the gangplanks, rather they watched their surroundings.

If these were soldiers, I might think they were guarding the ship, de Groot thought and peered suspiciously at the upper deck. Half a dozen officers stood there and observed the unloading. Other sailors ran with buckets of water around the deck and emptied them over the railing.

De Groot felt an itch under his scalp. Either the English were extraordinarily cautious, regarding Table Bay as hostile territory despite the Paris Peace Treaty of four years ago, or something was fishy.

On the spur of the moment, he walked directly toward the chief mate, who stood near the stern, stuffing his pipe, but he had second thoughts. De Groot did not want to draw attention to himself, and this would be a good opportunity to find out if Hiller had what it took to be his assistant.

The door to Master Willemsen's workshop was wide open. One could hear the sounds of sawing and the rhythm of hammers coming from inside. De Groot entered. When his eyes grew accustomed to the relative darkness, he saw several journeymen working on tables and workbenches. Hannes Hiller stood next to a hearth. He wore a leather apron over his shirt and breeches. A tool bag hung from his belt. He took a torch from the fire and walked over to a plank lying on two stands. The piece of wood was shiny with moisture, and clamped on one end. Hannes held the flame underneath the wood, used his free hand to crank the vise and slowly bent the plank downwards.

"August! Where are you?" He lowered the torch into a basin filled with water, where it went out with a sizzle.

His helpmate hurried over to him. In his right hand he held a brush, in his left a bucket. He dipped the brush into the bucket and sprinkled water on the hot wood. "You and I, Hannes, we're strong as oxen! We can even bend tree trunks!"

The Netherlander crossed the workshop without paying attention to the curious glances of the journeymen and stopped behind Hannes.

"Private Hiller," he said in flawless German. "I need a moment of your time."

"You!" Hannes raised his eyebrows. "What is it?"

De Groot rocked back and forth on his feet and decided to overlook Hiller's impolite address. "I wish to discuss a proposal with you. If you will be good enough to listen to me!"

"I don't have time. I have to repair the English ship on the pier."

"What's wrong with it?" De Groot could hardly contain his joy at hearing this information.

"It grazed a reef and is leaking. It's being unloaded so that it rises and reveals the hole above the water line. Then we'll fix it." He pointed to August, who stared unabashedly at the Netherlander.

"Get to work, Hannes. I'm not paying you to talk!" The voice of the master sounded through the shed.

De Groot expanded his chest and pulled his authorization from his jacket.

"My good sir, you are obviously unaware that you have before you a finance inspector of the honorable Company. I advise you not to interfere with my work; otherwise…" his eyes slowly scanned the shed, "I will have no choice but to verify whether you have been properly fulfilling your tax obligations."

Willemsen's plump cheeks shook. He grunted something unintelligible and disappeared into the back corner of the workshop.

Hannes raised one eyebrow. "Out with it, de Groot, what do you want?"

"I want you to have a look around the English ship. Specifically, below deck. I would do it myself but I fear the British would hardly allow a Netherlander on their ship."

"There is nothing to see down there. All the cargo holds have been emptied."

"Perhaps there is something to see after all." De Groot casually pushed back the flap of his jacket and revealed a plump little coin bag. "I am merely interested in anything unusual you might notice."

Hannes stared at the bulging sack and thought feverishly. His work as a *pasganger* was hard and strenuous, but he was so exhausted in the evenings when he sank into his straw sack that he slept until the morning without any nightmares. The master paid him in Dutch silver gulden instead of paper money. He had saved thirty gulden so far and the Netherlander's bag also contained a nice little sum. He had no idea what the man was up to but the mission sounded easy and harmless.

Too easy for so much money, warned a voice inside. Indeed, this conversation was eerily similar to the one he had had with the recruiter. Von Langsdorff, too, had enticed him with generous pay. But all he had earned for his credulity was misfortune and vexation. He took a breath and was about to decline, when he thought of his mother. The thirty gulden pay for his work as a *pasganger* and the content of de Groot's bag could free her from worries for a long time. Admittedly, he had no idea how he would get the money to faraway Swabia. It was too likely to be stolen on the mail route.

"I'm offering twenty Dutch silver gulden," the Netherlander said. "That's my best offer."

Hannes grasped the silver cross on his neck.

"The money must go to my mother. She lives in a village near Stuttgart. I will accept your offer if you guarantee that every single coin will safely reach her."

De Groot frowned. "You don't trust me! Well, but here is how I will show my good will. The *Batavia* sails in two days. It is a Dutch ship owned by the Company. I will make out a bill of exchange and give it to the captain. Upon his arrival in Amsterdam, he will pay it to the Wisselbank."

Hannes looked at him warily. "What is a bill of exchange?"

"A paper which authorizes the bank to pay out money or credit an account."

Hannes had no idea what it meant "to credit an account". He did understand, however, that in this transaction no coins would be delivered.

"No!" He shook his head emphatically. "Paper money is worthless. That is something the Company has taught me. And anyway, it's meaningless to my mother if her money lies in Amsterdam."

De Groot rolled his eyes. "Of course, I shall write a promissory note for a cash payment to your mother. The money will be delivered by courier. Are you willing now to grant my little request?"

Hannes nodded haltingly. "But if you're trying to cheat me, you'll be sorry."

One hour later he and August stepped on the English sailing ship, carrying the plank. The ship was, indeed, lying higher in the water now, as evidenced by the wet line around the wooden hull. De Groot was not able to see the hole. He supposed it was on the side facing away from the pier.

He had Master Willemsen bring him a three-legged stool from the workshop, watched the goings-on and took out a pinch of snuff every now and again. The sun was high and hot on his black bicorne even though the master had placed the stool directly against the wall of the shed. His swollen feet were painful in his tight shoes.

He almost yearned for the brisk spring winds which had blown when he arrived but at the same time, he knew that the summer temperatures at the Cape were nothing compared to the tropical heat of Ceylon.

A shadow appeared over his legs. "There's not much to see below deck. Just a bit of clutter."

De Groot looked past Hannes. "Where is your helpmate?"

"I sent him into the workshop. You wanted to speak to me alone?"

"Yes, but not here." De Groot stood up and walked along the pier a few steps until he found a space between two storage sheds. Hannes followed him.

"Did you really not see anything? Did you look on all the decks?" asked de Groot.

"You must think I'm a real dunce! Of course, I did!" Hannes folded his arms across his chest.

De Groot furrowed his brow. Could he trust the statements of an uneducated tradesman and soldier? He really wanted to go on board the ship himself but, unfortunately, that was not possible.

"Don't you want to know what kind of clutter I discovered?"

De Groot's eyes grew wide. "Out with it!"

"A few hammocks," Hannes began, "a few pairs of breeches, a woolen blanket..."

"Are you trying to play me for a fool?"

Hannes grinned. "The blanket was stretched out in a corner of the steerage. Two sailors stood in front of it. They did not take their eyes off August and me, so I could not see what was behind it. But I could smell it. It was a flavor I have smelled only once in my life and have never forgotten. It was Christmas when I first came back to visit my mother after my journeyman years. She had baked gingerbread especially for me. It smelled spicy and warm like the stuff on the ship. My mother called the spice 'cinnamon' and said it was the bark of a tree on the other side of the world. She had bought it from a traveling salesman. It was such a small amount but it cost more than a whole side of beef."

"Hm." De Groot chewed on his lower lip. "Pity you didn't bring me a sample."

"You're underestimating me again." Hannes reached into his pocket and extracted a piece of a brownish bark. De Groot took it. The bark was damp but when he put it up to his nose, he could smell the typical cinnamon aroma. "How did you get hold of it?"

"Little pieces of it were lying all over the place. The whole deck must have been full of it. When the ship's hull was punctured, the cinnamon got wet and was of no use anymore. I suppose the English threw it overboard while they were at sea and stored what they were able to salvage behind that blanket."

"Of course! That's what must have happened. I can see you're nobody's fool."

Hannes studied him. "It was always about the cinnamon, wasn't it? The English are hiding it. This stuff is valuable."

De Groot took a deep breath. "I'm paying you well so that you keep this little meeting to yourself and don't give it any unnecessary thought. You have carried out your assignment to my satisfaction. Tomorrow, before you come to the harbor, stop by my house. I will make out the bill of exchange for your mother and we will discuss whether you want to earn more money."

Immediately after the morning muster, Hannes headed over to the Heerengracht. Rufus met him at the door.

"Good morning, sir. *Mijnheer* de Groot is expecting you."

"Good morning, Rufus. I've told you before not to address me as 'sir'. It confuses me because I don't know who you mean."

The slave smiled politely and, with a deep bow, bade him enter. Hannes looked at the crystal mirrors on the walls, the multi-branch candelabras on the ceiling and the opulent curved stairs. After turning his attention to the slave himself, he stopped short.

"Where is your turban, Rufus, and why are you barefoot?"

"In the Cape Colony, slaves are not allowed head coverings or shoes," Rufus explained. "Now if you would please follow me."

"Do we have a visitor, Rufus?" a pleasant voice called. Bethari stood on the landing. She froze when she recognized Hannes. He, too, felt uncomfortable. He had acted like an absolute fool during their last encounter and had been very unfair to her. He bowed to her hesitantly.

"Greetings, *Demoiselle* de Groot." Since he had arrived at the Cape, where people from the most diverse backgrounds came together, he had picked up fragments of many languages.

She raised her chin. "Private Hiller. What are you doing here?" Her condescending tone irritated him and before he could help himself, he retorted, "I'm not here because of you, if that's what you mean, miss."

She flinched and he immediately regretted his words. What had gotten into him to make him act like a puddinghead again!

"I, uh, I..." he started out awkwardly but she cut him off with her hand.

"How could I ever have believed that there is a gracious person somewhere inside you when, time and again, you have shown me what an utter brute you are."

He watched her leave with sadness and as he did, he noticed the difficulty with which she still moved, favoring her right leg. He turned to Rufus.

"Is her knee still not healed?"

The servant had a deep furrow between his eyebrows. "I do not appreciate it when the mistress is not treated with respect."

Hannes lowered his head. "I deserve to be admonished. But I would like to apologize to the *demoiselle* and I must know how she is doing. Please. Do you think you might arrange for me to meet her after I'm finished with her father?"

The servant hesitated. "You must promise not to insult the mistress again."

Hannes placed his hand on his chest. "May lightning strike me if I lose my temper again."

Rufus gave him a penetrating look. "I sense your earnestness. But it will be up to the mistress."

The head of the household stood, slightly bent, over a wooden orb covered with different-colored patterns. It was mounted in a ring on a movable stand.

De Groot's fingers slowly rotated the orb. Without turning, he called, "Please bring us two cups of coffee, Rufus."

When the servant disappeared, he beckoned. "Come closer, Hiller."

Hannes gazed inquisitively at the orb. He saw irregular patterns, and dotted lines going up and down and across on the surface as well as many words.

Atlantic, Africa, Indian Ocean. His lips moved slowly as he deciphered each word.

De Groot watched him. "Is reading difficult for you?"

"Not at all," Hannes assured him and repeated loudly, "Atlantic, Africa, Indian Ocean." He pointed to the words as he read them. "I'm pretty good at writing too. But especially at arithmetic."

De Groot tapped lightly on the orb with one hand. "Do you know what this is?"

"I've never seen such a thing before but I think it must be some kind of likeness of the earth. Africa is between the two oceans, the Atlantic and the Indian Ocean. And so, the lines must represent the routes the ships take."

The Netherlander nodded approvingly. "This likeness of the earth is called a globe. Here," he tapped on the upper half of the orb with his forefinger, "is Vlissingen. This is where we started out." He traced one of the dotted lines sideways to Brazil and then all the way down to the lower half. "And now, we are at the Cape."

"This is amazing," Hannes said, full of wonder. "I'm looking at the world like a bird although I cannot fly. No human can fly and yet there are some who are able to take the place of the bird. How do they do it?"

De Groot smiled. "Actually, I'm not sure myself. That's for scientists called cartographers to know. They survey the land and calculate the distances." De Groot turned the globe; the vast Indian Ocean was now exposed. Asia appeared, as well as a much smaller land mass.

"That's Australia," de Groot explained. "The civilized world knows almost nothing about that continent but we Dutch explored its coasts about two hundred years ago. We have traveled to the countries on the other side of the Indian Ocean for some time and trade with many of them. Nutmeg, cloves and pepper come from Indonesia and Malaysia."

His finger moved around several islands, some of them tiny, which extended almost all the way to the northern coast of

Australia. "We import porcelain from China, cotton from India. The cinnamon that the English had on board comes from Ceylon."

He pointed to an island the size of his thumbnail that seemed to hang onto the southern tip of India. "All of these commodities, especially the spices, are the source of my country's prosperity."

"And what about the English?" Hannes wanted to know. "Do they also have trading rights in these countries?"

"Let's just say, they're trying to—they use methods that the Dutch East Company does not approve of."

"Now I understand why you were so obsessed with the British sailor," Hannes noted. "It had been loaded with cinnamon that the VOC wanted."

"The trade in this spice is our traditional right. We have concluded contracts with the king of the island of Ceylon."

"When you say 'we', do you mean the Dutch or the trading Company?"

De Groot laughed and pulled out his snuff box. "Those are one and the same."

He opened the box and held it out to Hannes, who was so bewildered by the offer that he shook his head.

De Groot took a pinch and continued, "Without the honorable Company, the Netherlands would not have access to remote markets and their goods. And without these goods, my people would not have been living in prosperity for almost two hundred years. We are a small country but our reach extends to the remotest corners of the world."

"Shall I hazard a guess, good sir, that your task is to extend and deepen that reach, particularly in Ceylon?" Hannes studied de Groot's face. "What concerns you, in particular?"

De Groot purposely fumbled in putting away his snuff box. "You have convinced me that you are a capable man and that your support would be very helpful to me."

Hannes observed the expression of respect and squared his shoulders.

"Before we continue our conversation, I should like to see the letter of exchange you promised me."

"Of course. If you will follow me." De Groot went to his desk and opened a leather portfolio lying on it. "The promissory note, made out to your mother."

Hannes leaned forward. The letters were hazy because of his excitement but he was able to make out his mother's name and the sum: fifty Dutch silver gulden. His earnings as *pasganger* and the wages from de Groot.

"Is everything in order?" the Netherlander asked.

"Almost." Hannes reached into his jacket and pulled out a folded piece of paper. "I have written a letter to my mother. Can you send it with the promissory note?"

The previous evening, he had sat in the courtyard of the Kasteel until darkness fell, trying to commit to paper all of the events of the past year. Reading was difficult for his mother too, but the village priest would surely help her.

"Of course." De Groot took a round seal, a stick of wax and some tinder. Hannes watched as de Groot closed both letters and pressed the seal with the three entwined letters "VOC" on the wax. Hannes still mistrusted the paper but he knew that he had no other way of sending the money he had promised to his mother in faraway Swabia.

Rufus knocked and entered with a tray of two steaming blue and white porcelain cups.

"Over there."

De Groot pointed to a round table in front of the window with two comfortable armchairs. "It's best to discuss business in peace and quiet with some refreshment."

"Please. Help yourself." De Groot pushed one of the cups over to Hannes. A rich aroma wafted to his nose and made his mouth water. He had never tried coffee before because it was much too costly for a simple carpenter.

Curious, he took a first sip and made a face. "This stuff really turns your insides out!"

De Groot smiled. "If you consume it more often, you will begin to appreciate the bitter taste. To say nothing of the stimulating effect. Unlike beer or wine, coffee lends clarity and focus to your thoughts—an indispensable advantage in business."

Hannes bravely took another sip.

"Do you want me to find more cinnamon for you? That should not pose a problem. Most of the ships that dock here need repairs."

De Groot nodded pensively. "I need a capable man to keep his eyes and ears open in the harbor and report to me anything that seems of importance. And I believe that I have found him."

"What are you offering me if I accept?" Hannes asked, trying to keep his voice steady.

De Groot got up and went to his desk. He opened one of the drawers, removed a plump linen sack and set it on the table.

"Every Monday evening after dark, come here and report to me. Not more often, as that would attract attention. Every Monday you will receive ten Dutch silver gulden. But you've got to keep silent, do you understand? Under no circumstances are you to speak to anyone about our arrangement."

As if in a trance, Hannes reached for the sack and stowed it in his jacket. The Netherlander offered him many times over what he earned in the regiment, just for a few, easily-gained pieces of information. He suspected there was more behind the matter than de Groot was divulging, yet what did he care? What mattered to him was being able to provide his mother with a comfortable life. He himself would have his pockets full of money when he returned home.

I shall be rich, he thought and felt his skin tingle.

He suggested eagerly, "I could go out drinking with the sailors at night. I'm sure to find the odd bit of information when their tongues are loosened. You'll have to see to it that I get a pass and don't have to be at the Kasteel for taps. And, of course, you'll have to cover all of my expenses."

"An excellent idea. Henceforth, you will no longer be a soldier of the regiment but will follow my directions. You can continue your work as *pasganger*. But find yourself other accommodations and exchange your uniform for civilian clothing."

"You mean you've arranged all that already?" Hannes stammered in disbelief.

"Certainly." De Groot leaned back comfortably in his armchair. "The regiment exists solely at the behest of the VOC. It is part of your mission to accompany me to Ceylon. I am expecting one more important shipment from Amsterdam. As soon as it arrives, we shall leave."

A feeling of relief washed over Hannes. He would leave the regiment and the painful memories behind him. He had nothing against traveling to Ceylon. Strange lands about which he knew nothing aroused his sense of adventure.

Suddenly he thought of August. Without Hannes, he would be mercilessly tormented by the soldiers and officers.

"I have a friend, you met him in Master Willemsen's workshop," he started out. "Might you have some use for him too?"

"Oh, you mean the simpleton?"

"Well, he might not be the sharpest tool in the shed but he's been quite useful to Master Willemsen," Hannes rejoined.

De Groot shook his head. "I'm sorry. I have no use for an oaf like that."

Hannes chewed his lower lip pensively. He had expected that answer.

"Well, what about it? Do we have a deal?" De Groot extended his right hand.

Hannes shook his hand. He would find a different solution for August.

Rufus waited in the hallway, though Bethari was not with him. After de Groot had bade Hannes goodbye, the servant escorted him to the front door.

"Go to the back of the property, where the stable and the carriage house are," he said quietly. "I'll meet you there."

Hannes ran up the Heerengracht, turned left onto a cross street, then another, and came back to the stable. Rufus stood by the gate. "The mistress is waiting inside."

"Thank you." Hannes took Rufus' right hand and shook it vigorously. The servant withdrew his hand and looked around, but the two men were the only ones on the street.

"I'm helping you because the mistress has agreed to the meeting. And anyway, I like you," he said. "Still, if anyone were to see us being familiar with one another, we would both get in trouble."

"I hope you won't refuse a little sign of appreciation all the same." Hannes reached for the money bag de Groot had given him and took out one gulden.

The servant shook his head. "Only free people may possess money."

"This might be your first step toward freedom." Again, Rufus shook his head. "I was the de Groots' servant when I was not yet a man and the mistress was still an infant. I have never possessed so much as a copper coin. If a silver gulden were to be found on me, I would be taken for a thief and punished severely."

"I cannot imagine that your mistress would do something like to you," Hannes countered.

"Oh no, she would not," Rufus agreed. "But the master does not appreciate people who go against the established order."

Hannes sheepishly put the gulden back in his money bag. "You will not have trouble on my account."

The servant smiled. "I will consider myself paid if you and the mistress put aside your differences."

"You are a pippin, Rufus."

The servant bowed his head slightly. "I'll whistle if someone approaches. You'll have to hide immediately."

Bethari took a carrot from her pocket and held it to the horse. Slowly, the large dark brown head descended, the long whiskers tickling her skin before the soft lips gently took the treat from her flat palm. While the animal chewed languidly, she stroked its warm, smooth neck.

"Soon my knee will be healed and I'll ride you on Table Mountain," she said softly.

As soon as she heard the gate creak, she turned around. A wide stream of light fell on the barn aisle. One of the horses snorted and she heard the sound of boots, which stopped after every few steps as though someone were pausing to look into each of the six stalls. The closer the steps approached, the faster her heart beat.

When Rufus had first told her that Hannes wished to have another word with her, she had said no. His renewed display of impertinence had hurt her, and she had no desire to be hurt again. Then she remembered two of Hannes' traits that she had also come to know: the courageous and resourceful Hannes, to whom many owed their lives after the shipwreck, and the unhappy, distraught Hannes, whose soul bore such a heavy burden. When Rufus added that Hannes wanted to apologize, she agreed to the meeting.

The bootsteps stopped and she saw him in the aisle. His hat brim hid his face but when he removed his hat, she saw that his expression was serious.

"*Demoiselle* de Groot—I wholeheartedly regret my idiotic talk." He placed his right hand on his chest.

She suppressed a smile. "Which idiotic talk would that be? The one in Vlissingen, in Vaals Bay, or the one this morning?"

"All of it, miss," he replied hoarsely. "I cannot undo it but I honestly beg for your forgiveness."

She pushed the horse aside and stepped into the aisle. "I can sense that you mean it." She wanted to shake his hand but that would not have been proper so she confined her response to a smile. "Are we not old friends who have been through much?

Old friends forgive each other when one of them makes a mistake."

"That is exactly how I see it, miss!" He seemed relieved. "And how is your knee? I can see that walking still gives you trouble."

"The doctors are puzzled. They recommend that I continue to favor it."

Hannes nodded. They stood silently facing each other. He rocked back and forth on his heels. Bethari wrapped a strand of hair around her right index finger and examined it as though there were nothing more interesting in the world. Hannes was equally at a loss for words. One of them had to restart the conversation.

"I…" she began.

"Yes, miss?" He looked at her eagerly.

She shook her head. "It's nothing."

"Yes, it's something."

"I should like to know, why were you so unpleasant when we first met? What was the reason?"

"Miss, you secretly watched me and drew a picture of me!"

"Did you not like my drawing?"

"I did, miss. But you should have asked me first."

She frowned. "I understand, and I am sorry. But why were you so rude to me in Vaals Bay? All I wanted to do was thank you."

"I thought you were a married lady, miss."

"Yet even a married lady would have thanked you," she riposted. "Did you think that I wanted more from you than was proper?"

He was silent, suddenly feeling very foolish. She persisted. "Do you seriously think that after we had just come within an inch of losing our lives in a shipwreck, the first thing on my mind was to flirt with you? Is that how childish you think I am?"

"No, miss," he conceded.

She thought of the night when she had observed him on the *Drie Gebroeders*. "Were you so gruff because you had been hurt by a married woman?"

"Miss, of course not!" he countered angrily. "I beg your pardon, please, I did not mean it like that. What I wanted to say is that I have made mistakes for which I had to pay dearly."

"All will be well. I promise." Boldly, she laid her hand on his arm, yet quickly withdrew it when he furrowed his brow.

"Please forgive me if I offended you."

He cleared his throat. "I must be on my way to the harbor then, *demoiselle* de Groot. Master Willemsen doesn't like me to be late." He put on his hat.

"But you cannot take your leave so soon!" She did not want him to go. Perhaps it was because he awakened thrilling and confounding feelings in her. Perhaps it was because she had no friends in the Cape Colony and often felt lonely, or perhaps simply because it was fun to tease him and sometimes even quarrel a little with him.

"You still owe me the answer to another important question."

"Do I, miss?" His eyes were obscured by the hat brim; his voice sounded restrained.

She thought feverishly, then it came to her.

"Why did you come to see my father?"

"It concerns a confidential matter, miss" Hannes explained. "What I can tell you is that your father has asked me to enter into his service and that I have agreed."

"Why does my father require the services of a carpenter? Or of a soldier?"

"I cannot speak to you about that, *demoiselle*. But I can reveal to you that I will accompany you and your father to Ceylon."

She looked at him in astonishment. At that moment, a short, shrill whistle could be heard.

"Someone's coming," Hannes whispered.

De Groot's voice could be heard bellowing in front of the stable. "Rufus, have you seen my daughter?"

Hannes placed a finger to his lips and as he slipped past her, his body lightly grazed her arm. His skin smelled of leather, soap, and wood glue. She briefly closed her eyes and breathed deeply. Then she called loudly, "I'm coming, Father!"

Before disappearing, Bethari turned back to Hannes and whispered, "I hope we shall have another opportunity to chat again soon."

CHAPTER THIRTEEN

CAPE TOWN, SOUTH AFRICA, 1788

The Schotsche Tempel was located in the Cape Colony's entertainment district, at the foot of a long hill in front of Table Mountain.

Sunday was the soldiers' day off, though they did not necessarily observe it as a day of rest. Beginning on Saturday night, the men of the regiment typically spent their time, as well as their gulden on watered-down beer and the services of seductive mulatto women. Many of them even skipped Master Spönlin's Sunday morning sermon in order to continue the fun. Yet this Saturday evening, as he hastened through the dark alleys, Hannes encountered only sailors and a few "respectable" Cape Colony burghers.

Schotsche Kloof was the name of the area at the southeastern end of the colony. Squeezed in among the bars, bordellos and small stores were countless squalid wooden huts where the Cape Malays dwelt. They were former slaves from China, Malaysia, Madagascar, or Mozambique and made their living from trade with the sailors anchored in Table Bay. Widows rented rooms to sailors whose ships lay anchored in Cape Town for longer periods.

Hannes clasped the handle of his knife with his right hand while with his left, he clutched the bulge in his jacket where he had sown a little sack of coins into the lining. After nightfall, the chances of being robbed in the Schotsche Kloof increased. This was not Hannes' first time in the Malay district. He knew the narrow passages well and reached the Schotsche Tempel unimpeded. The tavern was regarded as the best bordello in the colony and was situated between the Blaauwe Anker and Laatste Stuivertje, two notorious drinking and gambling dens.

The broad-shouldered young Black man in front of the entrance greeted him with a handshake.

"Well, Hannes, feel like some fun?" He swung his hips back and forth.

"Every man needs it now and then," Hannes answered in a jovial tone. He had frequented the establishment a number of times recently, not for a drink or a tup, but in an effort to find sailors from ships that transported cinnamon.

As Hannes stepped into the bar, the smell of sweat, cheap perfume and tobacco swirled around him in the crowded tavern. The undefinable din was a mixture of the shouting of drunken men, the screeching laughter of women, and the playing of bizarre music. Near the door, sitting on a stool, a Chinese man played a Chinese wind instrument called a sheng, accompanied by a chorus of drunken sailors. Two of them snatched up one of the young barmaids, lifted her on to a table and caterwauled enthusiastically as she gathered up her skirts and swayed her hips suggestively.

Hannes avoided a puddle of beer and pushed his way to the long bar along the side wall. A couple of barmaids in low-cut dresses tirelessly poured beer and spirits.

Clara Tant, the proprietress, sat on a chair next to the shelf with the bottles and watched the activities with eagle eyes. A muscular character armed with a club stood next to her. Hannes knew the boss and her bodyguard and greeted them with a hand gesture. Clara Tant had once been the property of the VOC but had long been a freedwoman. Hannes had heard rumors that at one time she had sheltered fugitive slaves in this house. For this, the governor had tortured her and sentenced her to three additional years of slavery.

Hannes stepped up to the counter and beckoned a server. "I'm looking for one of the sailors from the *Northampton*, a Charlie Peck."

"Over there." The girl pointed with her chin to the back of the tavern. "He's already a bit top heavy, that one."

Hannes looked over to Charlie, who was stretched out on a mattress along the back wall. He had one arm wrapped around a young mulatto woman, whose ample bosom threatened to burst out of her tightly wound bodice. In the other hand he held a pewter cup which he used to toast a second woman.

Hannes thanked the barmaid for the information and placed a few coins on the counter. "Brandy for Charlie and the two girls, generously poured, and a beer for me."

Holding the drinks, he made his way to the back, past the tables where sailors played dice and cards.

"Evening, Charlie." Hannes placed the drinks on a small table and pushed it over to the other man.

"Hello, mate. Here's to you. Go on, sweetie, say thanks to my chum here." Peck nudged one of the girls in Hannes' direction. She fell against him on the mattress with a giggle and felt his chest.

"Strong man. You have the power to sway me as you please."

He gently pushed her aside. He was here because of Charlie, not the for a chance at amorous congress.

"Did you get me what I asked for?"

"A sailor always keeps his word." Charlie fumbled in his jacket and retrieved a handful of pieces of brown bark. "I swear to you, this is the genuine stuff from Ceylon," he slurred and let the pieces trickle into Hannes's outstretched right palm.

"This here is so good, I put some aside for me. I'll flog it off when we're back in London. And when I'm finished with the seafaring, I'll buy myself a little house, yoke myself to a nice girl and open an inn. What about that, mate?"

Hannes nodded absentmindedly and looked at the pieces of bark in his hand. De Groot had shown him how to tell the valuable from the cheap Chinese cinnamon.

"Chinese cassia has a dark, reddish-brown rind which barely unfurls. When Ceylon cinnamon is harvested, it is exclusively the young shoots that are peeled. The bark is thin and coils tightly," the Netherlander had impressed on him.

The samples Charlie had brought were the color of wet sand and no thicker than paper. The Englishman was speaking the truth. Hannes leaned forward and sniffed.

"Ceylon cinnamon has a sweet and delicate aroma. Cassia cinnamon, on the other hand, smells pungent and a little earthy," de Groot had explained to him and provided him with samples of both varieties.

The cinnamon in his hand emitted the familiar warm fragrance that reminded him of his mother's gingerbread. He briefly closed his eyes and thought of the squalid little hut of his childhood. With the money he was earning thanks to de Groot, his mother would be able to build a new house with an impermeable roof and a large hearth to warm her in the winter.

"Hannes," the girl next to him whined and traced a finger along his thigh, bringing him back from his thoughts. "May I sit on your lap?"

"Not now, but if you keep quiet, I'll give you a stuiver." He held out a coin.

"Shall we go up to my chamber? A little two-handed put would do you good. And if it please you, we can take Charlie and my girlfriend up as well."

"Well, let's see."

He turned back to the sailor. By now Hannes had been in de Groot's employ for three weeks and had yet to deliver any information about the transport of cinnamon. Very few foreign-flagged ships had come to the Cape Colony. All of them had anchored far out in Table Bay and sailed on as soon as they received provisions and fresh water from the boats of Malay merchants. No crew members had come ashore.

Yesterday, however, had yielded possibilities. The English ship *Northampton* docked at the pier. Hannes had been brought aboard to assess damage to one of its two pumps and immediately noticed the delicate fragrance of cinnamon. He had wasted no time in approaching Charlie Peck, the sailor who guarded the hold on the steerage deck.

Hannes knew well what a man craved after months at sea and offered to trade information: he would tell Charlie where to find the most willing strumpets and the cheapest brandy in Cape Town, in return for particulars about the *Northampton*'s cargo. In short order, Hannes learned that the English sailor carried one hundred bales of the finest Ceylon cinnamon. And in exchange for a few more drinks at the Schotsche Tempel, Charlie had held out the prospect of a few more bits of information. Hannes thought now was the time.

"Think you, how cunning must one be to trick the Dutch into giving up their cinnamon?" Hannes asked casually as he wrapped up the pieces of bark into his handkerchief and tucked it into his jacket.

"Oh, we English are very clever. The Dutch haven't had their precious cinnamon all to themselves for an age." Charlie grinned broadly.

"But the Dutch don't even let you into their ports in Ceylon." Hannes folded his arms, leaned against the wall, and studied the Englishman.

"That is correct. But at the moment, docking there would be suicide."

"How so?" Hannes perked up his ears.

"They have an outbreak of smallpox there. All along the southern and western coast."

"How do you know this, if you have not docked there?"

"We have an agent. We get our cinnamon from him and he told us about the pox. Say, would you spot me another of these?" He pushed the cup across the table. Hannes leaned forward and grabbed Peck's wrist.

"What agent?"

The sailor looked at him bleary-eyed. "Not before you get me another one."

One of the girls joined in this demand for more tipple; the other snored on the mattress. Hannes was reluctant to interrupt the tale but calculated that he would more quickly get his information if Charlie had another brandy in hand.

Yet, by the time he returned with the liquor, Charlie was asleep with his head on the table. This would never do. He grabbed Charlie by the scruff of the neck.

"Arise, we've not finished here! The agent! Who is it?"

Very slowly, Charlie began to grin broadly.

"Well, he's not a Netherlander." He reached for his cup of brandy and emptied it. Then he flung his arm around the girl next to him and kissed her noisily.

"What was his name?"

"Mate, the name was so funny, it tied my tongue and my head in knots. If ever you're in London, come and see me. Ask for the inn with the best ale. I shall pour you one on the house." Charlie sank against one of the pillows and closed his eyes.

"Arise! Damnation!" Though Hannes shook him, he prompted only a mighty belch. He pounded the table in frustration. He was so close.

Bethari sat in an armchair in her room. She held a book but her gaze continually wandered to the bronze clock between the two windows. Ten minutes to nine. It would surely not be much longer before Hannes rang the doorbell.

For the last three weeks, he arrived every Monday evening, disappeared into her father's study and departed a little later.

"Why don't you invite him for dinner some time?" she asked her father.

De Groot had protested, "Bethari, please! Since when do we socialize with tradesmen or common soldiers?"

"Perhaps today would be a good time to start," she retorted, though her father did not agree.

She asked herself more than ever about the kind of personality that might be hidden inside Hannes Hiller. Was he the standoffish, unfriendly boor who made her see red? Or was he the sensitive, attentive man who touched her heart?

She closed her book and went to the window. She looked at her reflection from the bright light of her room and picked at the lace trim around her neck. Did Hannes appreciate that she expressed her opinions without reserve? Was he interested in her art? Did he find her attractive, or did he prefer sophisticated ladies like Anna Maria von Hügel? Once again, she thought of the interaction between Hannes and Baroness von Hügel on the *Drie Gebroeders*. She had sensed a powerful passion in their quarrel.

Whatever it is between them, I want it to stop, she caught herself thinking.

The small clock behind her rang nine. Where was Hannes? She opened the window, heard boot-clad feet approaching, and withdrew at once.

She heard Hannes softly call out, "*Demoiselle* de Groot?"

Embarrassed, she returned to the window. "Good evening."

He smiled up at her. "What are you doing? Were you waiting for me?"

She was not happy that he had guessed the truth and responded coolly, "I merely felt like looking at the stars."

His smile deepened.

"In that case, I do not wish to disturb your observations any longer." His hand grasped the bell rope.

"Wait!" She was not yet ready to see him go.

"How long is your meeting with my father?"

"About an hour, I reckon. Why do you ask?"

"Come to the stable afterwards. There is something important I wish to tell you."

"One hundred bales of cinnamon! That's seven hundred pounds! At five gulden a pound, that's a loss of thirty-five thousand gulden! What do you have to say, Hiller? Hiller! What's the matter with you?" He pounded his fist on his palm.

Hannes jumped. "Thirty-five thousand gulden? Sweet Mother of God, that's a lot of money. What do you plan to do with it?"

"Nothing!" de Groot snorted. "That's how much the cinnamon on the *Northampton* is worth. I expect you to pay attention to me! Come on, out with it! What's going through your head?"

Hannes cleared his throat. He could hardly reveal to de Groot that his thoughts were with the boss' daughter. Her invitation preyed on his mind though he had not yet decided whether to accept. Bethari had openly expressed her interest in him and awakened his desire. Still, past experience made him extremely cautious. He strained to listen to de Groot.

"Sir, what is your plan? Seize the *Northampton*?"

"And tip them off, those villains? Certainly not. I am going to put an end to this abomination once and for all. If only I knew where the English had loaded their cinnamon." De Groot massaged the bridge of his nose.

"It is likely taken aboard in some remote bay."

"That's an excellent point!" De Groot ran over to a shelf along the wall, took a rolled-up map and spread it out on his desk. "It could have been here." He pointed to a few little bays on the western coast of Ceylon, a finger's width above Galle. "Or here." His finger wandered north. "At the mouth of the Bentota."

"No," said Hannes. "I don't believe that."

"And why not?"

"Charlie Peck maintains that an epidemic of smallpox is raging all along the southern and western coast. His captain would not risk infecting himself or his crew."

De Groot stared at him. "Smallpox? Are you sure?"

Hannes nodded. "At least that's what Peck told me."

"What terribly bad luck! This complicates the search for potential transfers."

"Peck mentioned an agent," Hannes interjected.

"That means he loaded the cinnamon and met the *Northampton* at a previously agreed-upon location." De Groot stomped over to the globe and turned it impatiently.

"It might be the southern coast of India or perhaps one of the countless islands of the archipelago of the Maldives. Theoretically, the *Northampton* could have taken on the cinnamon off the coast of Madagascar or the Philippines, even though the waters over there are teeming with pirates."

"Or the agent is himself a pirate."

"That's quite possible. The English will try anything to invade our markets. God Almighty, finding that transfer spot is going to be like trying to find a needle in a haystack. We must find this agent. What's his name?"

"I'm afraid I don't know. Peck was too drunk for me to be able to get that out of him."

De Groot glared at Hannes. "You shouldn't have allowed this tosspot to drink so much!"

"If you know exactly how to obtain the information, you should do it yourself," Hannes retorted. He felt offended.

"Watch your mouth!" the Netherlander snapped. "I pay you more in one week than you would earn in the regiment in months! I expect something useful in return!"

"I have brought you all sorts of information," Hannes responded coolly. "Or maybe you think that the sailors at the Schotsche Temple would have trusted a dressed-up arrogant fop like you? And incidentally, it was quite costly to make Peck so talkative."

De Groot pressed his lips together. So far Hannes was the only one in whom he had confided. If he stopped the payments, his silence could no longer be guaranteed. "I deserved the rebuke," he grumbled. "Your information has, indeed, helped me make a great deal of progress."

Hannes nodded lightly, mollified, while de Groot adjusted his powdered wig.

"How shall we proceed now?"

"Today my replacement funds arrived from Amsterdam and we can prepare for our departure. In the next two to three weeks, we shall set sail on the *Edam* and put a stop to the activities of the English for good."

De Groot removed a little linen bag from his desk.

"Your earnings, Hiller. What else do I owe you?"

"Five gulden." Hannes watched as he counted the additional silver coins. "I shall have another talk with Peck. He should be sober by now. But I'm telling you, you get more information out of a drunk person, and later they don't remember all that they shared."

"Give it a try. Maybe you'll be lucky. And don't worry about the money. Let's not allow it to get in the way of this sailor's talkativeness." He closed the drawer.

"Please don't hold my little outburst against me. I am counting on your help in this difficult task."

"How long is the trip the Ceylon expected to take?"

"About three months. Why do you ask?"

"Do you think that there will still be an epidemic of smallpox when we get there?"

"Maybe, maybe not. Are you afraid?"

"I would prefer not to die from it, sir, that's all."

De Groot scrutinized him. "You are free to leave my employ and return to the regiment. Of course, I would have to describe the details in my report to the commanding officer. I don't suppose that he will take kindly to a soldier who displays fear. Quite apart from the fact that you will be giving up an awful lot of money. Will you still be able to support your mother?"

Hannes had, indeed, planned to send half of his earnings to his mother. He swallowed hard.

"You're giving me the choice between the devil and the deep blue sea. How considerate of you."

"Come on now!" De Groot took hold of his shoulder. "I do not plan to become infected with smallpox either, and will take every precaution. Now, let us focus on the task at hand. If we're successful, it will benefit all of us."

"From your lips to God's ear."

De Groot tightened his grip on Hannes' shoulder. "I am a God-fearing man but in order for this endeavor to succeed, we have to depend on each other. Can I count on you?"

"You can." Hannes nodded. "Only don't treat me like your errand boy."

No sooner was he alone than de Groot leaned against the wall, his face distorted with pain. For hours he had been afflicted with such severe stomach cramps that he almost lost his composure with Hiller. He really did need this young man, who in a very short time had found out more than de Groot had hoped.

He staggered to the cabinet along the wall and removed a bottle and a small pewter vessel. He stumbled to his desk and fell into the chair, breathing heavily. He pulled out the stopper and poured out the light, gold-colored liquid, breathing in the rich aroma of malt and juniper. He closed his eyes and drank the brandy in one gulp. He grimaced and shook himself as he felt it run down his esophagus. The pain became more bearable. Two weeks before, overcome with nostalgia, he had purchased a dozen bottles of the best Dutch jenever from a Dutch captain. Later he thought he must have been crazy to pay three times as much as he would at home. Now he congratulated himself on the purchase.

The day had actually started well. The bell rang early. A sailor had been sent by the captain of the *Edam*, an East Indiaman that had come into port at Table Bay yesterday afternoon, to deliver a letter from Frederik Alewijn. The replacement funds were on board the *Edam*.

However, upon inspection, de Groot determined that instead of the five crates he had requested, only two had been delivered, and one of those contained only copper coins. He had almost flown into a rage. The greater part of the silver coins would go to von Hügel for the uniforms. That left hardly anything for living expenses. He would not be able to pay Hiller's salary any longer. There was only one explanation for the disregard of his request to the Lords Seventeen, and that was that the financial situation of the Company was significantly more dire than he had assumed.

His stomach pains began with this alarming discovery. They increased when he returned home and withdrew to his study with Alewijn's letter.

> *Most Esteemed Sir:*
>
> *It troubles me most greatly to inform you that the British East India Company sold contraband cinnamon at the spice auction it hath lately held in London. The lot represented 4,500 pounds, almost ten per cent of the annual cinnamon harvest.*
>
> *I need not explain to such an esteemed finance inspector as your good self, that this loss has torn a deep hole in the Vereenigde Oostindische Compagnie coffers. As you well know, the calls on our purse have lately been great, and profits down. We can ill afford to absorb such a loss as this.*
>
> *The Lords Seventeen, have decided to dispatch a unit of one hundred of the best soldiers of the Infantry Regiment of Württemberg. Under the command of Colonel von Hügel, the regiment will accompany you, most honest sir, to Ceylon, to assist you in your mission to expose the ambidexter thieves who steal from us. By any and all means necessary, you shall extract every whit of information from whomever you may apprehend in this plot. All traitors will be sent to Amsterdam for sentencing.*

We trust that you will understand why further funds are not forthcoming.

We await your conclusion of this investigation, post-haste. Your good name, and ours, depend upon it.

Yours most truly,

Frederick Alewijn
on behalf of the Lords Seventeen,
Vereenigde Oostindische Compagnie

De Groot poured more jenever into his vessel. He was not at all comfortable with the idea of military support. Von Hügel was his subordinate, but experience had taught him that the military did not like taking orders from civilians. If he was to put an end to a well-organized and wide smuggling network, he preferred to proceed clandestinely. He planned to find and stop the masterminds, and if he did that, the rest of the network would fall apart on its own. This course of action would require his full concentration. Having to rein in von Hügel at the same time would not be helpful.

"I should write my will," de Groot muttered and downed the jenever. Of course, Bethari was his only heir but he wanted to ensure that she would live in security and prosperity should anything happen to him in the course of these exploits. He took some paper, a quill, and an ink bottle from a drawer.

In addition to the will, he had other arrangements to make. With the outbreak of smallpox, it would be better if his daughter did not accompany him to Ceylon. He had told Hiller that he guessed it would be over within three months but the outbreaks he had witnessed in Amsterdam had all lasted longer. He had to find a place for Bethari to stay, as leaving her by herself in Cape Town was out of the question. He sighed deeply. A long, busy night lay ahead for him.

Hannes stood in front of the slightly open door of the carriage house and wondered if he were about to make the same mistake as he had with Anna Maria. Although Bethari had said that she had something important to tell him, he understood it as a subterfuge. She might not be a married woman but her father had even more power and influence than von Hügel. He could imagine only too well what de Groot would say to a secret rendezvous between his daughter and a common soldier and carpenter.

And yet, his feet had taken him to the stable and his hand now opened its door. The hinges creaked softly. Hannes instinctively looked over his shoulder. Here and there light glistened through the closed shutters. The street seemed empty. He stepped into the stable and carefully closed the door behind him. He smelled leather, horses, and hay, and heard the animals snort and rustle in the straw. An oil lamp sat on the floor at the end of the aisle. The flame was so small that the light did not reach the high windows. He could not see Bethari but sensed that she was waiting for him there.

Hannes, Hannes, he thought. *What are you getting yourself into?* There was no answer from his mind but a warm sense of anticipation expanded in his chest.

He slowly walked toward the light. His steps resonated on the stone floor. Behind the oil lamp he discovered a small corner in which hay lay ready for the next morning. Bethari sat on top of the hay, smiling at him.

"You have accepted my invitation."

"I very much looked forward to it, *demoiselle*. What was it you wanted to tell me?"

"Nothing. It's not proper to say directly that I wanted to be alone with you. So I cheated a little."

That was just as he had thought.

"Well, miss, you certainly don't mince words."

She giggled and patted the ground next to her. "Wouldn't you prefer to stop talking and come a little closer?"

He took off his hat and bowed perfunctorily. "Miss, your wish is my command."

She spread a woolen horse blanket on the hay and moved aside a little when he sat down. "You kept me waiting for a long time." She stroked the sleeve of his jacket.

Sweet Mother of God, he thought as he put his hat next to him. *You don't mince words or waste time.* Without thinking, he leaned forward and kissed her fingertips. When he looked up, he saw her eyes shimmering in the twilight. Hannes became aware that he wanted her to like him.

"You have a new suit," she remarked. "It looks good on you."

Now that he did not have to wear a uniform anymore, he had had a two-piece suit of dark green cloth made for himself and he had bought new buckled shoes and a black tricorne. Never before had he owned such a good suit before, and her compliment embarrassed him.

He asked a little awkwardly, "Do you consider a man's attire important, miss?"

"I don't know." She sounded surprised. "It might be useful, don't you think? Still, a man should never be dressed up like a peacock."

"But you recognize his importance by the way he dresses, don't you, miss?"

"I believe that his actions show that."

Her answer delighted him. He embraced her and drew her to his chest. "Do you know how your virtues have taken up nearly all my thoughts?"

In his exuberance, he neglected to address her formally, as was proper, though she did not seem to mind. She lay her arms around his neck. Their faces drew closer. But Bethari paused.

"Did you hear that?" There was a faint rustling sound. She pressed her fingers against his chest.

"What do you have there?"

"It is something I did not want at first but I cannot do without now." He left it at that because he absolutely did not want her to know that he had carried her drawing with him for an entire year. Her dark eyes came nearer.

"I have sensed that you are a man of mystery. But that makes you special. Is that how you say it in German?"

"Exactly like that," he answered softly.

She placed her palms on his face, leaned forward, and kissed him. He felt her soft lips and was overtaken by arousal and a feeling of profound, satisfying peace. He took her in his arms and reciprocated her kiss with a passion of which he had no longer thought himself capable. He longed to possess her and her thrusting body told him that she felt the same.

He pushed up her dress, felt the cool silk of her stockings and the warm skin of her thighs. She moaned softly and her hand fumbled with his waistband.

A loud bang startled them.

"What was that?" Hannes pushed Bethari aside and jumped to his feet.

"Just one of the horses," he heard her surprised voice say. "It kicked against the partition."

"Lord in heaven!" he groaned, falling back into the hay. He was embarrassed by his outburst, and by the fact that his heart threatened to jump out of his chest because one of the horses had kicked the wall. But the bang had sounded just like the shot in Vlissingen. In that instant, he was transported back to the day when he thought he would die.

She nestled up to him but he did not react. She withdrew.

"What's the matter?"

"Nothing. Why do you think something has to be the matter?" he replied unkindly.

She did not answer.

He immediately placed his arm around her. He regretted having been harsh to her.

"You really ought to return to the house before someone notices you're gone."

"No one will miss me. I've already said goodnight to Father and Rufus only enters my room when I call him. Why did this horse frighten you so?"

It's not the silly horse's fault, he thought. *It's these accursed memories that won't leave me alone.*

"Still, we shouldn't risk getting caught by your father. He'd challenge me to a duel."

"He certainly would not be thrilled to find you here. But he would not shoot you. He does not even know how to acquit himself with a pistol. Why don't you just tell me that you find my company dull?" She sat up and arranged her dress.

"But I don't. Just the contrary." He extended a hand and drew her close again. "Why rush things? There was a time when I wanted everything immediately. But with you, it is something special. I believe," he swallowed, "I am discovering love for the first time, not only lust. It is as though I have uncovered a treasure. Do you understand me?"

She nodded and took his hand. "That is the most beautiful thing I have ever heard. And I can hardly wait to discover this treasure with you."

CHAPTER FOURTEEN

CAPE TOWN, SOUTH AFRICA, 1788

"All I see is dots, lines and blots." Jan Pieter de Groot bent over Bethari's half-finished picture.

Father and daughter were in the courtyard. Ever since receiving her new art supplies, Bethari had been spending several hours daily here, painting. Mostly she depicted daily domestic scenes: a slave sweeping the courtyard or hitching up the horses, a cat sunning itself on the warm stones, and always Table Mountain as her motif, looming on the horizon like a mighty, dark hulk.

"You mustn't look at the picture up close." She placed her brushes and palette on the small table next to her easel and pulled her father a few steps away. "Now look."

He obediently studied her work and shook his head, at a loss.

"I can guess that the picture represents Table Mountain. But it's all so blurry, as though there's something wrong with my eyes."

"Father, you're not really trying," she called out impatiently. "The most important thing is not the mountain but the sky with its veils of clouds."

"Since when are cloud veils pink?" he grumbled. "And I've never seen lilac and golden flecks in the sky."

"I think you have never really looked at the sky," she retorted in a hurt voice. "It's not just blue. Its colors vary depending on the time of the day and the light. The wonderful thing about painting *en plein air* is that I can recreate the many light and dark shades much better than if I paint them from memory." She took the brush, dipped the tip into pink paint and placed another dab on her horizon. "If I were to paint this picture this afternoon, it would look completely different because the sun will be lower and cast longer shadows." She stepped back and looked at her work.

De Groot looked at his daughter. The smock covering her dress was full of paint stains, just like her hands. Her cheeks were reddened and some strands of her hair had become unfastened. He did not want to offend her but he believed that this painting was too odd to arouse any interest in future buyers. And that deprived it of all value.

"Your pictures have always been colorful but at home in Amsterdam I could at least make out what was in them," he said.

"Painting *en plein air* is not subject to the restrictive rules I was taught at the academy. My powers of observation determine the appearance of the picture. I studied the light for days just to capture this brief moment. Do you mean to say that you really cannot see how I have balanced the colors?" She looked at her father expectantly.

"Well, perhaps I just have to get used to the idea of a lilac, golden and rose-colored sky," he equivocated.

"It does not please you," she said sadly.

"I think all your paintings are marvelous, Bethari!" He took her in his arms and hoped that she would not notice his deception. "And I have always supported your artistic endeavors."

She laid her head against him. "You have indeed, Father. And that's precisely why I want you to like my paintings."

"I do, little one." He stroked her hair. "Don't hold it against your old father if he doesn't understand your art. I am so glad that you have something to occupy you, now that—" He broke off.

She raised her head. "Now that what?"

He swallowed. He wanted to inform his daughter that she would not be accompanying him to Ceylon but he found it difficult. They had never been apart for very long.

"Let's sit down for a moment." He led Bethari to a bench along the wall and took her hand.

"You're frightening me, Father."

"I have learned that there is an outbreak of smallpox in Ceylon."

Her expression grew serious. "That's terrible news. I hope the sailors don't bring the epidemic here to the Cape."

De Groot dabbed the perspiration from his brow. "That would, indeed, be a catastrophe."

Smallpox was a devastating pestilence that not even the best physicians had under control. Despite experiments that had been carried out for years to develop a vaccine, the epidemic of smallpox continued to kill thousands of people. There had been several outbreaks in Amsterdam. Each time, de Groot had fled to the countryside with his daughter to avoid getting infected.

"Does that mean that our onward journey is postponed again?" she inquired.

He shook his head. "Yesterday I received a letter in which the Lords Seventeen ordered me to leave for Ceylon at once. But only I will go. You shall stay here."

She looked at him, horrified. "You want to spare me and yet expose yourself to the risk of infection?"

"I can wait no longer, Bethari. The onward journey has been planned for months and was delayed only because of the *Drie Gebroeders'* shipwreck. One week from now, I set sail on the *Edam*."

"And I will worry the entire time that you'll get sick and die! Don't you at least want to get vaccinated?"

He stopped her. "There is no smallpox here and so there is no vaccine available. As you know, it is derived from the pustules of infected patients. And it is possible to get infected with the injection. That is why I never had you vaccinated."

She frowned. "Perhaps it would have been better if you had. That way I could accompany you and would not have to fear for you for months. What is this mission about anyhow? Is it not something you can take care of from here?"

He smiled weakly. "Unfortunately not."

She took his hand. "Promise me that you will be careful."

"Of course! I will not act recklessly."

"Is it a dangerous assignment, Father?" she wanted to know. "Is that why you won't speak of it?"

"No," he said evasively. "I merely have to investigate some irregularities concerning the transport of cinnamon." He changed the subject. "I want to talk about where you're going to live in my absence. What do you think about Baroness von Hügel? This morning I sent Rufus with a letter to her husband making the request. I await his answer but I don't think they'll decline."

In reality he had not asked, but rather ordered the Colonel to put Bethari in the care of his wife.

Bethari briefly recalled the hours she and Anna Maria von Hügel had spent on the deck of the *Drie Gebroeders*, painting and chatting. Then the recollection of the night when she had observed the colonel's wife with Hannes crept into her mind, and she suddenly she lost all desire for the baroness' company.

"I prefer to stay here in the house with Rufus."

Her father roundly rejected that suggestion. "You don't think I'm leaving you here alone with a few slaves! Why do you not want to live with Baroness von Hügel? You got on so well with her on the journey here."

Bethari was silent. She did not want to tell her father that she disliked Anna Maria's interest in Hannes because she herself had fallen in love with him. It was still too soon to talk about these feelings. And so she answered evasively, "At least I can take Rufus with me."

De Groot shook his head. "Rufus is coming with me. He and Private Hiller."

"You mean you're exposing not only yourself but two other people to this epidemic? What do you need Private Hiller for anyway? How will a carpenter help you audit the books?"

De Groot furrowed his brow. "Why should Hiller's fate concern you?"

The blood rushed to her cheeks. "I am concerned about you and Rufus too."

"Hiller is my assistant," de Groot replied. "I need him to carry out my mission. Nothing else should concern you."

When she looked down on her lap in silence, he put his arm around her and continued more gently, "Please, little one, let's not quarrel right before my departure."

Tears streamed down Bethari's face. One single day without seeing Hannes was sheer torture for her. She could not imagine being without her beloved for months on end.

"Are you going visiting?" inquired Theobald von Hügel.

"It looks like it, doesn't it?" Anna Maria von Hügel stood in the foyer in front of a gold-framed mirror and adjusted her hat. Their eyes met in the mirror.

"Where are you going?"

"I'm not one of your soldiers you can question in that tone." She was about to squeeze by him but he blocked her way.

"Why do you not answer my question?"

"I visit the governor's wife every Tuesday."

He stepped aside immediately. "Forgive me. I had forgotten."

She looked at him from under the broad brim of her hat.

"You're thinking that I'm meeting a lover? We had once come to the agreement that so long as we were discreet, we're not accountable to each other."

"It is that very discretion that you violated!" he snapped. "And to this day, I have not heard you apologize to me."

She lowered her head. "My behavior in Ludwigsburg was careless. It will not happen again."

"Are you still seeing him?" he gasped.

A door opened on the second floor, and footsteps hurried across the landing. Anna Maria looked upstairs.

"We should not have such conversations in front of the domestics. And anyway, I must be on my way."

"I have something else to discuss with you," he countered. "But not here, so come into my study."

She hesitated but then followed him. After closing the door, he moved a chair near the window for her and leaned against the brick ledge.

"This morning I received a message from de Groot. He is set to leave for Ceylon soon and asks us to take in his daughter in his absence."

Anna Maria seemed surprised. "On the journey here, she told me that she would accompany her father to Ceylon."

"Obviously he has changed his plans. Perhaps his mission has become more wide-ranging or dangerous."

"Dangerous?"

"There is said to be an epidemic of smallpox on Ceylon. I heard that from an English captain at the lodge meeting yesterday. His ship was to go into port at Galle but because of the smallpox, they sailed on."

"I understand." Anna Maria nodded slowly. "Well, I have no objections to the young girl. Her company is certainly more pleasant than that of the dull Cape Dutchwomen."

"I'm glad to hear that because it will be your task to look after her." He went over to his desk and rummaged in a stack of papers. "I received a letter yesterday from Frederick Alewijn, one of the Amsterdam Directors of the VOC." He pulled a sheet out of the stack and handed it to his wife.

She scanned the tightly spaced letter. "You depart to Ceylon with de Groot?"

"I, and a special company of one hundred soldiers of the Infantry Regiment of Württemberg."

"And when do you leave?"

"Soon, probably. I have written a letter to de Groot and requested a meeting. I'll ask him about the departure date."

"But can the VOC determine that a part of the regiment be moved? It was meant for South Africa!"

He took back the letter. "According to the subsidiary agreement, the Company can deploy us anywhere it sees fit."

"At least you'll be spared the smallpox. You did survive it as a child, didn't you?"

He nodded, happy to see his wife so concerned about his fate. "The Lords Seventeen want me to assist de Groot but they say nothing about his assignment, impeding my task considerably, of course. I'm hoping to receive some information from him but I'm not counting on it. He is an eccentric, self-opinionated person."

She thought for a moment. "Maybe the Lords Seventeen harbor some doubts as to de Groot's ability to carry out the assignment they entrusted to him. To ensure that it will be carried out, they are sending you as support."

He smiled at her. "I have always valued your shrewdness. But in what endeavors could the military assist a finance inspector?"

Anna Maria folded her hands in her lap. "That's what you'll have to find out." She got up. "And now if you will excuse me. It would be very discourteous to keep the governor's wife waiting any longer."

He watched her as she walked toward the door. When she placed her hand on the handle, he said, "You never answered my question."

She remained immobile for several seconds. Finally, she shook her head.

"I'm not meeting Hiller anymore."

"Then why are we not finding our way back toward each other, my dearest?"

She turned around slowly. "I have always striven to support your career and I have borne you three sons, who will follow in your footsteps. But I have no interest in any further intimacy."

His expression hardened. "Yet you're willing to give yourself to a scurrilous have-not like this Hiller? I don't understand you."

A little smile flickered on her lips. "The only reason that you, dear husband, are no longer a scurrilous have-not is my dowry." With that, she turned and left.

"Rufus!" De Groot stuck his head out of his study. The door of the library opened, though it was not Rufus, but a female slave with a duster in her hand, who stepped out.

"You called, master?"

"I'm looking for Rufus," de Groot grunted. "Where is that good-for-nothing hiding?"

"I saw him in the courtyard with the mistress."

"Send him to my study! It's urgent!" De Groot slammed the door shut.

He was impatient because the *Edam* was to set sail in three days and his trunks still needed packing. He wanted to discuss with Rufus what would to take and what to store in Cape Town.

He had spent most of the last week brooding over his mission. Unfortunately, Hiller had not brought any new information because his English contact had been sentenced to detention as a result of his tippling, and shortly thereafter, the English ship departed Table Bay.

De Groot wanted names, not only that of the agent but also potentially of someone in the Dutch colonial administration. He deemed it impossible that such large-scale smuggling of cinnamon could take place without corruption from within the ranks of the VOC. The patchy information prevented him from getting a clear picture, and the uncertainty made him irritable. He went over to his desk, where, among the charts and papers full of scribbling, stood the open bottle of jenever and a glass. He poured himself some and downed it in one gulp. There had been a time when it would have never occurred to him to drink spirits before lunch, but this was the only way to get his nerves and stomach pain under control.

His separation from Bethari caused him concern as well. He was not as young and resilient as during his time on Java. A creeping anxiety had befallen him that his farewell to Bethari might be forever.

He replaced the empty glass on his desk, walked to the window and looked at his daughter in the courtyard. Today she was not standing at her easel but sitting under an umbrella at a small folding table writing a letter. She wore a light dress made of pale blue Indian silk, held together by a sash under the bosom. He noted that her figure had become distinctly more feminine. Her face, too, had changed in the last few months. The childlike expression had vanished. She appeared more mature and self-assured. More than ever, she now resembled her deceased mother.

It is time to find a husband for her, he mused and determined to do just that, once they were back in Amsterdam.

Rufus stood next to Bethari's chair, and de Groot observed how the two talked and laughed together as his daughter folded her letter and sealed it. He shook his head. Bethari's familiarity with his slave still irritated him. She handed Rufus the letter. De Groot expected his servant to place the envelope with the other outgoing correspondence in the foyer, and yet he slipped it under his jacket. Then Bethari took his hand, and said something while looking intently into Rufus' eyes.

De Groot gasped. Familiarity or not, this behavior went decidedly too far. He opened a crack in the window.

"Tell no one," he heard Bethari say. "And be careful."

De Groot was dumbfounded. His beloved daughter was keeping secrets from him! And his servant of many years was helping her to keep them. He leaned forward to prevent a single word from escaping him. But at that moment the female slave appeared. She curtsied to Bethari.

"The master is asking for Rufus."

"Is it necessary?" she asked. "I need Rufus to do something for me."

Rufus stepped up. "The master does not like to be kept waiting. I will take care of your errand afterwards."

"Very well. But not a word to anyone. Not even to my father."

De Groot was shattered when he closed the window. Meanwhile, as his daughter gathered her writing materials, she looked up, saw her father at the window and waved to him. He slowly raised his hand and waved back.

"What is it you need, master?"

De Groot swung around. He had not heard Rufus enter. He was gripped by an overwhelming rage and wanted nothing more than to lunge at his servant and beat the secret errand out of him.

"Since when do you not knock, Rufus?"

The servant looked at him in surprise. "I did, sir. But you did not answer."

De Groot swallowed hard and studied the dark face of his slave. It was courteous and attentive as always. He remembered that in all those years, Rufus had never once disappointed him.

Maybe I am being unfair, he thought and decided to wait and give Rufus the opportunity to say something about the incident in the courtyard, thus proving his loyalty.

"My trunks need to be packed for the journey to Ceylon," he said, trying to sound amicable. "I want you to go through my clothes and see if anything needs fixing. Everything should be taken to the *Edam* the day after tomorrow. Anything I do not take with me will go into storage with the VOC."

"Certainly, sir. Do you want me to pack the young mistress' belongings as well?"

De Groot nodded. "Her trunks will go to the von Hügels."

Rufus looked surprised. His master had not discussed the details of the trip but he had expected Bethari to accompany her father.

"There is an outbreak of smallpox in Ceylon," de Groot explained. "I am afraid she might get infected. She will stay with the von Hügels for the duration of my absence."

"A very wise decision," Rufus agreed. "When shall we move?"

"Not you, Rufus," de Groot replied. "You shall come with me to Ceylon."

The servant's eyes grew wide. He also feared smallpox, but a slave was powerless against his master's orders. He bowed. "Very well."

De Groot scrutinized him, deeply disappointed that Rufus made no mention of the letter.

"You're concerned about the mistress, are you not?"

"Her wellbeing is my first priority."

"I have my doubts about that."

De Groot went to his desk, poured himself some jenever and swallowed it. "Misunderstood loyalty only does harm."

"Sir?"

De Groot slammed the empty glass on the desk. "Have you nothing to say to me?"

Rufus evaded his master's piercing look and remained silent.

De Groot's right hand gripped the back of the chair and his knuckles turned white.

"Have I not always treated you well, fed and clothed you, and never beaten you? Have you not always had a special position in my household?"

"Yes, sir." Rufus' voice shook slightly.

"Give me the letter!" de Groot barked.

Rufus flinched but otherwise did not move.

De Groot reached him in three quick steps, grabbed his jacket, and tore it open, making the buttons fly. He pulled out the sealed letter and held it up.

"This is how you deceive me and lie to me!"

He broke the seal and unfurled the page. He read the short missive.

"Why, this is outrageous! For whom is this meant?"

Rufus stood stock-still. His chest rose and fell visibly.

"Answer me!" de Groot screamed. "Or else I'll sell you off today! And trust me, I'll see to it that your life with your next owner will not be as comfortable as it has been with me!"

There was absolute silence. Master and servant stared at each other without a word. Then Rufus lowered his head.

"You disobey me?" de Groot raged. "Just you wait. I'll get to the bottom of your plot!" He stormed to the window, tore open it open and leaned out. "In my study, Bethari. Now!"

CHAPTER FIFTEEN

CAPE TOWN, SOUTH AFRICA, 1788

Bethari jumped up from her chair. Her heart was pounding. Never in her life had her father spoken like that to her. Occasionally, he grew impatient, and they argued at times, but he had never screamed at her or given her orders.

Rushing into the house, she wondered what the cause of his anger could be. He had summoned Rufus. Could he have seen her giving him the letter? At the door to the study, she stopped and listened, yet she heard nothing. She gingerly opened the door and entered.

Her father leaned against the window, his arms crossed and his eyes fixed on her. His lips were reduced to a thin line and his brows were furrowed. In the middle of the room Rufus, who waited with his head lowered, did not look up when she entered.

She stood next to the servant. "What have you done to Rufus?"

Her father laughed sardonically. "Obstinate and contrary is what he is. Doesn't answer my questions. But maybe you will."

He reached into his pocket and pulled out the letter she had entrusted to Rufus, unfolded it and read aloud, *"Come to our usual spot right after sundown today. I will be waiting."*

Bethari felt heat surging up in her. At first, she panicked. Then she told herself that her father was angry because she had secrets from him, not because he knew to whom the letter was addressed.

"Are you cross because this is how you have learned that I have fallen in love?"

"So, you have fallen in love, have you? Well, well."

De Groot slowly folded the paper. His voice was so cold, so full of painfully restrained rage, that anger flared up in her.

"I am an adult and yet you treat me like a naughty child."

"This disgraceful missive is undignified for a grown woman," he cut her short. "Have you forgotten your obligation to me and our reputation? To whom is this addressed?" He waved the letter in the air.

Her lips trembled. Her father's anger frightened her. But at the same time, her own indignation grew.

"If you're going to treat me like a criminal, I shall tell you nothing."

"Please, miss," Rufus piped up carefully. "Perhaps you ought to tell your father everything."

De Groot put the letter back in his pocket. His gaze wandered over to his servant. "Do you remember to whom you owe obedience?"

"You, sir," Rufus answered in a toneless voice.

"Then why are you conspiring with my daughter? If her behavior is unbecoming, it is your duty to inform me. Instead, you are complicit in secret mongering under my roof!" De Groot lunged at the servant. Rufus raised his arms protectively. Too late. The blow struck his head. He stumbled backwards and struggled to stay on his feet.

"Father! Have you taken leave of your senses?"

De Groot looked Rufus in the eye and again raised his hand. "To whom is this letter addressed?"

Bethari's eyes filled with tears. "To Hannes Hiller."

Her father blanched. "You offer yourself to a man like Hiller? Someone without rank or name?"

Aghast, she cried out, "Do you think I offer myself? As though merchandise? Father!"

"What else shall I call it when you throw yourself at some uncouth, uneducated fellow who has no manners? That rogue!

Were he to boast of his conquest, your reputation would be ruined!"

She clenched her fists. "If you think so little of him, why did you hire him as your assistant?"

"I did not choose him; von Hügel would give me no one better."

She looked at him dismay. "You do remember, that it was Hiller who saved your life after the shipwreck?"

"No decent man has secret encounters with a respectable young woman! He asks her father if he may come calling!"

She straightened her shoulders. "He did not try to seduce me. It was I who asked him to meet me. And it was I who kissed him the first time."

"Ahhh!" De Groot clutched his stomach and doubled over.

"Father? What is it?" She rushed to his side. "Rufus, go and fetch Major Liesching!"

"No doctor!" De Groot strained to get up and pointed to his desk. "Only a nipperkin of jenever!"

"Of course, sir." The servant rushed to fill the glass to the brim and took it to de Groot, who hastily emptied it.

"It's your fault," he gasped in Bethari's direction. "Never would I have imagined that you, of all people, would disappoint me like this. I am only thankful your mother, bless her God-fearing soul, is not here to witness this day."

"Mother?" Bethari stammered. "What...?"

De Groot stared at his empty glass.

"Lord knows I loved your mother. But I never married her. I was not allowed. The honorable Company forbids marriage between its Dutch employees and indigenous people in the colonies. It was a source of great shame. You were never supposed to find out that our union lacked the blessing of the church; I promised her that on her deathbed. But you leave me no choice." He looked into her distraught face.

"As God is my witness, Bethari, all these years I tried to live down your parentage, silenced malicious tongues with money, and set up a dowry for you that would be worthy of the daughter of one the Lords Seventeen. But I cannot change your parentage and your skin color! You must counterbalance these stigmas on your own–with conduct that is above reproach! If you throw yourself at this have-not, you destroy everything I have built for you!"

"Father! You accuse me of keeping secrets and are yourself doing the same?"

Bethari was crushingly disappointed. Until today, her father had been the person who was closest to her, and who held her absolute trust. And yet, his story confirmed certain realities. She had always observed that people treated her differently. She thought it strange that she was often asked about her mother, directly or indirectly, and though she usually believed it was due to her exotic appearance, it did not always seem a satisfactory explanation. Of course, the Company's marriage regulations were well known in Amsterdam and she realized now that her father had not fooled anybody.

She raised her chin. "Henceforth, I will no longer keep company with people who pay attention to such trivial matters as my skin color. And even less with people who look down on my mother." She had never cared a whit for what others thought.

Her father looked at her angrily, unable to appreciate how his unfaltering support and devotion had nurtured this independence in her. Unlike Bethari, who felt as though she did not entirely belong–and relished the feeling–de Groot craved acceptance.

"You are incorrigible. And after all that I have done for you! To prevent you from bringing yourself and our good name into disrepute, I see no option but to lock you in your room until my departure. You will have your meals there as well. Alone."

"Never have I seen you like this, Father. But if it is your wish." She had tears in her eyes.

"It is my wish to protect you from yourself, Bethari, even if you cannot see that at this moment. And as for Rufus, he, too, will be punished," de Groot said frigidly.

She ran to him and took his hands. "Please spare him! As you have said, it's all my fault."

De Groots face hardened even further. "God teaches to punish the sinners before we forgive them. Rufus was disobedient to me, his master. I believe my kindness toward him has gone to his head. He must learn his lesson. Come with me. Both of you!" He stomped to the door.

Bethari went to Rufus and took his arm. "Had I imagined what—" She sobbed loudly and could not finish.

"Do not concern yourself about me, mistress." The servant gently loosened her grip. "Come now. We should not keep the master waiting."

Without looking back even once, de Groot marched to the horse stables. The house and courtyard were empty but Bethari was certain that the servants were watching, through the curtains and cracked doors. She tried desperately to invent ways to help Rufus but was incapable of thinking clearly.

The horses snorted and laid back their ears as de Groot tramped down the aisle. He turned into the tack room, scanned the shelf, and pointed to an iron padlock used to lock the stables at night.

"Take that, Rufus!"

"Father, what are you doing?" He tramped past Bethari without saying a word. The last stall was empty, save for a little heap of hay on the ground. An iron ring with a chain was mounted on the wall above the fodder rack.

De Groot turned to his servant. "Do you remember Brazil, Rufus? The slaves we saw there?"

"Yes, master."

"Do you remember what the men had on their feet?"

"Chains, master."

De Groot nodded deliberately. "Then you know what you have to do?"

"Father! You cannot chain him up!" Bethari could not believe her ears.

"I shall not do that," de Groot answered coolly. "He will do it himself."

"Under no circumstances!" she called out in horror. "He is a human being, not a horse or an ox!"

"He has forgotten where he comes from and what his position is in this house. It is my duty to remind him." De Groot gestured to Rufus. "You will stay in this stable until my departure."

The servant moved forward without a word but Bethari blocked his way. "All this because of a little letter–the content of which Rufus did not even know? I cannot believe that you would do that, Father."

"Clear the way!" he barked at her. "It is high time that order was restored to my house!"

"All will be well, young mistress." Rufus gently moved Bethari aside, stepped into the stable, wrapped the chain around his right ankle and locked it with the padlock. De Groot pocketed the key.

Tears ran down Bethari's cheeks. She rushed to Rufus and embraced him. "I am so sorry! Please forgive me!" She then turned to her father. "Give me a chain and a lock. Rufus' fate is mine as well."

De Groot yanked her into the aisle. "Do not press your luck, Bethari!"

Through her tears she looked directly at him. "I am glad to be spared your company until your departure!"

Jan Pieter de Groot stood on the pier with the captain of the *Edam* and Colonel von Hügel. He looked into Table Bay, past the ship's slightly bobbing bow.

It was the middle of May and fall was making its way to the Cape Colony. Gray clouds, driven by the wind, rolled over the town, bringing light rain with them. And yet it was still much warmer than in the Netherlands at this time.

"Think you that a storm is coming?" he inquired of the Captain, looking at little whitecaps dancing on the water.

"The wind will definitely freshen. But at least it's coming from the west." The bearded captain took a long drag from his pipe. "That's more useful than the southeasterly in the summer. But if, out of the blue, I have to find room on my ship for one hundred more souls, not to mention the additional provisions, well then, our departure will be delayed, of course." He shot an angry glance at von Hügel.

The commanding officer shrugged his shoulders. "I mere following the directions of the honorable Company, who is your employer too, if I am not mistaken."

The captain growled but did not answer. The three men watched as a long line of soldiers marched up the gangway onto the ship.

Von Hügel chose one hundred men from the regiment's companies; on de Groot's recommendation he had made sure that they were all young and healthy. None of the recruits had any combat experience.

"I am grateful that you are taking in my daughter," de Groot told the commanding officer. "I really am glad not to expose her to the smallpox in Ceylon."

"It is no trouble," von Hügel replied. "My wife is glad for the company."

"Master, your luggage lies in your cabin. Do you wish me to unpack it?" Rufus suddenly appeared behind de Groot.

De Groot nodded. "Make sure that everything is there. The box with my charts and documents is especially important."

"Yes, master."

"Oh, and lash the box with my jenever with an extra strap."

"Certainly." Rufus bowed. "Will you permit me a question, master?" He continued when de Groot nodded, "Will I still be in South Africa when I am on the ship?"

De Groot frowned. "Why do you ask?"

"I would like to put on my shoes and cover my head. But only with your permission, of course."

"I will allow you that," de Groot agreed, "but only once we're on the open water."

"Thank you, sir."

De Groot watched his servant as he walked toward the ship, his shoes in his right hand, the scarf for his turban in his left. Ever since he had thrown Rufus the key to allow him to unlock his chain, he had behaved impeccably. And yet de Groot wondered if he were affording him too much independence by granting his request.

"For God's sake, what are those blockheads trying to do over there?" The Captain stormed away to oversee preparations by his crew.

Colonel von Hügel moved closer to de Groot. "I want to thank you for defraying my costs for the uniforms so promptly."

De Groot acknowledged him briefly. "I promised to do it as soon as my money arrived from the Netherlands."

Von Hügel moved a little closer still.

"This money is meant to cover the costs arising from your mission in Ceylon, am I right?"

"If you know all this, why do you ask?" de Groot grumbled.

"It is time you told me the details of the mission. How else am I to assist you?"

"I will determine when you assist me–if at all," de Groot retorted.

Von Hügel had tried repeatedly to obtain the particulars of the assignment. The last time had been two days earlier, at the farewell at the lodge. But de Groot always put him off, saying that the matter was highly confidential.

"The Lords expect a detailed report about the deployment of the soldiers," von Hügel tried again. "They will be angered to hear that you are hindering me."

"At this moment it is not clear that your men will be deployed at all," de Groot countered. "As long as smallpox is going about in Ceylon, they will remain at the barracks in Galle, unless you want to expose them to certain death. That would not please the Lords Seventeen either."

"I see that you want to act alone," von Hügel remarked smugly. "Or perhaps with your so-called assistant. Where is he?"

De Groot did not answer although he silently asked himself the same thing. He was sure that Hiller was not at the von Hügel house. He himself had deposited Bethari there that very morning, relieved that it would be impossible for her to meet Hannes. The farewell between father and daughter had been frosty. That hurt him, but was to be expected he judged, given Bethari's character.

"You must be pleased that you've moved me safely out of Hannes' way," she had said as she snidely evaded his embrace.

Yet when he handed her the envelope with his will, she began to cry. "Promise me you'll return safely, Father," she had said. "Write to me often, so that I know you are well. And stay away from places where the smallpox is raging."

"I'm going aboard," Von Hügel jolted de Groot out of his gloomy thoughts. "We will have ample opportunity to discuss the matter during three months at sea."

Wracked by indecision, de Groot paced up and down, but just as he had made up his mind to follow von Hügel, Hiller turned the corner by a storage shed. He carried a linen sack of his belongings over his shoulder. When de Groot noticed his leisurely pace, he became enraged. Why was this malapert late? Might he have found a way to meet Bethari, despite all of de Groot's precautions?

Hannes spotted de Groot and began to run, laughing all the while. "You will not believe what I just found out!"

"Where have you been hanging about, Hiller?" de Groot cut him off. "If I order you to be at the harbor at sunrise, you are to be at the harbor at sunrise!"

"Well, that's a fine greeting!" Hannes dropped his sack on the ground, within inches of the Netherlander's feet. "What did you think? That I had been fooling around with my sweetheart?"

"I'm warning you!" De Groot grabbed the collar of his jacket. "If it ever were to reach my ears that you are not behaving like a man of honor!"

Hannes freed himself with one move. "Unhand me! I am not your servant!"

De Groot fought to keep his composure. "You are my assistant and as such, you must justify yourself to me! Why were you late?"

Hannes furrowed his brows. Briefly, he was on the verge of saying, *Why don't you gather the information yourself, you maundering old fool!* But it was of no advantage to him to keep the information to himself; it was in his best interest to carry out his mission in Ceylon as successfully as possible.

"I met Charlie Peck," he said. "That sailor from the Schotsche Tempel."

"He's still in Cape Town." De Groot was incredulous. "The *Northampton* left long ago."

Hiller grinned. "When he was released from detention, he bolted from the *Northampton* and signed on with an American sailer that's still anchored here. He was so angry with his old captain that he even wished the smallpox on him."

"Yes, but did you get any information out of him?" de Groot interrupted.

Hannes nodded. "I invited him for a beer and he told me that the agent is Polish."

"Excellent! What is his name?"

"Charlie did not know, unfortunately. The man was always called 'the Pole'."

"Then he probably also didn't know where and how this Pole gets the cinnamon on board?"

"Sadly, no."

"Hm." De Groot stroked his chin with his thumb and forefinger. "That's not really a lot of information."

"I should call it better than nothing at all," Hannes retorted, hurt.

"Well, it remains to be seen if we can put this information to good use. Now let us board." De Groot stepped over Hannes' linen sack and headed to the narrow gangplank.

At that moment a loud voice called out, "Hannes! Wait for me!"

The boy ran in huge steps along the pier and stopped directly in front of Hannes. "I want to go with you! I'm your friend, remember?"

Hannes sighed. "You will be much better off in Cape Town, August. Aren't you happy that I got you a job in the Company's gardens?"

"Yea." August nodded eagerly. "With the nice flowers."

"You see. You can care for them all day and even get paid for it." Hannes had not only arranged a job for August as a *pasganger* in the Company gardens but also negotiated with the administrator for August to be paid in Dutch gulden. They were to be kept in the regimental chest until Hannes' return, and then paid out to the boy.

"I'll be back soon." He laid his hands on the boy's shoulders.

August looked at him fearfully. "Tomorrow?"

"No, not tomorrow. But soon. I promise."

"Well." August looked down sadly at the tips of his shoes.

Suddenly, he beamed, threw his arms around Hannes, and embraced him. "A promise is a promise."

"Don't suffocate me, boy!" Hannes freed himself with a laugh and picked up his sack. "Farewell, August. We'll see each other again."

"Hello there, Hannes!"

"Are you going to keep us company?"

"It's quite crowded down here but you'll find a spot in the very back."

Many different voices called over to Hannes from all the corners of the steerage deck. The soldiers arranged their sleeping hammocks among baskets filled with vegetables, crates of bread, cheese wheels, water barrels and cannons positioned in front of the gun ports.

Hannes looked around. "What are you all doing here?"

"Well, what do you think? We've been ordered to Ceylon with you! Off to new adventures!" a soldier clapped Hannes on the shoulder.

"It may be a questionable adventure, with smallpox in Ceylon," Hannes said dryly.

"What?" The man raised his eyebrows. "Nobody told us. But an order is an order; that's the life of a soldier. I shan't be intimidated by smallpox!"

"Well. I must find a place to sleep." Hannes tried to get past him.

"Wait," The man stopped him. "Do you know about the orders? Are we going to war?"

"I do not know. If you want to find out more, ask the commanding officer."

"Why so gruff?" the soldier called after him.

Hannes strode on. He found a hammock and a place to hang it. It was dark there but he was guaranteed some peace and quiet.

"Hannes. Please, I do not wish to offend you." The soldier had followed him.

Hannes nodded. "All is well. Know you, is the Netherlander's daughter on board already?"

"The little dark-haired one? What lies between you two?"

"Nothing!" Hannes had hoped to see Bethari once more before their departure, but she sent no message. He believed her to be busy with preparations for the trip, and anticipated seeing her on the pier with her father. But she had not been there. He had been tormented by an uneasy feeling ever since.

The soldier put his hands on his hips. "With all due respect, Hannes—"

"I surrender. 'Tis true, the brightness of her cheeks has taken up my thoughts," Hannes conceded reluctantly.

"Hm." The man chewed his lower lip. "In that case, I'd tell you not to get your hopes up. She did not board."

"Is that true?" Hannes stared at him.

The man nodded. "She's staying with the commanding officer's wife. I heard the Netherlander and von Hügel talking on the pier."

Hannes was dumbstruck. Why had Bethari not told him that she would remain in Cape Town? And why had she not bid him farewell? He thought of her soft voice in the darkness of the stables, of her delicate little body in his arms and of the yearning in her kiss. Could it be that the most beautiful experience in the last few months was over before it had begun?

"Will you come on deck?" His fellow soldier touched his arm. "We're about to put out to sea."

"I think not." Hannes turned away. "There's no one to wave goodbye to me anyhow."

De Groot and Colonel von Hügel stood on the foredeck and looked over the railing. There were two boats in front of the bow, tethered to the foremast of the *Edam*. They were to tow the mighty sailer from the pier into the open waters. Sailors kept lookout for reefs from the starboard and port sides as well as from the crow's nest, while a pilot operated the wheel, all under the Captain's anxious eye.

Slowly the great ship moved away from the pier. "Why, there's your daughter," von Hügel shouted, "with my wife!"

De Groot swung around. There was Bethari, close to the edge of the pier. Baroness von Hügel sat behind her in an open carriage.

De Groot cupped his hands around his mouth and leaned over the railing. "Bethari! What are you doing here?"

But the wind and the noise from the harbor drowned out his words. Bethari's eyes searched the *Edam*'s deck. He distinctly felt that it was not him that she sought.

CHAPTER SIXTEEN

CAPE TOWN, SOUTH AFRICA, AND AT SEA, 1788

"I have never seen pictures like yours," said Anna Maria von Hügel. "It's simply wonderful how you've captured the light. I can almost feel the sunlight on my skin." She gazed at Bethari's depiction of Table Mountain. It was the same picture in which her father had said he could see only dots, lines, and blots.

Bethari brought all her paintings, canvases, and other art supplies with her to the von Hügel house. When Anna Maria asked to see her work, Bethari anxiously feared a verdict like her father's, but the baroness saw her painting with different eyes. Bethari was delighted.

"You really like it?"

"An astonishing technique," Anna Maria assured her. She leaned over the view of Table Mountain, then took a few steps back.

"Really extraordinary. Who taught you to paint so that up close one can see only blots of color but from a distance one recognizes the subject?"

"I taught myself to do that," Bethari explained. She was flattered by the interest her hostess showed. "First I sat in the open to look at the light and to feel the warmth on my skin. When I began to paint, I tried to reproduce these feelings in colors."

"Is this painting for sale?"

"I've never thought about it. How much are you offering?" Anna Maria was Bethari's first potential buyer and she was pleased. At the same time, the idea of parting with what she considered to be her best work pained her.

Anna Maria smiled. "Name your price."

Bethari thought feverishly. The Amsterdam Arts Academy regularly held exhibitions at which potential buyers could see the students' artwork. The prices were usually between ten and twenty gulden per picture. While Bethari had never sold anything, she wanted more than that price. It was her favorite picture and she thought it was good, whatever her father might have said. She took a deep breath and said, "Fifty gulden."

The Baroness looked astonished. "Trained artists who already have a certain reputation ask such prices."

Bethari held her gaze. "Well, it is a very fine picture; there are no others like it anywhere."

Anna Maria examined Bethari's other paintings. "Give me the one of the cat sunning itself on the steps as well then."

"Agreed," Bethari replied after briefly hesitating. The corners of her mouth twitched with pleasure. The image of the kitten was pretty but not nearly so impressive as the view of Table Mountain. And it was much smaller.

"It's a deal then." Anna Maria extended her right hand and Bethari shook it in agreement. "Come to my salon with me, and I shall pay you right away."

They went downstairs together and entered a small room facing the garden. Anna Maria took a key out of the embroidered sack on her belt and unlocked an iron strongbox.

"Here you are, *Mademoiselle* de Groot, fifty silver gulden." She counted the coins, filled a small linen sack with them and handed it to Bethari. "You bargained well. You must have inherited your business sense from your father."

Bethari placed the sack in her dress pocket. The coins clinked softly and she was pleased to feel their weight. "You are my first customer."

"Really?" Anna Maria looked surprised. "Your father will be proud of you when you tell him. I'm sure you miss him."

Bethari was silent, but she could not prevent her eyes from welling up. The rage and cruelty with which he had treated her and Rufus had disturbed her far more than the revelation that he had not been married to her mother. She did not know whether she could forgive him and feared that their once close relationship had been destroyed forever. Almost two weeks had passed since his departure and she had still not written him. She had made one attempt but found herself with nothing to say.

She flinched when she felt Anna Maria's hand on her shoulder. "Your father will return safely."

She nodded silently. Of course, she wanted her father to return safely from Ceylon but it was Hannes whom she missed. Even her painting did not provide her with solace and distraction. She lay awake nights longing for his embrace and his kisses. During the day, she worried that he might become infected with smallpox, be exposed to danger during his mission or have to suffer her father's anger.

"Why were the Colonel and soldiers sent to Ceylon? Is there a war going on? Is their job to protect my father and Hannes Hiller?"

Anna Maria shook her head. "The VOC ordered my husband to assist your father in his endeavors. I'm afraid I don't know any of the details."

"Are you aware that smallpox is rampant in Ceylon?" Bethari inquired softly. "Are you afraid for your husband?"

"He had the illness as a child. Of course, the tropical climate is detrimental to one's health but danger is part of my husband's profession. He knows how to deal with it."

Bethari frowned. "It sounds as if you don't care about what happens to him."

Anna Maria locked and replaced the strongbox as she said, "You're passing a harsh judgment, *Mademoiselle* de Groot. Army life makes it necessary for him to be away for long periods of time. Tormenting myself changes nothing."

"Do you yet love your husband?" Bethari found herself asking. Again she thought of Hannes and the encounter between him and the Baroness von Hügel that she had observed on the *Drie Gebroeders*. All of a sudden, she felt she must know.

"Does your heart belong to another?" *Please do not confide that your heart belongs to Hannes*, thought Bethari, *because mine does*.

Anna Maria cleared her throat. "Marriage means duty, loyalty and creating a good future for the children. But after a while, even the best marriage becomes routine, and love, longing and desire do not tolerate routine. That is why these feelings are seldom found in a marriage."

"I observed you and Hannes together, at an hour when a married woman might have been with her husband."

The Baroness nodded, "So that's what this is about."

"What do you mean?"

"You are in love with Hannes Hiller. And you are jealous of me."

Bethari said coolly, "Oh, I am not sure that I need be jealous. From what I saw, it appeared as though the embers of this love affair had long gone cold. If there were ever any love to speak of."

Anna Maria blanched. "I refuse comment. What may happen between Hannes Hiller and myself does not concern you in the slightest."

"I ask of you, Baroness, release him from your mind and heart! Hannes loves me and I love him. We are each other's rising sun to be adored, and I am sick 'til I see him again! Please excuse me. I must take some air." She turned on her heel and left the room.

Bethari stopped in the hallway, and briefly closed her eyes. She touched her fingers lightly to her to chest while she took in a deep breath. She had not planned this outburst. Her heart was in her mouth but she had spoken her mind, and her heart.

Bethari walked down the Heerengracht, tormented by her thoughts. She was perturbed by her quarrel with Baroness von Hügel and felt not the slightest desire to spend many months, perhaps even a whole year, in her company. She no longer understood why she had let her father lock her away! How foolish she felt, and certainly how empty, since it had cost her the opportunity to bid farewell to Hannes. Hannes ... she did not know how she would endure being without him. She longed to hear him, see, and feel him. It was all that mattered, to be in his company, and she was full of anxiety that it may never happen again.

To regain her inner peace, she had to see with her own eyes that he was well. And once she was with him, she would not let anyone displace her from his side. But Hannes was so far away, and as a rule, women were forbidden to take long journeys without a male chaperone.

I am going to try, just the same, she thought, feeling around her dress for the pocket. The sack with fifty gulden for the sale of her pictures bulged under the fabric. Giving up without a fight was not an option.

The wind whistled between the storage sheds and the workshops at the harbor. The small supply boats rowing back and forth between the pier and the mighty East Indiamen bobbed up and down on the waves like nutshells. When Bethari reached the wooden pier, the spray wet her shoes. A strong breeze grabbed her hat but she managed to save it at the last second. She held down her skirts with the other hand.

She was the only woman in sight and the workers, tradesmen and sailors eyed her surreptitiously. She raised her chin defiantly. There was no law forbidding a woman to visit the harbor. A slave came in her direction, carrying a basket of firewood. She quickly raised her hand.

"Pardon! Where can I find the harbormaster?"

"Over there, mistress." The man pointed to a narrow, gray building, barely twenty steps away, between a storage shed and a ropemaker's workshop.

She reached her goal in no time, pulled open the heavy door and stepped into the office, a small square room with filing shelves on the back wall and a desk by the window. Two men stood with their backs to Bethari.

"Here are your freight documents. The receipt for fees and tariffs is enclosed," said one as he handed several papers to the other.

"Have a safe trip, Captain, and may you have wind in your sails and a hand's width of water under your keel! When do you set sail?"

"As soon as I'm back on the ship." The man tipped his bicorne and turned to leave. He stopped short when he saw Bethari but then rushed by her and into the open without a word.

"How can I help you?" The harbormaster raised his head. His eyes grew big when he saw his visitor; women did not ordinarily visit his office.

"*Goedendag, mijnheer.*" Bethari lowered her head respectfully. "When does the next ship leave for Ceylon?"

"Why do you want to know?" The harbormaster scrutinized her with suspicion.

"Why not?" she riposted, irritated.

"Look, if you've come here to quibble with me, you can leave right now. I have enough work to do without you!" The harbormaster rustled his papers.

She forced herself to smile even though the man's gruffness annoyed her.

"I have not come here to bother you, *mijnheer*, my question is serious: when does the next ship leave for Ceylon?"

The harbormaster grumbled something and answered, "Early tomorrow with the tide, the *Petronella*, the *Oranje* and the *Harmonie* leave Table Bay for East India. The *Oranje* is departs for Ceylon, the other two for Batavia."

"So soon!" Bethari gasped. "Is there a later ship to Ceylon?"

The harbormaster laughed derisively. "Certainly, if you want to wait until March. Beginning next month, the sailers are touching in Vaals Bay. But at that time there are fewer ships from Europe anyhow."

Bethari frowned, "So I have less time than I thought. But if I hurry, I'll be ready first thing in the morning." She smiled at the harbormaster, "I would like to book a passage on the *Oranje*."

He looked at her, thunderstruck. "I must be hearing things! Since when are gracious ladies such as your good self allowed to travel alone?"

"Since when are there rules which prohibit it?" she asked snidely.

The harbormaster cleared his throat. "Well, maybe not. But no captain is going to risk upsetting his crew by allowing a woman on board without a male chaperone. Don't you know what sailors say about female passengers? They say a woman on board is bad luck."

"Sell me a ticket anyway. I pay well." She pulled the linen sack out of her dress pocket and weighed it in her hand. She had no idea how much a trip to Ceylon cost but thought it would not hurt to try to make an impression.

The harbormaster scrutinized her sternly. "Even if I wanted to–and I stress that I do not want to–the passenger cabins on the *Oranje* have been occupied since Amsterdam by employees of the Company. Who are you anyway? Give me your name!"

Tears of anger sprung to Bethari's eyes. "I almost think that it gives you pleasure to place obstacles in people's way!" She turned around, ran to the door, and slammed it shut behind her.

She stopped on the pier, pulled out a handkerchief and dried her eyes. Eight large merchant ships belonging to the Dutch East India Company seesawed in the water in Table Bay in front of her. One of them was the *Oranje* and if she wanted to get to Ceylon, she would have to be aboard it first thing in the morning.

But how? Her nimble mind danced through a list of possibilities. Should she disguise herself as a boy and try to sign on as crew? This adventurous idea appealed to her until she realized that she did not know where to find men's clothing in her size in such a short time. And the crew on the *Oranje* was no doubt complete by now. Another possibility would be to speak with the Captain personally. Like all Dutch merchant ships, the *Oranje* belonged to the VOC. If she told him that her father was the Company's finance inspector and wished her to join him, he would have to find room for her on his ship. But then he might have her father confirm her identity in Galle. And then all hope of seeing Hannes again would be dashed. She was deep in thought when she left the harbor and rushed along the Heerengracht toward town.

"Miss! Look out!"

She was startled and at the last second managed to avoid an ox cart loaded with wicker baskets of fruit and vegetables.

Without noticing, she had reached the Company garden. Several carts stood in front of the wide-open gate. Slaves pushed carts with baskets full of fruit, cabbage, nuts, and potatoes out of the garden. Overseers with loud voices directed the men toward the different ox carts, supervised the loading process and checked the goods off their lists. In the midst of this activity, some pedestrians tried to shoulder their way into the garden. Because, although its primary purpose was to provide fresh food for the ships' crews, the inhabitants of Cape Town were permitted to stroll along the wide alleys on the grounds. Old people sat on the benches, newlywed couples kissed behind the laurel bushes and mothers with small children fed breadcrumbs to the ducks.

Bethari made her way through the crowd until she noticed a young man whom she recognized. He pushed a wheelbarrow to the ox carts.

"August!" she called out and waved. "Well, this is a surprise!" The young man put down the wheelbarrow and looked in her direction. She ran up to him, laughing. "I'm Bethari. We were on the *Drie Gebroeders* together. Do you remember me?"

Finally, he nodded hesitantly. "Your leg was hurt very badly and Hannes and the Black man carried you. But later, Hannes was not kind to you," he added sadly.

Bethari remembered the evening in Vaals Bay; August sat next to her and Hannes at the campfire and heard their argument.

"That's right. But we've made up." She looked at the baskets of lemons. "Do you work in the Company garden?"

"Hannes wouldn't take me with him," August replied sadly. "He says I should look after the nice plants until he comes back."

"August! The lemons aren't going to jump into the ox cart by themselves!" One of the overseers rushed over. "What are you doing standing around? Get to work!" He gave the boy a resounding slap across the face.

"Yow! That hurts." August whimpered and held his cheek.

"Move along, halfwit!" The overseer raised his hand again.

August gave him a frightened stare, but he took the handles of his wheelbarrow and hurried away.

The overseer turned to go but Bethari blocked his way.

"How dare you slap the boy!"

"If you had not kept him from his work, I would not have had to slap him!" the overseer riposted angrily.

"I should report you to the garden supervisor!"

The overseer snorted derisively. "Go right ahead, my esteemed lady; he will tell you the same! We're in a rush here. The *Oranje* sets sail at first light tomorrow and we still have to load more than half of the provisions they ordered and take them to the harbor."

"The *Oranje*?" Bethari pricked up her ears. "Is that not the ship that departs for Ceylon?"

"Precisely. And now please excuse me. We have to finish before nightfall. Hello, hello, put the walnuts on the second cart with the apples. The first one is reserved for lemons. How many times do I have to tell you, you good-for-nothings?" He ran away.

As she watched him leave, Bethari's mind began to form an idea of how to get to Ceylon even though the ship was fully booked. She looked for August. He was just entering the garden through the gate. She gathered her skirts in her hand and ran after him.

"August, wait! I have to talk to you!"

Bethari listened intently in the impenetrable darkness but all she heard was the soft sound of waves against the ship's side. After stowing the last baskets and sacks in the lower steerage of the *Oranje*, the sailors had closed the hatch and no one had come since then. In the blackness surrounding her, she had lost all sense of time. She did know, however, that she had to get out of the cramped basket where she had been crouched under several layers of lemons, which had weighed like lead on her shoulder muscles.

She freed her hands and stretched her arms horizontally until she felt the side of the basket. Then she carefully felt her way to the top edge.

There was a thud. And then another. Two lemons rolled out of the basket and fell on the floor.

Although she knew she was alone, she anxiously held her breath.

"Yow!" a male voice interjected.

She twitched. Instinctively, she clutched two lemons in her right hand. She used her left hand to hold the edge of the basket and pull herself up abruptly.

More thuds. The lemons fell on the wooden planks like little balls.

"Yow!" a male voice again said. "Why do you throw things at me?"

Bethari thought her heart would stop from fear. Then she recognized the voice.

"August?"

"Yea," someone in close proximity said. "'Tis I! August!"

"Why are you here?" she called. "You were only supposed to cover me with lemons and make sure I wasn't discovered when the basket was carried out of the garden and lifted on to the ox cart."

"And that is what I did," he said proudly in the darkness. "I put so many yellow lemons on your head. And then I got into the cart next to your basket and went to the harbor with you. There I told them that I had to help get all the baskets on the ship." With a giggle, he added, "And then I just stayed with you."

Bethari was astonished. She would not have thought August capable of so much cunning. "Why did you not return to the garden?"

"Because I don't want that man to beat me anymore," said August. Bethari could hear the hurt in his voice. After a while, he added, "And you need a protector."

She suppressed a sigh. It remained to be seen who was going to protect whom. But first, she wanted to get out of this basket. She gathered her skirts with one hand and tried to straighten a leg. *At least my knee isn't giving me problems anymore*, she thought, relieved. However, no sooner had she lifted her foot, pain shot through her stiff muscles.

"Oh! It feels as though I'd been cut with a knife."

"You've cut yourself with a knife?" August sounded alarmed. "Are you bleeding?"

"Quiet, August. No." Bethari tried to pacify him. "I have not injured myself. I only said that because it hurts so much when I move my leg. I've been in the same position for such a long time that I am stiff. I believe you have to help me out of this basket."

"I'm already there, miss!"

August padded across the floor and collided with Bethari's basket. "Where are you?" she heard his voice.

"Here, right in front of you." She extended her arms until she felt his chest. She felt her way up to his shoulders, down to his hands and placed them around her waist. "Now you have to lift me."

"Yes, miss."

Within a few seconds she was floating upwards. She clung to his shoulders but he had already placed her gently on the floor.

"Oh, my legs," she groaned. "They're tingling horribly. If I let go of you, I think I'll fall over."

"I'm going to make sure that you do not." The boy held both of her arms. "You see, I'm protecting you."

"Well, you're very strong, that much I know." She had to laugh despite her pain. Then she suddenly had a terrifying thought.

"Do you realize that you are now a deserter, August?"

"I don't know." He sounded perplexed. "What is that?"

"A soldier who secretly runs away from his regiment. If he is caught, he is punished very severely."

There was silence. Then August asked in a trembling voice, "Will I be beaten again?"

If all they do is beat you, you'll have gotten off easy, flashed through her mind. But as she did not want to frighten the boy further, she said aloud, "Nobody will beat you, August. I shall see to that."

With a soft groan she sat down on the floor and stretched her legs. She had not expected it to be easy to travel to Ceylon as a stowaway but she had thought it possible. Now there were two of them and thus it would be doubly difficult to hide under deck for three months. But giving up was not an option.

The hatch to the lower steerage deck creaked softly as it opened. Bethari took August's hand. They cowered behind two stacked boxes in the corner of the hold. After a few seconds, Bethari straightened up and peered over the edge of the upper box.

She could not make out much because, despite the open hatch, it was so dark, but she heard wooden clogs clattering down the steps. She cautiously stretched a little higher and saw the outlines of a pair of legs in breeches. Then a male body wearing a vest and a shirt appeared, as well as a hand holding a lantern and an arm with a basket hanging from it. The man slowly felt his way down the stairs, the only person to stray into the lower steerage deck. He had come six times before, probably once a day. She assumed he was the ship's cook because he collected food for his basket and disappeared again. The last three times he had inspected the contents of the boxes and baskets more closely. She watched him smell the lemons and heads of cabbage, shaking his head and looking around in the hold. All the while he could be heard sniffing.

She knew all too well that after only a week, the smell in the place was anything but pleasant, since there was no way to dispose of their bodily waste. She had attempted to alleviate the stench by crushing lemons and drizzling the juice over their waste but the rank smell grew worse with each passing day.

The man had just reached the steerage deck when the bootsteps of a second person could be heard, followed by the light of a second lantern.

"You're right, cookie, the stench in here is atrocious!" He sounded disgusted. "Why didn't you report this sooner?"

"With all due respect, it wasn't like this at first, Chief."

"Do you think the salted meat is going bad in the vats?" the other man asked with concern in his voice. "The crew needs more than just cabbage and lemons. We're not going to be getting fresh supplies until we reach Galle."

"Spoiled meat smells different," the cook replied. "Besides, I checked all the vats before they were loaded. Quite frankly, the smell in here is that of shit, Chief!"

"So you think we have stowaways on board?"

By now the chief petty officer stood in the room. "Well, we'll find that out soon enough!" He turned toward the hatch and bellowed, "We need reinforcement! We may have some stowaways down here!"

Bethari froze. Should they surrender? August and she had gone to great trouble to arrange the boxes and baskets in the corner in order to hide behind them. Their arrangement provided a solid barrier and allowed almost no access to their part of the deck. They had a chance, however tiny, to remain undetected.

"We'll get started with the search," she heard the chief say. "From one side to the other, working toward the back."

"Maybe the stowaways are armed." The cook sounded uneasy.

The chief retorted, "And we have knives. Listen up, you cowards. Show yourselves before we slit open your bellies!"

August moved restlessly but Bethari clutched his arm and whispered, "Stay still."

The footsteps moved about the cargo area, sometimes stopping, and then starting again. She clenched her free hand, pressed it against her mouth and said a quick prayer.

"Would you look at this!" the cook called. "Their latrine's right here."

"Disgusting! But it proves you're right. It won't be long until we've got'em."

Bethari bit her knuckles and cowered even lower. The two men's footsteps came ever closer. Boxes and baskets were pushed aside until, at last, the lantern shone behind her, then was lowered slowly. Finally, two faces appeared behind the edge of the highest box.

"I knew it." The cook grinned triumphantly. "A man and a woman."

The chief pulled his knife out of his belt and pointed it at Bethari and August. "Get up and hold your hands so I can see them."

"Aye aye, sir!" August shot up, both hands stretched over his head. "Please don't slit open my belly."

Bethari got up more slowly, with partially raised hands.

"Well, aren't you a nice little pair!" The chief wrinkled his nose. "Are there any more of you stinking rats hiding down here?" She shook her head.

"My companion and I are alone and we ask for your help. We absolutely must get to Ceylon."

The man scrutinized her dispassionately. "Personally, I don't care in the slightest what you need or want. The captain is the one to decide what happens with you."

"These vermin!" The cook snorted indignantly. "How on earth did they manage to sneak on board?"

Voices could be heard from the opening of the hatch. Feet rumbled down the stairs and the chief officer and five sailors appeared. The chief turned around and snapped to attention.

"Sir! Respectfully report that the cook and I have discovered two stowaways!"

"Well done!" The officer scrutinized Bethari and August. His face expressed utter revulsion. "I'll take these culprits to the captain right away. In the meantime, you search the entire ship. I don't want us to overlook another one of these degenerates. And everything has to be cleaned meticulously. The reek down here is unbearable!"

The officer escorted Bethari and August to the captain's cabin, knocked and entered.

The captain leaned over a nautical chart that was spread out before him on the table. "I said I didn't want to be disturbed."

The chief officer snapped to attention. "Respectfully report: two stowaways were discovered on the steerage deck!"

The captain glanced at Bethari and August before turning to the officer. "Thank you, officer. I'll handle this. Have you ordered all the decks thoroughly searched to see if there are any more of these rats?"

"Yes, Captain." The officer bowed and left.

The captain shoved the chart aside. He looked at the stowaways with a stony expression. "What are you doing on my ship?"

Bethari quickly elbowed August in the ribs. *Let me handle this*, she thought.

"I tried to buy a, uh, I mean two tickets from the harbormaster but he told me the *Oranje* was completely booked. I urgently have to get to Ceylon. I simply didn't have time to wait weeks or months for the next ship."

The captain furled his bushy eyebrows. "What is the relationship between you two peculiar characters?"

August stuck out his chest. "I am Bethari's protector!"

"Is that so?" The captain leaned across the table. "And who exactly are you?"

Bethari stepped on August's foot. "Yow!" He looked at Bethari reproachfully and retracted his foot.

The captain gave Bethari an austere look. "I am more inclined to think that the protector is you. Let us begin again. Your names! Immediately!"

Bethari thought for a second. Then she said, "My name is Bethari Hiller. I am the wife of Hannes Hiller, who is in Ceylon in the city of Galle at this moment. My companion is named August. He is my husband's brother and lives with us."

"I'm Hannes' friend." August beamed at the captain.

The captain crossed his arms, leaned back in his chair, and looked at Bethari.

"Why does your story not add up?"

"I'm telling the truth. You can see for yourself that August cannot live alone. He needs our help," she protested. Above all else, she wanted to prevent the captain from probing further and discovering that August was, in fact, a deserter.

"Hm." The captain rubbed his stubble. "There's something about this that sounds fishy. On the other hand, why else would you bother with this simpleton? And why do you need to get to your husband so urgently? Why do you not wait for him at home, the way any decent wife would?"

"We've only been married one month. I cannot bear the thought of being separated from him for a year or more." Bethari cast down her eyes. "I am sick 'til I see him."

The captain drummed his fingers on the table top. "You stole onto my ship because of newlywedded yokedom? And you saddled yourself with this nicky ninny on top of it? I don't mind saying that this situation is a gallimaufry of chaos, and that is not how things are managed on this ship."

Bethari looked at him in horror. "What do you mean?"

The captain got up and slowly circled the two stowaways.

"Rats like you walk the plank."

"Walk the plank?" Bethari repeated tonelessly. "What is that?"

"You will have your hands tied behind your backs, be blindfolded and try to balance on a plank extended over the ocean. I think you can imagine what happens when you reach the end of the plank."

Bethari's neck hairs stood up. "You're not going to throw us into the ocean," she said in a tremulous voice. "You're merely trying to frighten us."

The captain scrutinized her with narrowed eyes. "I won't throw you into the ocean. You two vagabonds will take care of that yourselves."

She froze. "I don't know what you have in mind but I'm sure that it's not allowed."

The captain laughed raucously. "On my ship, I alone decide what's allowed and what's not."

There was a knock. The chief officer stuck in his head. "Respectfully report, Captain, there are no other stowaways in the hold. We're now searching the rest of the ship." He disappeared.

The captain positioned himself in front of Bethari and August, his legs spread apart. "Because you're a woman and your companion here is obviously simple-minded, I'm going to temper justice with mercy. We're still quite close to the coast of Africa. You'll be given provisions and water for one week, as well as one of the longboats. You can row to the coast in that."

"You're planning to put us out in the ocean?" Bethari cried out. "Then you might as well throw us in the water! And even if we were to make it to shore, I don't believe that there is a settlement so far east of Cape Town. We would have to make our way through the wilderness all alone."

The captain shrugged. "At least you'd have a chance."

She straightened her shoulders. "*Mijnheer*! My husband holds an important post at the honorable Company in Ceylon. When he finds out that you put me out on the ocean, he will make you pay a bitter penance a hundred times over."

The captain harrumphed. "And I'm the Emperor of China! No highly placed Company functionary would allow his wife to undertake a journey as a stowaway in the company of a simpleton."

"My husband will confirm my identity once we arrive in Galle," Bethari asserted. "And anyway, I am perfectly capable of paying for the passage for me and my companion." She knew that employees of the Company usually traveled for free but as the captain had already threatened to set her and August adrift, she thought it wise to soften him up. She took out her small sack. "There are fifty gulden here."

The captain took it and weighed it in his hand. "This will not take you far."

She did not bat an eye. "Normally, as the wife of a Company employee, I would not have to pay anything at all. But I am offering this to you as a sign of my good will and I advise you to accept my offer—while it stands."

"Very well." The captain's fist closed tightly around the sack. "I'll have a cabin made ready for you, *demoiselle*," he now answered in a markedly more courteous tone. "The simpleton stays below deck with the crew and will make himself useful. If you two strictly abide by my rules, nothing will happen to you."

CHAPTER SEVENTEEN

INDIAN OCEAN, 1788

By the beginning of August, de Groot, Hannes, and Colonel von Hügel had been traveling for three months. The *Edam* had sailed in a convoy of ten ships on the southern route to Asia. When the lookout on the port side reported the two tiny islands of Amsterdam and St. Paul, the convoy split up. Seven ships sailed toward the northeast in the direction of Java, while the *Edam* and two other sailers turned north-northeast toward Ceylon. At breakfast, on the ninety-second day of their journey, the captain informed his passengers that they would be arriving in Galle in a few days.

Subsequently, de Groot ordered Hannes and the commanding officer to his cabin for a meeting. As he unfurled a map of Ceylon on his desk, a cabin boy brought a jug of watered-down wine and three drinking vessels. De Groot, however, took out a bottle of jenever from a box next to his bed. Throughout the journey Hannes had observed how often the Netherlander reached for his brandy. He claimed that it protected him from the harmful effluvia of the hot humid air. Hannes looked at his sunken face and the waxen, perspiring skin and asked himself whether de Groot would survive the rigors of the journey.

Although it was not yet midday, the tight cabin smelled of sweat and stale air. The men took off their jackets and rolled up their shirt sleeves. Colonel von Hügel walked over to the washstand, dipped his neckcloth into the water carafe and laid it around his neck, heaving a deep sigh.

"Are we finally about to be told what is really behind your trip to Ceylon?"

De Groot ignored the snide tone and replied, "I am sure you are aware that the honorable Company has the cinnamon monopoly of Ceylon. But for some time now, cinnamon that is not ours has been turning up in considerable amounts, primarily in London. The directors have asked me to look into these activities."

"So, this is about smuggling. And why do you tell us this as we reach our destination?" Von Hügel took a sip from his vessel and grimaced. He glanced at Hannes.

"Did he know about this?"

"He collected information for me in Cape Town," de Groot said. "He found out, for instance, that there is a Polish agent."

Von Hügel slammed his vessel on the table. "Curse it! You trust an ordinary soldier, yet keep me in the dark?"

"It was you who assigned Hiller as my assistant," de Groot reminded him. "What's more, this matter is sensitive. If it becomes known that the Company can no longer control the cinnamon trade, our competition will try to seize the monopoly entirely."

"I assume you speak of the English." Von Hügel's laughter sounded brittle. "You Dutchmen lost the last war against them. Your power in India, as well as the lucrative cinnamon trade, is slipping away to them. This is not a business matter, but a question of military might. I'm here to wield strong military action against all those who are active in smuggling in Ceylon."

"That's precisely what I am not planning!" De Groot wiped his forehead with the back of his hand.

"With such an initiative we would catch only the porters, guards and low-level clerks, who turn a blind eye for a couple of gulden," Hannes interjected. "The people with power, who plan everything and collect the lion's share from the sale of smuggled goods, are left unscathed."

Von Hügel's face, already reddened from the heat, turned even darker. "And what is it you know about military tactics?"

Hannes straightened his shoulders. "In this case, it seems more than you!"

"How dare you! Show your commanding officer some respect, soldier!"

"This undertaking puts us all on an equal footing. And besides, you haven't been my commanding officer for some time now." Hannes crossed his arms obstinately.

De Groot clapped his hands. "If you gentlemen could please turn your attention back to the mission at hand! If it is to succeed, we must depend on one another and act in secrecy."

"But we must share information," Hannes objected.

De Groot nodded. "We will do so when necessary. I will determine the place and the time. Other than that, we will send messages with alternating messengers."

The colonel frowned. "There's one thing you still haven't explained to me, dear de Groot: why has the Company delegated me and one hundred soldiers for your support? It seems to me that you mean to reject my assistance."

De Groot silently stared at the map on the desk as though he wanted to bore holes in it.

Von Hügel upped the ante. "I believe it to be the wish of the directors that my men and I proceed forcefully against the smugglers. It is our duty to set an example. Only then can we discourage others from doing the same."

"We will do nothing of the kind," de Groot replied calmly. "The locals should know as little as possible about our difficulties. That might give them the idea to revolt against us."

"Not at all," von Hügel contended, "if we strike quickly and purposefully. What are the natives, compared to my perfectly trained and armed soldiers?"

"Quite a bit," de Groot retorted. "Ceylon is made up almost entirely of dense, impenetrable jungle. Completely unsuitable for military formations and battlefields. To say nothing of the climate. Once we get to Ceylon, your men will fall ill so fast, you won't be able to keep up with the body count." De Groot pulled a handkerchief from his pocket and wiped his forehead. "I'm leading this operation and will determine how to proceed. If you do not conform, you are out, you understand?"

Hannes stood up and opened the window. He felt a light breeze blow across his face. Hot, but still a breeze. He leaned against the window frame. "I believe that we're dealing with a smuggling ring because no individual is capable of conveying large amounts of cinnamon out of the country on his own. People like that know every trick there is. We will not defeat them with soldiers, but with cunning."

Von Hügel was disinclined but de Groot nodded.

"That's exactly right. I'll sum it up like this: The only thing we know absolutely is that there is a Polish agent. We must discover how the cinnamon is transferred out of the VOC's warehouses, past all the guards and customs inspectors, and transported off the island."

"Fork out some of your gulden and you'll get your information soon enough," von Hügel interjected testily.

De Groot again wiped his forehead. "Unfortunately, the honorable Company did not see fit to send me the coins that I had requested for that purpose. We will, therefore, have to come by our information stealthily. As soon as we get to Galle, each of us will move to his quarters. Colonel von Hügel and the soldiers in the barracks, Hiller and I in town."

"When will we confer again?" the colonel wanted to know.

"As soon as Hiller or I have uncovered something," said de Groot, rolling up his map.

"Considering it's taken all morning, we didn't accomplish much. *Mijnheer* de Groot, I am going to retire a little before lunch." He tromped to the door without deigning to look at Hannes.

"I wish to discuss some of the details of your course of action in Galle," de Groot informed Hannes. He poured himself some jenever and gulped it down.

"I want you to find work as a carpenter in Galle, just as you did in Cape Town. Keep your ears open for the Pole. The taverns and bordellos are probably good places to do that."

Hannes shook his head forcefully. "I shall not go to the alehouses for you. Smallpox is rampant in Ceylon and the best places to get infected are taverns and bordellos."

"The epidemic will be long gone by the time we arrive."

"That remains to be seen. Until I can be sure I will stay away from such places."

De Groot stared at him angrily. "You are under my orders. You are to do as I say."

"I am under no one's orders. Remember that." Hannes could feel his anger slowly rising.

"Never mind. Don't get excited, Hiller. But how else shall we get information about the Pole? I don't have the means for bribes." De Groot placed his hand on his stomach and breathed deeply.

"I know. You owe me my pay as well," Hannes reminded him. "Quite a sum has accrued since we set sail."

"You have nothing to do at the moment," de Groot parried. "You get paid only for working."

"Our agreement is that I am to get paid ten gulden every Monday," Hannes countered calmly. "And don't think for one moment that I am going to let you off the hook."

De Groot gnawed at his lower lip. "I shall keep my word. But you must provide me with first-rate information."

"Agreed." Hannes pushed away from the window. "But I won't have you meddling. I'll do it my way, do you hear?"

Hannes stomped up to the deck. He was angry that de Groot had once again treated him like an errand boy, not a collaborator. He looked for a place along the starboard railing in the shade of the main sail, laid his arms on the wood of the railing and looked out at the ocean. Far ahead of the *Edam* he could see the two other ships in their convoy, two small, dark dots on the horizon of the vast Indian Ocean. The color of the water was the same vibrant blue as the sky. There was not a cloud anywhere on the horizon.

The journey had begun in pleasantly cool conditions, with occasional rain. But ever since they crossed the 23rd degree latitude, the temperature rose steadily. Not a drop of rain had provided relief. And yet the air was so saturated with humidity that everything, even the sheet with which Hannes covered himself at night, felt clammy.

He thought of Bethari, as he had done every day since they departed from Cape Town. Initially, his thoughts were filled with bitterness because, while he had come to find magic and tenderness in their connection, she did not feel the same. In fact, she banished him from her life most carelessly. But after almost three months, his rancor gave way to confusion. Bethari was not like the baroness, who had simply sought a pleasurable adventure; Bethari always expressed kindness and interest. She even forgave him for his unjust and close-minded behavior after the *Drie Gebroeders* shipwreck. He asked himself why she had concealed from him the fact that she would not travel to Ceylon, and why she had not even bade him farewell. No matter how he racked his brain, he found no explanation. The farther away the *Edam* took him from her, the greater his longing.

"Master?"

Hannes was startled. "Rufus! Sweet Mother of God, must you frighten me like this? And what is this mullock; I have asked you not to address me so damned formally!"

The servant bowed slightly. "You are too kind, Mr. Hannes."

Hannes grinned. "Does not the heat bother you at all? If I had to wear a turban, my brain would start to boil. Is it this hot in Ceylon?"

Rufus smiled. "I have never been there but I imagine it is. Yesterday the master said that we shall arrive during monsoon season."

"Monsoon season?"

"That means the season of great rain. I experienced it often in Java. It comes every year for several months, drenches the earth with water and makes the plants grow in the fields. But it can also transform rivers into raging torrents in which humans and animals drown. The mud flows from the mountains into the valleys and buries entire villages."

"That sounds like a Biblical flood." Hannes looked at him in disbelief.

Rufus nodded. "That's what my master says too." He looked over his shoulder and leaned toward Hannes, "I have some important information. About the mistress."

"What?" Hannes snapped. "And you've waited until we've been at sea for three months?"

"Forgive me, but I had to be cautious. My master is watching me."

Hannes looked at Rufus in surprise. "I had the impression that he trusted you."

The servant's face grew dark. "My master trusts no one."

Hannes grabbed his arm. "You know how much Bethari means to me. If she gave you a message for me and you have kept it to yourself until now, I'm going to wring your neck."

Rufus shook his head. "She is well but was prevented from giving me a message for you."

Hannes tightened his grip. "Why? What happened?"

"Rufus!" De Groot stomped down the steps to the afterdeck and came directly toward them.

"At your service, master!" Rufus quickly freed his arm from Hannes' hand and stepped away from him.

"I've been looking all over for you," de Groot blustered. "Why are you loitering about on the deck?"

"Forgive me, master, but this morning you complained of stomach pains. I wanted to ask the cook for some broth for you. It will do you good."

"Where is the broth?" De Groot pointed to Rufus' empty hands. "Do you deceive me again?"

"No, master." The servant lowered his head. "I was just on my way."

De Groot waved his hands about petulantly. "I don't want any broth in this heat. And now, away with you."

"Yes, master." Rufus hurried away.

De Groot gave Hannes a hostile look. "What did my servant want with you?"

"Nothing. As he told you, he was on his way to get some broth for you. I stopped him and asked how he could bear to wear a turban in this clime." Hannes squinted out at the ocean, pretending not to notice the Netherlander's strange behavior. His mind reeled. Why did de Groot sound him out about Rufus? And what had occurred at his house before their departure?

He pushed his shirt sleeves up past his elbows. "Does your servant no longer please you?"

"Where do you get that idea?" De Groot looked at him suspiciously.

"You were rather harsh with him just now."

"A servant's job is to serve," de Groot snorted. "If Rufus continues to disobey my orders, he will earn a whipping."

"He fetches broth for you and you threaten to whip him?"

"Are you one of those who advocate for these newfangled ideas of equality and liberty?"

Hannes shrugged his shoulders. "That does not sound wrong to someone like me; I was not born to riches and privilege."

"You speak as my daughter does," de Groot grunted.

Hannes threw him an oblique glance. Was now a good time to find out what had happened at the de Groot house? He asked, "Does your daughter not accompany you due to the outbreak of smallpox?"

De Groot stared out at the sea, his lips pressed together into thin line. Finally, he replied, "You are to concentrate on your tasks in Galle and I shall worry about the rest."

After the midday meal, Hannes looked for a quiet place on the quarterdeck. He wanted to think without disruption and the best way for him to do that was when his hands were busy. Before him on the planks he placed a bowl of warm water and a clean linen cloth, both of which he had been given by the cook. He felt for his mother's chain, carefully pulled it over his head and looked at it. Not only had the silver cross become tarnished but the chain too was unsightly with grime. He lowered the two into the water, and rubbed vigorously with the cloth.

It had been almost two years since he had seen his mother in Württemberg. The money he had sent her must have arrived. He hoped that it made her life more comfortable. As soon as he returned from Ceylon, he would send more.

He took the chain out of the water and examined it. *I should write her another letter*, he thought, *so that she knows I still exist.* As he polished the cross, which began to gleam once again, his thoughts wandered to his impending mission in Ceylon. It was obvious that de Groot did not yet know how to put the cinnamon smugglers out of business.

When it comes to gathering information, he relies on me completely, yet he cannot say thank you. Again, anger flared up inside him. The Netherlander was growing altogether more and more irascible. Initially, Hannes had attributed this to his uncontrolled tippling. He had often thought that de Groot looked unwell, and today Rufus confirmed that de Groot was in severe pain. If he were seriously ill, it would make their mission in Ceylon all the more challenging.

Hannes returned the chain to its place around his neck and under his shirt. He had the distinct feeling that Rufus feared his master. He began to suspect that something had occurred in Cape Town between Bethari and her father, and that Rufus knew what that was.

After returning the bowl and cloth to the galley, Hannes hastened to the cabins on the afterdeck. De Groot's accommodations were directly behind the captain's mess on the right side. He expected to find Rufus there, but the area in front of the door was empty. Hannes bit his lower lip. He urgently wanted to speak with the servant to find out what had happened to Bethari.

At that moment, he heard a commotion in de Groot's cabin and immediately placed his ear to the door.

"If you think for one moment that I believe that nonsense about the broth, you mistake me!" de Groot raged. "Why did you huddle with Hiller?" he slurred.

"Master, I—"

The rest of his sentence was absorbed by the sound of heavy steps and de Groot's bellowing. "Did you try again to bring him news of my daughter?"

"I did not see the mistress after you chained me in the stable and locked her up!"

"Do not feed me this Banbury story! Lies! Three days in the stable did not teach you? I want to know how she got out of her room and to the stable!"

"She did not, master," Rufus protested. "I swear it to God!"

"And I think that she secretly gave you a letter for Hiller! Where did you hide it, you miserable bastard?"

Hannes heard a muffled clapping sound before Rufus groaned, "Even though you beat me, master, I swear that your daughter did not give me any message for Hannes Hiller."

"We shall find out," de Groot thundered. "Undress!"

The silence sounded unending to Hannes. He heard only the blood rushing in his ears and his heart racing as though he had sprinted across the deck. Should he enter de Groot's cabin, help the servant, and interrupt this humiliation? After what he had heard, he thought de Groot capable even of killing his servant. He placed his hand on the door handle, then heard de Groot's voice say, "Dress yourself."

"No letter. Now do you believe me, master?"

"I cannot prove otherwise. But hear me well, Rufus, because this is my last warning to you: my daughter shall have no contact with Hiller. I will not suffer her to sully her reputation in such a way. Furthermore, I also forbid you all further contact with him. You are not to speak to him unless I expressly instruct you to do so. Is that understood?"

"Yes, master."

Hannes heard steps approach the door and withdrew quickly. He quickly opened the door of the cabin opposite and slipped in just before de Groot appeared. Through the narrow slit he left open, he watched de Groot unsteadily making his way down the corridor.

He was stunned by what he had just heard. At the same time, he felt happier than he had for a long time because he knew that Bethari still loved him.

CHAPTER EIGHTEEN

GALLE, CEYLON, 1788

Three days later the sailor in the lookout shouted: "Land, ho!"

Hannes ran to the bow. The first thing he saw was a gray veil of clouds floating in the distance above the blue ocean. Next, the southern tip of Ceylon appeared to rise out of the Indian Ocean and finally, as the ship approached, Galle came into view. The fortified town was situated on a rocky peninsula. It was surrounded on three sides by the ocean and on the fourth by dense green jungle. It was protected by ramparts fortified with cannons and a tall granite wall.

"The defenses are pitiful. They will never withstand an attack from the sea."

Hannes turned his head. Von Hügel and de Groot stood next to him. The colonel looked through his telescope, then handed it to de Groot.

"The ocean is to blame for the lamentable condition," the Netherlander said, after having examined the entrenchments thoroughly. "The salt water and surf assault fortifications so much that repairs are unending."

The captain joined the three men.

"Well, the fort commander will be pleased with our arrival. My entire hold is filled with granite that he ordered over a year ago. Pity that it must be unloaded. It made for good ballast."

By now the *Edam* sailed along the coast. Hannes looked at the holes the ocean had worn in the fortifications. The ramparts were washed out and the walls broken down. Yet he saw almost no workers making repairs.

A shrill whistle sounded. The chief officer on the main deck bellowed, "Mainsail backwind! We have to slow down! Ready to reef the sails!" A little while later the *Edam* reached a long stretch of coast on which the harbor was located, surrounded by ramparts flying the red, white, and blue flag of the Netherlands. Warehouses and workshops lined the shore, as in Cape Town. Behind those, Hannes saw the red-tiled roofs of Galle and the white walls of a church, and a tower looming above them. Houses crowded the rocky little peninsula. The town seemed squeezed between the ocean to the south and the jungle to the north. The harbor was considerably less busy than the one in Table Bay. The only ships anchored here were two big East Indiamen, a few two-masters, and some rowboats.

"Here comes the harbormaster." The captain pointed to a boat rowing toward the *Edam*. "He's got the pilot with him."

"We need a pilot?" Hannes asked. It seemed to him that the wide bay offered more than enough room to enter the harbor.

"Take a look at the dark patches in the water. Only someone with intimate knowledge of the conditions here can circumnavigate them." The captain pointed to the harbor entrance and now Hannes, too, could see that underneath the clear, light blue surface of the water lurked a rocky menace. Unlike the rough South African coast, the rocks here had been polished by the water but still presented a treacherous situation for every ship.

Again the whistle sounded. The chief officer bellowed, "Lower the jack ladder!"

Two sailors ran to the railing with a rolled-up rope ladder, attached it to the railing and lowered it along the exterior of the ship. Two men used it to climb aboard and introduced themselves to the captain as the harbormaster and the pilot.

The pilot immediately went to the helmsman on the afterdeck. The harbormaster stayed with the captain and leafed through his files. "What is your cargo?"

"Blocks of granite, tools and household goods. And a box of Bibles and hymnals," the captain answered. "Oh, and we also have three sacks of mail on board."

The harbormaster took notes with a graphite pencil.

"Commander Sluijsken has been waiting for the granite. It is urgently needed for the repairs of the city ramparts. Unfortunately, we've had hardly any workers since the smallpox epidemic."

"Is it that bad?" de Groot asked. The harbormaster nodded. "We tried to isolate the sick in the hospital but the epidemic spread like wildfire. Hardly a household in Galle has been spared. Commander Sluijsken even had to postpone his youngest child's baptism because the parish priest died. We finally have a clergyman again. A new one came from Colombo with the governor a few days ago."

"The governor is in Galle?" de Groot sounded surprised.

The harbormaster nodded. "He wanted to get an idea of the situation here. He has already visited the hospital."

"So the epidemic is over?" Hannes inquired.

"By and large, yes. But in the harbor, there's still the odd case here or there. Therefore, I urge you to stay away from certain establishments."

"I shall have my soldiers march directly from the ship to the barracks," von Hügel declared. "There will be no passes for the time being."

"My men will remain on board," said the captain. "Once they're ashore, it will be impossible to keep them away from the brothels and taverns. And so, harbormaster, I suggest we head to the freight hold. Then we drop anchor and unload as quickly as possible. I don't want to stay in the vicinity of the smallpox epidemic any longer than I need to."

"Kind of a backwater, this Galle," Hannes declared once the harbormaster and the captain had left. "How many people do you think live here? Eight hundred, a thousand?"

"According to my files it says somewhere that almost two thousand people live here. But that was before the smallpox outbreak," de Groot replied. "And don't be fooled by the small area of the town. After Batavia, Galle is the Company's most important harbor. Even elephants are shipped from here, and these warehouses," he pointed to the long buildings in the bay, "temporarily store the entire cotton output of India before it is transported to Europe. In addition to ivory, coconuts and, of course, cinnamon."

"Coconuts?" Hannes laughed. "I've never heard of such things."

"Their flesh is pleasantly sweet and their water refreshes you in the heat. You must take some general rules to heart if you want to survive this climate. First: get yourself a thin net to hang over your bed at night so that the mosquitoes don't bite you. Second: drink only boiled water. And third: follow the example of the natives. Forego excessive consumption of meat and opt instead for steamed vegetables and rice."

"Rice? What is rice?"

"It's a grain cultivated all over the tropics. Once boiled in salt water, it is quite palatable."

"If you say so," Hannes grimaced. "Since you've lived in this climate before, I shall learn from you."

"You shall not regret it." De Groot took a pinch of snuff.

Hannes observed him askance. It appeared as if the Netherlander had calmed down after his outburst three days ago. Perhaps he was simply exhausted from the heat. At least Rufus had not suffered any more from his fits of anger. Hannes had seen the servant in front of de Groot's door, upright and impeccably dressed as usual. He had asked Rufus if all was well and the servant had politely answered in the affirmative. He had said nothing about the dispute with his master. Hannes had the impression that he wished to discuss neither that nor Bethari, and so he did not intrude. He did not wish to cause Rufus any additional trouble.

Though unable to discuss Bethari with anyone, Hannes thought about her daily. Ever since discovering that loved him, Hannes felt empowered. He decided to fight for their love as much as she had fought for it. Until he saw her again in Cape Town, he must focus on his work.

He placed his elbows on the railing and looked out at the bay.

"Do you think there is so little activity here because of smallpox?"

"Quite possible." De Groot tucked away his snuff box.

"The warehouses might be bursting at the seams. The two East Indiamen might be anchored here because they are going to take on cinnamon. But they also might be coffee ships from Mocha, taking on provisions before returning to Europe."

"And what about the two-masters?"

"They belong to small merchants and commercial agents and usually commute between Ceylon and Java to provide the Dutch in the colonies with provisions."

"Perhaps one of these vessels belongs to our agent."

De Groot looked at him in astonishment. "What makes you say that?"

"They look agile and fast and are small enough to head into hidden coves and then blend into the vast ocean afterwards."

"You could be right." De Groot frowned. "Their hold is sufficiently large to transport cinnamon."

Hannes glanced at the long warehouses. "Do you think those are full of cinnamon? Is it possible that our agent has sold off all the cinnamon to the English by now?"

De Groot grimaced as though he felt a fresh attack of stomach pain coming on. "You imagine the worst. On the other hand, whatever it is, I think the English are capable of it."

"Where is cinnamon cultivated, anyway?" Hannes inquired. "On plantations?"

"The trees actually grow wild in the jungle here and they belong to the king of this island. Only the Sinhalese workers know where to find them."

De Groot thought about the extensive files he had read on the journey to Cape Town, to familiarize himself with the topic of his mission. "Several years ago, Governor van de Graaff cleared land along the coast and started trial plots. As far as I know, the harvests have not been satisfactory. In the beginning, the trees were planted too closely together to develop properly. This mistake was corrected but the trees are still dying and no one seems to know the reason."

"Why does the governor not employ Sinhalese people as growers? They obviously know best what the trees need."

"It's not that easy. The Sinhalese consider their king holy, and working for him is a religious duty. We, on the other hand, are foreign intruders from the other side of the world. They tolerate us in their country. Nothing more."

Hannes looked across the harbor, at the red rooftops, and across the jungle, all the way to the clouds that gathered to become a seething, dark mass on the horizon. This land was more alien than anything else he had seen on his journey thus far. He wondered if this was the place where he would find the paradise the duke's recruiter had promised him, almost two years ago in Tübingen.

The first time Hannes and de Groot agreed to meet was at lunchtime, two weeks to the day after they disembarked from the *Edam*. Hannes suggested a meeting at the church. Although it was situated in the immediate vicinity of the commander's office and the Governor's Residence, anyone who watched them enter the church would take them for two believers seeking meditation, stillness, and prayer. In addition, they were unlikely to be seen at the church during lunchtime, when everyone else was busy with their own meal.

Hannes arrived with the twelfth strike of the clock. One of the monsoon storms, the power of which still filled Hannes with amazement, gathered over the town. As he entered the graveyard, lightning flashed and the first heavy raindrops fell from the heavy, slate-colored clouds. He ran up the steps to the entrance and slipped inside the house of worship just in time, before the skies opened up.

As he expected, the church was empty. De Groot was nowhere to be seen. The forecourt was already several inches under water and the street was flooded, despite the canal that one of the commander's predecessors had built. Then he spotted the Netherlander. His shoulders hunched; he ran toward the entrance. He made the water around him splash with every step.

"God, how I detest this weather! My house is just a stone's throw away and yet I'm soaked to the bone." De Groot took cover under the portal and shook himself. His black suit was soaked; raindrops dripped from his wig and flowed out of his shoes.

Hannes was tempted to grin because he had stayed dry while de Groot looked as though he had been thrown into the Indian Ocean. "Don't worry. At least the water is warm. Do you know what? I have even gone outside and stood still in such a downpour before. It's a wonderful feeling to have the sweat washed off one's body like that."

"Don't let me stop you," de Groot countered caustically. "I'll be happy to wait. It won't take long for you to be as drenched as I am."

"No offense meant," Hannes said peaceably. "I was lucky and you weren't, that's all. Incidentally, your advice about the mosquito net has proven very useful. Without that protection, those monsters would suck me dry at night."

A thunderclap drowned out his last words. De Groot took off his soaked wig and ran his hand over his thinning hair.

"Let us move away from the entrance."

They crossed the interior of the church. Above them the rain pelted the roof and absorbed the sound of their steps. The lightning periodically illuminated the congregation's carved wood benches along the side wall. Tombstones engraved with skulls, skeletons and scenes from the Biblical apocalypse were set on the floor.

De Groot turned into the transept in front of the pulpit, with the simple communion table on one side and the organ on the other. He stopped in the farthest corner, where they were least likely to be seen.

"So, Hiller, how did you fare? Did you find a job?"

"That was easy." Hannes moved his hand dismissively. "The master in the wharf is desperately looking for carpenters because he lost almost all of his journeymen to smallpox. That's the reason I easily found a room with an older widow, whose husband and son died in the epidemic. I told her that the Company hired me as a carpenter and that I liked her house because it's not far from the wharf. My room is cheap and comfortable and the landlady is a nice woman who cooks well. So it wasn't too terrible that the very first night I found a snake under my bed. And I keep the shutters closed so the monkeys don't come inside and cause all kinds of mischief. They are crafty beasts! When I leave the house, they sit in the palm tree in front and throw coconuts at me. I reckon they don't like being locked out. But their missiles are tasty." He grinned.

De Groot looked impatient. "Did you just have fun with the monkeys or did you actually attend to our mission?"

"I could ask you the same thing!" The Netherlander's arrogance always annoyed Hannes.

De Groot cleared his throat. "The day before yesterday I paid my respects to the fort commander. He was appalled when he heard how much money the Company is losing to smuggled cinnamon, and he pledged his unmitigated support. He agrees that proceeding in a covert fashion is likely to lead to success."

"Talk is cheap. After all, huge amounts of cinnamon disappeared from this island right past his administration."

"If you're intimating that the fort commander doesn't have a handle on his administration, I have to disappoint you. He is keenly interested in the success of my mission and has already made all relevant books and records available to me. He has the most senior warehouse manager and the most senior overseer of the cinnamon peelers report to me so that I can question them at length."

"Yes, but have you had any success?" Hannes wanted to know.

"Unfortunately, not yet," de Groot replied. "And what about you?"

"I may have a lead." Hannes crossed his arms on his chest and leaned against the stone wall behind him. "And I witnessed cinnamon being smuggled."

"You did what?" De Groot's surprised exclamation could be heard over the thunder.

But Hannes stopped him. "It wasn't smuggling on a grand scale. And probably not of any significance to us."

"Still, tell me exactly what you observed," de Groot pressed him.

"I was called to one of the two East Indiamen to replace a broken yardarm. While I was on the ship, it was being loaded with cinnamon. I saw how all the cinnamon leaving Ceylon is weighed in front of the cargo hatch. During this process, the weighmaster overlooks the odd bale. The sailors hastily put it aside and pay a small sum for it. Does the VOC know about that?"

De Groot nodded in resignation. "What you're describing happens from time to time. The men view the smuggling as compensation for the harshness and uncertainty of the East India trips. The captains let them get away with it because they have to rely on every hand to ensure that the ship and its freight arrive safe and sound at the home port. The directors, too, abstain from bringing the culprits to court. This small-scale smuggling does not justify the costs. I certainly hope that this is not your so-called lead."

Hannes propped one foot against the wall. "Well, as I said, this was an observation I made incidentally. As soon as I found my job, I asked around for our Pole. There is a man in Galle who's called 'the Pole' because he had once been employed by a Polish merchant who traded wares between Ceylon, Batavia, and Manila. He is, in fact, a Portuguese man who took over the business after his master died. At this time, he trades elephants for the king. He has a ship built expressly for that purpose, the *Estrela*, one of the two-masters you saw in the harbor."

"Hm," de Groot grumbled. "What's his name?" Hannes took out a crumpled piece of paper and unfolded it. "Domla–uh, Domlau–re–nzoo ... Sweet Mother of God, names like this shouldn't be allowed!"

"Let me see." De Groot snatched the paper from him and tried to make out the scrawls. "That might be Dom Laurenzo Carlos Olivero de Mascarenhas. But do you think that he is really our agent?"

"I mean to find out." Hannes took the paper and tucked it up his sleeve.

"An elephant is going to be loaded in one week. Before that can happen, its cage has to be repaired. Apparently, the last elephant damaged it. I have offered to assist with the repairs."

"Fair enough, but how does that help us?"

"I'm going to look around the ship and keep my ears open. I might even meet the Pole. Whatever happens, there will be a lot of opportunities to find out all sorts of interesting things."

"I don't know." De Groot looked doubtful.

Hannes looked at him provocatively. "Have you ever considered the fact that the hold of a ship, even that of a small two-master, is not nearly filled with one elephant?"

"Setting out with only one elephant on board would, indeed, not be cost-efficient," de Groot conceded. "But who says that several elephants are not being loaded?"

"I say," Hannes countered. "Because I asked the master and he confirmed that only one elephant cage is in the hold of the *Estrela*."

De Groot watched the rain streaming down the window on the other side of the church. "I'm not completely convinced of your theory but we don't have any better leads."

"You're mistaken," Hannes replied. "It is a very good lead, or do you think there are many Poles in Ceylon, or men who are called 'the Pole'? Our agent has got to be Charlie Peck's man."

CHAPTER NINETEEN

GALLE, CEYLON, 1788

"Good work!" The wiry little man with the sunburned face and the black ponytail shook the braces on the elephant crate, each as thick as a man's thigh. Then he checked the fit of the ropes with which the crossbars and vertical posts were tied.

"This one here must be tied again. It will not hold." He pushed through two fingers and gave one of the ropes a slight jolt.

Hannes stepped forward. "I'll take care of it."

For almost a week, he had been working on the *Estrela*, a two-mast brigantine belonging to a man known in Galle as 'the Pole'. Today he finally stood face to face with him.

The Pole nodded briefly. "Make sure you thoroughly apply lots of pitch so that the elephant can't open it with its trunk. Those beasts might look ungainly but they're clever and nimble."

"I'll handle it," Hannes answered. "Any idea yet when the elephant is being loaded?"

The Pole's dark eyes looked Hannes up and down. "I value workers who do decent work–and don't ask unnecessary questions."

Hannes smiled. "I cannot imagine how such a huge animal gets over the railing and into the hold. I assume it does not clamber up ladders and stairs?"

The Pole grinned and revealed a row of white teeth. "He can't clamber but he can fly–with the help of belts on the hoist of the main mast."

"Will you need me when the elephant comes aboard?" Hannes asked hopefully. "Perhaps it will step on something that needs to be repaired."

The Pole shook his head. "When the time comes, only his *mahouts* and the sailors operating the crane can be present. The procedure makes the animal nervous; any additional people could make it rage. And a kick or even just a blow with its trunk can kill you." When he saw Hannes' disappointed face, he gave him an encouraging slap on the shoulder. "Watch the spectacle from the harbor. All of Galle will be assembled and you won't miss a thing."

He turned then to the ship's carpenter. "How long before you complete the cage?"

"As soon as we knot the rope again, all we have to do is saw the beam to close the cage."

"Dom Laurenzo! You have a visitor!" The captain thundered down the steps to the hold. Hannes knew that his name was van Schouten and that he, like most of his crew, was Dutch. Yet the *Estrela* sailed under a Portuguese flag. Van Schouten ran to the Pole and whispered a few words to him. Hannes understood nothing but indistinct mumbling.

"Did he say what he wanted?" the Pole inquired.

The captain replied, "No. He wishes to discuss the matter with you personally."

The Pole frowned. "I'm counting on you," he told Hannes and the ship's carpenter before hastening away with the captain.

"Must be someone important for him to drop everything like that. Do you know what it is about?" Hannes probed.

"Do I look like a clairvoyant? Must have something to do with the elephant." The ship's carpenter tugged on the loose rope.

Hannes realized that the man would not provide any information, so he retrieved the bucket of pitch and a brush from the corner of the hold.

The two sailors who had been setting up sandbags since morning grinned at him.

"Ahoy, friends," Hannes greeted them. "Do you distribute ballast?"

"Nay, the sand goes in the elephant cage," said one of them. "The animals like playing with it. They suck it up with their trunks and throw it on their backs." He gave a demonstration.

Hannes laughed. "I'm sure a creature like that gets ravenous!"

"And thirsty," the second sailor added. "He'll drink an entire barrel of water a day and guttle colossal heaps of palm leaves."

"The hold must be filled to the brim with elephant food then."

The sailor doubled up with laughter. "Oh, certainly!"

"Hey, Hannes! You're not here to chew the fat! Get to work!" the ship's carpenter shouted.

"On my way!" Hannes, disappointed, took the bucket of pitch and a brush and walked through the hold. Perhaps he had been mistaken; perhaps it was truly only the elephant and nothing more to transport. If so, he would have to re-start his search from the beginning.

A gong sounded and a voice at the entrance to the hold called, "Come and get it!"

The sailors ran up the steps and the ship's carpenter looked at Hannes, "Join us for chow, Hannes?"

He shook his head. "No, today I prefer to stay and finish the cage. I wager that the Pole will return to check our work. Anyway, the meal I'll be getting from my landlady tonight is worth waiting for. I need to arrive with an empty stomach."

"I hope your landlady is as pretty as her food is delicious." The ship's carpenter grinned.

"Nonsense, the Widow Kleijn is older than my mother! And now, off with you!" Hannes made a movement as if to push him away.

"No need to tell me twice!" The ship's carpenter ran up the steps.

No sooner was Hannes alone than he placed the bucket of pitch on the floor and climbed up the side of the elephant cage as though the cross-braces were steps on a ladder. He stopped when his hair touched the dark wooden beam of the ceiling because he knew the captain's cabin was directly above. He turned his head on the side, with one ear almost touching the ceiling, and listened intently.

Heavy steps stomped above. Next, an unfamiliar man's voice said, "You're a savvy scoundrel, Dom Laurenzo. Your idea to use the elephant as camouflage was splendid! Will we be able to load the bull at the appointed time?"

"Everything proceeds according to plan, *Mijnheer* Sluijsken," the Pole replied.

Sluijsken, Hannes reflected and furrowed his brow. *Where have I heard that name before?* And then he remembered: it is what the harbormaster called the fort commander!

He pricked up his ears as he heard the Pole continue, "I was informed this morning that the elephant arrives in two days. We set sail as soon as it is on board. In one week, we'll unload the elephant in the port of Travancore, and from there we proceed to Ari Atoll, where the English await."

"And tomorrow we bring the cinnamon aboard?" the captain inquired.

"Yes, *mijnheer*. By that time the carpenter from the wharf will be gone and we'll be alone again. How go your preparations? Are your porters ready?"

"Perfectly. The cinnamon's already been packed. Just this morning I inspected all one hundred twenty bales of palm leaves. There is no way for anyone to suspect that they contain anything but elephant food."

"How extraordinarily fortunate it is that your residence is located at the gates of Galle," the captain interjected.

The fort commander laughed heartily. "That, my dear Captain van Schouten, is not luck, but design. I had the mansion built specifically at this location so that we would have a place to store our cinnamon in close proximity to the harbor."

"And no one would come up with the idea of searching your grounds for secret storehouses of cinnamon," the Pole added.

Again, the commander chuckled. "How would they, since I'm the one who would have to order such a search?"

"And someone would have to be aware that cinnamon is being smuggled," Captain van Schouten added.

Hannes could no longer suppress an exultant grin. "*Sweet Mother of God*," he said to himself softly. "*I've just uncovered something really big.*"

There were a few moments of silence above him. Finally, Sluijsken said, "In fact, someone in Amsterdam is, aware of the smuggling itself, if not the details. The Lords Seventeen do not yet know how their cinnamon is getting to the English. To find out, they've sent over a spy, someone by the name of de Groot."

"Holy nipples of Neptune!" van Schouten cursed. "Maybe we should let him quietly disappear?"

"Not yet," the fort commander replied. "It might raise even more questions in Amsterdam. I gave de Groot access to our official books for the last twenty-five years. That will occupy him for weeks. And I've advised him to speak to a few people, none of whom can tell him anything because they don't know anything, of course."

Van Schouten roared with laughter but the Pole said, "One of these days, this de Groot is going to realize that his search is fruitless."

"When that happens, I'll throw him another nugget," Sluijsken countered. "Incidentally, I've invited him to watch the loading of the elephant. I shall do my best to suppress my laughter when a ship filled with cinnamon is anchored right under his nose!"

This time, all three of them chuckled. Then Sluijsken continued, "The ship on which de Groot arrived also brought one hundred soldiers from the Cape Colony. But this is no cause for concern either. The commanding officer, a certain Colonel von Hügel, assured me during his first official visit that their mission is to replace the soldiers of the garrison who were lost during the smallpox epidemic. And with that, gentlemen, I bid you farewell. My wife wishes to discuss our son's baptism with me. We will see each other again upon your return from Ari Atoll. Dom Laurenzo, Captain van Schouten, I wish you a safe trip and look forward to future lucrative business dealings with our English partners!"

Hannes heard footsteps then a door close. The Pole said, "I shall take another look at the elephant cage."

When he came down the stairs to the hold a little while later, Hannes stood in front of the crate, busily stirring the pitch in his bucket. He could hardly wait to give his report to de Groot.

"Hey you!" Hannes approached a young boy who sat on the pier, dangling his legs over the edge, his fishing pole at the ready. "How would you like to earn a little money?" He loosened the opening of the money sack on his belt and fished out a copper coin.

The boy beamed and nodded enthusiastically.

"I want you to deliver two messages for me." Hannes pulled a graphite pencil from behind his ear and a scrap of paper from his work apron. He tore the paper in two and scribbled something on each half. He gave the boy the first piece.

"Take this to the barracks and give it to Colonel von Hügel."

"Barracks," the boy repeated. "Colonel von Hügel."

"Very good," Hannes praised him and gave him the second piece.

"Now, do you know the house behind the church yard? The one that has the tree with red blossoms in front of the porch?"

The boy stretched his arm high. "Red flowers up to the roof."

"Exactly. *Mijnheer* de Groot lives in that house. This message is for him."

"*Mijnheer* de Groot." The boy stuck his fishing pole between two planks on the pier and stood up. Hannes gave him the copper coin. "You must not give these messages to anyone else. And now, hurry!"

When the child disappeared through the city gates, Hannes proceeded to the wharf on the western end of the harbor.

"You're just in time," the master said when he saw him. "Someone is asking for you."

A bearded man appeared behind the master. His long, wide pants, short jacket and sunburned skin identified him as a sailor. He introduced himself to Hannes as the boatswain of the *Oranje*. "My captain wishes to have a word with you."

"What about?" Hannes frowned.

"That's all I can tell you. Only the captain can say more. Come with me."

Hannes followed the sailor to a little rowboat that was tied up to the pier, though he could not imagine what this strange captain could want to say to him. He had never heard of a ship named *Oranje*. Maybe it was a misunderstanding?

The boatswain rowed over to the *Oranje*, a large East Indiaman anchored at the southern end of the bay. She must have arrived while Hannes worked on the *Estrela*. He followed the boatswain up the rope ladder onto the ship and was taken to the captain's cabin.

After the boatswain had left, he knocked, entered, and froze. "Sweet Mother of God! I must be losing my mind!"

In the middle of the cabin stood the captain, with Bethari and August next to him.

"Hannes!" Bethari tried to rush over to him but the captain was quicker and blocked her. His eyes rested on Hannes' leather work apron and tool belt. "This one here is supposed to be a high-ranking functionary of the honorable Company? He is a workman! And it has yet to be established whether you are his wife and the simpleton is his brother. I think, miss, you have spun quite a yarn here."

Hannes was thunderstruck as he stared at Bethari. She placed her finger on her mouth and he nodded imperceptibly. Whatever had caused Bethari and August to be on this ship and whatever might have taken place there, he would deal with it. And thus, he took a deep breath and declared, "My name is Hannes Hiller. I am a carpenter in the employ of the Dutch East

India Company. I demand that you release my wife and my brother."

The captain grinned broadly. "If you say that these two good-for-nothings here are who they say they are, I'll take your word for it. I found them in the hold of my ship because they wanted a free ticket to Galle. I could have thrown them into the ocean and nobody would have faulted me. But I'm not like that. I've been supporting them for all this time and I'm due some compensation."

Hannes placed his hand on the money sack on his belt. "How much do you ask for their release?"

"Fifty gulden."

Without hesitation, Hannes emptied his money sack on the captain's desk. "Here are sixteen gulden and twenty-five stuiver. That's all I have."

The captain shook his head. "That won't do."

"I've already given him all my savings," Bethari called out. "Fifty gulden. And August worked the entire time. He helped the cook."

Hannes crossed his arms across his chest. "I see. This is how you support people on your ship."

"You're in no position to bargain with me," the captain said harshly. "Either I get fifty gulden or you can visit your wife and brother in prison!"

Without taking his eyes off the captain, Hannes rolled his shirt sleeves up to his elbow. "I suggest you let my wife and my brother go right now. Unless you wish to find yourself on the floor with a broken nose. We carpenters are known for our strong fists."

The captain's eyes darted to a hand bell on his desk but Hannes noticed and quickly seized it. "No one will come to help you."

The captain grunted something and shoved Bethari and August in Hannes' direction.

"Here, take these rats and get off my ship!"

While a longboat transported the three of them to shore, Bethari told Hannes how she and August had slipped aboard the *Oranje*. He was horrified to learn that they had barely escaped being put out to sea. Bethari continued, "I really didn't expect that horrible man would try to cheat you out of everything!"

Hannes' hand took hers. "At least he passed on the price I was willing to pay with my fists."

His hands gently stroked Bethari's. He had to resist the urge to take her into his arms in front of August and the sailors. He could hardly believe that she was actually with him. How easily he might have lost her, possibly without ever knowing what had happened to her.

They reached the pier. Hannes disembarked first, then he grasped Bethari's waist and lifted her on to the dockside. Her eyes glistened. His hands again found hers and held them. Not being able to express his joy the way he wanted to, he took a light-hearted approach. He made a serious face and looked Bethari over.

"What's the matter?" she asked anxiously. "Why do you look at me like that?"

"I'm trying to remember when we got married."

"The day on which August and I were discovered in the hold of the *Oranje*," she replied, her heart pounding.

"And so you pretended I was your husband and August's brother?" Hannes asked sternly.

"Yes."

Hannes turned to August although the boy, not unnerved in the slightest, laughed with abandon.

"I'm so happy to see you, Hannes."

"I agree with you, brother!" He slapped August on the shoulder.

August gave him a slap so hard that he stumbled. "Friend!"

Bethari giggled. Hannes feigned a stern look. "Well, this is a fine family I got myself!"

"You'll never get bored with the two of us," Bethari countered.

Hannes' eyes radiated. "I can believe that! Anyway, I'm in too deep now."

"Truly?" She cocked her head.

"Truly," he replied firmly. He could no longer stand it; he took her in his arms and kissed her.

"I would never have let you leave for Ceylon without saying goodbye," Bethari told him breathlessly when they finally let each other go. "I was at the harbor the day of your departure, but I was too late. The ship had already left. It was my father's fault."

He gently stroked her cheek. "You don't need to tell me. I know."

"Rufus told you?"

He took her hands and kissed her finger tips. "He was about to tell me, but your father intervened in a rage and beat him."

Bethari looked at him in dismay. "Are you sure?"

He nodded. "The walls on a ship are thin."

"I no longer know my father," she said sadly. "I don't know why he rejects you. Does not every father want his daughter to give her heart to a good man?"

He was so moved by her words that he felt a lump in his throat. To avoid being overwhelmed by his feelings, he changed the topic.

"I'm not a good catch at all right now. I currently own no more than seven gulden because you two had to insist on playing stowaway."

She looked at him in astonishment. "Excuse me? I thought you had given that captain all of your savings!"

"Do you really think that I was going to hand over all that I own to that greedy old coot?"

He grinned broadly and patted his jacket. "I've still got a little nest egg sewn in here. I'm going to need it, now that I have a family to care for."

"You are not angry that I said you were my husband?"

"Don't talk nonsense! Happy is what I am," he replied. And that was true. Even though his life at that moment was anything but easy, he had never felt happier.

Bethari nestled up to him. "I am even happier than you. But I don't want to go to my father. I want to stay with you."

"I would hope so." He pulled her close. "First of all, I'm going to take both of you to my landlady. She'll be happy to meet you."

He was loath to let go of Bethari but there was one thing he absolutely had to clarify before anything else.

He placed his hands on August's shoulders and looked straight into his eyes.

"You must not leave the house to which I'm about to take you, under any circumstances whatsoever. You ran away from the regiment in Cape Town. That is strictly forbidden for a soldier. The men here know you. If they were to see you, they would have to report it to Colonel von Hügel and he would punish you severely. That is why we have to leave now. We shouldn't tempt fate."

Shortly before sunset, Hannes entered the church and met Rufus. For a moment, he considered telling him that Bethari was there but he thought better of it. If Rufus did not know anything, de Groot could not beat it out of him.

Thus, he merely said, "Good evening, Rufus. Are you keeping watch?"

"As my master requests. He awaits you on the bench in front of the pulpit." Rufus pointed to the dim interior.

Hannes approached de Groot, greeted him, and sat down. He found that the Netherlander looked worse than ever. His cheekbones protruded, his eyes were hollow and he had lost a considerable amount of weight. Hannes wondered if he still suffered from his stomach ailment or if he had been stricken by one of the notorious tropical diseases he had heard about. He himself felt well, affected neither by the heat nor the humidity.

He had adhered to de Groot's advice; his youth and robust health were also on his side.

Hannes and de Groot heard steps and turned around simultaneously. They watched as von Hügel approached them down the aisle.

De Groot furrowed his brow. "You invited the colonel to this meeting?"

"The information I have concerns him as well," said Hannes.

"Good evening, *Mijnheer* de—" von Hügel hesitated as his gaze fell upon Hannes. It required an effort for him to include Hannes in his salutation. "Good evening, gentlemen. I had begun to fear that you might decline my support in this mission."

"On the contrary," answered Hannes. "My research may have taken some time but I now have quite a bit of information to report."

De Groot said, "I am eager to find out if your information justifies this gathering."

"I should say so!" Hannes revealed the conversation he had eavesdropped on between the Pole, the captain of the *Estrela*, and the commander.

When he finished, there was a moment of silence. At last, de Groot spoke, "So, Sluijsken is the leader of this smuggling ring. And his manor is the hideaway for the cinnamon. I must say, this is extremely clever."

"You don't seem too surprised," von Hügel remarked.

De Groot smiled weakly. "The Company has had to battle such problems from the outset. Our colonies are too far removed from the homeland for the Lords Seventeen to control. It is extremely rare for someone to be dispatched like me." De Groot withheld the fact that an additional reason for his dispatch was punishment for his own corruption.

"So that means that the Lords have sent you here because the situation becomes more serious," Hannes observed.

"I assume so. If one smuggling operation alone involves one hundred twenty bales, how does the fort commander manage to divert such quantities for himself?" von Hügel questioned.

"After the peeling of the trees, the bark is taken to collection points in the vicinity of Galle," de Groot explained. "There it is dried, packed into bales and stored ready for transportation. I suspect that several of the porters don't go to these collection points but take the cinnamon from the harvesting location directly to Sluijsken's residence."

"This means that the Sinhalese king, as owner of these trees, has to be a participant in the smuggling operation," Hannes said. "Surely he has exact information about the amount of bark removed from his trees and expects to be paid for it."

De Groot sighed. "I would be surprised if he did not make a profit from it."

"Once more, I venture to point out the importance of military action," von Hügel remarked. "It would demonstrate not only to this Pole, but also to the king, that we are in control here."

"The king lives secluded in the interior of the island and, as I already explained to you on the *Edam*, it would be extremely difficult to perform any sort of military action in this terrain." De Groot sounded irritable.

"Then we should strike at the fort commander's country estate at least," von Hügel said.

"If we were to do that, Sluijsken will claim that the smuggled cinnamon is an official shipment for the Company," Hannes countered. "We have to wait until the cinnamon is on board the *Estrela*. She sails under the Portuguese flag and is thus not allowed to carry any cinnamon for the Company. You strike immediately when the *Estrela* sets sail, as soon as the elephant has been loaded."

"And we will arrest the commander at the same time," de Groot finished. "I cannot wait to serve those culprits to the Lords in Amsterdam, on a silver platter."

"A good plan," von Hügel said, "yet there is one hitch."

"What is that?" de Groot asked nervously.

"My men are dying like flies in this climate. I've already lost two dozen. Many more are sick. I want to show up with as many soldiers as possible in order to intimidate the smugglers. But if the rate of sickness and death continues … You're furloughed from the regiment, Hiller, but I could use every man."

"Fair enough," Hannes said after quick consideration. "The men can count on me."

"What would you think about priming the cannons on the two bastions at the harbor entrance?" de Groot asked. "I don't mean to say that we should sink the *Estrela*, since our evidence would go down with her. But if the Pole were to resist arrest, your soldiers could fire some warning shots."

Von Hügel agreed. "I'll see to it that my people are on duty on both bastions."

De Groot rose with some difficulty but his face radiated in a way that Hannes had not seen since the outset of their journey.

"Two more days to accomplish our goal! We'll be homeward bound soon!"

It was dusk by the time the three men parted. Hannes had learned that nightfall came quickly in the tropics, so he hurried back to the Widow Kleijn's. As soon as he reached the porch, delicious aromas wafted his way, and he heard voices and laughter coming from the kitchen in the back of the house.

"Well, you're all in great spirits. Are you having a party?" He stepped into the kitchen and grinned as he looked from one to the other.

"Hannes, I'm cooking!" August stood in front of the fire, busily stirring a copper pot hanging over the flames.

"Your brother is quite a deft cook. He needs help only now and then." The widow scooped some water from a bucket next to the fire. "So that the rice doesn't get scorched."

As she was about to pour the water into the pot, August took the ladle from her. "I'll do that!"

The old lady looked at him affectionately. "My boy loved to cook too."

Hannes took a knife from the table, slit open the seam of his jacket and removed a few coins with his thumb and forefinger. "How much do I owe you for the additional meals, Mrs. Kleijn?"

The widow smiled. "Give me what you can spare for your wife. I won't take anything for August. He gives me such pleasure, almost like my Klaas. He had a good heart, just like August."

Hannes counted a few coins and pressed them into the widow's hand. "Your son must have inherited his kind heart from you."

She shyly tucked the coins into her apron. "The Lord will reward you and your wife for not putting this poor devil August here into a sickhouse."

"Did you hear that, darling?" Hannes turned to Bethari. She sat at a table in the middle of the kitchen cutting a long, green vegetable resembling a cucumber. The widow called it "luffa". It grew in her backyard.

"I didn't know you could cook." Hannes took a stool and sat down next to Bethari.

She made a face. "To be honest, today is my first attempt. I may end up cutting off part of my finger."

The Widow Kleijn laughed. "I take it your brother, *Mijnheer* Hiller, cooks at your home."

After their meal of rice and steamed vegetables, the widow retired for the night and August disappeared into the small room behind the kitchen. Hannes and Bethari stood at the table and scrubbed the dishes with water and sand. They could hear the calls of the night birds through the closed window shutters and when Bethari followed Hannes upstairs to his room, the wooden floorboards creaked under their feet.

He opened the door and allowed her to enter.

"I hope you're not expecting anything grand," he said sheepishly and placed the oil lamp on the floor next to the bed.

Bethari looked around the plain room. There were no pictures on the whitewashed walls nor rugs on the wooden floor. A pair of breeches and a shirt hung on hooks next to the door. The only piece of furniture was a narrow bed with a palm straw sack. A sheet served as blanket.

"So, this is where I shall sleep tonight," she said with a smile.

He stepped behind her, took her in his arms and kissed her neck. Her skin was soft and warm and tasted slightly salty.

"I hope that we shall spend many more nights of our lives together."

She turned to face him and wrapped her arms around his neck.

"I missed you so much. I simply had to follow you."

He looked into her eyes.

"That means that you are serious? It wasn't just a pretext when you told the captain that we were married?"

"I am absolutely serious about you, Hannes Hiller. I am yours."

He traced the small scar on her forehead with his fingertips and recalled what they had endured together.

"The grace of eloquence is seated on your lips, my dear. I must say that your previous life was spent in much greater affluence than you will ever experience at my side."

She placed her hands on her hips. "Since when can you predict the future, Hannes? True, I've grown up in affluence but I am certain that together we will accomplish much. You are a carpenter and I am a painter. There is no reason that we should not be able to support ourselves."

He leaned toward her and gently kissed her.

"You make me a very happy man, Bethari. To think that I almost lost you. That captain—"

"I don't want to think about that old fool anymore."

She took his hand and led him to the bed.

"Let us not waste our first night together."

Hannes sat down, pulled her on his lap and again, they kissed each other long and passionately.

"I have never felt like this before. The brightness of your cheeks shame the stars, and I am filled with love for you," he said hoarsely.

He ran his fingers through her hair, took a handful and buried his face in it.

"And I am filled with love for you."

She felt for the knot on his shirt and pulled it open. Her fingers ran over the rough linen and over his chest. She stopped abruptly.

And before he could stop her, she pulled out a folded and crumpled piece of paper from his shirt.

"May I have a look?"

He nodded without a word and watched with interest as she unfolded the paper and looked at it for a long time. At last, she lowered her hand.

"All this time, you have carried so close to your heart the drawing I made of you in Vlissingen."

"It is special," he answered sheepishly. "Even then, with your pencil, you were able to look inside of me like no one else."

"And yet you didn't treat my picture very nicely." She waved the sheet and the paper rustled.

He placed his head against hers.

"There was a time when I almost threw it away. At a moment when I wanted to throw away my whole life."

She took his face in her hands and looked at him.

"Your words frighten me."

"Don't be afraid," he said flatly. "That moment is gone."

She took a deep breath.

"Was it on the *Drie Gebroeders*?"

He frowned. "What do you mean?"

"I watched you on the ship one night. I had the feeling that a very heavy burden was weighing on your soul."

He freed himself.

"It's almost eerie the way you can look inside of me."

"So, I'm right. What is it that haunts you so?"

He laughed sharply. "I told you, it's over. And now let us stop with the talking."

He was about to kiss her but she pushed the palms of her hands against his shoulders.

"If we are to live our entire lives together, we should not have secrets standing between us."

"I agree," he said, placing his forehead against hers. "Yet it is so hard to speak about it."

She gently caressed his stubble.

"Try."

He raised his head and looked into her eyes.

"Shortly before we set sail from Vlissingen, I experienced the worst moment of my life."

He related to her how he had dared to fight for the pay which he and the other soldiers were owed, and how Colonel von Hügel had incarcerated him for it, then punished him with the mock execution.

Bethari could not believe her ears.

"How cruel people can be! How frightened you must have been!" She squeezed him close to her.

"The moment I thought my life was over was terrifying."

He stroked her hair.

"But reliving that moment for many months was even worse. I did not know how to free myself from the memory. I'd like to have killed von Hügel for what he did."

"I can understand," she replied in a muted voice.

"Your drawing helped me to see the Hannes I once was," he continued. "After our shipwreck, I became aware of how much life did mean to me. Little by little, I came to believe in a good future for myself. The nightmares became less severe until they finally disappeared altogether."

They sat in silence for a while, each lost in thought.

At last, Bethari said, "You should bring charges against von Hügel."

"He did me wrong but he has the law on his side," said Hannes. "I'm no longer out for revenge. I want to look toward the future, not at the past."

He prevented her from replying by kissing her. His hands loosened the fastenings of her bodice and found her full, soft breasts. He grew more aroused as she moaned softly and leaned into him. He pulled her backwards onto the straw sack. Their feverish fingers removed their clothing. All of Hannes' painful memories dissipated as their bodies melted into one.

Later, when the flickering light of the oil lamp had long gone out, they lay in a close embrace on the straw sack, his arm around her shoulder. His fingers played with her hair. Her head rested on his chest, rising and falling slightly with his breathing.

"My mission here will be finished in a few days," he said softly. "Will you return to Cape Town with me? We'll find a pastor and turn your white lie into reality."

"Do you mean to marry me?"

"Precisely."

"You know, Hannes," her breath tickled his neck, "I feel connected to you with all my heart and soul but I don't need a pastor to give me permission to spend my life by your side."

"But you wouldn't turn me down, would you?" He kissed her hair. "It is important to me to introduce you to my mother as my wife."

"If it means so much to you, we'll get married. I look forward to meeting your mother. Will it be dangerous for you to complete your mission?"

"Not if all goes according to plan."

"It's about cinnamon, isn't it?"

He raised his head with a jerk.

"How do you know?"

"Shortly before he left, my father told me that he had to investigate irregularities in the shipments of cinnamon. Does that mean that cinnamon is being smuggled out of Ceylon?"

He shifted uncomfortably.

"Your father has sworn me to secrecy. If you want information, ask him. He's staying behind the churchyard."

He felt her tense up.

"I don't want to see my father."

"Don't you miss him at all?"

"I miss the person he used to be." Her voice sounded hard.

For one brief moment he contemplated telling her that her father looked unwell and was perhaps sick. But then he recalled how disgraceful de Groot's treatment of his only daughter and his servant had been. He felt anger well up in him.

"We must face him when we return to Cape Town. You must know that I will fight for us even if your father opposes our union."

"I love your determination, Hannes."

"And I love your courage, Bethari."

He took her in his arms and gently rolled her on her back. Their mouths found their way to a tender kiss.

CHAPTER TWENTY

GALLE, CEYLON, 1788

"They have nerve, thinking they're getting away with this." Colonel von Hügel shook his head as he looked at the *Estrela*.

The Pole and the captain stood at the railing and waved toward the dais at the end of the pier, where the governor, the fort commander and his wife, de Groot and several other dignitaries had taken their seats.

"Do you think everything will go smoothly?" asked Hannes. He stood at the window next to von Hügel. The commanding officer took two steps to the side and stared straight ahead. Hannes pretended not to notice this renewed insult although it irritated him. He no longer harbored any feelings of revenge and yet he had not forgiven him for the mock execution. Deep inside he felt the need for some sort of atonement.

The two men watched from the window of a warehouse that was built on the city walls, located no more than fifty paces from the dock. Directly below them lay the entrance to the fort which separated the harbor from the city. The path to the pier bustled with onlookers, who were held back by fences built expressly for the purpose. Their voices and laughter could be heard in the warehouse. It was not every day that elephant bulls were loaded on a ship and hardly anyone in Galle wanted to miss the spectacle.

Von Hügel puffed out his chest. "We'll overwhelm them before they understand what's going on! It shall take no more than five minutes."

"There are all sorts of objects on board that can serve as weapons, such as rods, wooden logs, knives, to mention a few." Hannes felt for his rapier. For the first time in many months, he wore a uniform. Not his own, because that was at the barracks in Cape Town, but one that had belonged to a dead soldier.

Von Hügel jeered. "Those aren't weapons that can compete with our rapiers, guns and bayonets. And if the smugglers get really brazen, we still have the cannons on the two bastions."

Thirty soldiers and the sergeant now stood in the large room where normally bales of cinnamon, cotton or sacks of coffee were stored, waiting with anxious faces for the order to storm the pier. The Colonel's two adjutants were responsible for arresting the commander.

The pier had been converted expressly for the elephant. Workers had covered the wooden planks with a thick layer of sand and lined the sides with palm leaves to give the animal the impression that it was the jungle. Even the side of the *Estrela* facing the pier was covered with palm leaves, so that only the bowsprit and the two masts were visible. The long arm of the hoist hovered over the pier; the straps to lift the elephant on board lay ready on the side.

Yesterday dozens of Sinhalese porters had taken the elephant fodder on board the *Estrela*. Hannes was still stunned by the audacity of carrying the concealed cinnamon in plain sight through the harbor area. He wondered how many people in Galle knew what was camouflaged by the green palm leaves. Did everyone who had the authority to prevent the smuggling get paid to turn a blind eye?

"Here comes the elephant," said von Hügel. He stepped away from the window and indicated to his adjutants and Hannes to do the same.

The pier grew quiet. Everyone, from the crowd behind the barrier to the people on the dais, looked in the direction of the city wall. A few moments later, the elephant appeared on the street.

"Sweet Mother of God!" Hannes whistled softly. "He is colossal!"

The elephant bull was the largest living being he had ever seen. He was so large that he did not fit through the city gates and had, instead, been led around the city. His massive gray body moved in rhythm with his swaying steps. Yet his legs were bound with ropes. On his neck, directly behind his flapping ears sat a Sinhalese boy holding a wooden stick with a hook. Four other Sinhalese boys ran next to the animal. Their only protection against the powerful bull was a stick with an iron hook. Barefoot and dressed in a knee-length loincloth, they looked tiny next the enormous animal. Hannes felt sure that the elephant could kill them with one blow of his trunk before they ever had a chance to use their stick, to say nothing of the strength of his tusks.

The *Estrela*'s carpenter had told Hannes that these Sinhalese boys were the elephant's keepers, *mahouts*. The most important one was the one on his back.

"He's the one who's tamed and trained him. He's going with him to India too and they will stay together until one of them dies," the carpenter had explained to him.

The elephant reached the pier and stopped. The tip of his trunk moved across the sand. He snorted, raised it and, to the great amusement of the spectators, sprayed some sand over his head. And yet when the *mahout* touched his back with his stick, he obediently walked on and stopped when they reached the *Estrela*. The four *mahouts* on the ground guided leather straps under his rounded belly, which the man on his back attached to a sturdy hook on the hoist. Then he used the stick to touch the bull on his right shoulder. Hannes was spellbound as he watched the animal lift his front leg and the *mahout* walked down as if on a ladder.

The Pole leaned over the railing, raised his right arm and bellowed, "Come on, men! Put your backs into it!"

One dozen sailors, who had been hiding behind the railing, got up, took the hauling rope from the hoist, and lifted the elephant amid loud calls of "Heave-ho!". As soon as his front legs left the ground, the bull began thrashing about. He swung his trunk wildly and emitted a scream so bloodcurdling that Hannes' hairs stood on end. Again and again, the elephant trumpeted and roared. He acted so wildly that not even the *mahouts* ventured near him. Once his hind legs were completely suspended in the air, he gave up his resistance. He helplessly rose higher and higher in his harness, was lowered into the cargo hatch, and slowly disappeared from sight.

There was thunderous applause. The Pole and the captain bowed in the direction of the dais.

Colonel von Hügel turned to his adjutants. "Let's go!" He pulled his dagger and went to the head of his soldiers. Hannes felt the handle of his rapier and stormed down the stairs with his fellow soldiers, right behind von Hügel.

Colonel von Hügel marched, flanked by his two adjutants. They were followed by the sergeant and the soldiers, lined up in ten rows. The rhythmic steps of the men's boots aroused the curiosity of the spectators behind the barrier, who looked puzzled as they watched the troop, armed with muskets and bayonets, bearing down on the pier. The two adjutants peeled off and ran to the dais, their daggers drawn. Out of the corner of his eye, Hannes saw spectators jump out of the way. On the dais, the governor and fort commander rose to their feet and gesticulated wildly. De Groot, too, stood and held a piece of paper under Sluijsken's nose. The two adjutants rushed up the steps to the dais and stopped in front of the fort commander.

Hannes reached the end of the pier, together with von Hügel and the sergeant. Five soldiers had begun to remove the palm leaves from the *Estrela*'s hold, and they stared at them, mouths open.

Von Hügel signaled the sergeant, who ordered, "Attention! Present arms!"

Hannes and his fellow soldiers pulled their muskets from their shoulders.

"Cock your guns!" the sergeant commanded.

Thirty clicks were heard by all.

"What's this about? Have you gone mad?" The Pole stood at the railing next to Captain van Schouten and stared down at the colonel.

Von Hügel puffed out his chest. "Dom Laurenzo Carlos Olivero de Mascarenhas! By order of the VOC, this ship and its entire cargo are impounded! You are strongly suspected of having stolen one hundred twenty bales of cinnamon from the honorable Company, with the intention of selling it for your own profit. I call on you, Dom Laurenzo, Captain van Schouten, and your entire crew to surrender and leave the ship."

The Pole leaned over the railing. "Listen to me, blockhead! I don't care a whit about any of this. And now, please excuse me. I have an elephant for the Maharajah of Travancore and his Lordship shall not be kept waiting." He nodded to the captain. "Order the gangway lifted!"

Hannes and the soldiers took off for the gangway at the same time as the sailors, but they were too late. Before the first one could put a foot on it, van Schouten's men retrieved the narrow walkway.

"You will regret this, Dom Laurenzo!" Von Hügel shook his arms in the air.

After a moment of complete silence, a deafening crash was heard from the direction of the harbor entrance. From each protective bastion, one from the right, another from the left, an explosion of smoke could be seen. Then, the cannon balls flew high in the air and splashed into the water a few feet from the *Estrela*, creating a giant water spout. Adding to the din and confusion, the elephant made bloodcurdling trumpeting sounds and the sailors on deck screamed curses.

"God's wounds!" van Schouten thundered. "They'll sink us!"

"Nay, they have only shot across the bow!" the Pole screamed. "They shan't intimidate us! Right, men?"

The sailors screamed their agreement as van Schouten directed them toward the belaying pins that secured the rigging. The sailors tore the pegs out of the boards as multiple rope ends dangled onto the deck, positioned themselves along the railing, gripping and waving the pegs and smacking them into their hands while screaming in unison, "Ahoy! Ahoy!"

Van Schouten shook his fist at von Hügel, "If you try to board my ship, you will be sorry!"

"And you will be sorry if you do not give yourself up," von Hügel bellowed from the pier. "Dom Laurenzo, I call upon you to avoid a blood bath!"

The Pole guffawed. "You do not frighten me!" He pulled his pistol from his belt, pointed it at von Hügel's head and cocked it.

There was a metallic click. Hannes jumped up and rammed von Hügel using all of his body weight so that he hit the sand with a thud at the same moment the shot was fired. Hannes felt the bullet whiz past his head, with a light but precise breeze. The next instant, the bullet crashed into a wicker barrier on the side of the pier. Not to be thwarted, the Pole again aimed his smoldering gun at von Hügel. Hannes knelt, raised his musket, and shot. His aim was true.

Dom Laurenzo's eyes widened; the pistol slipped from his hand onto the pier. A rapidly expanding red stain appeared on his topcoat. The man known as the Pole stumbled along the railing and fell. Though he attempted to pull himself up, he slumped and fell onto the pier in a display that ended with a dull thud.

Von Hügel, meanwhile, pointed his pistol directly at Captain van Schouten. "If you and your men don't wish to be riddled with bullets, give yourself up!"

The captain slowly raised his hands. "It's not my fault," he said hoarsely. "I was forced."

Hannes retrieved the Pole's pistol. When he straightened up, von Hügel stood before him with a glint in his eyes. "If not for your presence of mind, Hiller, I would be lying on this pier right now." His voice sounded rough.

"So now you have had a taste of your own medicine," Hannes countered. "Do you recall Vlissingen, Colonel?"

The Colonel did not answer and avoided his gaze.

"Do you? Look at me if you're not a coward!" Hannes snapped at him. Reluctantly, the colonel complied.

"How does it feel to fear for your life? Did you feel any regret when you thought it was over? Did you think of your wife? Of your children? Or did you piss yourself because you were afraid?"

Von Hügel's face grew dark red. Hannes seized his arm and placed the Pole's pistol in the palm of his hand. His eyes bored into the commanding officer's.

"Remember this, von Hügel: You owe me a life."

"Master, Colonel von Hügel announced himself. I wanted to send him away but he insisted on seeing you." Rufus entered de Groot's bedroom.

The interior was hot and smelled of the sour stench of vomit. Very little light penetrated the closed window shutters even though it was the middle of the morning.

"You have barely touched your breakfast." A piece of bread lay on the plate. Next to it sat a bowl with the foul-smelling contents of de Groot's stomach. The pieces of mango and banana that Rufus had arranged in the bowl were strewn all over the tray.

"I tried to eat." De Groot's voice sounded weak. "But my stomach doesn't tolerate anything."

"Please allow me to call a doctor, master." Rufus opened the shutters. Bright sunlight streamed into the room.

"I don't need a doctor to tell me that my condition is wretched," de Groot croaked. "Close the window. You're only making it hotter in here."

"The air is so bad that it alone will make you sicker," Rufus replied as he closed the shutters again. "Do you wish me to make your excuses to Colonel von Hügel?"

"No. Remove this sick tray from the side of my bed, and then show the Colonel in."

"Very well, master." Rufus took the tray and disappeared.

As soon as de Groot was alone again, he used a corner of his night shirt to wipe the sweat off his forehead. He had planned to return to Cape Town on the next ship, collect Bethari, and then travel directly to Amsterdam. But he had just suffered a sleepless night with frightful stomach pains. This morning, for the first time, he felt too ill to leave his bed. He lay there, tormented by the fear of never seeing his daughter or his homeland again.

There was a knock, the door opened and Rufus admitted von Hügel.

"Pardon me, de Groot, are you unwell?"

"I'm feeling a little weak this morning," de Groot grunted. "Why do you disturb me?"

Von Hügel sat down on the chair by the washstand. "I have two pieces of news, neither of which will please you. First: Captain van Schouten was found dead in his cell this morning."

"What?" De Groot sat bolt upright in his bed before slumping back, his face distorted with pain.

"Do you need help?" asked von Hügel, alarmed. "Shall I fetch your servant?"

De Groot shook his head and breathed deeply. "How could this happen?"

"He hanged himself on the window bars with his kerchief." Von Hügel extended his legs. "And yet my adjutants have assured me that when he was incarcerated, everything he might use to hang himself was taken from him."

"That means either that they weren't thorough or that he had help," de Groot said flatly. "But why did he hang himself?"

"Well, perhaps he feared he would be tortured and divulge information to the Lords Seventeen that had to remain secret at all costs. That might also be a reason to help him along to his demise," von Hügel noted.

"Do you imply that he was murdered?" de Groot grunted.

"It's possible. And that brings me to my second point." Von Hügel cleared his throat. "Fort Commander Sluijsken was released from custody. Apparently last night. It happened without my knowledge. Even my adjutants did not learn about it until this morning, but they informed me at once, of course. When I questioned the guards outside Sluijsken's cell, they handed me this."

Von Hügel pulled a folded piece of paper from his jacket. De Groot looked it over quickly.

"A directive from the governor to release Sluijsken immediately! Why, this becomes more and more outrageous! Why does the governor undermine our work?"

"My good man, is it possible that Hiller's information was incorrect? Perhaps the fort commander is not involved with the smuggling after all?"

"Nay, Hiller has been most reliable. I am convinced that Sluijsken is the head of the snake." De Groot leaned forward with difficulty and reached for the bell on his nightstand. "I shall pay the governor a visit and get to the bottom of the matter."

Von Hügel looked at him doubtfully. "Shall I accompany you?"

De Groot shook his head. "Some affairs need to be settled one-on-one."

The Governor's Residence was the biggest and stateliest building in Galle. It consisted of two stories with whitewashed walls, Palladian windows and shiny, red roof tiles. The Dutch East India Company's coat of arms, resplendently carved in stone, took pride of place, centered above the imposing two-columned portal. Next to it, a flagpole displayed the Company's red, white and blue flag.

The residence was within sight of de Groot's lodgings. Still, the short distance was so taxing for him that he repeatedly stopped, with one hand pressed to his stomach and the other leaning heavily on his servant's arm. When they reached the entrance, he instructed Rufus to wait and announced himself to the guard.

"My name is de Groot, Finance Inspector of the Dutch East India Company. I must speak with the governor."

Soldiers met him in the hall and escorted him to a salon on the second floor. As soon as the door closed behind him, he slumped into the brocade upholstery of the sofa. The pain almost took his breath away and the temperature rose under his velvet jacket. He placed his bicorne next to him, took a handkerchief out of his sleeve and dabbed the sweat from his face.

If you want to see your daughter and return home, you must stay strong, he reminded himself silently. But his stomach burned worse than the fires of hell and he found it impossible to concentrate on the matter at hand.

To distract himself, he let his eyes wander about the room. The governor's principal residence was in Colombo but even here in Galle, the opulence matched even the court of a European prince. He took in the Chinese lacquer furniture, the bulbous, blue-white porcelain vases, the silk wallpaper, and the oriental rug, which covered the entire floor. He had seen similar displays of luxury at the residence of the General Governor of Batavia during his time there as a young auditor and he was aware that the VOC neither approved of, nor paid for, such profligacy.

He observed the portraits of all the Dutch Governors of Ceylon; there had been forty-one in almost two hundred years. The most recent likeness was of the current officeholder, Governor van de Graaff. It depicted a man with intelligent dark eyes and a cool, appraising look. The powdered white hair pulled back at the nape of his neck lent his appearance additional sternness.

The door opened and De Groot hastily tucked his handkerchief up his sleeve and pushed himself off the sofa to greet the Governor. Van de Graaff was slightly older than his portrait indicated. He looked affluent and elegant in a gold-embroidered jacket, blue breeches, and silk stockings. He walked energetically toward his visitor, extending his right hand with the gold signet ring of the VOC on the ring finger.

"*Mijnheer* de Groot! Have you come to apologize for yesterday's blunder?"

De Groot barely smiled. "I have no cause."

The two men faced each other, de Groot on the sofa, the governor in an armchair. The latter crossed his legs and twisted his signet ring with his left hand.

"Oh? I was quite surprised by your performance at the harbor yesterday. Whatever gave you the idea to accuse Fort Commander Sluijsken, a good man of much merit, of these outrageous crimes? And without consulting me first?"

"Whatever gave you the idea to release the fort commander on the same evening, without consulting me first?" de Groot countered. "I am in Galle at the behest of the Lords Seventeen of the VOC, whose coat of arms graces your door. Their concern over the smuggling of cinnamon from the colony under your authority is great. They will be most happy to learn that by arresting Fort Commander Sluijsken, I have captured the head of the snake."

Van de Graaff leaned back in his chair and laughed heartily. "My dear de Groot, that is utterly absurd!"

"I assure you that it is not." De Groot leaned forward and fixed his eyes on the governor. "Unfortunately, this Polish elephant trader and his captain are dead, but I will take Sluijsken back to Amsterdam in chains and hand him over to the Lords."

Van de Graaff's mirth evaporated. "You have no proof."

Now it was de Groot's turn to laugh heartily. "You must be joking. I have seized a whole ship full of cinnamon and the crew as well."

"The *Estrela* belongs to Dom Laurenzo. There is no evidence against Sluijsken."

"According to my information, there is a warehouse on the fort commander's estate, where the cinnamon lies in temporary storage before, he secretly moves it on board the *Estrela*. There can be no better proof that Sluijsken is involved in the smuggling."

Van de Graaff furrowed his brow. "Who is this informant? I wish to question him myself."

"That is not for you to do." De Groot crossed his arms. "Why do you protect the fort commander, *Mijnheer* van de Graaff?"

The governor gnawed at his lower lip. At last, he looked de Groot in the eyes and said, "Sluijsken is my son-in-law. I agree that he has committed a grave error but I guarantee that he will never again act contrary to the interests of the Company. You yourself know well how hard life can become, so far away from the motherland. The honorable Company is not known for its generous compensation, and one never knows how long one can endure in this climate. Perhaps you have heard that my son-in-law has just become a father. Does not every father want to offer his child a sunnier future? In order to do that, one has to perform social duties and cultivate one's connections. Every favor must be reciprocated. You know that as well as I."

De Groot was silent. He, too, had pursued side businesses and enriched himself at the expense of the VOC, and deeply understood a father's motivation to provide and secure his child's future.

The governor, encouraged, slid forward in his seat. "Yesterday you spoke to me of your daughter. I know that you are as caring a father as I am," he said, as though he had read de Groot's mind. "Would you not do everything in your power to spare your daughter a dishonor as great as the one my daughter would suffer, if news of her husband's transgressions were to become public?"

Van de Graaff unlocked a cabinet and removed a carved chest from one of the compartments.

"If you are willing to show mercy to my son-in-law, you will be saving the future of my daughter and grandson. I am willing to give you the contents of this chest. One thousand gold ducats."

De Groot stared at the little chest, which was filled to the top with shiny coins. Instinctively, he placed his hand on his stomach. It was possible that after his death, Alewijn and the

Lords Seventeen would seize his assets to recoup the money lost to his prior fraud. But if he accepted this gold, Bethari would not be left empty-handed.

"There are others privy to this information who could cause your son-in-law difficulties. First of all, there is the *Estrela*'s crew. Then Colonel von Hügel and his soldiers. You might make a simple fusilier or grenadier believe that the fort commander's arrest was the result of mistake or misunderstanding, but not von Hügel. He knows the details of my assignment. And lastly, there is my assistant, who provided me with all the relevant information."

Van de Graaff closed the little chest and placed it on the small round table next to his seat. "How much longer is the term of service for the soldiers?

"Just under three years."

Van de Graaff nodded slowly. "We will not return them to Cape Town but leave them in Ceylon for the rest of their service. We can thus check all of their mail going through the fort commander's office and prevent rumors from reaching Amsterdam."

"Do you have the authority to keep the soldiers here?"

Van de Graaff smiled. "Of course, I will inform the Lords Seventeen that they must replace the soldiers whom we lost to smallpox. They are badly needed to protect Fort Galle against possible attacks from the British. My letter will reach the Lords in a year, their reply will arrive here in two years at the earliest. If the Lords insist on their redeployment to Cape Town, they will have to provide space for them on their ships. And that is where I can exert some influence. The Company always considers the transfer of salable goods more important than that of soldiers, who only cost money without bringing any in."

"You propose to keep the soldiers here in Ceylon indefinitely?"

"If need be, until they die. And that can happen rather quickly in the tropics." Van de Graaff stretched his legs. "I can also dispel all your other concerns. The *Estrela*'s crew will remain incarcerated for the time being. There will be no objections because no one sheds a tear over smugglers."

"True." De Groot felt the tension leaving him. The governor was a shrewd man who had a remedy for every uncertainty. "A solution is required for von Hügel and my assistant."

"Might they be receptive to a financial settlement?" the governor asked.

"The Colonel, certainly." De Groot related how he had paid von Hügel for the uniforms so that he would put an assistant at his disposal.

"I could grant him permission to pay for the entire military requisites out of his own pocket, buy them from him for a good price, and then charge the Company. That way both the Colonel and I will benefit from the transaction," said van de Graaff. "What is your assistant's price?"

De Groot recalled how Hannes had fought for the regiment soldiers' pay in Vlissingen and shook his head. "He is a simple man but if he feels something is unjust, he will take action against it."

"It's people like that who do the most damage to successful businesses," von de Graaff grumbled. "But there are ways and means of dealing with those with an exaggerated sense of justice. What is his name?"

De Groot glanced over at the little chest. He would be able to present Alewijn and the Lords with one hundred twenty bales of confiscated cinnamon, and the names of the Pole and the Dutch captain as masterminds. But if that did not satisfy the directors in Amsterdam and they seized his assets as restitution for his previous fraudulent activities, this money would afford his daughter a secure future.

The price was the name of the man for whom his daughter had almost jeopardized her reputation. It was not a price that would hurt him. "My assistant is named Hannes Hiller. He works as a carpenter at the wharf. What are you planning to do with him?" he added after a short pause.

"Let me worry about that," the governor replied.

"Send him to Java," de Groot suggested. "To the Maluku Islands or to Sulawesi, for all I care. He'll never get away from those godforsaken islands at the edge of civilization."

"I'll find a good solution," said van de Graaff. "Do you accept my offer?"

De Groot nodded. "I accept it."

A while later the governor stood at the window and watched de Groot and his servant on the street below. He observed de Groot's slow gait and stooped posture and felt certain that he could have saved himself the gold ducats. But certain investments were inevitable if the ultimate profits were great enough.

A barely visible door in the wall silently opened and closed again. The sound of approaching steps was muffled by the rug.

"So that busybody's gone?" Sluijsken inquired.

"He had his price but I managed to silence him. And the others shouldn't cause us any problems, with one exception. A certain Hannes Hiller."

"I heard what de Groot suggested to you. You're not going to banish him to Java, are you?"

"Of course not," van de Graaff replied. "He must be silenced permanently. He must not find out that the English and I are partners in the cinnamon business. I assume he plans to leave Ceylon soon, so we must be quick."

"We'll eliminate this Hiller," Sluijsken said. "And then we'll look for a new agent and a new captain. We still have the ship and its crew."

CHAPTER TWENTY-ONE

GALLE, CEYLON, 1788

"Today we have a lot of work to do," the master said to Hannes. "The *Susanna* arrived yesterday. A longboat came loose during a storm off the coast of Madagascar and made a hole in the upper deck. There are several planks that need repairing."

It had been two days since the *Estrela*'s crew had been arrested. Hannes stood in front of the workshop with the master. It was almost midday and the two men look at the great East Indiaman in the harbor. Hannes wondered if de Groot, von Hügel and the soldiers would return to Cape Town on that ship. Bethari, August and he himself would also be on board and that was where the difficulties began. De Groot was sure to seethe with rage once he discovered that the punitive measures, he had taken against Bethari had been ineffective. On the contrary, they had brought Hannes and Bethari as close as a man and woman could possibly be. And then there was August, the deserter.

"You owe me a life," Hannes had said to von Hügel. He intended to claim August's life with that statement and would not give up until von Hügel had met his demand. There was no other solution, since desertion was punishable by death.

The master interrupted his deliberations. "The *Susanna* will be loaded with the cinnamon from the *Estrela*. I heard that once we finish our repairs, she'll head to Amsterdam."

Hannes watched the small rowboats commuting between the pier and the great three-master. The *Estrela* was docked at the quay. No longer was the red flag with Portugal's crown and coat of arms flying from her main mast. It had been replaced with the flag of the Netherlands with the entwined letters, VOC. Soldiers guarded the ship and made sure that the cinnamon was properly transferred. A dozen bales were stacked on the pier, each wrapped in a thin layer of leather to protect it from the humidity. In place of the earlier barriers, several small boats were now moored and being loaded by workers. Only the sand on the pier was a reminder that an elephant had been loaded here not too long ago.

"I would love to have seen that colossal bull being lifted out of the hold," said Hannes.

The master looked at him sideways. "What exactly are you, Hiller, a soldier or a carpenter?"

"Both." Hannes laughed. "I am the regiment's carpenter for the Company."

"Then why aren't you in the barracks with the other soldiers?"

"Because I have permission to work as *pasganger* and earn a little extra. The Lords of the VOC are real misers, you know."

At that moment, loud trumpeting could be heard coming from the *Estrela*. "The elephant is still on board?" asked Hannes in astonishment.

"And that's where he's staying," answered the master. "The Maharajah of Travancore is waiting for his gift, after all. As soon as the *Estrela* has a new captain, she'll set sail. By the way, have you heard that van Schouten hanged himself in his cell?"

"Mercy God, no!" cried Hannes. "That is how much he feared the Lords Seventeen?"

"Looks like it." The master shrugged his shoulders indifferently.

"So the crew will be taken back to Amsterdam without their captain," Hannes noted.

"Wait and see," the master countered. "I'd guess that Fort Commander Sluijsken is going to release them within the next few days."

"How will he do that?" Hannes was astonished. "He's still behind bars himself!"

"My dear fellow, you really don't know anything, do you?" The master put his hands on his hips. "The governor released Sluijsken on the evening of his arrest. I heard about it when I went for a beer at the Three Jugs."

Hannes was dumbfounded. "You must have misheard. He's being taken to Amsterdam and put on trial."

"Nonsense." The master made a dismissive gesture. "In the Three Jugs, they're talking about how that Netherlander just got overzealous and that there is no proof that Sluijsken was involved in the smuggling of cinnamon. If you ask me, the governor has a finger in the pie but then everyone knows that the rules the rich live by don't apply to the likes of you and me. Whoever has the gold, makes the rules. So his father-in-law got him out."

Hannes grabbed the master's arm. "Did you just say that Sluijsken is the governor's son-in-law?"

"Yea. Governor van de Graaff does not want his son-in-law is in prison. It does not reflect well on the rest of the family. Do you know what I mean?" He poked Hannes in the ribs.

Hannes did not answer. He was thinking that something was going horribly wrong and that he must warn de Groot. "I must go."

The master snorted indignantly. "Do you think you can come and go as you please?"

"This is urgent." Hannes took off his leather apron, threw it to the master and hurried away.

"I'll deduct this from your pay!" the master shouted.

No sooner had Hannes disappeared than a man stepped out of the shadow of the workshop building. He was dressed in inconspicuous gray clothing, his tricorne pulled down over his face.

"Sir! Was that Hannes Hiller?"

"What's it to you?" The master looked the stranger up and down. "Do you have a name?"

"Answer my question and nothing will happen to you." He raised his right forearm slightly, allowing the blade of the knife in his hand to flash.

"It was," the master grunted reluctantly.

"Where was he going?"

"I don't know!" The master stepped back. "Really."

The stranger seized his arm. "If you're lying to me, you'll be sorry!" He turned and ran after Hannes, who vanished through the city gate.

Hannes ran to de Groot's lodging. He was drenched in sweat as he reached the house behind the churchyard. He pounded against the wooden door with both fists.

There were footsteps; a bolt was pushed aside. Rufus opened the door. "Mr. Hannes!"

"Take me to your master immediately!" Hannes gasped, completely out of breath.

Rufus' face grew serious. "The master is very ill. He is not receiving visitors."

"I must see him!" Hannes pushed past Rufus into the hall.

The servant bolted the door. "I will take you to him. But he really is very ill."

Rufus went up the stairs to the second floor. Hannes followed. The servant went toward one of the doors on the landing, knocked and opened the door carefully. "Please enter, Mr. Hannes." He stepped aside.

The shutters of the windows in the room were open but the white cotton curtains were drawn. A clock on a dresser was ticking. In the twilight Hannes could make out a wide bed with heavy, carved wooden posts. A mosquito net hung from the ceiling. A jug, a glass and a bowl of water stood on the nightstand. Once his eyes had adjusted to the light, Hannes recognized a head on a stack of pillows.

He almost did not recognize de Groot. His scalp, without the wig, was almost bald. His skin was taut over his facial bones and his eyes lay so deep in their sockets that in the twilight they looked like dark holes. De Groot's arms lay on the sheet covering the emaciated body, his hands folded on his chest–almost as if he were dead.

Hannes lifted the mosquito net slightly with one hand. "*Mijnheer* de Groot. Can you hear me?"

A weak moan was his answer. Then the room was once again silent.

Hannes leaned forward. "Your servant has told me that you are ill and I would not disturb you if it were not important. Please give me a sign that you understand me."

Slowly, de Groot turned his head until his dark eye sockets focused on him.

"The fort commander is free again," said Hannes. "The governor has let him out of prison. You must do something. You are the one whom the Lords Seventeen vested with all powers."

De Groot's mouth opened slowly. Hannes leaned forward until his ear almost touched de Groot's lips.

"Speak. I am listening."

"So much ... pain...," de Groot wheezed. "Leave ... peace..."

"I would, but something here is very rotten."

He could hear a deep rattle.

"Please, *mijnheer*, how am I to proceed?" Hannes urged.

But he received no answer.

Frustrated, Hannes dropped the mosquito net. He had hoped to be given advice, some direction, but he realized that de Groot was no longer capable of giving him advice.

Before leaving the room, he threw one last glance at de Groot. His breath rattled; a thin stream of spittle ran out of the left corner of his mouth. He would not have the opportunity of making his peace with the world. The only thing that Hannes could do for him now was to grant him the possibility of seeing his daughter one last time.

Rufus waited on the landing.

"How much longer does he have, do you think?" asked Hannes.

"A few hours. Maybe until the morning."

Hannes nodded. "I'll be back. And don't worry. Once he is no more, we'll bury him and then we'll leave this damned island."

When Hannes stepped onto the street, thunder rumbled in the distance. Lead-colored clouds hung over the town. The rain fell in dense silver laces from the sky, dancing in the puddles and pelting the roofs of the houses. As he took great leaps to avoid the puddles, he thought about Bethari and how much he looked forward to seeing her. Ever since she had been with him, when he left the house in the morning, he could hardly wait to take her in his arms again in the evening.

As he turned a corner, he saw a man hasten from the front gate of the churchyard.

Seems I'm not the only poor devil who has to be out in this lousy weather, he thought as he hurried along. A few steps later, he came to a complete stop as the stranger blocked his way.

"What do you want?" Hannes wanted to know.

The stranger grinned. "Your life." His right arm shot forward.

Hannes without thinking, jumped backwards. The blade of his attacker's knife found empty air. The man immediately attacked again. This time he moved his knife back and forth quickly aiming for Hannes' internal organs.

With lightning speed, Hannes crossed his arms over his abdomen. The blade sliced open his right sleeve and went through his shirt down to the bone. He felt no pain and paid no heed to the blood streaming from the wound over his arms and fingers. He was seized by a steely determination. He had to win this struggle, or his life was over.

Again, the stranger reached back with his knife. Hannes' left hand accelerated forward against the hand holding the knife and blocked it. At the same time, he bent his right arm and rammed his elbow into his attacker's larynx. He heard a scrunching sound. The stranger gurgled, his eyes bulged and he dropped his knife. Hannes kicked it to the curb. Next, he kicked the attacker in the abdomen with all his might. The stranger stumbled backward and fell on the street with a dull thud. Water splashed around him, his tricorne swam in a puddle and he lay motionless on the ground. Hannes kneeled next to him and grabbed his collar. "Who sent you?"

His opponent's breath rattled. Then his gaze turned rigid.

Hannes jumped to his feet and looked around. The street was empty, the stores around him shuttered because of the weather. He picked up the knife, pushed it into his waistband and swiftly pulled his shirt over it. He had to make the weapon disappear. It was probably best to throw it into the ocean. First, however, he had to look after his wound. Blood ran from under his sleeve, over his hand, and dripped on the ground. Luckily, the rain washed the telltale red from the soil. He took off his jacket and wrapped it tightly around his injured forearm.

Hannes threw one last glance at the dead man. He was certain that the attack had something to do with the *Estrela*, the seizure of the cinnamon and the arrest of Sluijsken. The other two heads of the smuggling ring were dead. Did that mean that the fort commander had ordered his attempted murder?

Hannes could not return to the dock. Soon the person who had ordered him killed would learn that he was still alive. And then he would send the next one to hunt him down.

He raced down the narrow street leading to the Widow Kleijn's house as though a pack of rabid dogs chased him. He reached the small house on the city wall and threw himself against the door, which was always unlocked during the day. He stumbled inside, closing the door with his foot. Then he leaned against the wall, catching his breath.

"Who's that?" Bethari came from the kitchen. "Hannes! What—?" She looked at his pale face, the jacket wrapped around his right forearm and the blood dripping onto the widow's clean floor.

"Good heavens! Did you have an accident at the shipyard?"

"No." He stepped away from the wall but he felt dizzy and stumbled. "I think I have to sit down."

"Come with me." She took his healthy arm and led him.

The smell of food wafted from the kitchen. August and the Widow Kleijn, who were sitting at the table with plates filled with rice and vegetables, turned when Bethari and Hannes entered.

"My goodness!" The widow stared at Hannes. He was soaking wet. Blood poured from under his jacket.

August looked at his friend fearfully. "Did you hurt yourself, Hannes?"

"August, go and fetch the doctor." Bethari led Hannes to her chair. He slumped down.

"I will!" The boy jumped up but Hannes stopped him. "No doctor."

"Why not?" Bethari was upset.

Hannes pulled his attacker's knife out of his waistband and placed it on the table. "Here is why. I was attacked."

"Some common thief was going to rob you?" she cried out.

"No, I think it has something to do with the people in the smuggling ring your father, von Hügel, and I had arrested."

"Well, then we should inform the town guards!"

Hannes shook his head.

"Don't do that. First of all, I think that the fort commander of Galle is involved and secondly—" he swallowed, "I killed my attacker when I defended myself. The town guards will sooner arrest me than protect me."

"Mercy!" Bethari slapped her hand to her mouth.

The widow placed her hand on Hannes' shoulder.

"You have nothing to fear from me. I know you're a good person. And according to everything I've heard, our authorities have something to answer for."

"I killed two people in two days. That's two crimes."

Bethari squatted down in front of Hannes and laid her hand on his knee.

"You had no choice. The first time you saved Colonel von Hügel's life and the second, your own."

"You really do love me," he said softly.

313

"I do," she replied earnestly.

"We should see to the wound and get your husband out of his wet clothes before he catches a fever," the widow remarked. Her gaze wandered to the bloody blade on the table. "But this has to disappear."

She seized the knife, went to the stove, and threw it into the fire.

Bethari stared into the flames. "I never even thought about such things."

"Oh, but I did."

The widow fetched some cloths and a bowl from a kitchen cabinet, went to the stove and ladled hot water from the kettle.

"To clean the wound."

She placed the bowl and the cloths on the table.

Bethari unwrapped Hannes' arm and threw his jacket on the floor. The shirt sleeve underneath was dark red. Blood still flowed from the wide tear in the material. She carefully took off the shirt, dipped the cloth in the bowl of water and washed the blood from his arm.

"Ouch!" He flinched when she began to clean the wound. "It burns like hell."

The Widow Kleijn looked over his shoulder. "That wound needs stitches."

"No stitches," Hannes replied. "We'll cauterize the wound."

Bethari asked, shocked, "Is there no other remedy?"

"I've seen this done often on the worksite when a carpenter was injured. This is the only way to avoid gangrene and amputation in the case of an open wound."

Hannes looked at the Widow Kleijn. "Your poker. Heat it in the fire until it is red hot. Then bring it to me."

Before the widow went to fetch the poker, she retrieved an earthenware bottle from her kitchen cabinet and handed it to Hannes. "That's rum. Finish it."

"You're simply the best."

He took the bottle, emptied it, and placed it on the table with a bang.

"If this doesn't work..." he stuttered, "... well, then I don't know."

He held Bethari's hand with his healthy one. Both of them silently watched as the Widow Kleijn heated the crooked end of the poker over the fire. When she removed it, it glowed red hot.

"Don't think about what you must do." She handed Hannes the poker.

For a moment, he stared at the glowing iron and lowered it over his injury. Just before it touched the wound, he stopped.

"Your hand is shaking, Hannes," August observed.

"Well, so would yours, if you had to cauterize yourself," Hannes answered. Although the rum was gradually taking effect, as he started to sense the glowing iron closing in on his forearm, he could not manage to press it into his wound.

"Damn it, damn it," he panted. "I am so afraid!"

"I'll do it!" Bethari took the poker out of his hand. "You take hold of his hand, August. Grab it so he can't pull his arm away."

"Don't be afraid, Hannes." August took hold of his friend's arm and pressed it on the table with his whole body.

Bethari took a deep breath. Then she pressed the glowing iron into the wound. There was a sizzle like fat in a pan and then the smell of burnt flesh, so intense that they all felt nauseated.

"Ahhh!" Hannes fell backwards. Never before had he felt such hellish pain. He saw stars. He clenched his teeth with all his might. To stop himself from knocking the iron out of Bethari's hands, he used his healthy hand to clutch the table.

When he could no longer bear the pain, Bethari lifted the iron out of the wound and handed it to the widow.

"Damnation, is it over?" Hannes panted.

Bethari leaned over and kissed his mouth. "You were very brave, my love."

He tried to look at his wound with blurry eyes. Blisters had formed along the margins but the bleeding had been stanched. The stench of his burnt flesh and his pain were suddenly so overwhelming that his stomach turned and he vomited on the kitchen floor. August ran off, retrieved a rag from the widow's kitchen cabinet and wiped the floor.

Meanwhile, Bethari carefully wrapped a fresh towel around the wound. When she finished, she smiled at him compassionately. "Are you able to tell me what happened or are you too drunk?"

"I'll try," he slurred.

Then he told, slowly and searching for his words, about the fort commander's release, the captain's mysterious death, and the attack on his life.

"My God!" The Widow Kleijn threw up her hands. "What a terrible affair!"

Bethari jumped up. "We must away from here on the next ship! You cannot leave the house, Hannes. The door must stay bolted!"

She placed her hands on the sides of her head and thought for a moment.

"I'll go to my father and ask for his help."

"That's pointless." Hannes shook his head ponderously.

"I'll remind him that the only reason you got into difficulties is that you had gathered information for him," Bethari persisted. "I realize he's opposed to our love. But I will badger him until he agrees to help us."

Hannes reached for her hand with his good arm and pulled her on his lap. He leaned his head against hers. "Your father is dying, Bethari. If you want to see him again, you must go to him immediately."

The rain had stopped as Bethari left the Widow Kleijn's house. The roofs were glistening in the sun, the monkeys were being rowdy in the coconut palm in front, and the neighbor was opening her shutters to let in the air that the thunderstorm had freshened.

And yet Bethari did not take notice of any of that as she hastened along the streets, automatically avoiding the puddles. Her only thought was: *My father is dying.*

She hoped against hope that Hannes was wrong. It simply could not be true that the person who had raised her, cared for her, loved her, laughed with her, and ultimately fought bitterly with her would soon no longer exist.

She turned by the churchyard and stopped abruptly. Before her eyes in the middle of the street was a group of people arguing animatedly. Others watched the spectacle from their balconies in the nearby houses.

Hannes had told her that he had been attacked near the church and so she approached the group cautiously. Suddenly she saw a pair of legs on the ground among the people. She almost screamed. Fortunately, the bystanders obscured the rest of the body.

One man noticed her and turned toward her. "Dead as a doornail, this one. Suffocated. I've seen this before, blue in the face as he is."

"Maybe he choked on something," a woman objected. "Or maybe he had that sickness with the short-windedness."

"He was in a fight!" called a voice above them.

Bethari swiveled around and saw a woman leaning out of a window. "When it started to rain, I wanted to make sure that my shutters were closed properly. I didn't want my clean floor to get wet, you see. When I looked through the slits, I saw two men fighting exactly where this dead man is lying. One gave the other such a blow to the face that he fell over and didn't get up again."

Bethari swallowed hard. "Did you recognize the murderer?"

"I'm sorry, no, young miss. It was raining hard and I didn't exactly get the best view through the slits. But he ran that way." She pointed in the direction from which Bethari had just come. "If he knew that I had watched him, I suppose I would have to fear for my life now."

"You look pale." The man who had said that the attacker must have suffocated caringly took Bethari by the arm. "There's no need to fear this fellow, young miss. The town watch is sure to catch him."

She freed her arm. "Please excuse me. I need to go."

More than anything, what she wanted was to run back to the Widow Kleijn's house but at that moment, the town watch turned the corner and she grew fearful. She passed the five uniformed men with her head down and hurried away. Her knees were weak as she stood in front of the white house with the blossoming flame tree.

Please, dear God, let it be that Hannes is safe and that my father is not dying, she silently implored before knocking at the dark green wooden door.

After a while, Rufus looked out. His eyes grew wide.

"Mistress! You? Here?"

"Is it true that my father...?" Bethari's voice broke. She began to cry.

Rufus pulled her into the hall and locked the door behind her. He hesitated before embracing her. "I am glad that you are here, young mistress." He stroked her hair.

"Did Mr. Hannes tell you?"

"I followed him here to Ceylon and have been here for a few days," she sobbed. "Have I come in time?"

"A doctor was here a little while ago and gave your father some tincture of opium. His pain is now somewhat more bearable."

"Will he recognize me?"

Rufus hesitated for a moment. "He might be a little drowsy from the opium but I think he will be happy to see you."

Bethari freed herself from his embrace. "Please take me to him."

They went upstairs and Rufus opened the door to de Groot's bedroom.

"Call me if you need me, young mistress."

Bethari stepped into the dim room. The clock on the dresser between the windows ticked loudly. The rest of the room was still. A bed stood in the middle of the room; next to it on a nightstand she could make out a dark brown glass bottle and a pewter vessel. Her father lay on the mattress, inert, the blanket pulled up to his shoulders.

Am I too late?

She tiptoed to the bed, pulled the mosquito net aside, and sat on the mattress. Her father's eyes were closed, his face so gaunt that she hardly recognized him. And yet his chest rose and fell weakly. She felt for his hand under the sheet and found it. It was as cold as ice. As she touched his fingers, he winced and opened his eyes.

"It's me, Father."

For a few seconds, he gave her a glassy-eyed look. Finally, he asked in a barely audible voice, "You, Bethari? How long ... here?"

She swallowed. "Quite a while, Father."

He rattled. Then he wheezed, "Tried to save your good name ... but you ... threw ... away."

His unforgiving words pained her. "Hannes and I will stay together, Father," she answered steadfastly. "We love each other. No one will separate us."

"He ... pauper."

"He is a good person." She could feel herself getting angry in spite of her concern over her father. "Today someone ambushed him and tried to kill him with a knife. I think that happened only because he is working for you. Your assignment has put him in danger."

De Groot suddenly raised his head, groaned, and slumped back on to the pillow. "Must stay here, Bethari ... safe."

She shook her head vehemently. "How could I possibly hide here when Hannes is in danger? My place is by his side. I had hoped you would help us."

Her father did not answer.

With tears in her eyes, she stared at her lap. The ticking of the clock on the chest seemed to be getting louder and louder and strained her nerves.

"Call Rufus."

She flinched. "Why, Father?" She anxiously studied his face. "Are you feeling worse?"

"Call Rufus."

She left the room and returned with the servant a short while later. Her father was half sitting up in bed and looked at them. "Bring ... things, Rufus..."

"Yes, master." The servant went to the dresser by the windows, opened one of the doors, took out a wooden chest and three sealed documents and brought them to his master.

De Groot motioned with his head, indicating that he wanted everything put on the mattress. Then he looked at Bethari. "This ... for you. After my death. Rufus was supposed ... but..." He broke off and doubled over in pain.

"Master. I think you need your medicine." Rufus took the bottle and poured some clear liquid in the pewter vessel. Then he supported de Groot with one arm and with the other hand brought the liquid to his lips. "You will feel better soon."

De Groot emptied the vessel and fell back into his pillows. His eyes fell shut and Bethari began to think that he had fallen asleep.

Suddenly he said, "In the chest ... a thousand gold ducats ... for you. Secret ... don't ... anyone." His fingers sought the envelopes on the mattress. "A letter ... Alewijn ... in person ... in Amsterdam. A letter ... my will. A third letter ... for you. Read."

She took the sealed envelope on which her name was written in her father's hand and opened it. When she had finished reading, she dropped the paper into her lap. "Is this true, Father? You defrauded the Company and that is why you were sent to Ceylon? And my mother was a slave that you bought on the market in Batavia?"

"Wanted ... emancipate. Loved..." de Groot wheezed. "But ... died ... before I..."

"I was five when Mother died. I think you'd have had enough time to emancipate her."

"Not ... important..." De Groot's left hand moved across the mattress until he felt his daughter's fingertips. "You too ... slave ... because mother ... slave. No one must know."

"There were always rumors about my provenance," Bethari answered. "Did you really think I didn't notice people whispering behind my back?"

"Truth..." her father gasped, "... incontrovertible. Rumors ... people ... not sure." Again, he paused and gathered his strength. "Promise me ... leave Hiller. Otherwise ... you ... grave danger."

"Why, Father?" The thought of Hannes and the ambush brought new tears to her eyes. "Why did you involve him in an assignment that could cost him his life?" Her hand came down on the paper in her lap, making it rustle. "Who are these people who are seeking to kill him?"

"Very powerful..." her father moaned. "Very dangerous ... the gold," he looked at the chest with the ducats. "From them."

"They bribed you?" Bethari called out, beside herself. "So that you would deliver Hannes to them?"

"Am not murderer. Gold ... for ... silence ... because of Sluijsken and cinnamon."

Bethari choked on her sobs. "Was it not enough that you defrauded the VOC in Amsterdam? Have I been so deceived all this time?"

"Bethari."

"What else, Father?"

"Forgive me ... please." His voice was reduced to a whisper.

"Oh, Father! If only you knew how difficult that is!" She threw herself on him and embraced him. She felt his chest rise and fall a few more times. Then he no longer moved. Nor did she. Tears streamed down her face.

She felt a hand on her shoulder. "Young mistress," she heard Rufus say. "Do not despair."

She sat up and looked at her dead father. His face, distorted by pain just moments earlier, now seemed relaxed, even peaceful. "Will you come to the church with me, Rufus? I want to say a prayer for my father."

They sat next to each other on one of the carved wooden benches. Bethari stared at the altar next to the pulpit. "So, turns out we're both slaves, Rufus." She turned and looked at him. "Can a slave emancipate another slave?"

Rufus smiled. "You are free, mistress. Your owner has died and there are no relatives to inherit you."

"You really are very clever, Rufus." She smiled in spite of her sadness. "Then I emancipate you here and now. From now on you can come and go and do as you please. I will issue you your papers this evening. But Rufus," she placed her hand on his arm, "I would so appreciate it if you stayed with me. And get paid for it, of course."

"I would be happy to, mistress." He lowered his head. "It will be my pleasure to continue to stand by your side."

"I do have one condition, however, Rufus. It is very important to me that, effective immediately, you stop calling me mistress."

"Very well, Miss Bethari."

She wiped her forehead. "I don't have any idea where to start. My father has to be buried. But I also have to go down to the harbor and find out how to get us all on the next ship to Cape Town. And I have to get back to Hannes as quickly as possible."

"I will pack the master's belongings," Rufus suggested.

"I would be very grateful. And when you're done, please come to me." She described how to get to the Widow Kleijn's. "One more thing, Rufus." She looked at him grimly. "Do you know anything about these people who are after Hannes?"

He thought about his answer. "I don't know if it is the same people but shortly before his death, I accompanied your father to the governor. When we left, he had the chest with the gold that he bequeathed to you today. I carried it for him. When we got home, he wrote the letters and instructed me to give them to you together with the chest after he died. But then you arrived."

Bethari stared at him. "The governor gave my father the gold? Is he involved in the smuggling too, then?"

"As I said, I don't know. But I assume that this information is in the letter your father wrote to *Mijnheer* Alewijn."

Bethari stood up and smoothed her wrinkled dress. "If it is indeed the governor who is out to kill Hannes, I don't want his gold. It is stained with blood."

Rufus also got on his feet. "You still ought to accept it, Miss Bethari. Your father feared that the VOC might not be satisfied with the results of his assignment, and might seize his assets. In that case, the gold is the only thing left to you."

CHAPTER TWENTY-TWO

GALLE, CEYLON, 1788

"How is Hannes?" were the first words out of Bethari's mouth as August opened the door at the Widow Kleijn's house.

"He's in the kitchen, eating broth with chicken. I made it for him," August reported proudly. "He's holding the spoon in the wrong hand because his other hand hurts him and so stuff keeps falling into the bowl and splashing everywhere."

Bethari ran into the bedroom. She hid the three letters from her father and the chest with the gold ducats under the bed frame before rushing to the kitchen.

Hannes sat at the table, slowly and deliberately supping up his broth. He was dressed, with his injured arm in a sling around his neck. Through the open door to the garden, she could see the Widow Kleijn kneeling in front of one of her vegetable beds. Next to her was a basket with cucumbers and onions. August was with her.

Bethari slumped onto a chair next to Hannes. "I'm astonished that you have the strength to be up and about." She herself felt so bone-tired that she wanted to put her head on the table, sleep and forget all about the terrible events of the day.

He put down his spoon and stroked her cheek with his healthy hand. "You're only beaten when you think you are." He took a deep breath. "Is your father dead?"

"Yes." The memories of the afternoon brought tears to her eyes again and she was unable to continue.

He clumsily caressed her cheek. "He is released from his pain."

"True." She smiled sadly. "And you? How is your pain?"

"The wound is throbbing quite a bit but there are no signs of infection. The widow put my arm in this sling and that has made it more bearable. She changed my bandage when I woke up. But it will be a while before I'm completely recovered." He gave her a lopsided grin. "And I have a headache from the rum."

She looked at his pale face, with the dark five o'clock shadow and the bluish circles under his eyes. "What you need is rest. Come, I'll take you to the bedroom. We can talk undisturbed there." She pushed back her chair and looked out at August and the widow in the garden.

Hannes heaved a deep sigh as he sank onto the bed. Bethari took off her shoes and snuggled close to him. He wrapped his good arm around her. "Was the body of the man who ambushed me still lying in the street?"

"When I left, I saw him. Well, at least his legs. There were quite a few people standing around." She swallowed. "One woman watched your struggle from her window. She didn't get a good look at you but she did know in which direction you fled."

"That means that the town guards will be after me as well. Seems I'm the most sought-after man in Galle right now," he tried to joke.

She grimaced. "That's not funny. We must leave Ceylon as soon as possible."

"And we will," he assured her. "The *Susanna* will soon sail for Cape Town–and we will be on board." *Even though I don't yet know how we're going to manage that,* he added in his thoughts.

But his words filled Bethari with renewed optimism. "I'll go first thing in the morning to book our passages. You see, I have something that will get us the best cabins on any ship." She leaned over the edge of the bed, pulled out the three letters and the chest, and placed them on the straw sack.

"What do you think of this?" She lifted the lid.

"Sweet Mother of God!" Hannes gasped. "Where did you get all this gold?"

"The governor gave it to my father because..." She stuttered, afraid to confess to Hannes how her father had come by this money. But at the same time, she did not want to keep secrets from him, so she burst out, "I think my father betrayed you to the governor for this gold. And now the governor wants to eliminate you."

"Well, I'll be damned!" Hannes cursed. But when he saw how downcast Bethari looked, he added, more calmly, "I know that he was your father and that he has just died. But to betray me like that when he had me to thank for all the important information about the cinnamon smuggling! Ambidexter!"

"I am so sorry." Again, she found herself crying. "Can you still love me?"

He sat up and looked into her eyes. "You didn't choose your father, and bear no responsibility for his actions. I love you, Bethari. And that shall not change."

"That makes me very happy."

He smiled. "It's probably a good thing that you have these ducats now. But we cannot use them to buy our passages. If you start showing off your gold in a town this size, you are sure to attract the attention of the wrong people."

"You're right." She nodded glumly. "Maybe there are some silver coins in my father's estate. Rufus is packing his belongings. I'll ask him."

Hannes slowly shook his head. "I don't like any of this."

"But what are we going to do?"

"As soon as Rufus gets here, I'll send him to von Hügel with a message. For now, you can tell me about these three letters here."

Late in the evening, Hannes crouched behind the first bench near the center nave of the pitch-black church. He listened intently. Next to him stood a candle whose dim light he covered with his hand. Rufus hid in the churchyard. If the colonel was being followed, Rufus would throw a few pebbles against the first church window to warn Hannes.

The heavy wooden door creaked and Hannes tensed his muscles. A single person stepped into the church and carefully shut the door behind him.

"Hiller?" von Hügel asked in a hushed voice. "It's so dark in here that I can't see my hand in front of my face."

"Here I am," Hannes whispered. He took the candle and stood up.

Von Hügel came closer. The two men sat next to each other on the church bench as though they were equals. Hannes blew out the candle. "I would prefer us to be invisible."

Von Hügel grunted in the darkness. He seemed anxious. "Did I just see your arm in a sling?"

"Someone was after me," answered Hannes.

"You're not by any chance referring to the dead man that was found in front of the churchyard earlier today?"

Hannes said nothing. Von Hügel waited a while before he said, "You don't owe me an explanation. But before we get to the objective of this nocturnal encounter, I've got some information that will interest you: Fort Commander Sluijsken came to see me this afternoon. He wants me to arrest you."

Hannes laughed derisively. "Did he give you a reason?"

"He called you an agitator who sticks his nose into things that don't concern him. And he said that you were intent on discrediting honest businesspeople by telling lies about them to the Company."

"Well, that's one way of twisting the truth," Hannes growled. "So, are you going to arrest me?"

"I am here because you asked me to meet you and I am waiting to hear what this is about."

Hannes decided to put all his eggs in one basket. He would know as soon as he left the church whether von Hügel was lying to him. "De Groot died today."

"God rest his soul," von Hügel muttered.

"I have to get out of here," Hannes continued. "On the *Susanna.*"

Now it was von Hügel's turn to laugh. "You're funny. The *Susanna* sets sail tomorrow morning."

"So soon." Hannes chewed his lower lip. "Are you sure?"

"Absolutely. Some of my soldiers supervised the reloading of the cinnamon from the *Estrela* to the *Susanna*. The officer in charge told me this afternoon that the last of the bales had been stowed and that the ship will sail with the next high tide. I could issue an order for you to return to Cape Town but since you are wanted, you can't officially go on board."

"That's true," said Hannes. "And anyway, I need passages for three other persons."

"Moderation is not your strong suit, it seems," von Hügel grumbled. "For whom would they be?"

"De Groot's servant, his daughter and…" Hannes thought for a moment, "… my servant."

"My wife did write to me that de Groot's daughter had escaped her custody." Von Hügel grew pensive. "Her letter arrived on the *Susanna*. I take it *Demoiselle* Bethari's precipitous departure had nothing to do with her elderly father. Is she here because of you?"

"We love each other," Hannes replied.

Von Hügel whistled softly. His tense bearing eased noticeably. "And since when do you keep a servant in your employ?"

"Will you help me or not?"

Von Hügel cleared his throat. "I have not forgotten that I am in your debt. Apart from us and de Groot's daughter, who else knows that he is dead?"

"Only his servant, Rufus. Why do you ask?"

"Because I have an idea how you can get on to the *Susanna* undetected. But it will work only if you can successfully disguise yourself. And if no one in Galle finds out that de Groot is dead."

A few moments of silence followed. Finally, Hannes said, "You're not suggesting I dress up as de Groot!"

"That's exactly what I'm suggesting."

"But I'm much younger and sturdier than he was."

328

"I said you have to disguise yourself."

Hannes thought for a moment.

Then he grinned. "I can manage that."

"You should. After all, your life depends on it," von Hügel replied. "When you pass yourself off as de Groot, you must come out of his house. You must not return to your lodging. De Groot's servant and his daughter must be with you. You will wear one of his suits. Have de Groot's servant alter one so it fits you. And be sure to put on his wig. But most importantly of all, you must appear frail, the way he did toward the end of his life."

"I understand," said Hannes. "But if anyone discovers de Groot's body before I am on board, it is over."

"You'll take de Groot with you! That's the safest way."

"But how will we convince the *Susanna*'s captain to take a decomposing body on board?" asked Hannes. "And how will we get the body on board without being noticed?"

"Nobody will take notice if a well-to-do young lady travels with a lot of luggage," said von Hügel. "Only one of her chests will contain a body instead of clothes. As soon as the *Susanna* is at sea, de Groot will be given up to the ocean. I will write to the captain and explain that the dead man is a very high-level employee of the VOC, whose final wish–burial at sea–is to be respected."

Hannes mulled over this proposal. "Bethari will be pleased if her father is given a proper burial."

"Excellent," replied von Hügel. "I will send a message to the *Susanna*'s captain first thing in the morning. And before he even has a chance to think about everything, you'll already be on board."

"I'll send Rufus to Bethari to let her know," said Hannes.

"De Groot's servant?" Von Hügel sounded perplexed. "Is he here?"

"He waits in the churchyard," Hannes answered. "He was going to warn me if you were being followed or..." He paused briefly, "... had betrayed me."

"I am an officer." Von Hügel was bewildered. "As such, I am a man of honor."

"Then you will not deny my last request," Hannes countered. "I want you to discharge me and my servant from the regiment. I cannot remain Regimental Carpenter Hannes Hiller. If the fort commander were to discover that I am still alive, he'd send his henchmen after me."

"I find that too farfetched," von Hügel grumbled.

"Not at all," Hannes retorted. "Just think of the busy shipping route between Cape Town and Galle. And besides, it is entirely possible for my company to be sent here to Galle."

Von Hügel's fingertips drummed rhythmically on the bench. "Before I accommodate your request, I want to know who this alleged servant of yours is. If you are asking for his discharge from the regiment, he is one of my soldiers and I have the right to know his name and the reason for his exemption from service."

Hannes hesitated. Then he said, "His name is August Eberle."

"August Eberle? I am not familiar with that name."

"I want you to discharge him because he is feeble-minded," Hannes continued. "He is as innocent as a young child. The men torture him because he doesn't understand what is being asked of him. I am certain that he would never kill a person, not even if he were ordered to do so. He simply cannot hurt a fly."

"You're not by any chance speaking about that halfwit who got himself a whipping at the consecration of the flag in Ludwigsburg? Did he not wave at some birds?" von Hügel asked.

"That's exactly the one."

"We really can't use someone like that in the military. He's still a deserter, though."

"He wanted to protect Bethari. That's the reason he came with her to Ceylon. If you dragged him in front of the Council of War, he wouldn't even understand what you're accusing him of!"

Von Hügel thought for a moment. "Agreed," he said at last.

Hannes heaved a sigh of relief. "Thank you."

"So, we're even now?" the colonel asked.

"Even," Hannes answered.

The following morning, shortly after sunrise, Colonel von Hügel and Fort Commander Sluijsken stood in the warehouse on the city wall and peered through the window down at the harbor.

Two palanquins with their bearers had come to a stop on the pier. Two transport crates, secured with locks, some sacks, and baskets were already on the pier. A dark-skinned man with a white turban supervised the workers as they loaded a rowboat tied to the pier. Then he walked over to one of the palanquins and opened the door. A graceful young lady stepped out. She wore a simple cotton dress and had a colorful shawl wrapped around her long black hair. Together the two of them went over to the other palanquin. Again, the servant opened the door.

Nothing happened for a few moments. Then a gloved hand appeared, groping unsteadily, followed by an arm in a black sleeve. A black shoe with a silver buckle appeared, then a calf in a silk stocking. The young woman took hold of the arm and the servant guided the foot. It took a while but at last the occupant of the second palanquin stood on the pier. He was an older man, frail and trembling. He lowered his head, as though the wig and the hat, pushed down over his face, were too heavy for him. The jacket, too, seemed to be weighing down his hunched shoulders.

The young woman placed her arm around his waist and the servant also supported him. They accompanied the frail man, step by step, to the rowboat.

"Wouldn't be surprised if he doesn't make it to Cape Town," the fort commander remarked with arched brows.

"He'll be lucky to make it out of the harbor alive," von Hügel agreed.

The two of them watched as the servant lifted the sick man into the boat, with the assistance of one of the rowers. The fort commander asked, "Do you have any trace yet of that other spy, Colonel?"

Von Hügel laughed. "I've put my feelers out, my dear Sluijsken, but you have to have a little patience. After all, I've only known since yesterday that you wanted me to find Hiller for you."

"Well, make a real effort." The fort commander tapped the window frame with his fingertips. "I didn't put you in charge of equipping the soldiers stationed here for nothing. By doing so, I am securing for you an income that will surpass your officer's pay many times over."

Von Hügel lowered his head. "I certainly appreciate your generosity. And I consider it an honor to put my competencies at your service."

Sluijsken's eyes wandered outside the window once again. "Phew! Would you look at that young lady climb into the boat. Who'd have thought old de Groot was such a rascal. He may be on his last legs but still manages to hide the sweetest flower in Ceylon in his house."

The two men watched together as the young woman took her seat in the boat next to de Groot. She laid her head on his shoulder and the wind played with her long black hair and the fringe of her scarf.

"I have to agree with you," said von Hügel. "She is rather lovely. No doubt de Groot's fortune helped cement the relationship."

"The women here have their own magic." Sluijsken's voice took on a wistful resonance. "You will discover that for yourself, my dear colonel."

Von Hügel watched as the small boat left the pier and was rowed rapidly in rhythmic movements toward the *Susanna*. "I already have a wife. She is still in Cape Town. But since it looks as if I am to remain a little longer on this beautiful island, and the smallpox epidemic seems to be over, I will send for her." He paused and then added, as if speaking to himself, "I want her by my side."

Bethari and Hannes stood in their cabin on the afterdeck of the *Susanna*. They held hands and looked through their window at the town of Galle as it slowly disappeared in the morning mist. De Groot's hat and his powdered white wig lay on the narrow bed behind them. The transport crates and the rest of the luggage stood at the foot of the bed.

"We did it," Bethari said softly.

Hannes leaned over her and kissed her. "Yes, we did. It is a shame, though, that August did not want to come with us. When you gave me the message yesterday that he wanted to stay with the Widow Kleijn, I could hardly believe it. I just hope that von Hügel issued his discharge papers like he promised."

"Why wouldn't he? After all, you received yours." Bethari leaned against Hannes' shoulder. That morning before dawn, a messenger had knocked on de Groot's door and delivered the sealed document. "I'm sure that August is going to be happy with the widow. He's looking forward to honing his cooking skills. And the widow sees him as a gift from God after she lost her son to smallpox."

There was a knock on the door. The captain stuck his head in. "You can come out now. The pilot just debarked."

"Captain Schwarz!" Hannes exclaimed. "You're the last person I expected to see here!"

"Yes, well, the *Susanna* is my new ship now." The man with the scruffy beard roared with laughter. "I was quite surprised when I received von Hügel's message!"

He looked over the luggage and then the passengers.

"As soon as we're out on the ocean, we will give old de Groot a proper burial. And my *Susanna* will take you safely back to Amsterdam."

CHAPTER TWENTY-THREE

AMSTERDAM, THE REPUBLIC OF THE SEVEN UNITED NETHERLANDS AND WEILERSBRONN, DUCHY OF WÜRTTEMBERG, FALL OF 1789

Frederick Alewijn sat behind a heavy oak desk in his office in the East India House of the Company, reading the letter lying before him.

Bethari anxiously watched the wrinkle between Alewijn's brows. She had her fingers intertwined in her lap.

The director finally raised his eyes from the letter. "I take it you are familiar with the content of this letter, Miss Bethari?"

She nodded. "Yes, my father informed me shortly before his death."

"And you know what his mission to Ceylon was about?"

"He was to put an end to the smuggling of cinnamon."

"That is correct." Alewijn's fingers stroked the letter.

"But you do also realize under what conditions your father accepted the assignment?"

She straightened her back. "I am not sure."

"That is just as I had feared."

Alewijn settled in his chair.

"It pains me to speak ill of the dead, and to add to your grief, but your father did not always behave honorably toward the Company. He enriched himself at our expense, on a large scale. And still, in light of his previous merits, the Lords Seventeen displayed their generosity toward your father by offering to overlook his failings, if he were to complete his assignment in Ceylon to their satisfaction."

"And he did that," Bethari replied. "My father completed his assignment."

Alewijn shook his head regretfully. "I see that differently."

"On what basis?" she retorted. "The Pole and the *Estrela*'s captain are dead. And I delivered one hundred twenty bales of cinnamon from Ceylon, seized by my father."

"Dom Laurenzo and Captain van Schouten were by no means the chief organizers of the smuggling operation. According to your father's letter here—" Alewijn tapped on the paper before him, "Governor van de Graaff and his son-in-law Fort Commander Sluijsken are still at large in Ceylon."

"My father was gravely ill yet still discharged his duties. He established van de Graaff's and Sluijsken's guilt. All you need do now is arrest them," Bethari countered with irritation.

Alewijn smiled indulgently. "My dear Miss Bethari, you are better acquainted with the distance between Amsterdam and Ceylon than I. Before we can arrange for van de Graaff and Sluijsken to be arrested, years will have passed and they will have cost the Company many thousands of gulden. That is why the Lords Seventeen had given your father all the necessary authority. He had been charged with arresting the two and bringing them back to Amsterdam. I am very sorry to tell you this, but your father failed to fulfilled his obligations."

Bethari looked down at her hands. "What does that mean exactly?"

"I take it you are your father's sole heir?" Alewijn inquired.

She nodded silently.

He slid her father's letter into a leather folder. "The Lords will lay claim to your father's assets. They have proof of his defrauding the Company and have a right to compensation."

Bethari laughed bitterly. "What my father did was not right and it is true that the Company is entitled to compensation. But you want everything and are doing me wrong, just as my father did you wrong!"

Alewijn reclined in his chair. "I assume you will receive a small pension. This is not a matter of revenge but of justice."

Bethari stood up. "We shall see each other again–in court!"

Half an hour later, when she entered her father's house, her heart was still pounding. She threw her hat on the chair in the entryway and stepped in front of the wall mirror to straighten her hair. She was shaking with rage inside. On the one hand, she was furious at Frederick Alewijn's intransigence and on the other, she resented her father for getting her into this miserable mess.

At that moment, she heard Hannes laughing behind the closed door of the sun parlor. The high, jubilant squeak she heard next magically transformed her frown into a smile. She hastily smoothed her disheveled hair and opened the door to the sun parlor.

Hannes sat in an arm chair and bounced on his armlap a little boy of perhaps three months, with thick black hair. The little one gurgled and squeaked. When he tried to bounce along, Hannes could hardly contain his laughter. Rufus stood next to him. He tickled the baby's chin, humming.

The two men looked up when she entered. "How was it, sweetheart?" asked Hannes.

"Disagreeable." Bethari leaned forward and gave him a kiss. Then she took the baby and reported on her meeting with Alewijn, as she rocked the little one in her arms. "I'm afraid that we won't be able to stay in this house much longer." She looked at Rufus. "Luckily, I followed your advice and kept the thousand gold ducats. Otherwise, we'd have to move onto a barge on the Amstel with our little Paul."

"You are too pessimistic." Hannes got up and laid his arm on Bethari's shoulders. "Whatever may happen, you and I are building our future together. I've been thinking about going to introduce myself to a workshop where I can produce my masterwork. Then I'll apply to the guild and open my own carpenter's workshop. There's no reason in the world why I should not be able provide for us, working with my hands!"

She smiled. "And I shall contribute to our livelihood with my painting. Starting tomorrow I will advertise in the daily newspapers and offer to paint portraits. I will convert one of the rooms here into a studio—well, at least while we still have this house."

Hannes turned to her and looked into her eyes. "That is a wonderful idea. But before we do all that, we shall take a trip."

"Again? So soon? We've only just returned to Amsterdam!"

He smiled. "Do you remember what I told you in Galle?"

She thought for a moment. Then she twinkled. "Though I may be tired of traveling, this is a trip I would not want to miss."

One month later, a stagecoach stopped in the church square of the Swabian village of Weilersbronn. A man dressed in a fine suit, and a neatly dressed woman with a baby descended.

The man took a large, leather bag; the woman carried the baby. They walked through the village, paying no attention to the curious looks, and stopped in front of a house at the edge of the village. It was a small house but the mud walls were freshly whitewashed, the roof covered with new wood shingles, and the fence surrounding the well-tended garden was made with solid, straight posts.

An old woman sat on the bench next to the front door, warming herself in the rays of the midday sun. Around her shoulders she wore a knitted shawl, and she caressed a gray cat on her lap. When the couple with the baby stopped in front of her garden gate, she looked up. The sun blinded her and she squinted.

The man put his arm around the woman with the baby. He used his other hand to open the gate.

"Greetings, Mother. I want you to meet my family."

Never miss a new book by Julia Drosten – subscribe to our newsletter: HTTPS://JULIA-DROSTEN.COM/

EPILOGUE

Some time ago, while watching a program about the museum treasures of Württemberg, we saw a somewhat dented, not particularly compelling soldier's helmet from the late 18th century. We subsequently heard the story of this helmet and found it to be so fascinating that we decided to incorporate it into a novel.

In order to write this, our seventh historical novel, we have traveled down new paths. This time our central character is a man and we explore the Age of Enlightenment. In the process, we realized that although daily life and technical achievements in the 18th century world might be vastly different from those in the 19th century, it was during the former that the intellectual foundations for the French Revolution and the development of modern democracies were laid.

As usual, we explored not only the historical details but also the locations. One of our most memorable experiences has been our research trip to South Africa, where we discovered an extraordinary country while tracing the history of the Infantry Regiment of Württemberg and the Dutch East India Company there. In 2016, we had visited the second significant locale of the novel, the town of Galle in what today is Sri Lanka, for our novel entitled *The Elephant Keeper's Daughter*. The information we gathered for that novel served us fortuitously well this time around also.

The Infantry Regiment of Württemberg was a mercenary army, an army made up of soldiers recruited in exchange for pay, who often served foreign rulers or, as in the case of the Cape Regiment, a trading Company.

In the 18th century, German princes were fond of selling soldiers as a source of income for themselves. Such was the case with Carl Eugen, the Duke of Württemberg, whose dissolute lifestyle and extravagant court had brought him to the brink of ruin. In 1787 he conscripted the Cape Regiment and sold it to the Dutch East India Company (VOC), which needed soldiers for the protection of its trading post in South Africa.

What was at first glance a well-paid adventure turned out to be a nightmare. The Netherlanders were savvy business people and took advantage of the Duke–at the soldiers' expense. As a result, the recruits were not only poorly equipped, but their sleeping quarters and rations left much to be desired, and their pay was offset against the expenses for uniforms or weapons. When the two battalions finally reached Cape Town after a grueling march from Württemberg to Holland, followed by a months-long sea journey in crowded quarters on congested ships, many of the recruits had become ill or had died.

At the end of the men's five-year term of service, the VOC was all but bankrupt and refused to pay for their trip home. In order to survive, most of the soldiers had to make a renewed commitment of service to the regiment. During this time they were transferred to Ceylon, Java, and the far-flung islands of Indonesia. Without any prospect of ever returning home and left to their own devices, they gradually lost the will to live. Within four years, half of the men in the Ambon Garrison had died of tropical diseases. On Java, they were put up in the most deplorable conditions in the swamps, where they died of malaria, alcohol, drugs, or suicide. Their pay, already meager, became less and less frequent until it stopped altogether after the VOC was disbanded completely in 1798.

In the mid-1790's, when the Dutch began losing colonies to the British, a number of Cape Regiment soldiers went over to serve the new rulers, while others became prisoners of war. At the beginning of the 19th century, the regiment was dissolved once and for all and the surviving soldiers were entirely abandoned to their fate. Only an estimated 100 of the 3,200 original recruits returned home in the ensuing years.

The last surviving soldier of the Infantry Regiment of Württemberg is thought to have been the land surveyor Gottfried Adam Kohler, who joined a class action suit in 1847 at the age of 79 to claim payments for his time as a squire in the Regiment. He recovered 80 gulden. Various estimates of what Duke Carl Eugen made range between 780,000 and 900,000 reichsgulden.

On March 20, 1602 several rival Dutch trading companies merged to become the Dutch East India Company, the *Vereenigde Oostindische Compagnie,* or VOC for short. It enjoyed a meteoric rise to become the most powerful trading company in the world, controlling the Asia market for almost 200 years. The VOC took from the Portuguese their colonies in Ceylon, Indonesia, China, Java and India, and monopolized precious, expensive spices such as pepper, nutmeg, cloves, and cinnamon. It also traded in salt, porcelain, gold, cotton, tea, coffee, silk, and copper. It became the world's first corporation, had command thousands of ships, and paid its shareholders dividends of up to 75%.

The VOC was in its heyday in the 17th century, a time referred to in the Netherlands as the Golden Age. This era of prosperity, technological advances and cultural blossoming would have been unthinkable without the VOC. It was the patronage of its merchants that provided Rembrandt and Vermeer with the means to create the masterpieces we still admire today.

By the middle of the 18th century the VOC's star began to wane. The reasons were costly wars, a change in consumers' needs and the loss of the trade monopoly of the lucrative spice business. Ultimately, however, it was the directors' inability to rein in the corruption within the VOC itself that contributed to ever-greater losses for what had been the richest and most powerful trading Company in the world. The letters VOC no longer stood for *Vereenigde Oostindische Compagnie*, its Dutch name, which means United East India Company, but for *vergaan onder corruptie* (destroyed by corruption). By the time the French invaded the Netherlands in 1795, the VOC was bankrupt and was dissolved, leaving behind a mountain of 110 million gulden in debt. The new world power, Great Britain, took over Cape Town and the Asian colonies.

Some of the characters in our novel are historical, although we have taken the liberty of adapting their biographies somewhat to make them fit into our plot:

Our recruiting officer von Langsdorff was the general recruiter for Duke Carl Eugen, whereas in our novel, he is an individual recruiting officer.

Willem Jacob van de Graaff and Pieter Sluijsken were the governor of Ceylon and the fort commander of Galle respectively, but Sluijsken was not van de Graaff's son-in-law. In describing their role in cinnamon smuggling, we relied mostly on the events in the late 17th century, when high-level employees of the VOC carried out large-scale smuggling operations between Ceylon and Manila. In the course of our research in this area, we stumbled upon a further historical figure, on whom we modeled our "Pole": Don Theodor De St. Lucas, who served as agent for the shipments to Manila, and who must have been a colorful character.

Clara Tant, the proprietress of the Schotsche Tempel, was also a real, historical figure, although she lived around the middle of the 18th century. Her tavern, as well as the neighboring establishments of Blaauwe Anker and Laatste Stuivertje, are historically documented.

Our von Hügels were also real. Anna Maria von Hügel, however, was untitled and the colonel married her in South Africa in 1788. He ordered the mock executions of two soldiers in Cape Town when they rebelled because of insufficient rations.

In addition, he proved to be a capable businessman, operating bakeries, butcher's shops, tailor's shops, or cobbler's shops in Cape Town and selling their goods to the regiment, thereby amassing a sizable fortune. His grave is located in the Groote Kerk in Galle, another of our novel's locales.

The *Drie Gebroeders* and the *Susanna* belonged to the VOC and were used to transport the Cape Regiment to South Africa.

Samuel Taylor Coleridge's ballad *The Rime of the Ancient Mariner* was the inspiration for the legend of the frigate with the black sails crossing the horse latitudes.

The mention of the bad luck a woman brings to a ship is a reference to the 1966 German/French television series *Treasure Island*.

We changed some historical facts in the interest of heightening the suspense of our narrative. The VOC, in fact, did not lose its trading monopoly for cloves and nutmeg to France until 1795. We abbreviated the procedure of the loyalty oath. We are not familiar with the exact make-up of the Council of War that convicted Hannes. Today's lodge building in Cape Town was not constructed until 1789. The lodge itself was established in 1772 but was not active in 1788. We referred to the two mountains near Cape Town, Lion's Head and Devil's Peak, by their Dutch names of *Leeuwenkop* and *Duiwels Kop,* since our novel takes place at a time when Cape Town was under Dutch rule.

ACKNOWLEDGMENTS

We do not want to end this book without expressing our thanks to those who, with their competence and kindness, have helped us by answering many of the questions that came up in the course of our writing:

Gerhard Bronisch of the *Militärgeschichtliche Gesellschaft Ludwigsburg e.V.* (The Society for Military History of Ludwigsburg), for information regarding the Infantry Regiment of Württemberg in Ludwigsburg.

Gerrit Menzel and his team at the *Internationales Maritimes Museum Hamburg* (International Maritime Museum of Hamburg) for information regarding seafaring in the 18th century.

The staff of the *Koninklijk Paleis Amsterdam* (the Royal Palace of Amsterdam), the *Stadsarchief Amsterdam* (Amsterdam City Archives) and the *Openbare Bibliotheek Amsterdam* (Amsterdam Public Library) for information on the Dutch East India Company.

Ruth Franke for her translations from and into Dutch.

We want to thank Christiane Galvani for her wonderful translation and her personal collaboration. And we are indebted to Elizabeth DeNoma and Maura McGurk, not only for their outstanding editing but also for their excellent collaboration and their great support in answering any questions that came up.

Printed in Great Britain
by Amazon